Birth of a Traitor

Thaddeus rocked back and forth, his body rattling like the air in the boy's torn throat. "No, please don't die. Please don't die." But against every pitiful plea he screamed to the wind, the boy's blood slowed with his breath until his chest rose one last time, then fell still.

"Wake up." Thaddeus shook the lifeless body, panic rising in his veins. "Wake up!" He beat against the boy's chest, hating how heavy the body had become, how unnaturally still.

"Oh, gods." He scrambled away from the body when the boy's glassy eyes locked onto his and the reality of the situation set in . . .

SON
OF THE
PROPHET

EFFIE JOE STOCK

Fourth Installment of The Rasaverse

©Copyright 2024 Effie Joe Stock

Son of the Prophet
Book 3/Prequel of The Shadows of Light

Paperback ISBN: 978-1-962337-07-6
Hardback ISBN: 978-1-962337-09-0
eBook ISBN: 978-1-962337-08-3

All rights reserved. No portion of this book may be reproduced, stored in a retrieval system, or transmitted in any form or by any means—electronic, mechanical, photocopy, recording, scanning, or other—except for brief quotations in critical reviews or articles without prior written permission of the publisher.

No AI training: Without in any way limiting the author's (and publisher's) exclusive rights under copyright, any use of this publication to "train" generative artificial intelligence (AI) technologies to generate text is expressly prohibited. The author reserves all rights to license uses of this work for generative AI training and development of machine learning language models. Permission must be granted by the publisher for any part of this publication to be used by AI.

Published in Hackett, Arkansas USA by Dragon Bone Publishing™ LLC 2024.

Cover and illustrations are created by and copyright of Effie Joe Stock. Interior formatting by Effie Joe Stock. Edited by H.A. Pruitt and Samantha Mendell

Publisher's Note: This novel is a work of fiction. Names, characters, places, and incidents are either products of the author's imagination, or used fictitiously. All characters are fictional, and any similarity to people living or dead is purely coincidental.

To Zachary and Blake,
Who taught me the importance of brothers
&
To everyone who has stood at the edge of life, who didn't want to continue but did so anyway, for better or for worse
This is your origin story too.

"While you remember the light, and while the Light is still in this world, believe in the light, so that you might then become

The Shadows of Light."

　　　　　　　　　　—A Long Forgotten Teacher

THE WILDS OF CHINOI

DUVARHARIA

RUMI 5310 Q.RJ.M

RABUR-FECHAMU

THE DRAGON PALACE

SUZEFRUSUM

ETA CASTLE
RUINS OF
ELTRINTH
XENELUCH-RANI
ULUFAKUSH
PEACE HAVEN
N
W
E
S
CAVOS DESERT
LOTA WOODS

Duvarharia
Dragon Palace
Sužefrusum
Yazkuza
Hatching Grounds
Trans-Falls
N
Ravenwood
Socrolle

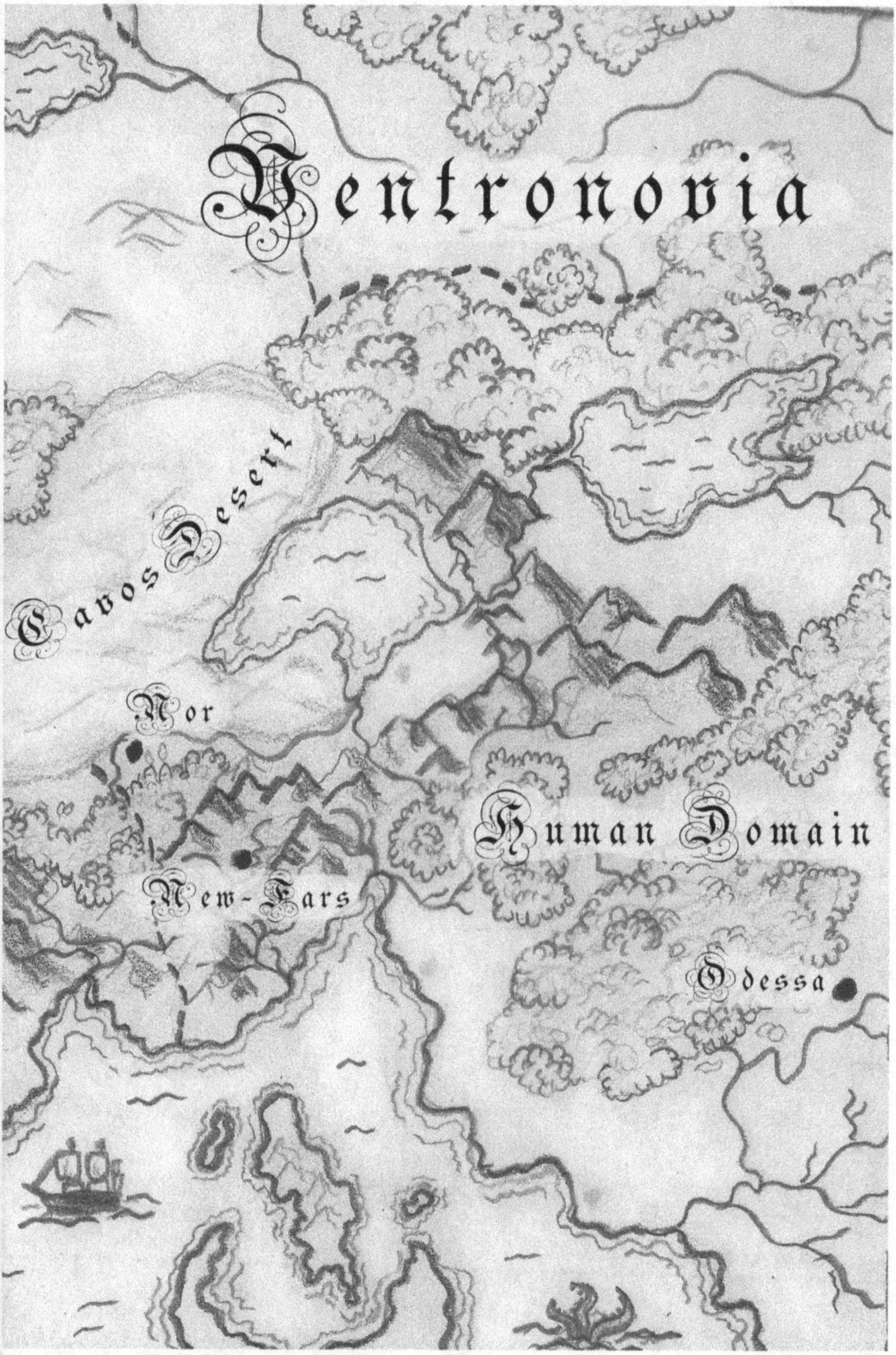

Ventronovia
Cavos Desert
Mor
New-Fars
Human Domain
Odessa

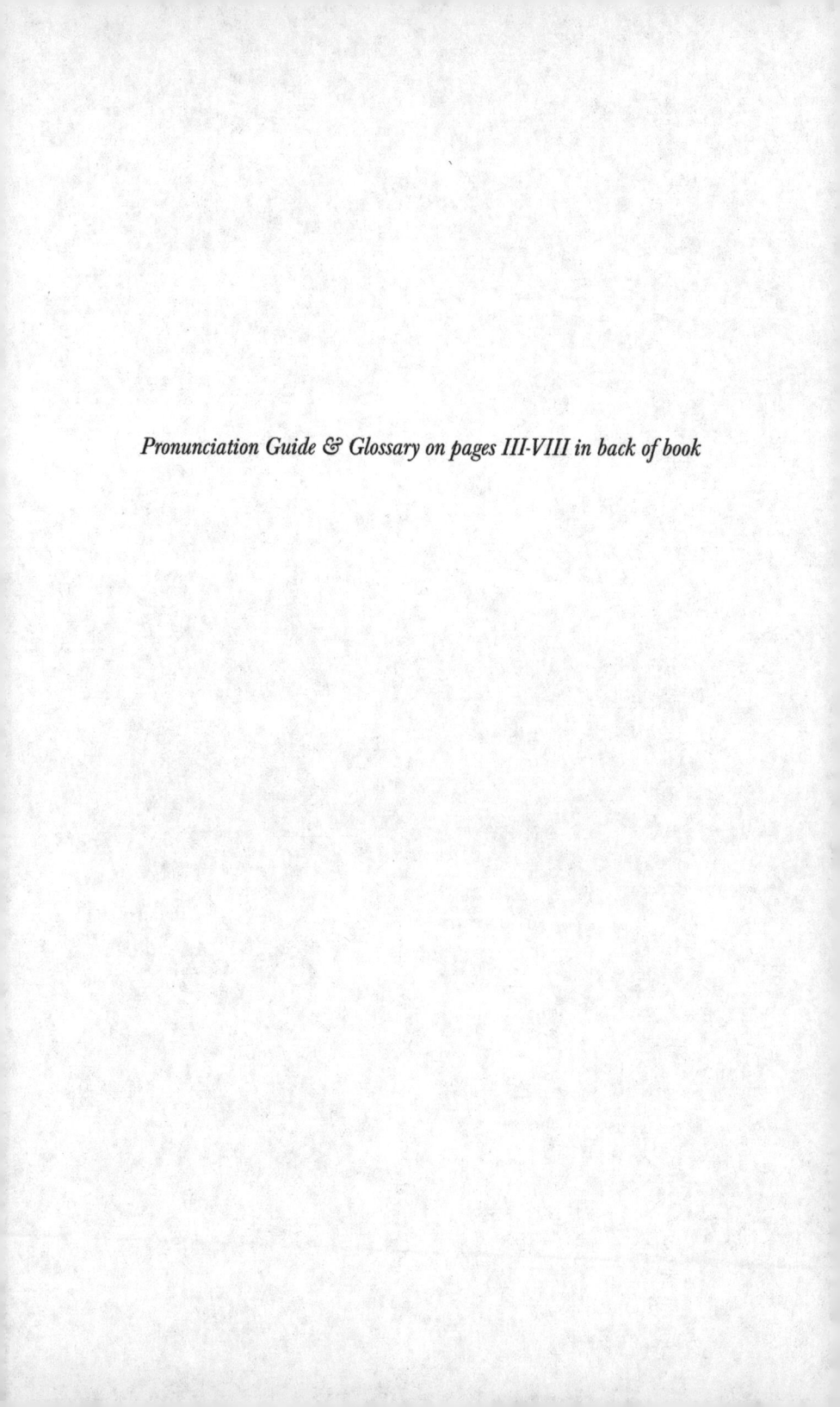

Pronunciation Guide & Glossary on pages III-VIII in back of book

BOOK 3
THE SHADOWS OF LIGHT

SON
OF THE
PROPHET

EFFIE JOE STOCK

Atonement of Sins

Trans-Falls, Ravenwood

Year: Rumi 5210 Q.RJ.M (Quźech raź jin mraha–After our Lord)
Time Counted Since the Beginning of the Great Lord's Reign

"I GIVE YOU ONE YEAR, *Esmeray. If Hanluurasa will not have you and the Great Emperor refuses you from Sankura, then Rasa has no need of you either. One year, and that is all."*

The Igentis Artigal's words rang clearly in Esmeray's mind as they often did on quiet, lonely mornings. As the memory faded, a long moment passed before her eyes blinked open. Darkness greeted her despite the patch of sunlight warming the rocks on which she had stacked her fur blankets.

A seed of rage worked at her heart, ready to spring free and grow into an all-too-familiar thorny vine. But she refused its nourishment and, after a few cleansing breaths, felt the rage, frustration, desperation, and hopelessness slip away.

With a yawn and an awkward stretch that reminded her rocky caves were not ideal Centaur homes, she took to her hooves and ran her hands across the cave walls, finding her small stash of berries and honey for breakfast.

Though the darkness that greeted her was the same every morning since losing her sight, today felt different. Today, she didn't have to live in bitter fear and resentment. Today, she had what the Igentis Artigal sought after: proof that she had paid fully for her mistakes and attained the forgiveness of the Great Divine.

It took her only a few minutes to gather her things: her staff, *Shazedow*, two *zheborgiy* mushrooms, a hooded cloak to cover her face, a small water flask, and a leather tie for her hair. She didn't bother slipping a brush through her thick pink and silver hair. She'd turned it to dreadlocks within the first few months of her banishment; why bother to maintain her once silky hair when she herself could no longer see it and strangers now only saw her as an abomination even Hanluurasa didn't want?

She paused at the mouth of her cave, one hand on the rocks beside her, the other touching her long, dreaded hair. It wasn't the first time she'd worn dreads. It wasn't the first time she'd stood on a precipice of her life either. Two paths stretched before her with no way back once the choice was made. A deep breath of resolve filled her lungs. This time, she would choose wisely.

Picking her way down the rocky steps leading to the forest below, she let her other senses guide her instead of the twine strung from her cave down the path. Eventually, the twine would run out. No use in relying on it now.

A *Ñáfagaræy*, startled from its morning forage, hopped across the road, its soft fur brushing her legs. With a quiet whinny, she shied from the contact, her heart thundering like Ravenwood's army of Centaurs.

Ñáshaid, she cursed at herself. *How will you stand before the Igentis if you are frightened by a Ñáfagaræy?* But try as she did, she couldn't muster the self-loathing she would've felt a year ago. Since her isolation from Ravenwood and during the time she'd spent listening to the stars and understanding the true heart of the Great Divine, she'd learned something about maintaining patience toward herself. However, she couldn't say the same about the other Centaurs.

As she continued along the stony path, thankful it leveled out as it snaked through the Trans-Falls Valley, she found it increasingly difficult to grasp awareness of her surroundings. Birds called, deer grazed, and, worst of all, more Centaurs traveled the road, none of whom were happy to be sharing it with her.

"By the stars. Is that really a Centaur?" A female's words cut deep into Esmeray's heart as a small rock smacked her in the back of the head. The perpetrator, a small child, laughed. The child's parent, presumably the rude female, did nothing to correct the behavior.

Esmeray's slender fingers tightened around her staff as she whirled to face the direction of the offending Centaurs, venomous words on her lips.

"It's hard to tell. Seems more like a walking corpse to me. Her skin is too white. And by the stars, look at the scars on her body. Do you think she's some kind of Warrior?" The father's comment about the disfiguring scars that lined Esmeray's once flawless black body stirred her blood.

Forgive me, Divine. Her fists tightened. *I cannot walk away and forget this one.*

Turning her white, unseeing eyes to the souls she felt lingering around her, she let her hood fall from her face.

Gasps of horror filled the air and the young rock-throwing Centaur screamed.

Black blood seeped from her eyelids, and she knew her fingertips were also stained with blood, knew the dark colors shone horrifically against her blueish, starlight skin and light pink hair, knew she looked like a monster.

"I would think twice before throwing another rock, *elu láshen*."

The air grew painfully quiet. She sensed movement as the young Centaur raised his arm.

Don't let my magic fail me now. Esmeray narrowed her eyes and bared her sharpened teeth.

The rock streaked toward her. With a snap of her fingers, she felt the magic jolt through her body, forcing its way through rusty barriers in her mind and struggling against promises she made to herself before finally leaving her fingers. Inches from her, the rock froze midair before changing course, careening back into the young Centaur's nose.

The forest erupted in crying, shouts of anger, and hooves as Esmeray turned and galloped away, praying the road didn't take too many sharp turns. Zuru *kid.* She spat on the road. *He deserves a crooked nose for the rest of his life. I hope they can't find a healer to fix it.*

Once the raging family had faded behind her, she slowed to a trot, her heart racing and mind dizzy from the small amount of magic. Releasing it had been harder than she'd hoped it would be. Hanluurasa had done a superb job of making sure she would never possess the power to repeat her mistakes.

Leaning heavily against her staff, she sucked in air that burned in her lungs. But a small smile spread across her sharp teeth. Despite the struggle her magic brought, she still wasn't as helpless as she had believed. Where once she had been bitter over the disfigurement of her body, now she was grateful. No one would recognize her as the Priestess of Hanluurasa who'd nearly brought ruin to Ravenwood. Instead, the horrors would fade away into legend and myth without a face or name to connect to Esmeray.

Like Artigal, she had been renewed by the Great Divine and given a second chance—a chance to change the world for the better. First, she would alert Artigal of the revelations she'd gathered from the stars; then she would find a way to undo the binding of the Corrupt Magic, *Kijaqumok*, that had suppressed the forest into the Sleeping. For even if all she accomplished was righting the wrongs she had committed against Rasa, it would be enough to be proud of, even if Artigal and the Emperor were the only ones who knew.

She only had to convince Artigal to let her try.

"Esmeray?" A familiar milky voice called gently to her.

It didn't take her long to figure out where he was. His magical presence was overwhelming, and she instantly recognized the Pure Magic, *Shushequmok*, within him. It was the same Magic whose channel she utilized to listen to the stars now that she couldn't read them directly. *I hope he can feel it in me just the same as I feel it in him.*

"Igentis." Though the aches in her scars screamed against the movement, she attempted to bow low before her ruler, the very authority she had once sought to kill.

A warm hand touched her shoulder. "No need. We are alone."

Thankful, she straightened, wishing more than anything that she could see his face, read his body language, look into his eyes, and read his thoughts. "How did you find me? You didn't know I was coming today. I sent no messenger."

A chuckle rang in his voice. "You are not the only one who can read the stars, Esmeray."

But am I the only one who can hear them? She kept the question to herself.

"You have something for me."

Throwing back her shoulders and finding a sliver of the pride she'd used to carry with such surety, Esmeray nodded. "I have read the stars, and by the powers that created Hanluurasa, I watched the Duvarharian deity, the Great Lord Joad, bestow a prophecy upon the Dragon Riders."

"When?"

"Two weeks from today when all the heavenly bodies dance the *Unurarujax*."

Esmeray sensed Artigal's demeanor darkening. "And what will the prophecy foretell?"

"The rise of a traitor and the destruction of the Duvarharians."

PART ONE
Dividing Secrets in Blood

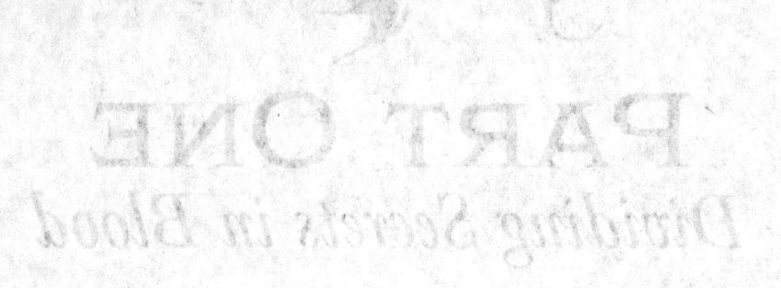

Chapter 1

Peace Haven, Duvarharia
Year: Rumi 5310 Q.RJ.M
100 Years After the Dragon Prophecy

DUST FLEW BEHIND the Duvarharian boy as he raced down the road, dodging a dragonet, vendors trying to sell their wares, and beggars seeking alms. "Thanatos, wait! Slow down!" Each breath burned his lungs as his legs screamed in protest.

Curses tumbled from his lips as his older brother only called back, "Last one home is a rotten hatchling!"

Putting on an extra boost of speed, the boy ducked under and between the towering legs of a dragon, narrowly missing being stepped on. The great creature rumbled in amusement as, only moments later, the boy collided with another Duvarharian Rider.

A sharp rap of pain jolted through his head as stars sparked across his vision. Rocks dug into his hands as he scrambled back to his feet, coughing against the small cloud of dust he'd breathed in during the fall. Frantically, he searched the crowd for the dark-haired boy he had been chasing. He couldn't spot him.

Ozi, he cursed.

"Well, don't just stand there, help me up!"

The boy winced at the young woman's tone and quickly stuck out his hand in assistance. Her own coughs mingled with the laughter of the market around them. His cheeks burned.

Once she was steady on her feet, she rubbed her eyes, muttering curses under her breath.

"I'm deeply sorry about that, miss. I'm afraid I wasn't really paying attention to where I was going." He clasped his hands in front of him and drew a line in the dirt road with his boot.

When his eyes met hers, burning with such hate and rage, he wished he'd simply left her sitting in the dust.

"*You* again. Are you always this stupid or just around me? *Žebu quhuesu dasuunab*," she cursed, reaching back to strike him across the face.

Before her blow could land, he ducked and pelted away as quickly as he could.

Heart pounding so rapidly he thought it would give up and burst, the boy didn't stop running until he could no longer hear the girl's screaming rage of how he had ruined yet *another* of her good dresses. Her threats of revenge were unfortunately not lost in the wind.

I wonder if she would let me pay the damages in femi *since she's always saying, "I'll pay"*. A small chuckle graced his lips, but the humor didn't last. The girl was Brina—the only daughter of a powerful Peace Haven council member. She had six wildly protective older brothers who made sure to teach anyone a painful lesson if they crossed her.

Tears stung the young boy's eyes, but he furiously wiped them away lest his blurred vision led to another unfortunate collision.

As he surveyed his surroundings, he realized he'd run so far, he wasn't sure what road he'd turned down. Thanatos was nowhere to be seen, and the suns were beginning to set over the treetops.

Dragging his feet, he took several deep breaths, trying to recall what Thanatos had taught him should they ever get separated.

The suns set in the west. The Council Hall's dome is south of home. From the top of the small hill he'd crested over, he could see the great circular walls of Peace Haven's arena. *That means I must turn around.* So, he did. *And now look for the tree.* He could just barely see the grand tree standing proudly above the rest of the forest near his home.

A sigh of relief left his lungs, and he changed his course. Now that the anxiety had faded, he allowed himself to study this new section of Peace Haven he found himself in.

This sector was significantly poorer than those he and his family frequented. Houses and stores weren't made with the familiar crafted granite or marble. Instead, they were built from brick, mortar, or stone. They didn't shimmer in the setting suns like the high sector establishments did, but he didn't find them all that homely either. He found something oddly comforting about the humble buildings, and he believed a certain beauty was hidden in the cracks and imperfections of the structures where water had worn them away or vines had pried them apart.

Taking a different road than the one that had led him on this adventure, he passed over a small bridge, stopping a moment to watch the *Qeżujeluch* lizards as they ducked underneath the large lily pads.

"By the gods, Thaddeus, where have you been?" Thanatos' voice caught the boy's attention. "Please tell me you didn't come all the way over here just to look at the *Qeżujeluch*?"

Thaddeus' face burned as he jumped away from the railing. "N–no. Of course not." He hated how guilty his squeaky voice sounded, despite being honest. "I ran into . . ." He nearly spoke her name but caught himself. Thanatos hated that he let her bully him, hated the thought of her brothers getting ahold of him. But Thaddeus didn't want his older brother to think him weak, as someone who always needed protection. ". . . into someone, and I thought they were going to skin my scales, so I started running. I didn't realize where I was going until I stopped." The road was full of hard rocks, and he kicked one before chewing the inside of his cheek.

Thanatos rolled his bright blue eyes and threw a heavy arm around his younger brother, playfully dragging him along. "What a story. Mother won't buy it for a second. Come on. Home isn't too much farther. Gods of all, you're a dusty mess!"

Thaddeus yelped as Thanatos playfully slapped his arms and legs, sending a dust cloud into the air. They took turns chasing each other until the roads grew familiar and gigantic trees loomed overhead, blocking the last few rays of the suns' light.

"Thanks for coming to find me." He snuck a glance at Thanatos, who nodded curtly.

"Don't mention it. Mother's too strict when it comes to curfew. I was planning on staying out late tonight anyway."

A smile decorated Thaddeus' face. He knew Thanatos never stayed out later than when Mother told them to be home. Neither of them wanted to face her lectures about rising crime and the increase in kidnappings of young men to fill the arenas with fresh blood. And even though neither boy had heard the statistics firsthand, the border wasn't far away, and all the stories said Wyriders were a vicious and bloodthirsty race.

Nearly a half hour after the suns dipped below the horizon, they arrived home. Even though their tardiness wouldn't go unnoticed, both boys took care to slip into the house as quietly as possible. If their mother didn't see them come in, they'd at least have the chance to come up with an excuse like playing predator and prey.

"Thanatos. Thaddeus. Do you have something to say for yourselves?"

The boys stopped dead in their tracks as the door clicked shut behind them, the small sound deafening in the sudden silence.

Slowly, they turned around.

A woman with long, hip-length black hair, olive skin, and eyes the color of emerald stood with her hands firmly on her hips, her lips pursed in a thin line.

After a quick moment of stunned silence and whirling thoughts, excuses bolted out of the boys' lips and tumbled over each other.

"Thanatos left me behind and—"

"Thaddeus was distracted and couldn't keep up—"

"I ran into someone! I had to help them up."

"He wasn't paying attention."

"I got lost."

"He wanted to look at the *Qeźujeluch*."

"I did not!"

"Did too!"

"Did not!"

"Did too!"

"Boys!"

Their attention snapped to their mother as their mouths clamped shut.

Her eyes sparkled with something that could be mistaken as mirth, though the rest of her body disagreed. "You know how I feel about curfew."

Thanatos groaned, and she shot him a scathing look that had him clasping his hands and twiddling his thumbs.

"The *Vuk Quseb* are always looking for young men just like you to kidnap and throw into the arena. They don't care if you think you're too fast for them and can lose their trail. They have hounds and tracking vultures and are always on the lookout for easy prey. Most of the kidnappings happen after dark on nights just like tonight! Is that what you want to happen?"

Both their heads hung low.

"No," Thanatos muttered.

"That's what I thought. Now, you'll be in this house before sunset from now on, or I'm not letting you roam the city alone. I'll send one of your tutors along with you."

"No!" The boys shouted a little louder than they meant to, so they each repeated their promise in a lower tone. "We promise to be home before dark."

"Good." Their mother's face softened, and she quickly planted a kiss on Thaddeus' head before turning to Thanatos. He dodged her kiss, and she lightly smacked the back of his head.

"Oh, Thanatos. Don't be so stubborn. You're not yet old enough to skip a mother's kiss." With surprising agility and strength, she dashed after her laughing son, pulled him into her arms, and showered his forehead and hair in kisses as he squealed and frantically tried to escape.

When she finally released him, all three of them were breathless with laughter. Thaddeus let himself be pulled into a group hug, feeling the comforting warmth of his mother's arms around him. He thought back and realized he'd never seen his mother truly angry before, no matter how much trouble he and his brother got into. Rumors lingered in the city of her wrath and something about her past, but as she whispered endearing words to him and Thanatos in her native tongue, he couldn't imagine her being anything other than kind, caring, and nurturing.

He sighed and squeezed them harder, ignoring Thanatos' playful groans of discomfort.

"Alright, *tyän setyäg*. Go change your clothes. I have a surprise waiting for you in the kitchen."

Thaddeus quickly broke away from her arms, racing to the long hallway that branched out of the grand living room they were in.

"Thaddeus! Walk, don't run please. This is a house, not an arena, and Arella the sun be blessed, try not to leave that dust cloud on the floor!"

"Okay!" He only slowed his pace to a fast walk.

"Yes, ma'am?"

He tried not to roll his eyes and thanked the gods she couldn't see his face. "Yes, ma'am," he called back.

As he entered the glass hallway, he faintly heard her call Thanatos back.

Hesitating near the entrance of the hallway and trying to appear as if he were watching the little stream that ran under the enclosed glass bridge, though it was much too dark to see, he strained to hear what his mother was saying.

"Thanatos . . . much younger than you . . . can't be left . . . in the city . . . your job to protect . . . keep that in mind."

Thanatos' voice was too quiet to hear, but Thaddeus sensed a sincerity in his tone—a tenderness toward his younger brother that he would never dare to show him face to face.

Before he could be caught eavesdropping, Thaddeus rushed through the rest of the tunnel and darted through the first door on the left of the hall, opposite his parents' room.

Dashing into the room he and Thanatos shared, he quickly stripped of his dusty clothes, tossed them into a pile on the floor to forget about later, and dressed in a fresh tunic and pants just as Thanatos stepped into the room.

"Who's the slow old dragon now?" Sticking his tongue out at his brother, Thaddeus dashed past him and back into the hallway, feeling a breath of air across his shoulders as Thanatos futilely swiped at him.

"You rotten hatchling!"

Thaddeus couldn't hold back his ringing laughter as he raced back across the glass bridgeway and into the living room, making sure to slow to a walk in case his mother was watching. Though he knew Thanatos would find a way to get even with him, the look on his face had been worth it.

Stopping at their collection of instruments to his right, he paused, knowing Mother would want him to wait for Thanatos so they could see the surprise together. He dragged his fingers across the side of their grand piano and danced them across the keys. The notes brought a sigh to his lips, and quickly, he played a short scale. Resisting the urge to sit down and practice, he meandered over to the plush couches, exercising all his self-control to not peek through the slightly open kitchen door.

I wonder what Mother made for us. He didn't smell anything cooking. Usually, her delicious creations would permeate the air with tantalizing scents. Today, however, he only detected the sweet scent of *zinligil-shätsh-gugi* drifting in from the garden with the crisp, cool summer air.

A hand reached around his head and locked him in a playful chokehold.

With a yelp of surprise, Thaddeus fought against his brother, trying every tactic his father had taught him to escape these sorts of holds. But despite Thaddeus' training, Thanatos' superior strength won.

The door to the kitchen opened, and their mother stepped out, a disapproving look on her face. She didn't have to say a word for the boys to jump apart, trying to act innocent of their mischief.

Gesturing for them to come over, she disappeared into the kitchen. They quickly followed, tripping over each other and pushing each other out of the way, trying to be the first to see the surprise.

After stomping on Thanatos' toes, making him bite off a curse and jump in suppressed pain, Thaddeus dashed the last few feet to the door, swinging it open exuberantly.

He froze in shock.

"What? What is it?" Thanatos was right behind him, just about to push him out of the way when he also froze.

"Father?" Thaddeus took one unsure step into the kitchen as the man sitting on one of the tall stools swiveled around to face them, a broad grin across his golden-stubbled face.

Tears of joy sparkled in his eyes as he nodded and opened his arms.

"Father!"

Without another moment's hesitation, the boys rushed to the man and descended upon him with playful wrestling and tight hugs.

The kitchen rang with joyful laughter and tears of delight from both parents. Soon though, the laughter was replaced with an endless stream of interrogation.

"Hold on, little dragonets!" Their father roared with laughter as he brushed them off him and pushed them toward their own chairs. With wide eyes, they jumped onto the seats, nearly climbing over the island counter to be close to him once again. Their bombardment of questions had yet to cease.

"Boys! Let your father catch his breath! He's only just arrived home and hasn't even had the chance to change his own clothes."

The blond man shook his head, waving his hand. "Oh, Naraina. They're only curious is all. Acting just like proper Duvarharians."

"Didn't you go to see the Centaurs, Father?" Thaddeus' question was quickly repeated by Thanatos. Though the dark-haired boy was nearly two years older than Thaddeus, his eyes sparkled with the same child-like wonder as his brother.

With a somber face, their father nodded. "Yes, I did."

The boys yelped with excitement. Their home of Peace Haven was so far north in Duvarharia, it wasn't often they heard stories of the Centaurs down south in Ravenwood. However, they were lucky enough to have an ambassador for a father who always brought home such wonderful stories. Sometimes Thaddeus wondered how much of the stories were true, but he never deemed it important to destroy the magic of his father's storytelling by asking.

However, today was different. A certain darkness shone through their father's eyes as if everything he were about to say was not only very true but also very serious.

"However, they weren't just any Centaurs."

An unusual hush fell over the kitchen.

"I met with the Council of the United Tribes of Centaurs and the Igentis Artigal himself."

Chapter 2

Aᴌᴌ ᴛʜʀᴇᴇ ᴘᴀɪʀꜱ of watching eyes widened. Naraina eased herself onto the stool next to Thaddeus and wrapped her arm around her son. "Igentis Artigal? The leader of all the Centaurs of Ravenwood?"

Their father's jaw ground on itself; his eyes spoke louder than he could.

She covered her mouth. "Quinlan . . ."

He nodded. "We talked a good long time about . . . the stars."

Naraina paled. "The *stars*?"

Thanatos scoffed and sat back on his stool, greatly disappointed. "What's so interesting about the stars? I thought you became an ambassador to talk about war and fighting and treaties and interesting things like that."

"I did. But you would be surprised at how much of that is already written in the stars, waiting to be read and understood by the great star readers of Ravenwood. Artigal is one of the greatest interpreters, so much so that he can see the future at times."

Thaddeus' brows furrowed. The importance of reading the stars was not lost on him, but he didn't understand why speaking with Artigal had caused such a solemn air to cling to his parents. When he glanced back at his mother, he was startled to find her biting her bottom lip—something he saw rarely, only when she was extremely worried. When she caught him glancing at her, she quickly smiled and hugged him close to her.

"What did he see in the stars?" Thaddeus' eyes locked onto his father's as he smiled in a strange, sad way. Thaddeus wasn't sure he liked how his parents were acting. Thanatos didn't seem to have noticed; he still appeared more worried about how reading the stars could be more interesting than talking about the arena games.

The man and woman shared a look before Quinlan winked at Thaddeus. "I'm afraid I can't disclose that information, my dragonet. Strict orders and confidentiality, of course."

Thaddeus nodded. *Of course. I couldn't have expected any more.* But he wasn't sure he believed his father. Usually, when the ambassador dismissed a topic as confidential, Thaddeus often caught him speaking of it in low tones to his mother later that night. And most often, any stories his father brought back from Ravenwood were never anything more than peaceful meetings between allied nations. *Why is this time so different?*

"Well, Naraina, are you just going to sit there and let me starve?" Quinlan's lighthearted comment broke the tension as Naraina jumped from her chair.

"With that kind of attitude, Sir Ambassador, I might just let you."

Quinlan groaned and rolled his eyes over to Thanatos. "See, son? If you don't treat your woman just right, she'll end up starving you. Either treat her well, or don't expect food. Got that?"

Though Thanatos laughed and brushed off the advice, Thaddeus made a mental note and stored it deep in his mind.

In only a few minutes, Naraina tossed a salad and pulled out herbed bread and roasted plain goat she had prepared earlier in the day. It was Quinlan's favorite food; clearly, she had known he would be arriving home today.

Joining hands with her family, Naraina repeated a familiar blessing in her native tongue, and they quickly dug in.

With a mouthful of food, Thanatos started to recount the adventure he and Thaddeus had gone on earlier that day. Excitedly, he described as they'd sneaked to the gates of the hatching ground and watched through metal bars as a dragon hatchling was chosen for bonding to one of the city's elite citizens.

"I'm amazed the mob didn't crush you!" Quinlan took a sip of the frothy *läshiglunov* before partaking in his meal once again.

Thanatos shrugged. "An arena game was going on. I guess everyone was there instead."

"I don't know why." Thaddeus scoffed through his mouthful of food. Naraina shot him a look, and he made sure to swallow before speaking again. "Dragons bonding with riders is so much more interesting than some stupid game."

Thanatos scowled. "It's not a stupid game. It's—"

"Ah, ah, boys." Quinlan's stern voice interrupted their would-be argument. He shook his head. "Not at the dinner table tonight, alright?"

The boys nodded and agreed, but not before exchanging dirty looks and sticking their tongues out at the other.

"Speaking of dragons, where's Krystallos?" Naraina directed the conversation to Quinlan's dragon, whom he had been bonded to since he was Thanatos' age.

Quinlan took a moment to swallow before speaking, taking only a second to do so before eating once again. "I do believe he went to *Ulufakush* tonight to take a swim in the sea after the long flight. I pushed him to make the trip in time for dinner and *läshiglunov*."

Thaddeus' interest was no longer on food. "Tell us about *Ulufakush*, the dragon island!"

"No, come on, Thaddeus." Thanatos rolled his eyes. "You always want to hear about *Ulufakush*. The Centaurs are so much more interesting."

"Please, Father. Please!" Thaddeus could barely keep from jumping up and down. Peace Haven was the closest Duvarharian city to the famous *Xeneluch-Rani*—the Dragon Sea—and yet not many Dragon Riders had ever actually been there. All matters relating to dragons were kept exclusive to the dragons since the passing of a law a few hundred years ago restricting the once free bonding of dragons. The law also restricted access to *Ulufakush* from all riders. Any news or tales from the sea and island were considered rare gems.

"*Tyän setyäg*, your father is very tired. He's had an extremely long trip home, and just like Krystallos, he probably wants to have a long soak and go to bed."

"Oh, I'm—" Quinlan started but then quickly changed his tone as he caught his wife's gaze. He stretched and faked a long yawn, winking at his sons. "She's right, dragonets. It's best I make my way to bed. A busy day awaits me tomorrow with relaying information back to the Council, and you know how early they like to start their days."

The boys groaned and complained despite their parents' halfhearted efforts to scold their attitudes.

"Tell you what." Quinlan scooped up his plate and began to wash it. "I was going to wait until tomorrow to surprise you both, but I might as well do it now. Do you think that's okay, Naraina?"

With wide eyes, the boys begged their mother to let them hear the surprise. Often stricter than most fathers in Peace Haven, Quinlan's surprises were few and far between, but when he had one, it was always worth the wait.

Try as he might, Thaddeus couldn't imagine what it could be. Usually, the surprises came close to their day of birth celebrations or some other big event. This seemed rather sudden.

Naraina nodded quickly, but she didn't seem as eager or excited as Thaddeus remembered her being when surprises were involved. However, all worry fled his mind as Quinlan's words spoke a dream come true.

"I've decided it's time for you boys to join the swordsman academy!"

A stunned silence filled the room before the boys erupted in whoops of laughter and excitement.

"Arella the sun be blessed." Naraina shook her head, trying not to laugh as the boys jumped on their father, thanking him and squeezing him as hard as they could.

Thanatos danced in a circle, hollering something he likely thought sounded like a Centaur battle cry, but Thaddeus thought it sounded more like a dying cow. The comparison brought another wave of laughter, and he had to clutch his stomach against the stitch in his side. He couldn't remember a time when he'd been so excited, but it was hard to tell when his entire life had been nothing but love and joy.

"Thank you, Mother!" Thaddeus ran to hug Naraina.

"Oh, well." She wrapped her warm arms around him and kissed the top of his head. "You really shouldn't be thanking me. I still think you're much too young."

Thaddeus broke away from her embrace and stood tall, puffing his small chest out as intimidatingly as he could. "I'm old enough, mother. I'm nearly as tall as Thanatos."

"You are not." Thanatos ruffled his hair, but the younger boy wouldn't be discouraged.

"And I can nearly run as fast."

Thanatos roared with laughter as he playfully smacked Thaddeus' small, undefined shoulder. "You cannot. You just proved that only this afternoon."

Thaddeus' face flushed red, and he tripped over his words. He knew Thanatos was right, but oh how he wished he were wrong! *I am nearly as fast as him. I could've caught up to him if I hadn't run into Brina.* "Well, I'm just as good with a sword as you." Those words were certainly untrue, and he regretted them as soon as they left his lips.

Thanatos guffawed at him. "You? Better with a sword than me? How stupid can you get?"

"Thanatos!" Quinlan's booming voice sent the entire room into silence. "That's enough."

Thanatos' face radiated with embarrassment and remorse.

"I'm sorry, Thaddeus. You're not stupid. Forgive me?" Though sincerity rang clear in his brother's tone, Thaddeus bit his cheek, his fingers digging into his palms.

He knew Thanatos never meant any real harm. They verbally sparred as brothers just as often as any other siblings did, but sometimes Thanatos' words cutter deeper than he knew. Brina's words rang in his head. *"Are you this stupid all the time or only around me?"* His stomach churned with helpless rage. *If only Thanatos knew what the other kids say. If only he knew they've said just the same—only they meant it. Would he agree with them, or would he defend me?*

"Thaddeus?" His mother's voice jolted him from his thoughts. Her bright green eyes shone down into his, expectant for his forgiveness to Thanatos.

Turning to Thanatos, he instead mustered up the courage to ask the question that always lingered in the back of his mind, hoping Thanatos would tell him no, even if he lied. "Do you really think I'm stupid?" He hated how his voice caught in his throat.

Thanatos' eyes widened in horror. "By the gods! No! Of course not! Why would you ever think that?"

Before Thaddeus could stop them, tears trickled from his eyes and slid down his pale cheeks. "I just—" He shook his head, wiping his nose with his sleeve and biting his lip. Naraina moved to embrace him, but Quinlan gently held her back, shaking his head.

"The other kids—" Thaddeus started again but found he couldn't continue without making a fool of himself by blubbering.

Thanatos' face flashed red, and his fists clenched. "They bully you, don't they?"

Thaddeus shrugged. "Not really. I just—"

"Those *eshisifoz džou!*"

Their parents' eyes widened at his foul language, but neither reprimanded him.

"You ran into Brina today, didn't you? That's why you didn't tell me who it was and acted all weird when I asked."

Thaddeus could only sniffle and try to wipe his tears and dripping nose. He didn't have to answer. Thanatos knew by the look in his eyes.

"I'll beat her up."

Thaddeus' blue eyes widened as Thanatos' narrowed.

"Yeah, that's right. I'm not scared of her or her *ñekol* brothers. They think they're all high on their hatching grounds because her father is one of the city elites, but they don't have any right to treat you like that. By Susahu, it's *my* job as your brother make fun of you, *not* theirs."

Despite his tears, Thaddeus couldn't help but laugh. Throwing his arm around him, Thanatos gave him a little shake. "Am I right? That's what big brothers are for, aren't they?"

Nodding, Thaddeus gave his brother a squeeze. "Yeah, you're right."

"Well, I don't know about beating up a girl." Their father raised a wary eyebrow, his arms wrapped loosely around Naraina in front of him. "But if you're planning on beating anyone up, you'd best get a good night's rest so you can pay attention at the academy tomorrow."

His tears and hurt nearly forgotten, Thaddeus smiled as Thanatos playfully boxed around him. "Father's right. Come on, hatchling. Let's get to bed."

Holding Thaddeus in a loose headlock, Thanatos pulled him out of the kitchen, their parents' quiet laughter fading behind them.

The boys raced to their room and into their night clothes, then waited patiently for Quinlan to say goodnight and Naraina to bless their sleep and wish away any evil spirits and nightmares.

When the door finally closed and the last flickers of light disappeared from the room, Thanatos rolled over, propping himself up in bed.

"Can you believe they're enrolling us in the academy?"

Thaddeus shook his head, fingers interlaced on his chest as he stared up at the dark ceiling. He really *couldn't* believe it. The Peace Haven Academy focused almost exclusively on fighting—for the military or the arena—and few Dragon Riders went only for basic education. However, their parents had always insisted on private tutoring by only the best teachers. Quinlan and Naraina had never particularly agreed with the academy's teaching system, so why enroll them all the sudden? *Mother didn't seem too thrilled with the idea, but I know Father wouldn't have done anything so serious without her consent.* He hated that his thoughts were draining away his excitement, but he couldn't seem to make them stop.

Thanatos was droning on about the academy and all the exciting classes they could take, particularly warfare and fighting, but Thaddeus hardly heard him.

"Are you listening?"

"Huh? Oh, yeah. I am." He could almost hear Thanatos' eyes roll.

"No, you're not. You didn't hear a word I said, did you?"

Thaddeus chose not to answer, wishing more than anything that his brother would be quiet for just a moment and let him speak of his worries. *Surely, Thanatos noticed something was off.*

But the older boy kept talking, and Thaddeus knew he hadn't.

"The girl we used to tutor with will be there, you know. I just heard from a friend that her guardian enrolled her just this season. Maybe she'll be in some of our classes."

This caught Thaddeus' attention. "Do you think so?"

"Oh, now you're interested." Thanatos sneered, and Thaddeus' face grew hot.

"No. I've been listening the whole time."

"Oh, you *like* her, don't you?" Thanatos made something that sounded like a mockery of kissing sounds.

"Shut up, Thanatos." Thaddeus rolled over, turning his back to his brother. "I was just wondering if she'll be in the classes between us, or if she'll have mixed classes. And besides," he grumbled, "it's been a long time since we've seen her. I don't even remember her name."

A loud sigh echoed in the room. "*Suluj.* I didn't even think of that. Too bad. What *was* her name again? Something like Sophia? No, that's not it."

They sat in silence, each trying and failing to remember her name. Thaddeus scowled with guilt but supposed names never meant much to childhood friends.

Finally, Thanatos shrugged and changed the subject. "Hopefully, she'll have more classes with me, then. Do you think you'll be alright being alone in your own classes?"

"Of course." Thaddeus' brow wrinkled in a frown. A strange silence stretched between them as an understanding grew. "Although I'm not sure if I want to take all their classes." Another long silence passed. "Maybe just the sword fighting and magic."

The sheets rustled as Thanatos nodded. "Right. I suppose that makes sense. But good luck on getting into the magic classes, if they even have any."

Thaddeus didn't like how uncomfortable the air had gotten. Now that the glowing excitement of their father being home had faded into the darkness of the room and their childhood dream of training at the academy was coming true, reality was settling in, and Thaddeus was beginning to find it was a lot scarier and bleaker than he could have imagined.

"Why do you think Mother and Father are fine with us enrolling all the sudden? I mean, you're fifteen and I'm thirteen. They've always said they'd only consider it when we turned fifteen. Why did they change their minds all the sudden?"

Impossibly, the air grew more uncomfortable and silent. Finally, Thanatos broke it, his words short and curt. "I don't know. We should just be happy they did. Does it really matter why? Why do you always have to ruin everything by thinking of such strange things?"

Pulling the furs closer to his chin, Thaddeus swallowed past the lump that had risen in his throat. "I don't know," he whispered very quietly. "I wish I didn't."

A loud sigh filled the room as Thanatos lay back down. "It's alright, Thad. Just go to sleep. You're just tired from the day. It'll all be better in the morning."

"You're right." His young blue eyes slid shut. But as sleep began to steal him away, he heard the front door open and shut, followed by the unmistakable hum of important adult conversation between his parents and a third presence he had never seen, only sensed—a presence that always brought a strange cold to the air and caused the shadows to stretch farther than natural.

Thaddeus waited until Thanatos' breath slowed to an even pace and he was sure he was asleep before sliding back the furs, tiptoeing to the door, and sneaking into the hall.

Chapter 3

He pulled the door shut behind him with little more than a soft *click*. It wasn't his first time sneaking to the living room, and by now, he had memorized everything that made sound in their house.

Moving in a snake-like pattern across the floor, he dodged the parts of the wood boards that creaked the most and stepped into the glass tunnel—the quietest place in their house.

Running his hand along the glass, he took a moment to marvel at the lack of seams. From top to bottom, the transparent material was flawless. Not a single ridge, dent, or scratch could be found. And though the world outside could be seen clearly, anyone standing in their yard would see nothing more than a solid tunnel built like the rest of the house.

Fashioned with magic, the tunnel was Naraina's creation. Thaddeus couldn't think of anywhere else she'd used magic, and it baffled him. Why, if she could create such beautiful architecture, did she not use her magic more often? Why didn't she get a contract designing homes for the elites in Peace Haven? He'd never seen anything built from magic that was quite like the tunnel, and he was sure she could make good money for the likes of it. Most strange, however, was how any conversation surrounding the tunnel had always changed to something else, as if his mother and father didn't like talking about it.

Realizing how much time he had spent in the tunnel, Thaddeus tore his attention away from the mystery and padded to the end of the hall where the two great oak doors hung on iron hinges, cracked slightly open.

Pressing his ear to the door, he used the technique his father had taught him to extend his conscious awareness into the next room, feeling for other presences besides his own. The voices were not coming from the living room as expected. They were coming from the dining room.

Satisfied he wouldn't be seen, he opened the door just enough to slide through, then closed it to a crack. Slowly, he picked his way to the dining room.

A low growl startled him, drawing his nervous attention to the great floor-to-ceiling windows behind him. Another growl rumbled through the house, shaking the chandelier. Movement outside the windows gave away the Crystal Dragon as he shifted his tail, moonlight catching on the crystal-like spines and scattering through the room.

Motionless, as if he were the dragon's prey, Thaddeus even refrained from breathing. If Krystallos was sleeping lightly, he would instantly notice Thaddeus' wakeful consciousness and alert Quinlan to his eavesdropping son. Thankfully, the dragon never opened his eyes, and his breathing quickly settled back into a slow, steady rhythm.

Thaddeus huffed a sigh of frustration when he realized the dragon's tail would not move again and he would have to contend with tiptoeing through shining reflections of moonlight illuminating the room like the suns.

Praying he hadn't missed anything important in the conversation, Thaddeus slunk to the dining room door, nestled into a dark spot on the floor, and pressed his ear to the wood. If anyone opened the door, he would be hidden between it and the wall, hopefully going unnoticed.

With a pang of guilt, Thaddeus realized how much his parents and their visitor were trying to keep their words private. But he hadn't sneaked all this way only to slink back to his room with no information gathered. Besides, this wasn't the first time he had eavesdropped on them, and it certainly wouldn't be the last.

After a few long moments of concentrated silence and controlling his breathing, he was able to discern snippets of the low conversation. Slowly, the words grew clearer and louder.

"Artigal's readings are never wrong." Quinlan's voice shook.

"More importantly, the Great Lord's words are never wrong." A raspy, ugly voice spat the words with overwhelming venom.

Thaddeus wished he could burst into the room and give the creature a good verbal lashing, but not only did he fear his father's wrath of his eavesdropping, but the creature's words held him fixated.

"Artigal aside, Quinlan, you must face the truth. The Dragon Prophecy said *your* sons. No one else. You chose to have these boys. You brought this fate upon yourself. Not anyone else. You have no one to blame but yourself."

Why is he speaking of the Dragon Prophecy, and what does that have to do with me and Thanatos? Why is Father at fault? As far as most Duvarharian citizens knew, the Dragon Prophecy, given to a scholar at the Dragon Palace nearly one hundred years ago, spoke of a renewal of the land that would bring a second Golden Age.

Brows furrowing, Thaddeus intensified his concentration. Heavy, fearful breathing filled his senses along with the soft sniffs of crying.

"But we didn't know." Naraina's whisper was almost inaudible. "We thought we couldn't—" Emotion choked the rest of her words.

The creature broke the silence, his words suddenly much softer. "I know, Naraina. I know. That's what you were told, that's what you believed. It's a miracle you had these boys at all, I know that. And forgive me for diminishing that blessing. But for the sake of Duvarharia, you could have chosen another option."

The blood drained from Thaddeus' face as a knot tied in his stomach. *Another option? What does he mean?* But deep down, he knew.

Naraina only cried harder until Quinlan gently shushed her, his own voice shaking with suppressed emotions, now including rage. "I know that, but their lives were not ours to take. Neither were they Duvarharia's."

The creature sighed and shifted in his seat. "That may be what you believe, but it is now the rest of us who are left to deal with the wreckage."

Quinlan started to say something else, but the creature interrupted him. "But it is nothing to speak of now. It cannot be changed. You made your decision, and we must deal with the consequences." He took in a deep, jagged breath. "So. Do you accept what I offer?"

"Do you really give us much choice?" Naraina hissed.

An uncomfortable silence stretched on.

"We do." Thaddeus almost didn't hear his father's answer, even with the magic he was using to hear better.

The creature grunted in acceptance. "Good. You will do with the boy what we have agreed. You know the words of the lesser prophecies. You must keep him from becoming what it prophesies."

Chairs scraped as they stood, startling Thaddeus to his feet. His heart pounded so loudly, he was sure they would hear it.

"We will do our best." Quinlan's voice was tight between clenched teeth.

The creature hissed. "You will succeed, Quinlan, rider of Krystallos. You and your *shekkamub* wife, Naraina. Duvarharia is counting on it. And if you don't—"

The door swung open, and Thaddeus flattened himself against the wall, a hand over his mouth to mute his ragged breaths and a gasp of shock.

Through the crack between the door and the wall where it hung on its hinges, Thaddeus caught a glimpse of the creature. It was hunched over with strange, mutated parts of its body lumped under a long, dark robe and cloak. As it breathed, the fabric over its face sucked in and out of an elongated mouth, which uncomfortably reminded Thaddeus of a wolf or large cat.

"I will take care of it myself. For both of them."

Quinlan towered his full six feet of height over the hunched creature, his voice rising, his Shalnoa, the Duvarharian markings on his hand and forearm, glowing a fierce, angry blue. "You will not lay a finger to a single hair on either of my sons."

The creature didn't seem at all intimidated. "Then make sure I don't have to."

Without another word, the creature turned and gimped toward the front door, scrapping something that sounded like talons across the floor. Just before it opened the door, however, it turned back.

Cold blood froze Thaddeus' limbs as its yellow eyes pierced directly into his.

In a moment's breath, the front door opened and closed behind the creature, leaving a sour note and sorrow in the air.

For reasons he didn't know, tears began to fall down Thaddeus' cheeks. He didn't understand anything he had heard, couldn't even begin to repeat it if he were asked about it.

Yet when he watched through the crack as his parents clung to each other, crying and gripping each other as if it were the last time they'd be together, and remembered how the creature's yellow eyes had burned into his soul as if to wipe away some sin he had committed, a dreadful feeling sank into his stomach. Somehow his life had just changed. Maybe not in a way he could understand now, but as he waited for his parents to retreat to their room before racing to his own, he knew nothing would ever be the same.

Chapter 4

"Thaddeus, hurry up, come on!" Thanatos yelled back from where he had pushed his way up in line.

Thaddeus groaned, shouldered his heavy pack, and politely excused himself through the line. Burning eyes stared at him with spite and frustration as Thanatos pushed them aside to reach his brother.

Taking his arm, Thanatos dragged Thaddeus behind him. Though he hated feeling like a small child being taken somewhere he didn't want to go, he was also relieved that only Thanatos looked rude now. To make up for their grievances, Thaddeus muttered apologies and tried to make sure he and Thanatos' gold elite student armbands were visible.

Though Thaddeus had wanted to accompany Quinlan to early registration instead of waiting until the lines stretched down the street, Thanatos had insisted they register on their own. He'd stated something grand about being independent and needing to grow up and do things without supervision. Of course, Quinlan agreed with the older son, despite Naraina's gentle pleading that Thaddeus not have to face the crowds. He and Thanatos' age difference had become painfully apparent when they'd arrived. Most of the crowd stood at Thanatos' height—at least a head taller than himself—and swallowed him in their mob.

The sheer number of people had immediately replaced his excitement with unmitigated panic.

Why does everyone insist on standing so close? Someone's elbow contacted his stomach, and he winced, unable to accept the stranger's apology as

Thanatos pulled him toward the gates.

Three dragons and their riders guarded the entrance. Only four potential students were let through at a time. When they reached the gate, Thanatos flashed his gold bracelet, Quinlan's crest stamped into it. The guard, standing a gawking six and a half feet tall, narrowed his eyes. Thaddeus' heart raced. He almost apologized for their imposition and pulled Thanatos back into the crowd, but finally, the soldier nodded, gesturing to the other woman and man to let the boys through.

Sighing with relief, Thaddeus moved behind Thanatos as the older boy stepped through the gate. But before he could join him, the gate clanged shut, and a large arm blocked his path.

"Ah, ah, ah. Hold it right there, boy. Let me see your band."

Thaddeus' mind froze as his eyes locked with Thanatos' through the gold gates. Thanatos rolled his eyes at his brother's panic and gestured to the guard, but Thaddeus only tripped over his own tongue, extending his shaking wrist.

"Boy . . ."

Thaddeus' throat went dry as he stared at his empty left arm, then up into the guard's flaming eyes. "Oh, um. Sorry." He couldn't believe how small and squeaky his voice sounded compared to the man's. Muffled laughs and jeers from the crowd turned his face bright red. Thaddeus stuck out his right hand; the guard grabbed his wrist—more gently than Thaddeus expected—and brought the small hand up to his face.

Trying not to think much about how easily this warrior could snap his arm in half, Thaddeus waited until he was standing on the other side of the gates before taking a breath.

It wasn't until his brother snapped in front of his face that he realized he had zoned out.

"Hey, did you hear me?" Thanatos waved his hand, and Thaddeus blinked himself back into reality.

"What?"

"Are you nervous or something?"

Thaddeus expected his brother to make fun of him, to laugh with mocking whispers only he could hear, but Thanatos didn't. Instead, real concern shone in his eyes.

A knot in Thaddeus' stomach unwound as he nodded. It took a few more deep breaths to find his voice. "Yes. I am."

Thanatos placed both hands on his shoulders and gave him a small shake. "Hey, Thad. Listen. There's nothing for you to be worried about. Little kids and hatchlings come to this all the time. They're not going to stick you anywhere that will require too much of you. They'll take care of you, alright? And at lunchtime, you can come find me, and we'll eat together. Father said these bands get us free food, so we'll chow down together, alright?

Thaddeus dragged his eyes from a group of girls who were whispering, giggling, and pointing at Thanatos, and turned his focus back to his brother.

"Alright."

Thanatos nodded and grinned before throwing an arm around his shoulders, ruffling his platinum blond hair. "Now cheer up, you grumpy dragon. This is the best day of our lives!"

Thaddeus wasn't sure he felt the same, but as he watched his brother beam and wave to strangers he didn't yet know, he did his best to try.

"WAIT, WHY IS HE going into a different class? He tested the same as me." Thanatos planted his hands on the desk, doing his best to stare down Professor Rakland on the other side of it.

Thaddeus drew a line in the carpet with his boot, doing *his* best to avoid eye contact with anyone, especially the uncomfortably familiar young woman who stood just behind Rakland.

A loud sigh filled the room as the professor leaned back in his chair, twirling a strand of his beard around his finger. "I'm sorry, Thanatos.

He may have tested into the same class as you, but for sword fighting, we separate by age group."

"That's *Xeneluch ue!*" Thanatos slammed his fist on the wood, causing Thaddeus and the young woman to startle, but Rakland himself remained unfazed. Thaddeus was convinced he dealt with overzealous upstarts on a daily basis.

"Is it, though?" His tone sharp, Rakland stood, suddenly not looking so old. He was much taller than either boy; Thaddeus gulped in surprise. Bulging muscles that looked ready to tear free of his shirt alluded to hours of sword fighting and took away any doubt in Thaddeus' mind: this man was the swordmaster of the school.

Thanatos took a single step back, but to his credit, didn't look any more intimidated than the swordmaster Rakland himself. "It is. Thaddeus is just as good as me in sword fighting."

Thaddeus' eyes widened at his brother's supportive comment before he frowned. When he caught the girl's eyes on him, he quickly wiped the uncertainty from his face and snapped his gaze back to the tips of his black boots, now dusty from the swords test.

"He should be allowed to fight with those equal to him."

Rakland's eyes narrowed. "Thanatos, let me show you something." As he opened his arm for Thanatos to step in front of him, he looked back to Thaddeus. "You too, boy."

Resisting the urge to grumble at the use of "boy" instead of his name, Thaddeus joined Thanatos as the swordmaster steered them to the large windows behind his desk and chair.

Clapping his hands, Rakland removed the covering of magic that had darkened the windows. Sunlight flooded in with a surge of brightness and heat. "Look below and tell me what you see."

After Thaddeus' eyes adjusted to the light, he found himself looking down into the arena. A great number of young Duvarharians were sparing with each other—aggressively. With wide eyes, he watched as a young woman threw a male fighter to the ground, her sword to his neck.

Only moments later, after the young man spat at her, she cast her sword aside and proceeded to pummel his face. She got almost three heavy strikes in, her knuckles spattered with blood, before the young man roared in rage and they tumbled in the dirt. The other students paused their own training for only a second, barely casting a glance toward the fight as two guards pulled the fighters apart. The boy's nose was broken and the girl's eye already bright red and swollen.

"This is the class you'll be enrolled in, Thanatos. They are your age and skill."

Thanatos' olive skin paled, but other than that, he did a rather excellent job of concealing any fear.

"Now tell me, do you really want your kid brother to be in this class as well? Or would you rather him be in a slightly less skilled class but with other fighters more his age and strength?"

Thanatos stared at Rakland, mouth open in protest, before he locked eyes with Thaddeus. Without shame, Thaddeus shook his head, heart racing with fear. He had no desire to be in a class where it was normal for swordfighters to beat each other bloody. If he must be put in a class that was under his skill level, then so be it.

Thanatos crossed his arms. "I suppose that's fine."

Rakland nodded. "Syrinthia." He waved the young woman over. Since her attention was on the professor and not Thaddeus, he was able sneak glances instead of diverting his gaze.

Instantly, he was convinced she was the prettiest girl he had ever seen. Her dark features were accentuated by the gold jewelry on her ears, neck, lips, nose, and woven through the thick braids that fell around her shoulders. The way her dark eyes shone golden in the bright suns and how she seemed to glow with an almost ethereal aura captivated Thaddeus' attention unyieldingly. And though he felt as if he were seeing her for the first time, he couldn't shake the nagging feeling that he knew her somehow.

"Would you please escort Thanatos to the forgery for a sword and then to his sword fighting class?"

Syrinthia bowed curtly before flashing Thanatos a reassuring smile that put jealous butterflies in Thaddeus' stomach. "Come with me, dragonet. Let's find you a sword, shall we?"

As if the brutality he was certain to face in his classes didn't faze him, Thanatos beamed, nodding eagerly. "Absolutely." Turning just before he followed her out of the study, he winked at Thaddeus. "Don't get into too much trouble without me, alright?"

Not wanting his brother to worry, Thaddeus pushed past the anxiety and smiled back, hoping he looked just as excited. "Nah. Not too much."

Nodding, Thanatos turned and disappeared down the long halls. For a long, quiet moment, Thaddeus stared after him. He couldn't remember a time he had done anything without Thanatos. They'd always been together, through thick and thin, getting into trouble, going on crazy new adventures; now he felt Thanatos' absence like a void opening inside him. He felt as if he were standing on the edge of a very steep cliff that stretched into a dark abyss and couldn't begin to see the bottom. A lump rose in his throat, but before he could chide himself for getting emotional over something so trivial, he felt a heavy hand on his shoulder, startling him from his thoughts. The vision of the void shattered into present reality, though he couldn't help but feel a certain darkness lingering at the back of his mind.

"You're close to your brother, no?" Professor Rakland's voice was much different than it had been when addressing Thanatos. Now it was as gentle and assuring as solid ground.

Thaddeus rubbed his eyes with the back of his hand, as if he could force the tears away with brute force. "Yes. I've always done everything with him." He wanted to say more, to explain this sudden, strange feeling of loneliness and dread opening inside him—a feeling he had been stranger to until now—but he couldn't seem to find the words. Besides, this man was a stranger himself. It didn't seem fitting to open his heart and soul to someone he had only met today. But though the words never left his mouth, somehow he felt the Swordmaster knew exactly what he was feeling.

"Walk with me, Thaddeus, please."

Feeling the request was more an order than suggestion, Thaddeus wordlessly followed.

As they walked down the long, open halls, Thaddeus took a moment to relish the heavy silence and observe this school he suddenly found himself enrolled in.

The hallways were impressively large—not necessarily large enough to fit an adult dragon, but certainly several dragonets. Even so, Thaddeus had only seen one or two dragons so far. Before he could stop the question, it jumped from his lips.

"This architecture is over a thousand years old, isn't it? It seems built to accommodate small dragons, as if this were originally built as a dragon school. Yet, I've only seen a handful since arriving here, if even that. Where are the rest?"

The master paused his walk before taking a deep breath and continuing. "You're well-versed in history."

Thaddeus shrugged, attempting to hide the burn in his cheeks. He knew it wasn't the most popular subject. In fact, at his age, anyone interested in anything besides fighting was considered a "wimpy scholar" and bullied. "It's my favorite subject, actually. My father always made sure we understood our country, its history, and therefore why we are the way we are. He says it's important."

"It is. Your father is a wise man."

Thaddeus nodded. He always did think his father wise, though it hadn't occurred to him that his father was unique in wanting his sons to learn academics over fighting.

"And yet . . ." The master stopped walking once again, this time turning to face past the columns they were walking by. The pillars held up the terrace of the covered bridge they were on. The land below them was another arena, and the sound of clashing metal and straining bodies filled the air.

Thaddeus followed the man's gaze to the fighters below. The sword fighters were impeccable. Their movements flowed like water on the sand or wind in the leaves—light, effortless, and powerful.

"I fear you've been enrolled in the wrong school."

Thaddeus frowned, turning his gaze to the swordmaster. "What do you mean, sir?"

With a sad smile, the man turned to Thaddeus. "I mean just that. This is not the school for you, son."

The dread in Thaddeus' stomach squirmed. "I thought this was the most advanced school in Peace Haven?"

"It is. For fighting. Not for history."

No, that can't be right. Father wouldn't enroll us in a school that didn't prioritize academics. Not after how he's raised us thus far. Mother certainly wouldn't let him. And yet her worried and unsure face wormed its way into his mind, and he wasn't so sure she *had* agreed with Quinlan's decision. "But I've heard this school has excellent scores in academia?"

Rakland shrugged. "It depends on who you ask and how much money was used to bribe the records."

The answer unsettled Thaddeus. "I'm confident my father wouldn't put us here if it wasn't advanced academically."

The master's eyes narrowed. "Son, I do not say this to turn you against your father. I know him personally, and he's always been a very good friend of mine. However, sometimes parents do things they think are best for their children that aren't. There is a reason your father has enrolled you here, and it is not because of what you want to believe."

Fists clenched with unwanted emotion, Thaddeus lowered his voice in an attempt to keep calm. "Why are you telling me these things?"

With a sudden intensity that Thaddeus wasn't expecting, Rakland grabbed his shoulders and knelt to his level so they could see eye to eye.

"You have the soul of an old Dragon Rider, Thaddeus. You are not the same as *them*." He jerked his head toward the training Duvarharians below. "Do you hear what I'm saying? You are not like them; you never will be. When you get to be as old as I and you have seen the things I have, you will understand; there is an unmistakable divide between us. We may all be Duvarharians, but we are not all Dragon Riders. Do you understand?"

Thaddeus nodded quickly, hating that tears were filling his eyes again. He most certainly *didn't* understand, but he didn't want to ask any questions that might anger Rakland. And though he raged against every word coming from the older man's mouth, Thaddeus couldn't help but feel as if it held some truth.

"Good." The man straightened and smiled, though the gesture did nothing to ease the knot tying itself inside Thaddeus. "I only say this so you are prepared for what you face here at this school, should you choose to stay."

Thaddeus nodded again, wishing more than anything that this interaction would end quickly, lunch would come even quicker, and he could be back with his brother, everything returning to normal. However, the horrid voice that manifested in his head last night told him nothing would ever be normal again.

"T–thank you, sir." Thaddeus nodded, and the man shifted uncomfortably.

I wonder if he regrets what he said? But Thaddeus could tell the professor was sincere and desperate for Thaddeus to believe him.

"Thaddeus . . ." The man's voice was so soft, so quiet, Thaddeus almost didn't hear it. "Please remember these things. Please remember the old ways. Don't . . ."

Eyes widening in disbelief, Thaddeus realized tears were sparkling in Rakland's eyes; he did nothing to hide them.

"Don't let the old ways die. Duvarharia can't be left to die, not the real Duvarharia, the land of the dragons. It needs young riders like you, riders whose souls carry the old magic. Please. Promise me you won't let the influence of others sway your love of history and magic."

Thaddeus bit the inside of his cheek and picked at a hangnail. "I promise." He wasn't quite sure what he was promising, but it felt like the most important promise he had ever made in his life. And though he wasn't even sure he meant it, a sudden weight pressed down on his shoulders as if he had just taken the whole of Duvarharia on his shoulders.

The man propped himself on his elbows against the railing and hung his head between his shoulders. "Thank you, Thaddeus. Thank you."

"Of—of course." Thaddeus took a few steps away and turned his attention to the fighters, though his mind was anywhere but.

When the silence grew unbearable, a light voice broke the tension.

"Sir, Thanatos is working with the blacksmith to find a suitable weapon. I'm ready to take Thaddeus to his fist mathematics class if he is ready."

His face devoid of all emotion or passion from only minutes before, Rakland nodded and gestured for Thaddeus to follow Syrinthia.

Thaddeus couldn't meet her kind gaze as she motioned for him to walk with her. Instead, his eyes locked on Rakland's face. For a moment, Thaddeus felt an unheard conversation pass between the swordmaster and Syrinthia. The interaction made him slightly uneasy, but when his eyes met Syrinthia's and she nodded, he couldn't help but feel that if she trusted Rakland, so could he.

As he followed her, hardly listening as she talked aimlessly about the kind of things he could look forward to at the school, Thaddeus found himself thinking of only one thing: the old Duvarharia and the lost, forbidden ways of the Dragon Riders.

Fists clenched, he made his own promise. Thanatos may long for the glory of the arena and the new Duvarharian ways, but he, Thaddeus, would make sure someone would carry on the old ways of magic and dragons.

Chapter 5

The rest of the morning flew by. Thaddeus found that because he had tested into the higher academic classes, he was the youngest student in them. A few of his classes overlapped with Thanatos', but it very quickly became apparent that Thanatos' many new friends were significantly more interesting than his kid brother.

Thaddeus couldn't be upset, though. Thanatos did try to include him in a few of their groups when the class called for team participation, but Thaddeus found he didn't like the knot that tied itself in his stomach anytime he was forced to interact with the strangers or how much he struggled with pairing names to faces. Once he realized he didn't want to be the center of attention, it became easier to let Thanatos go, though the ache of his brother's once constant presence never ceased to remind Thaddeus he was very much alone here.

When a dragon's roar announced lunchtime, Thaddeus couldn't believe the day wasn't over already. It wasn't hard to find his way to the gathering hall; the mob of hungry students racing to the food was impossible to miss. In the hall, eight large tables stretched from one end of the room to the other, and a great vaulted ceiling arched over them with a few dragonets roosting in the sturdy rafters.

However, once he was there, he found himself clueless as to what to do next. He could find no rhyme or reason in the students' chaos as they swarmed through the room, some with food they brought, others with food from the school, and still others who carried books and appeared to be studying instead of eating.

I can't believe it's this disordered. I thought this was supposed to be some sort of prestigious school. But the more he looked around and the more he was pushed into a forgotten corner of the room as he avoided being jeered at for his obvious confusion, the more he realized that Rakland was right. This school's reputation really did hinge upon who was asked.

"There you are!"

A heavy hand dropped on Thaddeus' shoulder. He startled with a sharp yip and whirled around, expecting to face his beaming brother.

"What a 'fraidy hatchling. You're not going find the food hiding in the shadows, *dasun.*"

For a second, Thaddeus thought it was Thanatos was making fun of him, and he almost laughed. Then he realized Thanatos's mouth hadn't moved one word but was instead morphing into an angry snarl.

"Hey, *Xeneluch ue.*" Thanatos pushed himself in front of Thaddeus.

From behind his older brother, Thaddeus could just barely see the bully. The red-haired boy stood half a head taller than Thanatos but didn't seem any more muscular or intimidating. However, a great sword as long as Thaddeus' full height was strapped to the boy's back, and that alone was enough to make Thaddeus' stomach do a nasty somersault.

"Don't you dare talk to my brother that way." Every muscle in Thanatos' body was coiled, his fists shaking with suppressed rage.

Thaddeus wanted to say something—*anything*—to defend himself, but the words lodged in his throat, and he instead took a step back, letting his brother take the full brunt of the blow as the bully's fist collided with his jaw.

The sound reverberated through the hushed hall. Thaddeus' face burned as Thanatos cupped his cheek, hunched over in pain and shock, baring Thaddeus to the hundreds of eyes now locked on him.

Horror clamped around his heart. He tried to reach out to Thanatos, to lift him back upright, to throw himself at the bully, to punch him and beat him senseless or until his blood ran down his hands, but he couldn't move. Not a single muscle in his body responded to him. Even his mouth wouldn't let loose the scream of horror and rage lodged in his throat. The only thing that found the strength to break free from his shock were the tears.

Then the laughter began.

What started as a snicker turned into a roar as the student body pointed their fingers and threw their jests and insults.

The bully cracked his knuckles and popped his neck. "That's for talking to me like that, *huladau*. Only I talk to anyone however I want. You'd best remember that. And as for your brother? He's worthless." Just as he was turning away, Thanatos straightened and looked back at Thaddeus.

A new fear rose in Thaddeus. His brother's eyes were narrow and dark with hate, anger, and something much deeper and primal. His fists tightened until his knuckles turned white. Brushing the blood from his cracked lip, he shook his head slowly. "No one treats either of us like that," he whispered very quietly.

"Thanatos, please—"

But Thaddeus' words were lost as Thanatos turned and, with the prowess of a fighter much more experienced than he was, lunged for the bully.

Time slowed.

With one quick movement, Thanatos knocked the boy's feet out from under him; he dropped like a stone. Grabbing the boy's long ginger curls, Thanatos brought the bully's face smashing into his knee.

Once.

Twice.

Thrice.

Blood spattered the ground.

Everyone watched with bated breath.

The boy's hazel eyes rolled into the back of his head as he slumped to the ground. With a groan, he struggled to his hands and knees, wildly flailing an arm, trying to catch Thanatos, who stood just outside his reach.

"You *nesa*!" The bully screamed several more insults before Thanatos brought his fist crashing into his temple. The boy dropped to the ground and didn't move.

Neither did anyone else.

"Get out of the way!"

"Move, children!"

Two burly male teachers forced their way into the circle of students that had formed around Thaddeus, Thanatos, and the bully. The ginger-haired boy's only sign of life was the ragged breath continuing to raise his chest.

One teacher knelt beside the boy, magic twining from his hands to the boy's face, stopping the gush of blood from his broken nose and straightening it with a sickening crack.

"What's going on?" The other grabbed Thanatos by the shoulders, shaking him like a dragon with a deer.

Finally, Thaddeus' body responded. "Stop! He's my brother! He was protecting me!" None of the students laughed anymore, not even when the tears flowed down his cheeks again.

For a brief second, the teacher stopped shaking Thanatos, his narrowed eyes locking onto Thaddeus instead. "Is this true?" His eyes moved between the brothers, who could only nod, their eyes wide.

Releasing his hold on the boy, the teacher turned to the crowd. "Is this true?"

A stiff silence hung in the air. Already, the bully was conscious and being helped to his feet. Though his face was horribly bruised, his nose swollen and ugly, he was glaring poisonously at the brothers. His piercing gaze landed on some of the onlookers, trying to scare them into lying.

A power struggle was ensuing, one Thaddeus didn't like being in the middle of. Even if Thanatos won, those who still feared the bully or followed him would want the brothers punished. And if the bully won, the brothers were as good as expelled, or worse, dead.

"Would someone stop cowering and tell me what on Rasa's green hills happened?"

A tall, slender woman glided into the circle and despite it not seeming possible, the room fell even more deathly silent.

The woman's eyes shone both green and gold. Her green hair hung to her ankles, and it was impossible to tell whether she was walking or floating across the floor, her long silver gown trailing behind her.

"You." With nails sharp like small daggers, she pointed to a small girl at the front of the students who hadn't ducked into the crowd fast enough.

"Um . . ." The girl's eyes flickered back and forth between the brothers and the bully. Sweat beaded on her brow, and she looked like she was going to be sick.

"Sweetheart." The woman's voice took on a much different tone as she knelt, drawing up the young girl's gaze with a long nail under her chin. A green spark twinkled in the little girl's eyes; instantly, her body relaxed under the headmistress' magic.

Thaddeus watched, baffled, as the young girl spoke in an even, calm voice, not once breaking eye contact with the woman, not even to blink. "The blond boy is right. Gordon was insulting and bullying the him. The black-haired boy was only defending his brother."

Pale lips spread across sharp teeth as the woman smiled. "Very good. And who struck first?"

The young girl sighed deeply. "Gordon."

Standing, the woman turned to face Thaddeus. As their eyes locked, he found he didn't like looking into her eyes. His stomach rolled as bile rose in his throat. Something very non-Duvarharian hung about her. Perhaps it was the way she moved, almost like a tree in the wind. Or perhaps it was how her hair seemed to move on its own, swaying as if in an imaginary breeze. But mostly, he knew it was her eyes. She didn't have pupils or sclera in her eyes—only swirling green and gold orbs.

He took a few deep breaths to calm his racing heart. When he blinked, he decided she didn't look so frightening. In fact, she almost looked familiar. But before he could place a finger on it, she smiled and nodded. "You are fortunate to have a brother like you do, Thaddeus."

A shiver ran down his back. *How does she know my name?* But he didn't have time to dwell on it. Thanatos was pushed to his side by the teacher and immediately started cursing Gordon and asking if Thaddeus had seen how well he had knocked him to the ground.

But Thaddeus paid him no attention. He could only see and hear Gordon as he screamed and pulled against the teacher holding him. The boy's hazel eyes burned like fire. "*Nufa seź!* I'll make sure you pay for this! I don't care who your father is you little *ue!* I'll make you wish you were never—"

Before he could finish, the woman waved her hand over the boy's face. All the healing the teacher had performed melted away. Gordon's nose broke again and began spurting blood over what had already begun to dry on his chest. His screams of rage turned to pain.

"Be glad you are your father's son, Gordon, for this is all I shall punish you with . . . the consequences of your own actions. Find another healer if you're not strong enough to bear the pain, but if you do, I'll make sure your father knows his son can't bear pain like a real fighter."

Gordon's mouth clamped shut, though his eyes still watered and knees wobbled. He shrugged himself free of the teacher when the woman nodded for him to be released.

He opened his mouth to slander Thanatos one last time but quickly shut it when the woman towered over him. Instead, he cast a hateful glance toward the brothers before slinking into the crowd, his friends and lackeys following him out of the hall.

Raising her hands to the crowd of students who still watched with wide eyes, she whispered softly, her words nearly inaudible. "Be dispersed." An almost unnoticeable wave of green energy left her hands and rippled through the crowd. Sparks of green lit up their eyes before disappearing. They blinked in confusion before turning without a word to resume what they had been doing before the fight broke out.

Did she just use magic on them? Thaddeus couldn't think of any other explanation for what he had seen, but he'd never heard of this kind of calming, deceptive magic.

"Thanatos." Thaddeus grabbed his brother's arm and shook it. The older boy hadn't stopped gushing about his fight. "Thanatos!"

"What?" With a roll of his eyes, Thanatos finally turned to his brother.

"Did you see that?"

"See what?"

Thaddeus pointed to the woman, but she was gone. "Wait . . ." He whirled around, searching for her, but all he saw were the two teachers as they left the hall. "The woman with the green hair. She used some kind of magic on the students."

Thanatos scoffed and slapped him on the back, pushing him in the direction of the food lines. "What are you talking about? That woman had brown hair, not green. And she's the headmistress of the school; Syrinthia told me so earlier. She wouldn't use magic on the students."

Thaddeus's jaw dropped as he stopped in his tracks. "No, what are *you* talking about? I know what I saw. She had long green hair, green and gold eyes . . ." He wanted to explain the magic he saw manipulating the students, but words failed him.

"Did your eyes get rattled? She looked nothing like that." Thanatos laughed. "You don't even know what you're talking about. Come on. All that adrenaline is making me hungry."

"But—"

"I don't want to hear it, Thaddeus. I don't have time for one of your ridiculous stories. Let's go."

Realizing he was fighting a losing battle, Thaddeus clamped his mouth shut, doing his best not to also clench his fists and grind his jaw. *I may not know how to explain it, but I know what I saw. She has a strange magic, one that can manipulate minds and change her appearance.* Though he knew he wouldn't find her, he searched the crowd for the woman once again.

Instead, his eyes landed on a familiar face looking in through the open doors of the hall. Rakland nodded slowly; without words being exchanged, Thaddeus knew exactly what he was saying.

For the first time since their conversation, Thaddeus knew Rakland was right. He *wasn't* like the other Duvarharians here. He didn't know how, couldn't even begin to comprehend it, but he wasn't.

Curtly, he nodded back. Without a second glance, Rakland was gone, and Thanatos was once more vying for his younger brother's undivided attention.

Conflicting emotions swirling inside him, Thaddeus let his brother pull him to the front of the line where their arm bracelets got them plates full of free food. Hundreds of eyes bored into the back of his head as the crowd parted to let Thanatos walk through. Though Thaddeus wanted to be anywhere but here, he knew the only place he'd be safe was next to Thanatos.

But this protection wouldn't last forever, and as Thaddeus watched his brother work his way into the table where Syrinthia sat with several other experienced students, fitting in like he had grown up with them, Thaddeus knew he had to either make his own friends or find a way to stand up for himself.

As much as he hated to admit it as he picked through the roasted meat, not feeling as hungry as he had an hour earlier, neither of his options seemed even remotely possible.

"TODAY WAS INCREDIBLE." Thanatos sucked in a deep breath and turned his face to the setting suns; the golden light played tricks on his olive skin and black hair in a way that would make the girls back at school swoon.

Thaddeus tried not to roll his eyes. "It was . . . something."

Punching him lightly on the shoulder, Thanatos danced around him, fists raised in a mock fight. "Oh, come on. You liked it. You know you did."

Thaddeus merely shrugged.

When Thanatos realized his brother wasn't up for messing around, he sighed and went back to walking at his side, his demeanor considerably less lighthearted.

"Tomorrow will be better." Thanatos nodded.

But Thaddeus wasn't convinced.

When they ate dinner that night, Thaddeus found himself picking at his food more than usual, even though it was *rusadabe* stroganoff and egg noodles—his favorite dish. Naraina seemed to have predicted Thaddeus' off mood, and he knew she had prepared it just for him. He tried to focus on that small act of love as Thanatos spent the entire dinner complimenting how incredible his peers and teachers were and how ecstatic he was to go back. The way he told the story of the fight was almost poetic, which surprised Thaddeus since Thanatos was more prone to using slang and taking any shortcuts with spoken or written language that he could.

All Thaddeus could remember from the day was the jeers and insults. *Hey, scrawny! Is that really Quinlan's son? I didn't even know he had a second son. Thought it was just the handsome one. He's not nearly as cute as his brother. Doesn't he seem a bit young to be in this class? Maybe he cheated on the entrance tests.* The words played themselves over and over in his head. The rest of the world faded around him until all he could see was his plate of food through a watery haze.

A hand touched his shoulder, jerking him back to the present. A piece of food stuck to his cheekbone when he quickly tried to wipe his tears away with his lap cloth.

"*Tyän*, are you alright?" Naraina's worried eyes searched his face.

Now all the eyes at the table were turned to him. It was clear by the look of annoyance on Thanatos' face that he wasn't happy his story had been interrupted.

"What? Oh. Yes. I'm alright." The smile he attempted to force on his face was as fake as the dragon-scaled clothes the elites of Peace Haven spent so much money on. "I'm just tired. Long day." His forced laughter sounded more like a sob.

"Oh, Thaddeus." Naraina stood, kissed the top of his head, and rubbed his back. "Help me take the dishes to the kitchen, and then you can go to bed."

He nodded and stood from his chair, realizing he'd only eaten a few bites of food while the rest of his family had seconds.

"I'll help too." Thanatos quickly jumped from the table, gathering the empty dishes and cloths in record time. His mouth didn't stop moving as every detail of his day came rushing forth.

Quinlan seemed just as excited as his oldest son, and though he hated to be skeptical of their father's joy for them, Thaddeus couldn't help but feel it was out of character.

"Why is Father so intent on us being at the school?" Thaddeus rinsed the dishes off, putting them in sudsy water before grabbing the silverware.

Naraina's mouth opened and quickly closed when Thanatos came back in the kitchen with the last of the glasses. She didn't speak until he left and the sounds of his and Quinlan's conversation filled the dining room.

A heavy sigh parted her lips as she fell to scrubbing the dishes, handing them to Thaddeus to dry.

"I think your father has always maintained a strict ideology about social education, but as he's been traveling more, I think he's coming to realize you boys are getting old enough to start seeing the world a bit more, making more friends, understanding your opportunities."

A long silence stretched between them where the only sounds were her sponge on the plates, the splash of water, and gentle clinks as Thaddeus dried and stacked them.

Finally, he spoke. "But you don't agree."

She didn't answer, and he suddenly felt uncomfortable broaching the subject.

"I don't like it." Tears rose into his eyes, but he bit his lip against them. *I've been crying as much as a little child lately. This won't do.* But no matter how much he scolded himself, his heart only beat its strange aching rhythm harder and the tears only grew more determined to choke his words and escape his eyes.

"Thaddeus." Naraina stopped from her work to turn to him. With a wet hand decorated in suds, she gently cupped his face. The scent of plum soap filled his nose, and the warmth of the water on his cheek was oddly comforting. For a moment, time was suspended. It was only him and his mother in the comfort of their kitchen, the cicadas chirping outside along with the gentle grumbles of Krystallos as he conversed with a friend. Thaddeus wondered if this would be something he would look back on and cherish as a memory or if it would fade and disappear in the movement of time.

"This is something your father believes very strongly about, Thaddeus. I know you don't like other creatures very much, but please at least give it a chance. If you still don't like it in a month, we'll talk about it again, alright?"

He chewed on his lip and turned back to his work as she did the same.

"Just give it a chance. For me."

Finally, he nodded. "Alright. For you."

CHAPTER 6

Only a couple weeks later, Thaddeus found himself slumped in a chair, back in Rakland's office, only this time with Quinlan. The two men were speaking in low tones near the windows. Thaddeus knew it'd be easy to use magic to hear what they were saying, but he couldn't find the heart. Something about having a black eye and bloody nose banished all motivation.

"Son?" Quinlan's strong but gentle hand tapped his shoulder. Thaddeus hardly moved; he was trying very hard not to cry. In fact, he couldn't think of anything he wanted to do less than cry in front of his father and the man who had quickly become his favorite professor.

"Thaddeus, look at me."

Struggling not to wince, Thaddeus lifted his good eye. The other throbbed and refused to open beyond a blood-hazed crack. Rakland had specifically instructed the medics to not heal him so Quinlan could see the damage.

"Why haven't you spoken to me about this before?" Kneeling, Quinlan searched his son's face and ran a hand through his white-blond hair—the same color as Thaddeus'.

Thaddeus only shrugged. "It's nothing—"

"Thaddeus, you promised you would let one of us know if it came to this." The harsh disappointment in Rakland's voice stabbed deeper than his own father's. Thaddeus sank farther into the chair, wishing it would swallow him whole and he would find himself in an open field as grassy green and soft as the chair itself.

The silence grew stuffy in the room as the sounds of metal on metal rang through the open window. Thaddeus couldn't remember a time when he hadn't heard fighting at this school. "All they do is fight," he muttered under his breath. "It's no wonder I look like this." He hadn't meant for either man to hear, but he'd forgotten he wasn't the only one who could use heightened Duvarharian hearing.

"So you admit this was done deliberately to you?" Rakland planted his hands on the desk, his stony stare drilling into Thaddeus. The young boy's eye widened before he looked away.

Ozi. "No." He tried to take back his incriminating words. The sound of his pounding heart was eerily similar to the meaty smack of the older boy's hand colliding with his face. "Like I said, I tripped and fell onto the table. The other kids laughed. It was stupid. I looked like a fool, and I don't blame them for laughing. That's all."

Quinlan stood, hands balled into fist, his face flaming red. *"Nufa qulu,"* he cursed. "I'm taking you out. I refuse to allow my son to be subjugated to this. I'll have a conversation with the headmistress if I must. This kind of behavior is unacceptable."

A familiar voice filled the room along with an overwhelming green haze. "If you desire to speak with me, all you must do is request it, Ambassador. You don't have to threaten it."

Quinlan's eyes narrowed as Rakland saluted.

The headmistress glided into the room, enshrouded in her usual silver gown, her long green hair moving in an unfelt breeze. Thaddeus only glanced in her direction for a split second. He'd learned making eye contact with her multicolored gaze was the first step to falling into the strange magic she used to control the school and its occupants.

Quinlan, however, didn't seem affected by her magic. In fact, as his Shalnoa glowed a vibrant crystal blue, Thaddeus got the impression Quinlan was familiar with this type of magic. *Perhaps he's encountered something like it on his travels.* Thaddeus knew that was likely, but he felt

Quinlan seemed *too* familiar with the magic, though he couldn't figure out how.

For the first time in weeks, Thaddeus found himself interested in something. He turned until he could see the hem of the woman's dress and his father standing before him, almost as if he were protecting his son from the woman. Maybe he was.

"I'm afraid the enrollment contract is for a full year. Even if he's only attended classes for a few weeks, withdrawing him now would be costly, and I'm afraid it would have to be a dishonorable expulsion. You know that wouldn't look good on his record. Most high-end tutors wouldn't risk taking on a student who's been expelled."

Quinlan's jaw worked against itself, and his knees locked. "Of course, I will take that into consideration, Headmistress. I'm not one to make rash decisions, otherwise I wouldn't be an ambassador."

Her eyes narrowed. "Of course. I mean no offense."

"But I'm concerned about my son's well-being. This isn't the first instance he's been bullied, and I fear this is only the tip of the egg. Just the first day my sons were here, they were threatened by another student and my eldest was forced to fight."

The woman's sickeningly high laugh filled the room. "Oh, young boys this age are so prone to exaggerating. I've no doubt your boys had disagreements with some of the previous students here, and I'm sure many are jealous of your boys' talent, but I assure you, nothing is unsafe about this school, and my students are not dangerous to one another. The fighting starts and ends in the arena."

Her voice was intoxicating, and Thaddeus found himself wanting to believe her. Maybe she was right. Maybe he *was* overreacting. Maybe Thanatos *was* exaggerating. Maybe the other students hadn't been so rude. Maybe Thanatos did want his younger brother around. Maybe the glamour of his new friends would fade, and he'd remember his first and truest friend.

But when Quinlan's hand came to rest on his shoulder, a warm clarity spread through him. Rage coursed through his veins. *How dare this woman disregard my suffering! I've been nothing but insulted since I've arrived here. My intelligence has been questioned, my appearance has been mocked, my claim to being Quinlan's son has been argued, and my very flesh has been bruised at the hands of her students.* The urge to stand and shout what a liar and manipulator she was nearly overwhelmed him. Instead, it rose into his throat, burned in his limbs, and eventually was choked by fear.

"Quinlan?" Another familiar voice rang through the room, breaking the tension like stained glass. The strange power struggle coursing between the woman and Quinlan disappeared, and the air cleared.

"Syrinthia, what are you doing here?" Rakland frowned, the green haze of confusion lifting from his eyes. His worried gaze turned to Thaddeus, as if afraid his student was in danger.

Thaddeus slowly stood, his father's hand still on his shoulder, as Syrinthia stepped around the headmistress, her eyes never leaving Quinlan's.

"I'm reminding Quinlan of a promise. A promise made to him, and one he made to someone else."

Every muscle in her body was tense. Thaddeus swore he saw tears in her eyes, but if she was going to cry, she did an incredible job of chaining it down.

Then Thaddeus watched something he'd never thought possible: his father giving up.

With a wavering gaze from Syrinthia to his son, Quinlan opened his mouth, closed it, then opened it again, releasing something like a murmur of pain. "Of course," he muttered before turning to Thaddeus.

Thaddeus stepped back, a well of dread filling his stomach. He didn't like the way his father looked at him and Syrinthia. He didn't like the bloodthirsty smile that spread across the headmistress's face or the strange plea in Rakland's gaze that Thaddeus desperately wanted to heed.

"Thaddeus." Quinlan patted his shoulder, but his touch, which had felt so familiar, loving, and protective only seconds ago, now felt like betrayal. "Listen, I know this is difficult for you. I know you don't like being here, your mother told me you wanted to leave, but I don't think you've given it enough time."

"But—"

Quinlan shook his head, a sharp look in his eyes that made it clear Thaddeus was not to speak.

"You need to be here right now. I know it doesn't make sense, but trust me when I say this is the best place for you to make friends and learn. Do you trust me?"

Everything in Thaddeus screamed *No!* But his own body betrayed him as he nodded and whispered, "Yes, Father."

A broad smile lit up Quinlan's face and, as if the rancid feelings in the air had dissipated, he stood and clapped his hands together. "Very well! Now, Headmistress, I would like to see that my son is placed in the advanced history class. He can stay in his current swords class if that suits him, but from now on, he will take whatever classes he desires, but he *must* take a minimum of three classes. Alright?" He turned to Thaddeus as if also asking him for permission, but as Thaddeus nodded and the headmistress responded with a crooked smile, he had the uncomfortable feeling his father hadn't needed to ask permission, not even from the headmistress.

No wonder the other students hate me and Thanatos for being his son.

Except they didn't hate Thanatos. Not one bit. That hurt more than anything.

"Syrinthia, would you please escort Thaddeus to the history class?" Rakland walked around the desk, placing his hand on Thaddeus' shoulder where Quinlan's hand had just been. Though his touch was not filled with the powerful magic that his father's was, Thaddeus found it more comforting.

"Of course." Her eyes didn't meet Thaddeus' as he followed her from the room. He turned back only to see Rakland. The professor was standing in the doorway, looking as if he wished to say something, but as Quinlan and the headmistress moved out of the room, Rakland only shook his head before retreating into his study.

The two young students walked in silence.

A million questions for Syrinthia raced through Thaddeus' mind. *What promise was made to my father? By whom? And what promise had he made?* But how could he ask questions when the adults had made it clear he wasn't to know? Anger filled his chest as he looked at Syrinthia, wanting to blame her for being stuck at this horrendous school. But as he watched the way she walked, as if afraid the very shadows would reach out and strangle her, the anger disappeared into quiet curiosity and pity.

Instead of every other question on his mind, he asked something Thanatos had mentioned two nights ago.

"Thanatos said we know you but won't tell me how. Says I have to figure it out myself." His tone came out more bitter than he intended.

She stopped walking and finally turned to face him, her eyes searching his face. Her expression too complicated to decipher, he avoided her gaze and tripped over his own tongue.

"I mean—I just—I thought you looked really familiar the first time we met, but you spend more time with Thanatos, and I haven't seen you much since then, and actually it's made me a little upset. I mean, not that I'm *trying* to see you. It's not like *that*. Not that I *wouldn't* want to see you. It's just, it's hard for Thanatos to be so popular and—gods, I'm a fool."

His face burned; his heart slammed against his ribs as if beating him for every ridiculous word he had rattled off. His eyes stayed glued to the tip of his boot as he dragged it across the granite, suddenly wondering how it was possible for rock to be so perfect and beautiful and wondering if it was made with magic. But eventually, the silence became so overwhelming, even the stunning architecture wasn't enough to keep his mind off his foolishness.

"Listen, Syrinthia, I'm sorry—" But he paused when he realized she was laughing. Not robustly, like most, but quietly, with her shoulders shaking gently and a hand over her mouth, as if trying to stifle a laugh she perhaps found embarrassing. After all, she sounded a little like a snorting dragon hatchling.

"How was that . . ." A frown dragged down his lips, but he was too baffled to feel embarrassed. "I'm sorry, what are you laughing at?"

She shook her head, taking a few deep breaths before she was able to speak a full sentence without breaking into laughter again. "You. I'm laughing at you, Thaddeus. Or rather, *with* you, I hope."

Heat rose into his face again as he prepared to defend himself, familiar dread filling him the same as every other time he heard what sounded like an insult.

"I've upset you." She quickly shook his shoulders, worry in her voice. "No, no, no. I only mean that you are so cute to look at."

The confusion and hurt in his expression weren't hard to imagine. "That doesn't make me feel much better." He tried to laugh to take the edge from his voice, but the sound came out more like a labored croak.

"Oh, *ue,* what am I saying?" Her hands flew to cover her face, which was as red as Thaddeus knew his own was. "Boys don't want to be called cute. Men, I mean. Or young man. *Ue!* What I mean is you are so nice to watch and look at and listen to. You're refreshing. You're not so worried about being tough, strong, or intimidating."

Thaddeus shrugged and muttered, "Well, that's because I'm weak, scrawny, and have no chance at being any of those things."

"Oh, stop being so pitiful." She rolled her eyes, but instead of being insulted, he trusted the sincerity in her eyes, which said she was only insulting him because she didn't want him feeling sorry for himself. "It's refreshing, alright? That's what I mean. I'm surrounded by meatheads every day. It's nice to be around someone who has something useful between their ears."

He couldn't help but chuckle. "I can't disagree with you. It does get a little . . . dull, doesn't it?"

Nodding, she gestured for him to follow her again. "Exactly. Which is why I'm not very eager for you to leave." She winked over her shoulder before pointing to a large door at the end of the corridor. "That's the advanced history class." Students were already trickling through the doors; they were considerably older than the other students Thaddeus had seen thus far, but notably, the class was small compared to the other studies. "It's the only class we have together, which is rather sad, I think. Don't you?"

Thaddeus nodded absently, having lost himself in the way the golden suns-set light glowed around her dark hair and skin. He did his best to jump back into the conversation. "I agree." This was the first time he had seen her genuinely smile, and he couldn't stave off the butterflies taking flight in his stomach because, somehow, he was the cause of that beautiful smile. A grin spread across his own face as he repeated himself. "I agree."

Before they entered the room, she paused to look at him, a strange sparkle in her eyes. "You said Thanatos told you we know each other. He was right."

Thaddeus' eyebrows rose, somewhat surprised Thanatos hadn't been messing with him. "How?"

She chuckled. "We used to tutor together. My guardian helped your father teach you and Thanatos sword fighting."

His eyes widened. *Not Sophia—Syrinthia!* He resisted the urge to smack his forehead. Memories of their lessons flooded his mind. She'd changed much since then, but her eyes and smile remained unmistakable. "Yes, of course. Why didn't I remember?"

She shrugged. "We were young."

Then he remembered something else—something that shifted a few more details into place. "Your guardian . . . he's Swordmaster Rakland." The man had been eerily familiar; now it made sense why he knew so much about Thaddeus.

"Yes! That's right! I'm glad you remember. You know"—she took his hand in hers, pulling him, surprised, through the huge doors of the lecture hall—"we used to be great friends back then." The smile she tossed over her shoulder made him forget the strange feeling that had settled in his gut. "And I have a pretty good feeling we're going to be great friends now too."

A bright smile lifted his cheeks as the doors closed behind them with a bang.

"THADDEUS, WHERE'RE YOU GOING?"

Jolting from his thoughts, Thaddeus turned, eyes flickering from Thanatos to the friend circle his brother had developed. Though they seemed eager to leave, Thaddeus was comforted by the genuine concern in Thanatos' eyes.

"I just"—Thaddeus gestured to the school gates—"I forgot my study notes in the lecture hall." Only a moment passed before he stopped looking his brother in the eyes. The prying gazes and whispers of Thanatos' friends tainted his once unyielding adoration.

"That's alright. I'll come with you." Thanatos broke away from his group, waving them on and laughing at something one of them said. "Come on. I don't want to be late for dinner. Let's hurry."

"No." Thaddeus' eyes didn't stray from the pebbles on the ground as Thanatos grabbed his arm, ready to pull him along.

"What do you mean? Let's go. I don't want you going alone."

"I'm fine." The words were a sour lie on his lips, but he wanted so badly for them to be true.

"Thaddeus." Thanatos rolled his eyes and scoffed. "Don't be like this. I know that Gordon has his eyes on you, and I know it's because he's jealous of me. It's basically my fault, and I don't want you to get hurt because of me."

A few of Thanatos' friends snickered, clearly eavesdropping on their conversation; Thaddeus felt his face burn.

"Don't listen to them." Thanatos turned to the students, shooting them a look that made them shuffle uncomfortably. "You're my brother. I'm going to make sure you're safe."

Thanatos would only let him go alone if he were convinced his younger brother would truly be fine. Forcing a smile on his face, he lightly punched Thanatos' shoulder. "I know. But seriously. No one's at the lecture hall anyway. Even Gordon doesn't want to hang around school after hours. I'll be home before you know it."

Thanatos' eyes narrowed, and for a long moment, Thaddeus wasn't sure he'd relent. His heart swelled with adoration for his brother who still cared about him despite rising to be one of the most popular students. But even so, Thaddeus couldn't accept this kind of care. Especially from his brother. He had to learn to protect himself. And if anything happened to him, maybe Mother could convince Father to let him withdraw, despite what promises Syrinthia had said he made.

"Alright." Thanatos stepped away, shrugging and shaking his head. He didn't look convinced by Thaddeus' wide, almost silly grin, but he moved back to his friends regardless. "Just be home before dark, or else Father will have your scales."

Thaddeus rolled his eyes as he turned away, grumbling. "I know." It took all his self-control to drown the sounds of the students laughing. Most of them didn't have a curfew and thought it childish to have one.

He didn't look back as he quickly made his way to the looming gates. They wouldn't be locked for another thirty minutes—just enough time to get in, grab his notes, and get back out. A glance at the sky told him the suns wouldn't set for another forty-five minutes; he wouldn't make it home before dark.

"Fantastic."

By this time, he had memorized the shortest routes through the school. Being able to traverse the long corridors as quickly as possible meant less time for the bullies to find and corner him and meant more time for reviewing lecture notes. With only three classes, studying wasn't difficult to keep up with, but that only made the lectures more boring. When he asked to be advanced, he was denied. The professors insisted he had to test out of his current level first, but they also wouldn't let students take the test before the end of the first half year, lest they help others cheat. The situation was frustrating. Though the thought of learning more intense curriculum excited him, it didn't nearly as much as being in the same classes as Syrinthia.

"Thaddeus!"

For a moment, he thought the voice was only in his head, but her hand on his shoulder was undeniably real, and so was the flutter in his stomach.

"Did you forget your notes in the lecture hall?"

A slight frown tugged his lips as he re-shouldered his bag. "I did. How did you know?"

She pointed to his left hand. "Empty. Very uncharacteristic of you. You're almost always clutching some sort of book."

Absently, he scratched the back of his neck. He was too flattered to be embarrassed. "I'm surprised you noticed."

She shrugged, already pulling ahead of him. They were nearly the same height, but she always managed to walk much faster than him. In fact, he was convinced she had a deity ancestor because of how ethereally and quickly she moved.

"You walk strangely." He hated the words as soon as they left his lips. "I'm sorry, that sounded so—"

Her snorting laugh cut him off as she waved dismissively. "I take it as a compliment. My guardian says it's because I danced a lot when I was a little girl. But I like to think maybe it's because I'm descended from the stars." Her eyes lifted upwards.

His gaze followed hers as their walk slowed to a stop, a soft silence wrapping them in the cool arms of dusk. Little pinpoints of light were beginning to shine in the darkening sky. They twinkled and winked as if alive and talking to one another, their reflection in the glass lecture hall dome enchanting in a way Thaddeus hoped he'd never forget. *I wonder what secrets they're revealing to the Centaurs tonight.*

"Do you think such a thing is possible?" Her question was soft, as gentle as the starlight itself.

"What?"

Their eyes met. "Being descended from the stars. Do you think it could be . . . possible?"

His heart skipped a beat as he considered it. It could be possible, couldn't it? Didn't they learn in history class that some Centaur and Faun legends stated their distant ancestors were stars trapped on Rasa? Staring into her black eyes, the galaxies above them shining in her curious gaze, he almost responded, *"I don't know, but if anyone would be so lucky to be a part of the stars, I think you'd be the one."* But he didn't. Instead, he shrugged. "It must be possible. Somehow. Otherwise, the Centaurs and Fauns wouldn't be so certain about it. In some aspect, truth is found in myths and legends."

Nodding, she turned her gaze back to the stars, drinking in every word as if he were an esteemed professor. "I think you're right. Maybe not physically, but maybe, somehow, our souls can be from there."

"Maybe so."

The silence between them stretched until she shook herself back to reality, a smile parting her lips. "Come on. We need to get your notes."

Thaddeus found it much more difficult to pull away from the heavens and the awe he felt as he watched them uncloak themselves from the day, revealing their splendor.

Stepping back into the long corridors, they started running to make up for lost time. Sooner than expected, he slipped through the massive doors of the lecture hall he'd grown fond of.

Wishing he could stay to reread the fascinating notes on governmental history decorating the black board, he forced himself to grab his notes, bind them shut with a leather strip, and slip back where Syrinthia was waiting.

"Ah, that's more like the Thaddeus I know." She gestured to the papers under his arm.

"Still surprised you cared to notice." He shook his head, a smile cracking on his lips.

"I notice everything." Though her words were prideful, a strange note in her voice made him pause to search her face; he saw confusion.

"Does that bother you?" Though they didn't have much longer before the school closed its gates, in that moment, time didn't hold them in its grasp.

Thick braids brushed against her cheeks as she shook her head. "No, it doesn't *bother* me. Why would you ask that?"

Shrugging, he clamped his mouth shut, feeling as though he had asked too much. But as they started their jog, her sullen silence convinced him she was more disturbed than she admitted.

The rest of the trip remained silent. Though he wanted to mend the gaping distance between them, he knew he'd been the cause of the weight settling over her shoulders. Not wanting to make it worse, he kept his mouth shut.

When they exited the last great doors onto the lawn, Thaddeus spotted a familiar figure waiting outside the gates.

"Thanatos!" Syrinthia's face lit up, and she waved.

A pang of uncomfortable emotion welled up in Thaddeus as his brother eagerly waved back. *Is this jealousy?* But he pushed the thought away and put on an extra burst of speed to catch up with Syrinthia.

"Just in time. Lucky your brother came back for you. I'd have locked you in." A burly guard leaned against the doorway of what Thaddeus presumed to be the gatehouse.

"*Shäshisä*. Thank you for waiting." His face flushed red as he nodded. "It won't happen again."

Instead of being upset—as Thaddeus expected—the guard only studied him a moment longer, then shrugged. "Maybe it will. Who am I to tell? I was young once too." His lips curled as he turned back into the building. "I suppose I could overlook it once more."

Thaddeus frowned, lingering a moment, as he watched the man disappear into the dark room. The gates started closing, the creak of metal jolting him back into the present. He slipped through the gate after Syrinthia as Thanatos sauntered over.

"Thanks for coming back, Than." Thaddeus kept his eyes on the ground. To his surprise, Thanatos wasn't upset either.

"Of course, don't mention it." Thanatos barely acknowledged Thaddeus. Instead, he focused on Syrinthia. "Would you let me walk you home?"

Syrinthia's face lit up before she frowned. "You should go with Thaddeus. I'll be fine."

The golden rays of the setting suns were just disappearing off the tops of the granite buildings; Thaddeus knew in only a few more minutes, the dusk would dim to night. None of them would arrive home before dark. Though he couldn't help being on the streets after dark, he had no intention of being out alone. Not after everything their mother had drilled into them.

"Maybe we both could—"

Thanatos cut him off. "You'll be fine, right, Thad? Home isn't too far. You know the way." A certain look in his eyes told Thaddeus he didn't want someone tagging along. A knot tied in Thaddeus' stomach.

"Sure. I know the way."

"Thanatos, wait—"

"It's alright, Syrinthia." Thanatos placed his hand on her back, gently steering her away. "It's not dark yet, and I'd rather Thaddeus face the streets alone than our mother's wrath because he was out late, if you know what I mean." He tossed a wink over his shoulder, and Thaddeus forced out a laugh.

"She's pretty strict when it comes to curfew." The words burned on his mouth and rotted in his own ears. "I'll be fine. It's not far."

"Alright." Syrinthia finally relented, but before Thaddeus forced himself down the street, he caught the worried look she cast over her shoulder. His stomach plummeted. Doing his best to brighten his face with a casual smile, he waved and turned away.

Resentment wormed its way into his heart as he kicked a rock and watched it tumble down the road. *You owe me now, Than. Big time.* His teeth worried into his bottom lip as he turned down one street after another, making sure to keep his landmarks in view. *Imagine that: letting your own little brother walk the streets alone at night just because you want a few minutes alone with a girl.*

But though these thoughts tumbled over each other in his mind, he knew they were drowning out the truth. He didn't resent Thanatos for forcing him to walk the streets alone. He resented him for something else entirely, and he hated every inch of himself for it.

Chapter 7

Keeping his promise to carry on the forgotten traditions of Ancient Duvarharia was proving to be much more difficult than Thaddeus had initially anticipated.

One of his teachers excitedly buzzed on about the *benierku*—arena games fought between Duvarharians or animals. As the professor's lecture focused on their laws and traditions, particularly the opening ceremonies and how they were developed, Thaddeus became increasingly disinterested. Digging his nails into the desk, he scratched little designs in the wood, concluding the other markings next to his were left by other previously bored students.

Gazing up for a moment, he surveyed the room; he was alone in his exasperation. Nearly every other student was paying rapt attention to the professor. The few whose focus drifted were clearly more interested in the actual fighting aspects of the games.

Just before he zoned out again, Thaddeus caught a sentence that made his skin prickle.

"During the golden age of Duvarharia, after the Etas were officially annihilated, the Great Lord officially banned the games, saying they were of the wicked Wyriders, but in the outskirts of Duvarharia, the games continued in secret until they were forcefully shut down about one hundred years later by the Shadows of Light."

Thaddeus' hand shot into the air before he could stop it. One of the old bedtime stories Quinlan used to tell him and Thanatos was of the

Shadows of Light. The story had been whimsical, speaking of powerful magic returning to the land. But as much as he enjoyed hearing the fall of the evil shape-shifting Etas, it hadn't been as factually informative as he would've liked.

"Yes, Thaddeus." The professor's lively face sagged as he took off his glasses, clearly upset at being interrupted.

"Professor, I was wondering, could you tell us more about the Shadows of Light? I thought they were a peaceful religion that didn't believe in force."

The professor's eyes widened. "Well yes, they were for a while, but we have many historical records of the Shadows of Light going against their own teachings to partake in violent, cult-like behavior, such as revolting against the games. Which"—he turned back to the rest of the class, determined to steer the lecture back to the original lesson—"was a huge attack on local communities since the games brought in foreign trade from the Wyriders and sometimes humans. Even now, the games benefit local councils with taxes and attracting consumers for local trade."

Thaddeus rolled his eyes while students eagerly scribbled in their study books as if this were important information they would need in the arenas. *How can they sit here, taking in this information, without seeing a sliver of evidence?* Though it was obvious he cared more about the truth surrounding the government and its struggle against the influence of the games than most of these students did, he failed to understand how easily they believed the trade surrounding the game was legal.

He raised his hand again; this time, the teacher ignored him.

"Excuse me, but what evidence do we have that the Shadows of Light had any part in those revolts? And where is evidence of the games benefiting our communities? Aren't the regular kidnappings a direct and dangerous result of the prominence of games in our own city?"

The entire class stared at him. Slowly, he lowered his hand, his face burning, his heart racing. *Maybe I shouldn't have said so much.*

The professor must've agreed because Thaddeus soon found himself standing in the hall, the door shutting none too quietly behind him. The man's words rang over and over in his mind, *"I can't have you being a disruption to my class. Remove yourself and think about your actions."*

Sliding down the wall until he was sitting knees to his chest, Thaddeus did just that. "What a worthless teacher and class. Who even cares about the opening ceremonies of the games? Doesn't anyone want to know why a peaceful religious movement was supposedly revolting violently against the games? Doesn't anyone want to talk about how much the games are tearing our city apart? I don't regret saying a single thing. Not at all. *Dasunab*. I'll show them."

But as he sat alone in the hall, cast out of class, unheard, and forgotten, he wondered what exactly he wanted to show them. How could a small, weak boy like himself ever be allowed a voice big enough to say anything at all?

Eventually, a dragon roared, and the rooms emptied into the halls, the once peaceful corridors suddenly torn apart by the chaos of students pushing and shoving their way around each other; teachers called after them, reminding them of extra studying they needed to accomplish.

Thaddeus scrambled to his feet, attempting to fade into the wall behind him. Every gaze from his class focused on him. Whispers passed between students but never quiet enough so he couldn't hear. He knew they wanted him to hear.

"What a loser."

"Who does he even think he is?"

"He just wants attention. I bet his family ignores him when he's home."

"I wouldn't blame them if they do."

"*Dasuun qevab*."

Thaddeus' head hung low as he clutched his notes to his chest. The fire he had felt when alone turned to cold ash as regret filled his heart. *I shouldn't have asked those things. It wasn't the right time. Wasn't the right class.* But if that hadn't been the right time or place, then what was?

"Thanks for ruining class, loser."

Thaddeus jumped, his heart leaping into his throat as a hand smacked the wall above his head, caging him between the granite and a much larger boy.

"What? I didn't—"

The boy bared his teeth and narrowed his shining green eyes, a lock of greasy black hair falling into Thaddeus' face. "Don't lie. You just don't like talking about the games because you know you're too weak to fight in them. Too pathetic to stand up to any of us, aren't you?"

Words tripped over themselves in Thaddeus' mouth; all he could think of was how the boy smelled like he hadn't showered in at least a week. From the looks of his clothes, Thaddeus was certain he was right. "Did your mother never teach you to shower and wash your clothes, or do you just not have one?"

The boy's eyes widened, his mouth hanging open.

"A mother, I mean. In case you were too dumb to know what I meant."

Blood flushed the boy's face as he roared with rage, pulling back his fist. Before his fist contacted with flesh, Thaddeus dropped to the floor. The sickening crack of bone against granite filled the hallway; in the split moment before the pain registered in the bully's mind, Thaddeus scrambled to his feet and took off running.

Screams of pain and rage chased him down the hall. Despite knowing he was running in the opposite direction of his next class, Thaddeus didn't stop. When he didn't recognize his surroundings, he finally slowed to a walk, lungs burning, legs screaming in protest. As he slowed his heart, trying to suck in a long, deep breath, he took a moment to survey the foreign halls.

Dark shadows stretched across the corridor. By the angle the shadows were slanted, he guessed this was the most eastern facing wing. Two large doors to what he assumed must be another study hall were cracked open to his left. To his right were massive stained-glass windows of a different style than the rest of the school.

Ignoring every instinct which begged him to turn around, find his way back to class, and obediently face the laughing students and annoyed teachers, he slowly walked toward the study hall. His footsteps echoed through the empty halls.

He hesitated at the carved doors. *You shouldn't be here,* he told himself. But a voice deeper in his mind whispered, *This is exactly where you need to be.*

Without another hesitation, he pushed open the door just enough to slip inside and shut it quietly behind him.

His breath froze in his lungs.

It wasn't a study hall. Not at all.

Instead, an exhibit stretched before him like a dream.

Pathways of stone weaved around staged displays under a glass conservatory-like dome. Strange plants spilled from the platforms and across the ground, snaking up trees or around rocks. Each platform displayed a different terrain: some forest-like, others grassy, some familiar, others exotic.

Thaddeus held his breath, feeling much too alive in a room so full of motionless objects. But it wasn't just the unnatural stillness making his stomach flop. Something else felt . . . off.

The form of a creature became clear, half hidden in a mass of vines. Then he spied another, and another.

They vaguely resembled Duvarharians, but Thaddeus knew they were anything but. Their skin tones ranged from pink to green to blue, while others resembled even the patterns of strange animals. Some appeared to be fashioned from bark or branches; others grew fur.

Though he knew he should turn back, Thaddeus felt himself drawn to the strange mutations.

Many of the creatures grew directly from the plants, their feet disappearing into flowering vines that curled up their legs, from their fingertips, and even their hair.

The other more animalistic creatures boasted long claws, tails, and the legs of large cats, goats, or canines. Eerily, they reminded Thaddeus of Centaurs and Fauns, but the longer he stared at them, the more certain he was they were something else. Something wilder.

A female creature knelt in a flower bush. He couldn't tell where the bush ended and she began; perhaps she was as much the bush as it was her. Her hands remained extended above her, her eyes the same soft pink of the flowers along the bush, her body, and her hair.

Subconsciously, he reached for her. Green and leaf-like, her skin seemed as delicate as a spring wind. Small veins sparkled in the suns, as if struggling to feel their warmth again. She looked so real, so life-like as her eyes stared into his; they almost pleaded with him, begging for life, for freedom. Only a breath of air hung between him and her. If only—

"Thaddeus? What are you doing in here?"

Snatching his hand away, he whirled around, struggling not to trip over another feline figure crouching behind him as if about to pounce.

His heart pounded against his ribs and rang in his ears as he searched for the voice.

As soon as his eyes met hers, he relaxed. "Syrinthia." A sigh of relief escaped his lips, though he didn't feel as relaxed as he wished to be. The eyes of the creatures bored into the back of his head as if waiting for him. "You startled me."

She shook her head, chuckling. "I see that." Sliding something she was holding behind her back, she nodded to the creatures around him.

Though he didn't ask, he wondered what she was hiding and what business she had in the exhibit. Clearly, she hadn't been expecting to see him, which meant she hadn't been looking for him.

"Aren't they so strange?" A quiet sadness hung in her voice as she moved to his side.

He couldn't look at what she was holding without appearing nosy, so he decided to forget about it. If she wasn't going to press why he was down here, he wouldn't either.

"Truly." Silence stretched between them as they took in the staged scenes. "What are they?"

Hesitation flashed in her eyes as if she were waiting for the right answer. "An experiment, I think." Her eyes landed on a creature whose body blended into something like a wolf, its face still uncomfortably human, its eyes dull and sad.

"For what?"

She shook her head. "I'm not sure exactly."

"Are they real?"

"I . . . don't know."

When he surveyed her conflicted emotions, he wasn't sure he believed her. She caught his gaze and turned away.

"They've been here a long time. Longer than most of the staff, I think. I'm not sure anyone really knows what it is. I just come here for the silence. It's mostly forgotten."

"It doesn't look forgotten." He didn't like how none of her words made much sense. Cobwebs didn't line the corners of the room, the windows were washed and clean, and everything appeared fresh, as if it wasn't as old or abandoned as Syrinthia insisted.

When she shrugged and turned away, she wasn't holding anything behind her back. He frowned. *Had she hidden what she was holding, or am I paranoid?*

A frown lined his brow as he followed her. He tried to glance back once more to the woman in the pink flowers, unready to let her go, but Syrinthia blocked his view.

"Like I said, I don't know much about it. Just what I've been told or the rumors I've heard." Seeming too eager to shut the doors behind them and start down the hall, she quickly changed the subject. "How are you liking your classes?"

A groan escaped his lips before he could stop it, and she raised her eyebrows. "That bad, huh?"

Shoving his hands into his pockets, he found the smooth stone he had collected to fidget with. "They're alright. I guess I just wasn't aware this school put so much focus on the games." A soft chuckle shrugged his shoulders. The incident from earlier almost seemed comical now. Almost. "I actually just got kicked out of class before coming here."

"Seriously?" She stopped to look at him. "What for?"

Not wanting to meet her eyes in case he would find disappointment in them, he watched his boots drag across the ground. "I guess I asked too many questions."

He could hear the frown in her voice as she answered. "About what?"

"The Shadows of Light. My teacher said only one hundred years after the Great Lord, they revolted violently against the *benierku* games, which were illegal at the time. I argued that didn't make sense since they were a peaceful religious group, so he told me to leave class and stop being a disruption."

"You're not wrong to ask those questions, you know."

He sneaked a glance at her face. Something like pride shone in her eyes, and his stomach did a somersault. "I don't know. I kind of feel like I was wrong for it."

She shook her head, her dark braids falling from the loose knot she had tied them into. "Not at all. In fact, I'm as intrigued as you are. Maybe if I can get a pass into the upper library, we could find some reading material on it. Did you ask if he had any references?"

Thaddeus shook his head as they began climbing the stairs he had run down not ten minutes ago. "He didn't. In fact, he got most upset when I asked for references."

Skipping up two steps at a time, she rolled her eyes. "Typical."

Thaddeus took the stairs one at a time, letting silence and space spread between them as she waited at the top. When he caught up, the clamor of the halls grew louder with each step.

Syrinthia looked at him and nodded as if making up her mind. "I'm going to ask my guardian if he'll give us two day passes into the upper library tomorrow. Are you alright with skipping a few classes or lunch so we have enough time to look around? They don't keep that library open after classes."

He didn't hesitate. "Absolutely."

Waving to the group of friends she shared with Thanatos, she made her way to them, calling over her shoulder, "Just don't get too used to skipping classes! I don't want to get in trouble for it!"

A small smile curved the corner of his lips as he answered, though she probably wouldn't hear, "Don't worry. I wouldn't let you get in trouble for anything I do." He wasn't concerned about becoming accustomed to skipping class; he already was. After being tossed from one today, he was sure he'd be skipping them more often.

"THIS IS RIDICULOUS." Syrinthia slid farther down in the chair she had thrown herself onto.

Thaddeus buried his head in his arms, sagging against the table where they'd stacked their books. He wasn't feeling any more positive about their research than she. Two hours had passed, and they'd only managed to find one book that mentioned the Shadows of Light. Every other book the librarians had suggested was either checked out or couldn't be found. When they pressed further, they were told the ones currently checked out had been so for over a year; the borrower obviously had no intention of returning the books, and it didn't seem like the library cared either.

Though Syrinthia assured him this was normal, even expected, he still wondered if books about the Shadows of Light had been purposely removed or even banned. Even so, Syrinthia was also frustrated, certain they should've found at least *something* more by now.

"Are you sure this upper library actually has 'better' material?"

She groaned in response.

"Because I'm starting to believe it has the same as the lower library.

I think they just want to enforce day passes so you *think* it's better or so they can charge more on late fees."

Shaking her head, she clenched her jaw and toyed with the hem of her shirt. "I don't know. Maybe you're right."

As much as he didn't want to draw attention to it, Thaddeus pointed to the massive clock in the center of the hall. "I think our teachers are going to notice we're missing if we keep sitting here."

Her eyes followed his finger, and she yelped, collecting the books as quickly as possible. "Quick, help me get these put away! I promised I'd help one of my teachers set up a demonstration today."

Paying attention to how cute she looked trying to stack a ridiculous number of books into her arms instead of hurrying, he collected his own stack of books and followed her deep into the towering bookcases lining the room. Rolling ladders ran the length of each one. In awe, he watched as a librarian used magic to levitate a stack of books next to her while effortlessly pushing herself across the bookcase on one of the ladders. Books reshelved themselves or landed gently on her floating stack with only the flick of her hand.

"Hey, a little help please?" Syrinthia's strained voice brought his focus back to her just before a book smacked his head.

"Ow! What was that for?"

"Well, if you would've been paying attention, you wouldn't have gotten hurt!"

A familiar knot tied in his stomach as he opened his mouth to defend himself, but when he looked into her soft gaze staring down at him, all bitter words died on his lips. Instead of being upset, she was struggling to hide her laughter. When she snorted, Thaddeus couldn't stay quiet and burst out laughing loud enough for echoes to travel down the shelves.

"Quiet down!" A sharp reprimand from the librarian he had been admiring earlier snapped his mouth shut. "I hear one more peep from you, and I'll seal your mouth shut the rest of the day."

Syrinthia's wide eyes stared into his. He resorted to biting his hand to keep from laughing.

Thaddeus handed the books to her while she did her best to reshelve them where she'd found them. Finally, he knelt to grab the book that had hit his head. A slip of paper fell from its ruffled pages.

The fall must've jarred it loose. He picked up the slip of paper, about to replace it between worn pages of old text, when the phrase *Darkness Grows in the Shadows of Light* caught his eye.

"What'd you find?" Syrinthia whispered, straining to see what he was holding.

"Oh, um . . ." The memory of her hiding something from him in the exhibit room flashed into his mind. On impulse, he decided not to share his findings. "Just an old day pass someone used as a bookmark." Crumpling the paper, he stuffed it into his pocket. "I'll throw it away. It's probably not something the librarians want pressed between pages in an ancient book."

Shaking her head with a smile, she took the book from his hands. "Yes, because a little piece of paper is going to be far more damaging than it being dropped on a young boy's head."

"Right." He hated how she said "young boy." Despite the closeness he'd felt over their shared research, he was suddenly reminded they were hardly friends. If anything, she only spoke with him because he was Thanatos' brother. Bitterness rose in his throat and heart. When she climbed down the ladder and shot him a questioning look, he didn't offer any other explanation besides a moody shrug of his shoulders.

When they exited the library, the metal gates outside the doors clanging shut with the click of a lock, the only goodbye they shared was a strained handshake and a "see you later."

Though he pretended to make his way to his next class, as soon as he was out of her sight, he ducked behind a pillar and stuffed his hands in his pockets, drawing out the paper.

Most of the writing was in what seemed to be Ancient Duvarharian, but it must've been a dialect he wasn't familiar with. The only words written in common tongue were *Darkness Grows in the Shadows of Light.*

Turning it in the green light of a stained-glass window, he realized it was from some sort of flyer or newspage. But what caught his eye most was the fairly new ink decorating the bottom of the scrap in small, flowing script.

Before he could try to decipher what it said, a dragon's roar broke the air, and once again the halls were flooded with students on their way to the next class.

Stuffing the note back into his pocket, he pressed himself away from the crushing mob, doing his best to fade into the background before one of his classmates decided they had enough time to bully him.

The note must have been written recently, perhaps from another borrower. If he was lucky, one of the librarians might let him look through the book's record and find who last checked it out. Then he could find a reference of their handwriting and eventually match it to the note.

It seemed farfetched, but it was the only clue he had. Right now, anything was better than thinking about all the other mysteries plaguing his mind and wondering when the next hateful word or "accidental" blow would land.

Chapter 8

"Hey, Thaddeus!"

Thanatos' piercing whistle dragged Thaddeus from the corner he'd pressed himself into while waiting for the lunch lines to dissipate so he could pick up his own food in peace.

Thanatos whistled again before Thaddeus saw him waving. He almost shouted back, but when he spotted the rest of Thanatos' friends, the words died in his throat. *What if I don't answer? What if I just . . . turn around and leave? They wouldn't really notice me missing. I'm sure Thanatos would just shrug his shoulders and forget about me.* Subconsciously, he started turning away, but then another familiar voice called after him.

"Oh, he's over by the columns." Syrinthia started waving, her bright smile crinkling her nose.

With a defeated sigh, Thaddeus waved back, his brother quickly making his way through the crowd, the students seeming to form a path.

"Hey! Where've you been? I thought we were supposed to eat lunch together, remember? I haven't been able to find you the last few days."

Thaddeus' stomach churned when he met his brother's shining blue gaze and saw the obnoxious way his black hair fell into his eyes—something the female students swooned over.

"Seriously? It's been over a month since I've eaten lunch with you." An uncomfortable silence stretched between them before Thaddeus continued. "I'm surprised it's taken you this long to realize."

"Come on, Thad, that's not fair." Thanatos' olive skin flushed red as he shifted his weight from one foot to the another—something he did when he was deeply upset.

Fine. Let him be upset. Can't feel any worse than how I felt the first few days he didn't even look for me.

"If you wanted to sit with me, why didn't you look for me? You can't be too upset since you didn't care enough to find me."

Thaddeus' blood boiled as hateful words brewed on his lips, but then Syrinthia joined them, and Thaddeus bit back his spiteful comment.

"Actually." He hated how calm and cold his voice sounded. It was so very unlike how he felt on the inside. "I did try to find you. You were just too busy with all your other friends to notice."

Immediately, he wished he could take back his words. Thanatos' eyes flashed with hurt, then cascading waves of anger. Syrinthia's eyes widened, her mouth opened in surprise at the venom in his tone.

"Well, I'm here now, aren't I?" Thanatos' teeth ground against each other. "Do you want to sit with us or not?"

I really don't, is what Thaddeus wanted to say, but when his eyes met Syrinthia's, another word replaced them. "Alright." Moments later, he was seated at the end of a crowded table full of Thanatos' friends—more people than Thaddeus even knew personally.

Syrinthia was on the other side of the table with Thanatos, and though she kept casting forlorn looks to Thaddeus, he found it hard to accept her pity without being infuriated. *If you feel so bad about leaving me alone, maybe you should trade seats with someone.* But she wouldn't. As much as she seemed to enjoy Thaddeus' company in the halls between classes, he had the crushing feeling it was only because she felt obligated to watch after Thanatos' little brother; he knew it because of how she looked at Thanatos and the way she laughed a little too loudly when he said a stupid joke.

Although, they're all laughing a little too hard. He isn't even that funny. Maybe they're all just dumb. Pushing his food around his plate after only a few bites, he found he didn't have much of an appetite.

An oafish fellow, who seemed capable of cracking Thaddeus' spine with flick, finally stopped eyeballing his plate and drawled the question he'd obviously been waiting a while to ask. "Are you going to finish that?"

"What?" Thaddeus followed the student's thick finger to the uneaten food on his own plate. "Oh." His lips curved downward. "I guess not." Before he'd finished talking, the young man was busy devouring the food.

Thaddeus caught a disapproving frown from Syrinthia; he shook his head and shrugged, hoping she wouldn't bring it up later. He sighed in relief when she turned her focus back to Thanatos, who spun a grand, exaggerated story. He hadn't said a word to his little brother since they sat down.

What am I doing here? I might as well be invisible. I can't believe Thanatos used to worry when I didn't eat much. If I stood up and left right now, I bet no one would notice.

All too eager to test the theory, he shoved his chair back and stood, but coincidentally, so did Thanatos. "I have an idea," he announced, a familiar mischievous glint in his eyes—a look that once stirred excitement in Thaddeus; now anxiety sparked instead.

The other students jumped to their feet, eager energy buzzing between them.

Thanatos leaned in as if to share a dark secret. "We should sneak into the animal pits and see what they're hiding down there. I heard they got a few new captures for the higher classes' training."

Before anyone could show support of the outlandish idea, Thaddeus spat out the first words that came to mind. "This is ridiculous." All eyes turned to him; the nausea rising in his stomach begged for him to take back what he said. Palms suddenly sweaty, he stumbled over a few words before a sentence finally emerged. "I just, I was thinking, wouldn't that—I don't know—wouldn't that get us kicked out?"

Worry emerged on the faces of the other students as they turned back to Thanatos, who looked at Syrinthia. Though she didn't seem happy to be dragged into this, she hid her frustrations well, aside from her nervous picking at her fingers.

Can't Thanatos see she's uncomfortable? No, of course he wouldn't. He can't see anything past his ego anymore. He couldn't understand why Syrinthia continued to play along with Thanatos' risky ideas, though they clearly disturbed her.

Instead of speaking her mind the way she usually did, she only shrugged, avoiding their gazes. "Technically, anyone can go into the pits. It's not a secret they use animals for training. The teachers would just rather us not skip class."

Thanatos was satisfied with that. "History, then. That's the class we'll skip. How's that sound?"

Everyone, except Thaddeus, readily agreed. History was his favorite class. In fact, it was the only class he looked forward to.

"Thaddeus?"

Hearing his name completely caught him off guard; for a moment, he couldn't believe Thanatos was talking to him.

"Are you coming or not?"

Everything in his soul begged him to walk away. He almost did as Thanatos moved toward him. But part of him remembered the fun he and his brother used to have together and yearned to feel that companionship again, even if it was brief and involved other people.

"Alright, I'll be there. I guess." Though he hated himself for agreeing, he was also deeply satisfied by the broad grin spreading across his brother's face as he clasped him into a rough side hug.

"I knew you still had some fun in you."

Hiding his grin, Thaddeus shrugged his shoulders, playfully shoving Thanatos away. "Whatever, Than." *Maybe I'm just projecting everyone else's view of me onto him. He's my brother after all; we're still best friends. Right?*

Minutes later, he found himself in the corridors ... alone. The warmth that had spread through his heart in the dining hall faded into a familiar, dark ache. A deep sigh left his lips as he forced his feet to move one after the other and carry him begrudgingly to his next class.

Time moved slowly through the class before history. Every possible outcome of this ridiculous plan repeated over and over in his mind. *What if we get caught? Will they blame the idea on me? Will I be able to claim I was forced into it? Am I being forced into it, or do I actually want to go?*

But as slowly as the day had been trudging by, the class ended too soon, and he found himself being pushed by Thanatos down an empty hall to where the other students waited: three girls, including Syrinthia, and two boys were waiting—the same group from lunch. They were hiding behind a few large columns, conveying their excitement in loud whispers.

"Whispering only works if you're actually being quiet." The words leaped from Thaddeus' mouth before he could stop them. He winced under the disapproving glares.

"I wasn't trying to be quiet," the blonde girl hissed, rolling her eyes. "I, unlike you, aren't afraid of getting caught."

"I didn't say—"

"Hey!" Thanatos clapped his hands, and Thaddeus clamped his mouth shut, trying to ignore how childish it was for the girl to stick her tongue out at him. "I don't want you guys to bicker. This is supposed to be fun, alright?"

"It *would* be fun if we didn't have a loser tagging along," the blonde girl's brother muttered under his breath.

Thaddeus' face burned as his hands balled into fists. Quickly, he glanced at Thanatos, hoping to be defended like on their first day at the academy. But instead, Thanatos ignored the comment as if he hadn't heard. Thaddeus' blood boiled as he ground his teeth. All the hope he'd felt earlier about his older brother still caring for him quickly dissipated.

"Let's go."

Thaddeus tried not to scoff too loudly as the group of kids sneaked away from the columns, thinking they were being covert when a three-hundred-year-old dragon a mile away could hear their giggles and footsteps. Hanging back, Thaddeus let the distance grow between him and the others. Syrinthia glanced back a few times, but when she tried to join him, Thanatos looped his fingers through hers and pulled her alongside him, whispering in her ear, making her blush and roll her eyes.

Sickening. But Thaddeus could think whatever insults he wanted; really, he wished he were the one whispering in Syrinthia's ears. Yet he wouldn't be dragging her somewhere she didn't want to go. *What does she see in him? Egotistical desert worm.* He knew exactly what she saw in him; he was handsome, strong, smart, and when he wanted to be, he was sensitive. *That's more than I have to offer. I have to stop thinking about this.*

All too soon, they had arrived at the dungeon-like pits beneath the school's largest fighting arena. As they neared the initial gates leading into the dark tunnels, a waft of animal feces and fear curdled Thaddeus' blood. All the muscles in his body froze; no matter how hard he tried, he couldn't take another step.

"Thaddeus. What are you doing?"

Sweat beaded on Thaddeus' forehead. His hands shook as he chewed his lip. He couldn't go in there. As if he were the animals, he felt fear rise into his muscles, hunger twisting his gut. He felt torn flesh tighten over his bones and mats of filth clinging to fur he didn't have. "No," he whispered quietly, backing up. "No, I can't."

"Scaredy dragon," one of the kids whispered. Soon, they were chanting slurs at him until Syrinthia yelled at them to stop.

Her hands cupped his face, finally breaking his gaze from the gates and cells beyond, tears filling his eyes as they met hers. "Don't make me go in there," he whimpered.

She nodded fiercely. "I won't. I promise."

Darkness swirled across his vision as his stomach flipped. She let him slip to the ground as she yelled at Thanatos.

Uncontrollable shaking rattled Thaddeus' body as his blood went from hot to freezing cold. He couldn't see anything other than blinding light spotting across darkness, couldn't hear anything except the ringing in his ears that sounded like dying animals screaming.

Finally, when he thought he couldn't bear it any longer, the yelling stopped as Thanatos stormed off with the other kids, the gate clanging shut behind them.

Slowly, the panic started to recede. His eyesight cleared, and he felt himself settle back into his own body. Syrinthia's hands gently rubbed his back, whispering a soft song that sounded like a lullaby his mother had once sung many years ago.

"Tell me what you're feeling, Thaddeus. Tell me what you felt."

Blubbering like a helpless child, he did his best to articulate his experience without sounding insane. "I was . . . I was *them*." With a shaky finger, he pointed to the cells. The animals were crying, pleading with Thanatos and his friends for help they would never give. "I could *feel* them. In me." Clawing at his chest, he sobbed against the memory of pain, fear, and hunger.

Cradling his head to her chest, she rocked him back and forth like a mother would, and he sagged into her touch. Warmth from her hands spread through his body and soul, reaching places he didn't know had ever been cold. The magic enveloped him, stilling and quieting the discontent he'd grown accustomed to the last few months.

Tears trickled down his face—tears of release and joy, tears that came from a place of peace rather than turmoil.

"It's alright. It's alright," she whispered. Then, as if she could read his mind, she said, "You're not crazy. You're not hallucinating. I think your compassion reached those animals, and you took on some of their suffering. A soul so tender as yours is a beautiful thing. Not many will ever feel something so powerful, loving, and compassionate."

After a long silence, he whispered the new question pressing on his mind. "Have you ever felt it?" Gazing up into her eyes, he felt as if he were looking at someone, or something, much older than just Syrinthia.

"Yes, I have. Many, many times."

Confused, he closed his eyes, surrendering to the warmth of her strange magic once again. "What do you see in him? Why do you stay with him?"

A tear fell on his face. The intensity of her grief took him by surprise. "Because I don't have a choice." Then she pressed her lips to his forehead, and everything went dark.

THADDEUS FIRST FELT the soft pillow under his head, then the blanket on his body, and a soft breeze blowing through an open window. Though he was desperate to grasp understanding of his situation, having no memory of what happened after his confusing conversation with Syrinthia, he groaned and rolled over instead, pulling the blanket over his face.

"Thaddeus?" A gentle voice called to him once and then again when he didn't answer. "Thaddeus, I'm sorry, but I can't let you sleep here. I'm only supposed to keep patients, not sleepy students."

Groaning again, Thaddeus rolled back over and cracked his eyes open. A cathedral-like ceiling greeted him. Without an elaborate mural painting upon it, this ceiling was much plainer than the rest of the school's ceilings. He found the simplistic design to be relaxing and a welcome change of scenery.

"Where am I?"

"The infirmary. Syrinthia called for me when you passed out near the arena corridors. She said something about fatigue and lack of nutrition. When was the last time you ate a full meal?"

Thaddeus frowned, ignoring the last question. Try as he might, he couldn't remember why he had blacked out; something deep in his mind pinned Syrinthia's magic as the culprit rather than hunger or fatigue. But he couldn't deny he wasn't healthy.

"And when was the last time you had a full night's sleep?"

Thaddeus hated how hard he had to think for answers. *When was the last time I didn't have any food left on my plate? Or slept through the night without a disturbing dream about school or overthinking something I said?*

A soft chuckle rang through the room. "I'm going to assume the answer to both of those questions is 'not recently'."

Thaddeus was too tired to be embarrassed by how amused the nurse seemed to be. Finally, he mustered up the strength to sit up, coming face to face with a most unlikely creature.

"Be careful a dragon doesn't fly into that mouth of yours."

Thaddeus clamped his lips shut, face flushing red. "You're—" He couldn't finish his question. What he stood before him seemed impossible.

The nurse had seemed Duvarharian upon first glance, but Thaddeus quickly noticed some things that proved this creature was something entirely different. Large, mouse-like ears poked out from the creature's thick, curly gray hair. Their nose was small and framed by little whiskers growing from their cheeks. Their two front incisors were unusually large, and a mouse-like tail curled around the creature's arm like an accessory. He would've thought it a costume if the ears and tail hadn't twitched. It was impossible to tell if the creature was male or female, and just when Thaddeus thought he had it figured out, he became confused again.

"If you're not planning on finishing that sentence, I'm going to hand you this"—the creature pushed a small bottle of herbs into his hand—"and this"—along with a paper. "These are just some sleeping herbs to help you get a better night's rest and instructions on how to brew the tea. And if your parents worry that we're giving you addictive substances, please remind them our school is supported by the Centaur's Inter-Ventronovian Medic Administration, and we only give our students substances their parents are able to purchase legally from any local apothecary."

The information went over Thaddeus' head, but he nodded anyway.

"Alright. Thank you so much."

With a twitch of their whiskers and a rub to their ears, the creature bowed. "My pleasure. Please tell dear Syrinthia I send greetings. I regretted not being able to speak with her longer when she called for me. Said she needed to find your brother, or something." Eyes widening, the creature snapped their long, slender fingers. "Oh! Please remind her that I have her prescription of *ui-mufak* for her."

Finally, some of the information sank into Thaddeus' mind, and he frowned. "*Ui-mufak*. Isn't that a potion made to suppress the conscious thoughts in dreams?"

The creature winked and bowed again. "How refreshing to meet a student who's smart *and* dashing. Yes, it is. Mostly for night terrors. But I've said too much. Please pass the message for me?"

Feeling as if in a waking dream and wondering if Syrinthia's magic had warped his perception of reality, he nodded. "I'll let her know."

"Wonderful, thank you!"

Then he was in the hall, the door shut, and the creature with all their secrets hidden behind it.

"Syrinthia has night terrors." He whispered the words over and over as he walked down the hall, his pace quickening to a run. Bits of their strange conversation just before he passed out came rushing back.

She said she was haunted at night and had felt what it was like to take on the sorrows of other creatures. The two couldn't be a coincidence. Not sure what was driving him, he found himself running back to the very place he'd dreaded going into.

He'd been at this school's mercy long enough. No more would he hide in its shadows. No more would he turn a blind eye every time something happened that didn't feel right. He demanded answers, and he was determined to have them.

Chapter 9

JUST DON'T LET *them in. Just don't let them in.* He'd been chanting the mantra to himself the entire trip from the infirmary, through several wrong turns, the crowds of students, and all the way back to the arena dungeons.

But now that he was standing only a few feet away from the wrought iron gates, tuning out the pain was almost impossible. The overwhelming amount of sorrow pouring from the animals was almost too much to bear. It welled up inside him, threatening to overtake him again. But this time, he focused on how Syrinthia's strange magic had flooded his senses with peace and strength.

Then he used all his will and focus to push that feeling into the minds of the animals he was so deeply connected to. Pressing against the hunger, pain, filth, and wounds was difficult, but a bit of the peace won over, and for a few long moments, the cells quieted.

Heart racing, he opened the latch on the gates and slipped inside. Gagging against the smell, he pinched his nose and slowly walked down the hall. Now that he was here, he wasn't sure why he had come back. Was it to face the animals and the reality of what this school was hiding? Was it to somehow understand the pain Syrinthia felt to the point she had to take drugs to help her sleep? Perhaps it was because he felt the sorrow of these creatures so deeply in his own soul that he was inevitably drawn to them and their pain. Whatever it was, it pulled him farther and farther into the halls until he was hopelessly lost.

Once he'd grown desensitized to the smell, he began to take closer notice of the creatures' physical appearances.

Earlier in the tunnels, though the creatures had been nearly unrecognizable due to mange, starvation, and wounds, he recognized them as familiar species: big cats, wolves, a few bears. But the deeper he went, the stranger and more mutated they became until he faced a locked iron gate.

An overwhelming compulsion transcending what he'd felt before reached out to him from the darkness beyond. This time, it wasn't just pain and suffering, it was familiarity, it was . . . home. Confused, he pressed his hand to the lock on the gate, wishing he could open it, wishing he could see what lay inside.

Just before he turned away, a vow on his lips promising his return, a hand reached out and clamped itself around his neck.

Though startled, he resisted shying away; the hand was gentle and nothing like anything he'd ever seen before. Instead of skin, the hand was made of bark, and each little fingertip grew into a leaf.

Strange mutterings drifted on the rank air, and he leaned forward. Despite the putrid smell, the scent of flowers reached his nose. A rush of wind brushed past him before something drew very close to the gate. Heart racing in his chest, Thaddeus rooted his feet to the ground, ignoring every base instinct telling him to run.

"Save us," the voice whispered.

Thaddeus swallowed air that rasped against his dry throat, wondering if he'd heard the creature right. "What?"

"Save . . . me," the voice repeated even quieter.

"Who are you?"

Another hand reached out of the darkness, moving slowly as if to not startle him. This one was fleshy, at least at first. As the tips of its fingers brushed his cheek, then his head, they began to grow into leaves and vines, tangling themselves in his hair. He was too frightened and astonished to move.

The vines in his hair then sprouted into the beautiful pink flowers, the scent of them filling his senses. They tied his hair into a loose braid, then swooped any stray locks into tiny braids woven with flowers.

Then, with a sickening snap, the creature jerked its arm away, leaving a stump where its hand had been, and all the leaves, flowers, and vines in his hair.

His eyes widened in horror until he saw little branches like fingers grow from the stump.

"Please . . ." With a breathy whisper, the creature drew its face close to the bars, just barely into the torchlight.

A sharp breath filled his lungs as he struggled to avoid recoiling from the creature. Flesh made up one half of the creature's face, but bark constructed the other half, a flower sitting in a sunken wooden eye socket. Thaddeus thought it alarmingly beautiful. Then he saw details that made his stomach churn. Swollen bruises decorated the creature's soft flesh. Caked with blood and oozing thick, yellow liquid, their eye could barely open; it reeked of infection.

"What do I do?" Tears rolled down his face. He yearned to touch this pitiful creature who stirred feelings of familiarity within him, but already they were drawing away, moving as if their whole body was in agony.

"Help us . . ."

"Wait!"

But the creature was gone. Darkness overwhelmed the room once more. Silence filled the aching cracks of the stone halls.

"I don't understand." Whimpering, Thaddeus sank to his knees, head in his hands. Hundreds of questions swarmed his mind. Who and what were these creatures? What was happening to them? But most of all, why did he feel as if he were the one dying instead of them? How did he . . . know them?

Staggering to his feet, overwhelmed by gut-wrenching sorrow pushing tears from his eyes, he dragged himself down the hall, letting his instinct guide him out of the twisting tunnels. He hardly paid attention to the other trapped creatures.

The first gate he'd passed through clanged shut behind him. Once clean air now tasted sour.

He didn't remember walking back to class or even sitting through it. All he could see was a blur of students as he walked out of class in a daze, tears still lingering in his eyes, flowers still woven in his hair. He barely even heard the insults thrown at him, mocking the flowers.

As if someone else were controlling his body, he made his way through the halls and down the front steps. Vaguely, he remembered needing to wait for someone so he wouldn't walk home alone, but he could only focus on the creature pleading for help. *Surely, they hadn't been alone.* He hoped it had been, and that more weren't trapped there, dying in the dark. But he knew he was wrong; he'd sensed more than a dozen of them, some only just clinging to life.

Then a clear thought rang through his mind. He had seen something like those creatures before—in the exhibit. Bile rose in his throat; his hands sweated. Collapsing to the stairs beneath him, ignoring the students shouting for him to move, he tried to quell his tears. A single thought consumed him. *They'll end up dead on the arena floor or in the exhibit. I have to save them. I have to save them. I have to save them. But how?*

Before he could process the weight of even considering breaking school laws to smuggle a dozen wounded creatures from a dungeon, a voice startled him from his thoughts, shattering the strange fog he felt he'd been walking through since the encounter.

"Thaddeus! What are you doing sitting in the middle of the stairs?"

Before Thaddeus could give an answer, Thanatos grabbed his hands and jerked him to his feet. Throwing an arm around him, Thanatos began to steer him away from the throbbing crowd pouring from the massive doors.

"What's gotten into you?" Though Thanatos smiled and nodded at the girls ogling him, Thaddeus heard the frustration in his tone. "First you embarrass me in front of my friends by being such a *umu qucha esh num*, then you pass out? Syrinthia said it was because you're tired and not eating, but seriously? You have all the food you need here. And what's *this*?"

He shoved Thanatos away as he snatched at the flowers. Anger coursed hot in his blood. "Don't touch it."

Thanatos' eyes widened. For a moment, it seemed he would back down, but eyes were watching them, and already Thaddeus heard whispers that the "great Thanatos" was letting his younger brother push him around.

A hardened look passed over Thanatos' face, and Thaddeus wished he were anywhere but here. *Don't do this. Please. Just let it go.*

"What in Susahu, Thaddeus?" Thanatos' face was beet red. "Seriously, what's wrong with you? They're just stupid flowers." Before Thaddeus could dodge him, Thanatos snatched one of the flowers from his hair, twisting it between his fingers.

"Thanatos, give it back." Embarrassment churned his stomach as he jumped up, trying to grab the flower back from Thanatos, who only waved it over his head, mocking him.

"Why? You have plenty more. Or are you trying to be like a girl?"

A darker rage filled Thaddeus. *What's so wrong about being like a girl? What's so wrong with liking flowers instead of fighting?* Before he could stop himself, he reeled his fist back and, with all his strength, punched Thanatos' jaw.

A gasp rang through the onlookers before they fell silent.

Thanatos staggered, the flower falling from his hand. His fingers drew away from his lips, speckled with blood.

Terror hit the bottom of Thaddeus' stomach like a rock. He and Thanatos had play-fought before, had even yelled and gotten physical, but never had one of them brutally attacked the other with the single intent to wound. *I didn't mean to. I didn't mean to.* He couldn't tell if the words were silent in his mind or if he were whimpering them.

With a cry of rage, Thanatos lunged forward, shoving Thaddeus to the ground. Thaddeus' ears rang, blocking out Thanatos' yelling.

As his hands rose to protect him from the kicks and blows he was sure would come, Syrinthia's angry voice tore through the air.

"What in Rasa and under all the gods of the Wyriders is going on?" She held out her hands to the boys, keeping them apart.

Not sure if he should lower his arms or not, Thaddeus' eyes locked onto Thanatos' flashing gaze. He towered over Thaddeus, Syrinthia's hand the only barrier keeping him from descending upon his little brother.

Tears flooded Thaddeus' eyes. How had their relationship come to this? His own brother was standing over him, the same burning hatred in his eyes as the other students.

No one wants me. No one will protect me.

New pain of a magnitude he hadn't known possible washed over him as he curled in on himself, cradling his head in his arms, the stairs digging into his knees. "No, no, no," he whispered, wishing he could run away, away from his own words and actions, from Thanatos, from the mocking students, even from Syrinthia, who was begging Thanatos to forgive his little brother, saying, "He didn't mean to."

"I didn't mean to. I didn't mean to." Thaddeus rocked back and forth, unable to span the gapping emptiness growing in his chest. But no matter how many times he whispered the words through the tears falling over from his eyes, down his neck, and to the ground, he knew deep down that he *had* meant it. He'd meant it for every time someone swung at him or mocked him for who he was.

Faintly, he was aware of Thanatos throwing up his hands and storming off into the crowd. Then Syrinthia knelt beside him.

"Thaddeus." Her hands shook his shoulders, but he hardly felt her.

"I want to disappear. I want to disappear," he whispered over and over, as if saying it would make it true. "I want to go with *them*." He thought of the creatures trapped beneath the dark halls of the school, feeling as if he belonged with them. The darkness they lived in seemed much more comforting than the blazing suns bearing down on him now. Didn't he too live behind bars, even if his were invisible?

Ignoring Syrinthia, he crawled to the little flower Thanatos had dropped. Sniffling through tears, he tried to pick up the flower; the blur in his eyes and the tremor in his hands made even that simple task nearly impossible. His fingers barely brushed the stem of the flower before he gave up and dragged his hand back to his chest, eyes shut tight, struggling to ignore the invasive gazes silently judging him.

"Thaddeus." Her voice was clearer this time as she pushed back his shoulder, gently pulling his hand from his chest.

"No—" he started, but when she pried open his fingers and he felt the softness of the flower in his palm, he let the plea die. Biting his lip against the seemingly endless stream of tears, he focused all his energy on the flower.

Her arm wrapped around his shoulder, pulling him close. Her voice, so quiet he wasn't sure he heard her right, whispered into his ear, "I will find a way for us to save them. I have to. I can't bear their pain any longer."

When their eyes met, he knew she felt the same connection to the creatures as he did. Just like himself, she couldn't rest having taken part in their pain and knowing it hadn't ended for them yet.

"I know why you can't sleep."

A mist rose in her eyes. "If you follow through with this, you may not sleep either."

"I don't think my heart could hurt more than it does now. Sleep evades me anyway. Sometimes I just wish I had something to actually feel this pain for, something truly worth suffering for. Maybe this is it." He was vaguely aware that the crowd had finally begun to disperse once they realized the action was over, but in this moment, all he could see, hear, and feel was Syrinthia and the overwhelming connection between them.

A sadness filled her eyes as she shook her head. Leaning forward, she pressed her lips to his forehead, a tear falling from her skin to his. "Be careful what you wish for. The gods have a thirst for suffering."

Then she stood and, after one last look back, turned to follow Thanatos.

THAT EVENING, after he had pulled himself up from the hard ground, he walked home alone. He wouldn't have cared about being home late, except he didn't want his mother to worry. The thought of her waiting for him with a warm cup of *elush* quickened his steps.

But once he'd crossed through their fence and he spotted Thanatos outside speaking animatedly with Quinlan and Krystallos, the flower in his hand turned to ash and his heart along with it. Just before he slipped inside, he caught Thanatos' gaze.

"Thaddeus—"

But he didn't wait for the rest. Instead, he slipped inside, closed the door behind him, and let out a long breath. For what seemed like an eternity, he waited for Thanatos to open the door behind him, embrace him in an uncomfortable, brotherly hug, and apologize for earlier. *I wonder if he's waiting for me to do the same.* But Thaddeus had always been the first to apologize. He wanted to see what happened if he didn't. When nothing but silence and disappointment filled the air, he had his answer.

Biting back the tears clogging his throat, he made his way to the kitchen to grab a glass of water and a small bowl of *suf'furruj*— his favorite snack—to stem off his growing, throbbing migraine.

The house always felt so much bigger when quiet and empty. Disappointment stirred in him as he wondered if his mother was already in bed.

"Thaddeus? Are you home now?" Naraina's voice was deep and slow, as if she'd just woken up.

His heart calmed as a rush of peace flooded him. He backtracked to the large couches in front of the floor-to-ceiling windows where his mother was just sitting up.

He hated seeing such dark circles under her eyes, hated that she stayed up to make sure he got home safe. Patting the light blue cushions next to her, she scooted over to make room for him.

Sitting down, he let the oversized cushions and pillows swallow him whole as he drew his legs up to his chest. Her gentle fingers ran through his hair, tucking wispy strands behind his ear and untangling little snags when she found them.

"Why have you been crying, *kinätyä segi?*"

Brushing a hand across his face, he scowled. "I haven't been crying."

A smile tugged the corners of her lips as she shook her head, pointing to the imported marsh nuts and water in his hands. "I know my son. When else do you eat *suffurruj?*"

I can't keep anything from her. The thought was both comforting and threatening. He wanted to keep everything from her: the bullying, how he felt both betrayed by and jealous of Thanatos, and the horrors he'd seen in the dungeons. At the same time, he wanted to get it off his own chest and listen to the comforting way his mother made everything seem bearable. Instead, he said nothing.

She waited patiently as he drank the last of the water before setting the glass and *suffurruj* on the table in front of them. Pulling him toward her, she rested her head atop his. He leaned into her embrace, eyes feeling very heavy. "Such beautiful flowers," she murmured and took a deep breath of their sweet scent.

She didn't ask where he got them from, didn't ask why they were in his hair, only wrapped her arms around him and held him close. He hoped she knew how grateful he was for her quiet comfort.

Very soon, sleep dragged him further and further down. Then, in the quiet place between dreams and wakefulness, he heard her whisper into his ear, "Save them if you must. But where they go, only sorrow follows."

A small frown wrinkled his eyebrows, but he was far too tired to make sense of it. Moments later, he slipped into a deep, dreamless sleep that eased the aching in his soul.

Chapter 10

Warm sunlight tickled his face. Squinting his eyes shut, he pulled the blanket over his eyes, rolled to face the back of the couch, and tried to wiggle back into the pocket of warmth he'd been sleeping in. For a long moment, he drifted into a lull of time where flowers bloomed around him as he sat in a large meadow with no end.

Standing slowly, he looked around. The horizon stretched where flowers and grass met sky; the rest of the world lay empty. Gone were the familiar mountains around Peace Haven and the thick forest surrounding his home.

The wind blew softly once then stilled, as if waking from slumber before deciding to sleep again.

Taking a slow step and then another, Thaddeus walked until the flowers changed from red, to orange, to yellow before he stopped.

A shape rose from the ground, fashioned from leaves and flowers, forming two legs, a torso, two arms, and a head. Vines grew from its head and blew in the wind, little flowers blooming along the length of it. The creature sucked in a breath and opened its shining eyes, revealing petal-like irises.

Thaddeus felt no fear, only awe and familiarity. "Who are you?" The question seemed unnecessary. This creature was as much a part of him as he was of it.

Lifting his hand, he watched as the creature mirrored his movements. When they touched, something deep awoke within him. He felt the field beneath his feet, the grass and flowers around him as if it were his own skin, the air a loving embrace, and the sun on his face filling him with the sensation of drinking warm soup when cold and hungry.

"I am the calling you feel when you touch the trees. I am the soul you feel when you embrace your mother. I am . . ."

But the creature never finished as the sound of a door jarred Thaddeus from the land between waking and sleeping.

His eyes cracked open as he heard Thanatos call after their mother, letting her know where he was going for the day. She told him to be careful, then the door opened and shut again.

The smell of fresh pastries filled his senses. The sunlight on his face, which had once seemed so warm, now felt cold after the dream faded away.

Clenching his eyes shut, he attempted to recapture the dream and find the creature among the flowers once more. But it had disappeared into the dust specks floating in the morning light, streaming through the windows.

Empty and tired, as if his sleep hadn't been restful, he felt the familiar dread of morning settle into his stomach. Another day awake, another day spent trying to survive until the next one. It was the weekend—two days out of school—but if he thought about it too long, then today was already over, and tomorrow had already begun, and the next day was school.

"Thaddeus, are you awake?" His mother's voice sparked memory of the words the creature from his vision had spoken: *"I am the soul you feel when you embrace your mother."* Her words felt very much like the sun had on his skin in the dream.

Instead of pretending to sleep, he pulled the covers down under his nose and let his sleepy gaze meet her shining eyes. A bright smile curved her lips as she ruffled his bed hair. "Come on, I made some fresh sourdough *shäsevel* with strawberry jam, and I want to show you something."

Awake with curiosity, he rushed to his room, tripped while putting on pants, hastily ran a brush through his tangled hair, and hurried back to the kitchen.

When he entered, she was waiting at the island, two plates of *shäsevel* and jam set out and a mug of *elush* in her hand.

A deeper emotion hung in her eyes, one he wasn't familiar with. Sitting on the spinning stool, he took a bite of the *shäsevel* and released out a content sigh. The sweetness of the homegrown strawberry jam paired delightfully with the tangy, sweet flavor of the bread. Washed down with a hot swig of home roasted strawberry cream *elush*, the breakfast assured him his mother was like a goddess with her garden.

"Thaddeus, I—" She shook her head, looking down into her drink.

His stomach flipped at her tone, but patiently, he waited for her to continue.

"I want to talk to you about what you found yesterday."

The breakfast went dry in his mouth. He slowly set it down, blood flushing his face as he stared at his plate. "How did you—"

Her gentle hand on his stopped his words. "I'm not stalking you or asking your teachers or Thanatos about you, if that's what you're worried about. I know because it's . . . more complicated than that."

She took his other hand. Expecting to see disappointment or anger, he winced when he met her gaze. Only love and a deep sadness shone back. The knot in his chest loosened.

"I'm not at all upset with you. I'm proud of you. I honestly never thought I'd get to have this talk with you. I thought you'd be safe from all that here, but . . ." She shook her head, drawing little circles on his hands with her thumbs. "But I can see you are more in tune with it than I thought possible. So, I want to show you something." Taking a deep breath, she released his hands, took the last sip of her drink, and motioned for him to follow as she walked into the garden.

For a long time, neither said a word as they strolled along the stone walkway. As long as he had been alive, the garden had always thrived, even during the most unforgiving circumstances. Eternally in awe of his mother's gift with plants, he watched as the plants stretched out to greet her, as if yearning to touch her skin and bask in her presence. If any had wilted, they sprang to life when she walked by. Thaddeus watched as blossoms opened to greet her.

A small whisper in his gut knew why they responded this way. He just wasn't sure he was ready to hear it.

Finally, they came to the small section of garden Naraina had asked Quinlan to fence in. Thaddeus and Thanatos had never been allowed into the space before, but on many occasions, he'd seen his mother disappear into it. She always called it her time with the spirits of nature.

Without a word, she opened the gate and gestured for him to follow her into the enclosed space. The space felt sacred. He paused at the doorway, noticing how vines crawled up the wrought iron fencing and dome, protecting whatever grew inside. Then he stepped in.

His breath caught in his chest. A small raised bed of flowers took up most of the room. The flowers spilled over the edges of the bed, yearning to be free. A gasp escaped his lips as he took in their red, yellow, and orange hues. They were the flowers from his vision. They were *home*.

Tears collected in his eyes. When he tried to speak, he found he couldn't form the right words. Tears glistened on his mother's cheek as she grasped his hand and led him into the flowers.

The little plants shifted to make room for each step they took. He and his mother sat down, and the flowers wrapped around their legs, twining into their hair. Then Thaddeus felt *everything*.

The sun beat down on his face, on the leaves, giving them life. The ground rested cold and dark beneath him, refreshing to the roots of the flowers. The petals filled the air with a scent that brought memories of a simpler life spent truly living, not just surviving. The entire garden hummed around him, each and every plant, flower, and fruit, every bee or butterfly, every blossom and leaf. The new sensations flooded through him, overwhelming his senses with life.

"You are of these flowers, Thaddeus, just like me," she whispered, taking his hand in hers.

"I don't understand." But deep down, he did. His heart raced, his palm sweated in hers, his grip tightening around the flower stems around him.

"I'm not . . . Duvarharian, Thaddeus."

He bit his lip, unable to tear his eyes from hers and the way orange flowers danced in her pupils. "What do you mean?"

"You know I don't have the same magic as everyone else."

He nodded, his mind racing with a hundred excuses, a hundred possibilities of why the single whisper in his heart was wrong.

"Because I don't have Duvarharian magic. I wasn't born in a small dragon tribe up north like I've said. The language I speak, the one I've taught you and Thanatos, isn't an old regional dialect, it's the Džoxsenä language."

His grip on the flowers tightened until one of the stems broke in his hand and a sharp pain ran through his back. Releasing the flowers, an invisible weight lifted off his shoulders. Only one explanation properly explained this connection.

"Džoxsenä," he whispered. "They're the . . ." He turned to her, shaking his head as she finished the sentence. He needed to hear her say it.

"Wyriders."

His heart skipped a beat.

"Which makes you half-Wyrider. You're as much a part of them as you are the Dragon Riders."

An empty chasm opened in his stomach. *No. This can't be. I can't be part Wyrider. They're vicious, lawless. They started the games in Duvarharia and hate dragons. This can't be true. My own mother can't be one of them.*

Her eyes didn't lie.

As if she knew what he was feeling, the flowers bridging a gap between their hearts, she did her best to dispel his fears. "They aren't what you believe. Yes, some of the Wyriders are greedy, bloodthirsty, and lawless, as your father and I have led you to believe, but . . ." Tears rolled down her cheeks.

The initial horror turned to heartbreak, settling in his stomach with a dull ache. He saw by the pain in her eyes how hard it'd been to teach her children lies about her own people. His fingers brushed a petal, and a shiver ran down his spine. "So, what are we?"

A small smile lifted her lips. "Terrestrial Zoics. Our ancestors have been bonding their souls to Rasa for as long as we can remember, specifically this flower." She brushed her hand across them, and they all rippled, responding to her touch.

"And so are the creatures you found yesterday, the ones who left flowers in your hair. They're not strange mutations like the Duvarharians want you to believe. They're our kin."

A cascade of emotions flooded him: excitement, realization, fear, confusion. *This explains the connection I felt with them. The meadow in their eyes is the same as the one I've always seen in my own mother's eyes.*

Then horror overtook all other emotions. The blood drained from his face. "The exhibit at the academy. Those were . . ." He tried to wipe them away, but tears escaped down his cheeks.

Naraina cupped his face in her hands and pressed her forehead to his. For a moment, they leaned against each other as the cruel reality threatened to crush them. "Now you understand why I *never* wanted you to go there."

Throwing his arms around her neck, he bit his lip against his sob. "Then, why? Why did you let us go?" A wash of bitter betrayal crashed over him.

"Your father doesn't know." Naraina whispered into his hair as she kissed the top of his head, her tears mixing with the flowers still entwined in his blond locks. "He doesn't know about the Zoics trapped there. He thinks the school has animal fights and nothing more. If he knew what the headmistress does . . ."

Thaddeus pushed her away, his blood boiling. "Then why don't you tell him? Why don't you *do* something?"

The distance between them felt like a mile. He wanted to bridge the gap, to let her hold him like a child again, but he wanted an explanation more. An explanation for why he had to suffer day in and day out in the gods forsaken academy.

"I can't," she whispered. "If I speak out, I'll be investigated as a potential threat. they'd realize I'm not Duvarharian, that I'm one of *them*." Her eyes pierced his, fear lacing every corner of them, driving the same terror into his heart. "Zoics have no rights in Duvarharia. I'm only able to live here because your father has protected me. But even his influence can only reach so far. I'm powerless to stop any of this."

Her fear sparked something feral in him. She didn't deserve to live in constant terror. Neither did he. It wasn't their fault the Duvarharians twisted the games and blamed the Wyriders. It wasn't a crime to bond with Rasa. It wasn't right for them to suffer. "You may be powerless"—his fists tightened into balls—"but I'm not."

The pride in her eyes shone behind a sea of worry. "I don't know what you'd do. It's too dangerous."

Thaddeus' heart ached as he bit back desperate tears. He wanted her to squeeze his hands and tell him he could bring down the two moons if he wanted or part the Dragon Sea. But she'd rather live in hiding than risk her security, and she wanted him to do the same.

But how could he? How could he stand idle while his kin were tormented by the games and school experiments?

"Something must be done. If no one else will do it, then I will." She opened her mouth to protest, but he continued. "The school is covering up any information about the Shadows of Light and the rouge faction that tried to violently end the games years ago. Then the attacks stopped abruptly, and the games continued. This is all connected somehow. I just have to put the pieces together."

"Thaddeus," she groaned, pressing her forehead to his, her dark hair falling into his face. For a moment, he saw her not as his mother but as a young creature displaced from her homeland to be with her lover in a country that hated her Kind. "Just leave the school. Tell your father you want to be tutored at home. Tell him the bullying has grown unbearable. Please, *anything*. I'll back anything you want to tell him, just let me get you out of there. Let me fix my mistake."

He shook his head. *I have to bring back the old Duvarharia, the one where the games didn't exist, where the other Kinds were welcome, where magic was embraced, and all could bond with the dragons. I have to at least try, and I need to be at the academy to learn how.*

Forcing a smile on his face, he stood and extended his hand. "I promise I won't do anything too dangerous"—the lie tasted bitter on his lips—"and I won't be alone. Syrinthia knows the school, the teachers, and the guards very well. She's been helping me, and I promise if anything bad happens, I'll stop."

Doubt shone in her eyes. He tried to keep the flowers from siphoning his emotions and transferring them to his mother, but the connection was too powerful. Panic churned his stomach, but she only sighed and let him help her to her feet.

Intimately, he was aware of the ground beneath his bare feet, her hand in his, and the flowers sticking through his toes, twining their way around his ankles, connecting him to the heartbeat of his mother and the soul they shared with Rasa. A single feeling pulsed from his mother to him through their stems: strength.

Though he knew she worried for him, he also knew she shared the inescapable calling stirring in his chest. She had been unable to answer, but he could. She knew that.

"I love you, Thaddeus." Her misty eyes searched his. "You're the light of my life. I couldn't live if anything happened to you."

His heart ached as he turned his eyes from hers. "Nothing will happen to me. I won't let it"

But they both knew it wasn't up to him.

With hands as soft as the light shining on them, she pulled his face to hers and kissed his forehead.

"Thank you. For telling me all this." Though he felt the connection to Rasa, to his mother, though all his logic told him he was Zoic, he still needed time to process being Wyrider, to process what that would mean for the rest of his life.

"Thank you for listening. I've never told anyone other than your father. It's been . . ." Tears fell onto his shirt. "It's been so long since I've truly felt at home and among family. I'm glad you finally know. I'm glad I can share it with you."

A smile curved his lips. "I'm so glad you can too."

As they broke apart and stepped out of the enclosed garden, she let him know he was welcome anytime. "Just don't let Thanatos see you. I doubt he'd understand as you have."

Though a new ache of loneliness pulsed in his heart, he nodded. "I promise I won't."

"Good." Then a smile brightened her face as she ruffled his hair. "Would you like to help me harvest some herbs to dry then browse the stalls at the market with me today?"

The gate shut, ending the intimate connection between them. Once again, she was only his mother, and he, her little boy. Relief washed over him. As much as he longed to feel the connection to Rasa again, he also yearned to simply be a child again, following trustingly after his mother as she showed him which herbs to pick and which to let grow a little longer.

He laughed with her, praised her handiwork with a bright smile, and helped carry her baskets of herbs and fruits to trade at the market. But under his cheerful façade, darkness swirled in his deepest thoughts.

They were living a lie. A lie that told them they could walk the streets without fear, without persecution. They deserved for it to be their truth, and he wouldn't stop until it was.

PART 2
Half of a Whole

Chapter 11

Peace Haven, Duvarharia
Year: Rumi 5310 Q.RJ.M

WHEN THADDEUS WOKE for school, he had an unusual spring to his step. Uncharacteristically, he was dressed and finishing his breakfast by the time Thanatos staggered into the kitchen, still in sleepwear and messy hair.

Rubbing his eyes and yawning, Thanatos cast a scoff in Thaddeus' direction before clambering onto one of the stools. "Why are you up so early? I thought you hated school."

Thaddeus scowled over the rim of his mug, hoping his father hadn't been around to hear Thanatos' words. "How would you know? You hardly talk to me anymore."

Before Thanatos could spit back a reply, Quinlan stepped into the kitchen, a grin on his face. "Good morning, boys. How are you both?" He planted a kiss to the top of Thanatos' head. Thanatos grumbled and fell to picking at his sourdough *shäsevel* while Thaddeus embraced his father.

"I'm fine, Father. Trying to get to school early. Syrinthia and I are doing some special research."

Quinlan's eyes widened at the mention of Syrinthia's name, but he seemed pleased with the news. "That sounds interesting. Can I ask of what, or shall I wait until you've changed the world with your thesis?"

Thaddeus smiled and looked at the floor. *Maybe I can change the world.* Though the task ahead of him seemed daunting, right now, anything seemed possible. "I think I'd like to surprise you."

Quinlan nodded, downing a hot cup of dark roasted *elush* in two big gulps. "Is your mother in the garden?"

Thaddeus nodded as he finished the last bite of his *shäsevel*.

Before Quinlan disappeared into the garden, he tossed a stern look to Thanatos. "I don't care if you hang out with friends on your own time, Thanatos, but if you let it affect when you wake up and arrive at school, I'll cut the wings from your back without hesitation, do you understand?"

Thaddeus' eyebrows shot up. He tried hiding his surprise behind his mug as he pretended to drink the last sip.

Thanatos' face burned red as he nodded. "Yes, Father, I understand."

Though Thaddeus usually hated when he or his brother were scolded, he couldn't help the satisfaction he felt at the look on his brother's face.

"What're you looking at?"

Thaddeus scowled and shook his head, unable to stop the words before they slipped through his lips. "Not much of anything." Immediately regretting the venom in his words, he deposited his plate in the sink, hoping to escape the kitchen before Thanatos recognized the insult in his words.

"Hey, Thaddeus?" Thanatos' voice stopped him just before he stepped into the main room.

Stomach flipping, he slowly turned. "Yes, Than?"

Thanatos pushed his food around his plate. "I just want to say . . ." He cleared his throat. "I'm sorry for getting so mad at you the other day about the whole flower thing. It was stupid, and I shouldn't have mocked you. The flowers were actually kind of . . . pretty."

Thaddeus' jaw nearly dropped. *Is this real?* But all doubt left his mind when he saw the embarrassment in Thanatos' cheeks and sincerity in his eyes. "Thank you, Than. That means everything to me." Guilt cascaded over him. "I'm sorry for punching you."

Thanatos huffed and tried to hide his smile. "Forget about it. You still punch like a girl anyway."

"I do not." Despite his efforts to remain stern, Thaddeus laughed. He pretended to punch Thanatos until the older brother ruffled his hair and shoved him away.

"Just go to school already, you crazy hatchling. What are you even doing with Syrinthia anyway?"

Thaddeus bristled. "We're just doing some historical research. Why do you care?"

Thanatos rolled his eyes and stuffed a spoonful of his food into his mouth. "By the egg, I'm just curious. Don't get so defensive. Next time, just sleep in and don't try so hard."

Trying to brush off his bad attitude with an even worse laugh, Thaddeus waved his hand dismissively. "You're just jealous."

"Am not! Get back here, you little—"

Thaddeus didn't catch the rest of the insult as he grabbed his stack of notebooks and pelted out the door, forgetting to be careful about shutting it gently. The door rattled the glass windows, and Thaddeus cringed, hoping no one heard.

Krystallos' glistening tail drooped down the side of the house from his perch on the roof. His voice rang in Thaddeus' mind. *I won't tell, as long as you say goodbye.*

Grateful, Thaddeus ran around the house to the looming garden fence; the iron bars supported the many flowering and fruiting vines his mother had planted along them.

"Goodbye, Mother! Goodbye, Father! I'll see you later tonight!"

He barely waited for their answers, pausing only a moment to return the kiss his mother blew before he ran down the road to the city streets. Krystallos' amused rumbles chased after him.

In this early hour, the city was only just coming to life. Usually, he had to force his way through an already bustling crowd, praying he wouldn't be late for class. Today he only passed a few other Duvarharians and one dragon.

Since he hadn't officially agreed to meet Syrinthia today, he decided to search for her in the lower library where she often spent the mornings studying. But he saw no trace of her there, neither at the study tables nor browsing the bookcases. When questioned, the librarian barely lifted her gaze from her own book long enough to shrug her shoulders and yawn.

"Thanks for the help," Thaddeus hissed through his teeth. He was scolded by a dramatic "Shhh" that echoed louder than his words.

His enthusiasm lessening with each step, he found himself standing outside Rakland's office.

Though he knew better, he crept closer to the cracked door. Using magic, he extended his focus into the room to eavesdrop.

"How are his grades?" The dark voice stirred a sickening feeling in his gut. He wanted to turn around and run in the opposite direction. However, the voice that answered wasn't Rakland's as he expected, but rather Syrinthia's.

"They're only just above passing. Any lower, and we'd have to review him for expulsion. Though the academy doesn't favor academics, it can't afford to have subpar students. Besides, some of the classes are important to the games."

Confusion churned in Thaddeus' stomach. Syrinthia could be talking about any student among hundreds. So why did the dread in his stomach say she was talking about him or Thanatos? But it couldn't be him. Though his grades weren't as high as they could be, they were still far above passing. *Could it be Thanatos? Is he really doing so poorly?*

"However, he is excelling at swordsmanship and any studies pertaining to the games." Rakland spoke now, sounding disappointed.

"Good. That's what we're hoping for," the dark voice said through a smile. "Our plan will only work if he's fully integrated into the games' culture. I want him on the champion teams next year. That will give him a taste of the games' money and fame."

Thaddeus' hands balled into fists as his blood burned. It mattered little who they spoke about. No one deserved to be manipulated into the games. Why they were so worried about a single student baffled him. *Is it for money?* But if it was, then why was Syrinthia speaking to them as well? And why did Rakland sound so defeated as if this was exactly what he *didn't* want to happen?

Ignoring his better judgement, he leaned farther into the doorway until he saw Syrinthia. She stood with her arms crossed and head down. Rakland's stance was familiar: in front of the windows, staring out over the arena.

Just a little farther. He leaned until his shoulder brushed the door, threatening to swing it open. Finally, he saw the third speaker.

His blood turned to ice.

It was the creature who'd visited his parents the night before he and Thanatos enrolled in the academy. Deep breaths kept him from blasting through the door and throttling the man. Hundreds of hateful accusations flooded his mind.

Before he could catch any more of their conversation, the cloaked man whirled around, his sharp eyes glowing under his hood and straight into Thaddeus' soul.

Thaddeus didn't waste a second before running, desperate to put as much space between him and the cloaked creature as he could. By the time his heart stopped racing and he allowed himself a moment of rest, his first class had already started.

He made his way to the classroom, keeping his gaze on the floor lest the cloaked man be in the crowd, stalking him, haunting him. The man never came. *Twice he's seen me, and twice he's let me go. What business does he have with my family? With Syrinthia?*

He couldn't interrogate her about it without admitting eavesdropping. So when lunchtime came, he ignored his question and instead pulled out the note he'd found in the library, pushing it into her hand.

"When you get done eating, come talk to me about this," he whispered in her ear as he passed her in the mess hall line.

Her face full of confusion, she tried calling him back, but he ignored her, ducking away before Thanatos and his friends spotted him.

Leaving the dining hall, he watched as most of the students gathered in the courtyard. They'd spend the rest of lunch hour there lounging in the sun, laughing, studying for the next test, or practicing new sword fighting techniques.

A familiar ache settled in his chest; why was everyone else surrounded by friends while he remained alone? Tightening his fists, he turned from the jubilant chaos in the courtyard and ducked back into the dining hall. By now, most of the food had been ravaged through; leftover scraps were being carted away to be fed to the animals locked in the dungeons below.

As usual, Thaddeus meekly waited until a familiar gray head bobbed just below the height of the counter. A grunt of exertion preceded the old woman as she climbed onto a stool so she could see over the counter.

Thaddeus couldn't hide his smile. "Good day, Miss Anrid. How's your morning been?"

The woman winced as she sat, her small legs dangling. "Oh, Thaddeus, you know it's the same every morning. Each day I get a little older, and each day everything seems that much farther above me." She shrugged, but despite her complaints and the wrinkles marking an unbelievable age upon her kind face, Thaddeus didn't miss the sparkle of youth still shining brightly in her eyes.

"You know I have to ask."

She shook her head and laughed, the laughing turning into an abrupt cough. "Such a polite one. Your parents raised you right, that's for sure. No wonder you have such a hard time fitting in. You need to learn to be crueler, if I can say that."

Thaddeus shrugged. She said the same thing every day, and he always told her the same in return. "The world needs more kindness, not cruelty and strength."

Her sweet smile spread her thin lips as her eyes disappeared into wrinkles. "Thaddeus, someday you'll be very popular with the ladies, I just know it."

He scratched the back of his head. Before he could trip over his words, she jumped off the stool, disappearing once more behind the counter.

The sound of plates against granite echoed loudly through the nearly empty hall. Small hands lifted the large plate above her head and onto the counter, pushing it as far to him as she could.

"I tried to save the best-looking sweet roll for you and the juiciest chop. But I'm afraid the older students got to the roasted goat leg before I could save any."

Thaddeus waved his hand, grinning at the sad-looking roll and ridiculously small portion of sinewy meat. By the time Anrid could scour the kitchens for extra food, most already sent to more demanding students and the leftovers were hardly decent. But Thaddeus had grown used to the small portions; he'd quickly learned hunger hurt less than a fist in his gut when someone accused him of cutting in line and took their out impatience on him.

"You're too good to me, Miss Anrid. How shall I ever repay you?"

She climbed back onto the stool, adjusting her loose green skirts around her legs. "Dear boy, you've no reason to pay me back. I've been where you are now, you know, even if it's hard to believe." She winked at him, and he shook his head, chuckling.

"I couldn't imagine why." He felt sick thinking of the bullying she must've endured because of her height. "But I mean it, truly. If I can do anything for you, just say the word, and it shall be done." He flourished his hand and bowed elaborately, eliciting a giggle from her.

"Well, when you put it that way, there is one thing you could bring me, though you may not want to."

"Anything. I will do my best."

She took a deep breath. "Because I'm an *elus-ugu*,"—she motioned toward her unusually short stature—"I've never been able to travel to the Dragon Palace. I've wanted to visit since I was a little girl, but traveling without a dragon or long enough legs to ride a horse is nearly impossible, and most of my jobs haven't paid enough for carriage fare."

Thaddeus's heart broke. Her only wish was to see the beautiful Dragon Palace, as every true Duvarharian dreamed, including himself. "How much do you need? I can get the money for you. My father is an ambassador. He knows the best and cheapest ways to travel. I'm sure we can figure out something—"

She shook her head with a sad laugh. "I'm far too old to travel now, love. It's hard enough running around on small legs, but once you get old and all the usual aches and pains add to it, it's far more comfortable to just stay home."

Thaddeus frowned, feeling helpless to repay this woman who had shown him nothing but kindness since he joined the academy. "Then what can I do?"

She stared into the distance as if imagining how beautiful the City of Dragons was. "If you ever visit the Palace, which I'm sure you will since your father is an ambassador, I would like very much if you could make a *Qumokuhe* or even a *Suźuheb*, if you can, of what you see. Then I could see it too, and that would be enough."

Shaking his head, Thaddeus reached for his plate, his fingers gripping it so hard his knuckles turned white. A *Qumokuhe*—a simple image capturing a moment in time—would be easy to make. But a *Suźuheb*—a complex art piece that trapped the artist's emotions—would be far more difficult. However, she deserved to not only see her dream but also feel the awe it invoked. "I promise I will do just that."

Tsking, Anrid waved her hands. "Ah, don't promise something you can't be sure you'll fulfill. A simple, 'I'll try,' is all I ask for. But don't you go chasing it. If you forget, you forget. And who knows, I might not even be around by the time you go to the Dragon Palace."

He shot her a scathing scowl. "You'd better be, Miss Anrid. I wouldn't know how to feed myself without you."

She winked before jumping down from the stool. "You'd find a way. You're cunning, and you have a mother who loves you. What more could you need?"

Before he could say anything more, she disappeared into the kitchen.

Staring at his plate, he carried it to a familiar corner of the room before hastily eating the little bit of food. *She's right, of course. I don't have much to complain about. Perhaps I'm mocked here, perhaps my views against the games are hated, but my family still loves me. Even if Thanatos can be a daufa. And though I'm small and weak, my body is still whole and serves me well. I don't have any handicaps or disabilities holding me back.*

But despite telling himself all these reassurances, his eyes still welled with tears. Dinner would be waiting for him at home, and his breakfast had been nutritious, but skipping lunch was taking its toll upon him. He reminded himself others suffered more than he, like the beggars on the streets or the trapped Zoics, and finished the last bite of his food, his stomach growling for more.

He slipped outside, trying to feel the warmth of the sun on his face while also staying hidden behind the pillars lining the covered walkway around the courtyard.

The lunch hour was nearly over, so he took to watching the other students and making up stories about them. Then a hand tapped his shoulder, startling him with a yelp. His heart racing, he whirled around to face Syrinthia.

Dark eyes wide, she did her best to stifle her laughter. "You should see the look on your face."

Trying to shake off the jitters from her adorable laughter more than from the scare, he rubbed the back of his neck and drew a line across the granite with his boot. "Why are you sneaking up on me like that?"

She mimicked him by scratching her head and standing on one foot. "Better question: why are you always hiding in the shadows?"

Thaddeus rolled his eyes, trying not to smile. *How can she mock me and it not hurt the same way as anyone else?*

"Scared the sun is going to burn that lily-white skin of yours? Can't tan like your brother?"

Groaning, Thaddeus smacked his head on his hand. "Please don't talk about Thanatos' skin tone. I hear it enough when I'm home and how much the ladies seem to love it. I don't understand why they're so interested in someone as young and dumb as him. He can barely walk up the steps with how big his ego's gotten." The words leaped from his mouth before he could stop them, but she didn't seem to mind.

She smirked. "Oh, the ladies love a young and dumb man. They're far easier to manipulate." Threading her arm through his, she dragged him along. "But I wouldn't complain too much about his age—remember, you're younger than him, you know."

Thaddeus' face fell, and eyes darkened. "Don't remind me." To lighten the mood, he asked, "Do you speak from experience?"

"Of what?" She waved to another girl her age, who waved back before shooting a judgmental look to Thaddeus.

He tried to ignore the girl's hateful gaze; she wasn't the only one glaring at him. It seemed no one approved of the older popular girl hanging out with the school's lowest of the low. At least no one dared to assault him if she was nearby. A few months ago, he would've been embarrassed by a girl protecting him; now he accepted it any chance he could. "Girls liking the young and dumb guys. Do you speak from experience?"

Her eyebrows darted up before she scoffed. "Please. I like a challenge. The smart ones are more my type."

A swarm of butterflies took flight in his stomach as heat rose to his face. Suddenly, she felt too close with her arm linked through his. Then he remembered the looks she flashed at Thanatos while listening to him talk or how she laughed at his stupid jokes. No matter their jokes, Thanatos was smart; they both knew that. He was nothing more than a friend without a chance, merely the brother of the boy she liked. Thaddeus ground his teeth, the tender moment between them spoiled.

The bitterness he felt reminded him of the conversation she'd had with the cloaked creature and Rakland that morning. Subtly, he put more space between them. She was speaking, but he hardly listened, only nodding and agreeing when it seemed appropriate.

Finally, he couldn't bear the overthinking any longer, and the words tumbled from his lips. "Do you think Thanatos is doing well in his academics?"

She stopped walking. The air shifted around them, and he knew she suspected his reason for asking. Her reaction assured him the conversation earlier had indeed been about Thanatos, not another student. His stomach turned.

"Why do you ask?" She brushed off her momentary hesitation but refused to meet his gaze.

He spun an excuse. "I don't know. I just don't ever hear him talk about his classes while he's home, just about the fighting and his friends. But Father keeps saying Thanatos is spending too much time with his friends and doesn't want Thanatos' grades dropping more than they have." It wasn't a lie.

Syrinthia relaxed. His excuse, though stretched, was easily believable. "Oh." She frowned. "I'm not sure. I don't really have any access to grades. Rakland would never tell me even if I asked, but I've noticed him not paying much attention in class. I'm surprised you're concerned about it."

Thaddeus shrugged. "He's wanted to attend this school as long as I can remember. He loves the games and has always dreamed of fighting in them despite what our parents taught us. I'd hate to see him waste this opportunity."

A tender smile spread her lips. "That's really sweet of you. You really are the perfect little brother."

Grumbling, Thaddeus detached her arm from his. "Not all the time. I can be a *daufa* sometimes too."

She laughed, moving her satchel to her other shoulder. "I suppose that's what being siblings is all about. Of course, I wouldn't know." A sadness settled in her eyes.

"I'm sorry for that."

"Oh." Her face brightened again. "No worries. Can't miss what you've never had."

Thaddeus frowned. *But you can. You can miss it in the same way I miss a meadow of flowers and the Zoic kin I've never met. Or the way I miss the dragon I've never been bonded to or the magic I've never been taught to harness.* Feeling the weight of those losses, he changed the subject.

"Did you get a chance to look at the paper? I found it in one of the books we looked at in the upper library." Part of him regretted sharing it with her because of the conversation that morning, but he couldn't proceed without her and the note already rested in her hands.

Her entire demeanor changed as she ducked down a smaller, less-crowded hallway. "I did, but I don't know what it means. How could the Shadows of Light have turned bad? We don't have any historical records showing that happening. And why would they have? They followed the Great Lord, who taught freedom and love. It was his teachings that led Duvarharia into the Golden Age. Why would a dark faction come from it?"

The intensity in her gaze startled him. For a moment, he tripped over his words. "I—well . . . I was thinking . . ." But he wasn't really sure what he was thinking.

Some of the Shadows of Light had seemingly broken their anti-violence pledge and attacked the games, then, not long after, ceased all such attacks suddenly and without cause. The games continued, but no records showed the rebel faction being put down.

Now Zoic Wyriders suffered in games created and brought to Duvarharia by Aristocrat Wyriders. In the middle of it all, this academy harbored captured Zoics and turned them into exhibits while claiming to be supportive of new freedom laws welcoming Wyriders.

None of it made sense, and instead of being able to find the words to voice his outlandish theories, he only fell into silence, shaking his head.

With a deep sigh of malcontent, Syrinthia pushed the note back into his hand. "Look, I don't understand why the school is trying to cover up the Shadows of Light, but it's probably something as simple as not wanting to let anti-game influence into the academy. We should focus on saving the creatures in the dungeons. That's something we *do* understand and can feasibly try to change. Alright?"

He disagreed. Strongly. It all had to be connected. He was just missing one little piece of the puzzle, he was sure.

"Thaddeus? Are you listening to me?"

He snapped back to the present, unable to meet her upset gaze. "Yes. I heard you. Let's just free the creatures. You're right. It's probably nothing."

She frowned. "You don't believe me, do you?"

He shrugged.

Shaking him gently, she forced him to look at her. "I know you hate this school. I know you don't fit in. I know you don't agree with the teachings. But your parents have you here for a reason, even if you don't know why. Don't get lost in some dragon's den and lose the opportunity to learn what you can from this school. Otherwise, your grades will drop, just like you're worried about with Thanatos. Promise me you'll forget this. Just focus on the things we can change and stop making such a big deal out of everything else."

Emotion choked his throat. He wanted to argue with her, to tell her everything his mother told him about the Zoics and how he *was* Zoic. He wanted her to understand that he needed to know why his father wanted him here despite the obvious danger and corruption But as Syrinthia searched his face for a promise, he felt very small and foolish, as if all the self-worth he'd begun to find shattered under her soft touch.

"Okay," he whispered against everything else in him screaming *no*. "I promise."

She sighed and forced a thin smile. "That's the spirit. Now, I've almost got a plan worked out for the creatures in the dungeons. Can you be free sometime next week after lunch?"

His heart sank further. A piece of him didn't want to trust her after she crushed his theories. But he had a duty to the Zoics, himself, and his mother, and he couldn't fulfill that duty without Syrinthia's help. "Yes," he whispered. "I can be."

"Good." She slapped his shoulder and bounded away, calling something back that he didn't quite hear before she disappeared into the crowd.

Hands balling into fists, he bit back tears and straightened his shoulders. *Despite what she says and the promise I made her, I know something deeper is going on here. I promised myself first I'd figure it out, and I intend to honor that promise, no matter how difficult or dangerous or who may stand in my way.*

Instead of heading to his next class, he turned down the opposite hallway and made his way back to the upper library. He would have to take matters into his own hands.

🐉

"THERE, THAT'S THE MOST comprehensive list I have of who's checked that book out." With a strange glint in his eyes, the young upper librarian pushed a slip of paper across an impossibly dusty desk.

Sneezing, Thaddeus reached for the list and squinted at it, daunted by the scrawling, confusing handwriting. "Thank you. I really appreciate your help."

The young man shrugged before leaning backward on the chair's hind legs. Pushing his glasses up, he cracked a half-crazy grin. "No need to thank me. This is the most exciting thing that's happened up here since I took this post. Honestly, I thought I'd be able to get my hands on some of the spell-weaving books I heard rumors about, but it seems the academy's confiscated anything they consider 'dangerous'." He rolled his eyes and scoffed as if spell-weaving wasn't the practice of draining magical creatures of their blood.

Laughing nervously, Thaddeus nodded, struggling to appear unfazed and apologetic. "You'd think they'd be more open to the freedom of information, seeing as they say they support the new freedom laws." He sighed in relief as the librarian hung on his every word, eyes sparkling.

"Exactly." He leaned forward, silver hair falling into his eyes; his long, sharp black nails rapped impatiently against the desk. "You know, you're not half bad. You come back any time. They may have confiscated some of the good stuff, but let me tell you, there's a lot more to learn from these books than the ones down below, if you know what I mean." He winked and licked his lips.

Thaddeus *didn't* know, but having easy access to the upper library was worth some discomfort. "I appreciate that."

The young man crossed one ankle over his knee and smirked as if he'd accomplished something great. "No need for thanks. Like I said, most exciting thing I've seen yet. Anytime you need anything strange, hit me up."

Chuckling, Thaddeus nodded, turning away. "I'll keep that in mind." Without waiting for anything more bizarre to come out of the student's mouth, he exited the library, walking a few paces quicker than usual. Once he'd put a few levels between them, he found a patch of blue light streaming through a stained window and began deciphering the scrawling writing.

Most of the names were unfamiliar except the name at the top with the most recent date next to it. A wave of emotion and confusion crashed over him as he read it over and over again.

Then, as if speaking it would make it more believable, he whispered, "Rakland."

CHAPTER 12

"I HAVE TO TELL HER." Thaddeus took one step forward, flinched, then took two steps back. *No, no, no. She already wants me to leave it alone, and I promised her I would. Besides, Rakland's her guardian. I can't possibly tell her.* But it felt wrong not to, as if it was worse to keep a secret than to break a promise.

He hated how long he stood at the top of the academy steps, watching as Syrinthia, his brother, and their friends gathered at the bottom of the stairs. "But maybe she'd want to know Rakland's hiding the information. She cared about it a week ago. Maybe he's forcing her to keep quiet." He took three steps down before halting again, his stomach flipping. *But why would Rakland hide this information? He specifically told me to hold onto the old ways; doesn't that include the Shadows of Light?*

Sinking to the steps, he covered his face in his hands, trying to tune out the passing students and their loud, judgmental whispers.

Why are things like this always so hard for me to decide?

When he looked up, his eyes locked onto Syrinthia's, and she waved. Faking a smile, he waved back and jumped to his feet, hoping she wouldn't feel the need to check on him. He brightened his smile, hoping she would ignore the dejected way he'd been sitting moments earlier.

She frowned but finally let another girl pull her toward the gate with the rest of the group. None of them looked back before disappearing down the roads to whatever they filled their late nights with.

Knowing he wouldn't be missed at home as long as the suns were still up, Thaddeus turned back to the academy and took the stairs two at a time. He didn't slow his pace lest he change his mind.

A few minutes later, he stood before Rakland's office, suddenly feeling very small. Never before had it looked so formidable and undeniably closed.

It'll be locked too, I'm sure. He'd seen Rakland unlock the door every time he went in and lock it every time he came out. But he didn't give up and return home. Deep down, he knew what he was looking for was in this room. *But is it worth the risk?*

Casting a glance down the hall, he frantically crafted a lie in case he got caught. The lie was only half-formed in his mind when his impatient hands reached for the doorknob, expecting it to halt when turned.

It didn't.

With a low creak, the door inched open.

Eyes wide and heart in his throat, Thaddeus stared through the crack, hand suspended where the doorknob had been.

For a long moment, he didn't move, unable to believe it'd been unlocked.

He swore his heart echoed traitorously loud through the halls.

Finally, he inched inside.

Hastily, he shut the door behind him, praying to every god he knew that no one had seen him.

When the halls and alarms remained quiet, he calmed his panicked breathing and began searching the room.

Knowing the professor wouldn't likely leave a book of forbidden knowledge out in the open, Thaddeus shifted his attention to the floor-to-ceiling bookshelves on the far end of the room.

The search proved exhausting. Each tome hid under a thick layer of dust, as if they hadn't been touched in years. The titles in scrawled cursive decorated the spines in confusing ways, many completely illegible. Sometimes he came across two or three of the same books, which only gave him the impression he was going in circles.

The room began to darken as the suns slipped below the ramparts of the school. He had maybe another half hour to find the book, exit the school's winding corridors undetected, and make it home before sunsset.

Fantastic.

Minutes later, he reached the end of the shelves, and the book he searched for remained lost.

Disappointment settled in his heart. Tears stung his eyes, but he quickly brushed them away, reprimanding himself for overreacting. *Syrinthia was right. This is ridiculous and a waste of my time. If I'm expelled, I'll bring shame to my family for nothing. Thanatos will never let me hear the end of it.*

Crushing under the guilt and self-pity, he dragged his feet back to the door.

Then his eye caught something on the desk.

He stopped but didn't dare turn around and let his hopes shoot back up like a hatchling flying. But he couldn't dispel his curiosity.

Hesitantly, he turned around.

A single book sat on the desk. A thick red ribbon snaked from its spine, tucked lovingly into the book to mark a page. The cover lay void of dust, the pages clean and white.

One step at a time, he crept toward the book, hands hesitant to grab it. *This can't be the book I'm looking for.*

But what else would it be, if not what he searched for? He'd never seen Rakland reading a book, nor had he ever seen one sitting on the desk. With gentle fingers, he pulled it toward him, the gold embossed title shimmering in the setting suns.

His heart skipped before racing. The title read: *Darkness Grows in the Shadows of Light*. When he opened the cover, the title page was marked by a torn newspage—the page the note he'd given to Syrinthia was written on.

Fingers trembling, he lifted the dense book, his body feeling weightless and unbelievably heavy at the same time. *Why is Rakland reading this book now of all times? If I take it, I'll be stealing. And if I'm caught, I could be expelled. My father would punish me for life.*

The page marked by the red ribbon drew him in. It started a new chapter with a black page and crème letters saying: *Jen-Jibuź*—A Dark Sect of the Shadows of Light.

Without any more hesitation, he tucked the book under his arm and sprinted to the door. Pressing his ear to the thick wood, he extended his magic to detect any life in the halls. Silence answered. Thinking this was too good to be true, he turned the doorknob and pulled.

The door creaked and he flinched but nothing stirred, not even a bird outside. The silence felt more concerning.

Not waiting to be spotted, he shut the door and sprinted down the hall, careful not to let his heels strike the stone floors.

When he reached the gates, he searched for a guard, his mind spinning a thousand excuses why he'd been late to leave the school. Not a guard stood in sight. His heart sank into his stomach as he cursed. *Just my luck.*

Then he realized the gate *wasn't* fully shut. Blood pounding through his veins, he slunk to the cold bars and slipped through the opening. *Too easy. Is it a trap?*

But when he stood outside the gates, not a single alarm blared. He was free, except for the overwhelming sensation clawing at his shoulders, warning him that someone, or something, watched him.

Without stopping to catch his breath, he rushed home. Every shadow startled him, flooding his mind of stories of kidnappers.

His conjured lies went to waste as his mother welcomed him with relieved, forgiving arms, simply happy to see him safe. Busy scolding Thanatos for the alcohol found in his satchel, his father barely minded his late entrance. Thaddeus thanked the gods his brother took the brunt of their parents' frustration.

He ate a few bites of dinner before quickly tidying the kitchen. Then he sneaked to the glass walkway under the light of the rising moons to read.

The tome held far more information than he'd initially imagined. Not only did it contain dark theories surrounding the Shadows of Light, but it also detailed records of their beliefs and practices. But despite how interesting it was, Thaddeus was most drawn to the dark sect that split from the Shadows of Light—a group of radicals called *Jen-Jibuź*. According to the book, they'd taken it upon themselves to fix the world with more than just the love and freedom the Shadows of Lights taught.

But what disturbed him most was the end of the chapter:

Abruptly, all attacks on the games ceased. The Jen-Jibuź faded from public view, and without reason, the true Shadows of Light began to dwindle. Soon, they were nothing more than another religious voice lost in the confusion of the radically changing Duvarharian government. Though many thought they disbanded, I have it on good authority the Jen-Jibuź *has survived by way of mercenary work; additionally, they have sought to implement their extremist, traditional ideals into the government and armies of Duvarharia, acting as a hidden political party.*

Though they strive for a traditional Duvarharian culture, their morals do not seem to abide by the old laws. It has become clear their driving conviction is "The ends always justify the means." Despite their core beliefs, they see little wrong with evil as long as it perpetuates their goal of reshaping Duvarharia, striving for the same power the original Shadows of Light once held.

I fear for the life of anyone reading this book the same as I fear for my own. They let no one stand in their way. They are everywhere. They are always watching.

Chapter 13

OVER THE NEXT WEEK, Thaddeus devoured the tome. It spoke of forgotten facts he'd never been taught by his tutors, father, or academy teachers. The knowledge was foreign and exciting and even somehow addicting.

He learned the Shadows of Light hadn't been one of the many false religions to rise and fall in Duvarharian history. Instead, they'd followed Joad—the Great Lord who led Duvarharia into its Golden Age. He'd been the one to destroy the cult of elites who monopolized dragons and magic. Joad taught that every dragon and rider was born with the same rights to bonding, magic, and most importantly to *Shushequmok*, a power only the elite religious leaders of the time were allowed to use.

The idea of the *Shushequmok*, a vast, ancient power, seemed more like a myth than history, but the more he read about it, the more he believed it. According to the book, *Shushequmok* was the magic creation upon which Duvarharia was founded thousands of years ago. It was the magic that bonded riders to their dragons and gave Duvarharians control over the land itself, shaping it to their will. It only made sense it was same the power used to build the Dragon Palace—an entire city fashioned of nothing but magic.

Joad had taught that all Duvarharians should be bonded with a dragon and be instructed to hone their individual abilities. those were the teachings that motivated the Duvarharians of that time to overthrow the corrupted Council, annihilate the last of the foul shape-shifting Etas, and enter a Golden Age that lasted thousands of years.

These were the beliefs Thaddeus wanted to bring back. By some power of the universe, perhaps even the *Shushequmok*, he'd been meant to find this book. Deep down, he knew Rakland wanted him to read this book. The ancient teachings and magic of Joad the Great Lord yearned to be found, to be in the minds and hearts of the Duvarharians again. And he believed he'd been chosen as the vessel of this renewal.

The proclamation awakened a steadfast purpose, sending it burning through his veins.

Each day in school became a little easier to bear. He raised his hand more often and spoke his mind more freely. Each time he was sent to the hall to think about his actions, he sent a prayer to Joad, hoping his words had made some impact on the other students, possibly even the teachers.

The more outspoken he grew, the more the bullying increased. But now the blows, words, and threats didn't hurt as much. Thaddeus knew the children mocking him had been brainwashed into believing violence was their only worth. So, no matter how many blows struck him down, he continued to find the strength to keep picking himself up. He never returned the attacks, but he'd resolved to fight back in a different way. He would bring back the old Duvarharia and instill a new age—one where institutions like this academy were long destroyed and forgotten, one where no young Duvarharian would have to suffer the same as he.

***

"SYRINTHIA, YOU HAVE to listen to me." Thaddeus' hands shook, his gaze latched onto the ground. He loathed every harsh word between them, but over the last week, he'd argued with her almost every time he saw her. It wasn't until she found the book in his satchel that she started yelling.

"No! I told you to drop this. Don't you see how it's consuming you? Where did you even find that book? It's been checked out longer than you've even been here."

Thaddeus opened his mouth to protest, but she snapped back. "Yes, I asked around. The main upstairs librarian was more than happy to fill me in on all the exciting questions you've been asking."

"Syrinthia, something is wrong with this school and—"

"Seriously, Thaddeus? Don't you think I know that? Isn't that why we're planning on freeing the creatures from the basement?"

Thaddeus ground his teeth. "I know. But I'm trying to tell you, I think it goes much deeper than just that." He glanced around, uncomfortable with the students turning inquisitive gazes toward their rising voices. "Come on." Grabbing her hand and ignoring her protests, he led her away from the crowds and into the column's long shadow. "I know what those creatures are, Syrinthia. They aren't just some random animals."

"What are you saying? What else would they be? The headmistress uses magic to distort the creatures in her sick experiments. That's what the exhibit is for."

Thaddeus shook his head. "Maybe she does, but not those creatures. Those are—" the words halted in his throat. If he told her they were Zoics, she would demand how he knew. He could never say his mother was one, that *he* was one, but he had to make her understand. He couldn't do this alone, but he didn't know who else to trust. Yet the way she stood—eyes narrowed, arms crossed firmly—made him question if he *could* trust her. The conversation between her, Rakland, and the cloaked creature raced through his mind. His blood ran cold with realization.

"You know." Painful silence stretched between them as tears collected in his eyes. "You know *everything*. That's why you want me to stop. You know about the dark sect of the Shadows of Light, and you know they're running this school."

Her arms dropped with her jaw, fear filling her eyes. "No, Thaddeus, you don't understand—"

Hands balled into fists, he tried to stem the rage boiling inside him.

"Then you'd better explain, because for all I know, you're baiting me to free those creatures so I'll be expelled and the school won't have to worry about me searching for their secrets."

Tears flowed down her cheeks as she struggled to form words—starting, stopping, then starting again.

Arms crossed, he waited until her crying had slowed enough for her to draw breath. "Thaddeus, please. I hardly know more than you. I've only just been learning these things as you have. Rakland—" She stopped herself, but his scolding gaze forced her to continue. "He's been deep within this school for decades, trying to uncover their deception. He's only now beginning to find ways he can expose them without risk of another cover-up. He only told me because I found those creatures and the exhibit just the same as you did and I started asking questions. But, Thaddeus, if you keep asking questions—" She covered her face and sobbed.

An overwhelming wave of guilt washed over Thaddeus. Throwing his arms around her, he held her close as she clung to him and cried. "Syrinthia, I'm so sorry. I know you'd never harm me or support something as cruel as the sect. I know that. I was just paranoid. I was just . . . scared."

Nodding, she pulled back from him and turned away. Thaddeus thought she would leave, but she didn't. Instead, she lifted her shirt.

Horror filled him.

Her back was lined with ugly scars, some in the shape of strange symbols. "This is what will happen if you keep asking questions like I did." She pulled her shirt back down, struggling through her tears. "Rakland is the only reason I wasn't killed, but that's because they forced him to hold the knife. I just—"

Thaddeus didn't want to hear any more. "I'm sorry, Syrinthia. I'm sorry." He wanted to hold her, to smooth away her fears the way his mother did for him, but he couldn't bring himself to touch her; he feared his touch would violate her the same as the others'. Tears filled his eyes. "Why do you want to free them if you know this is what awaits when you try?"

Her eyes, full of old wisdom and pain, shone unwaveringly into his. "Because I have no choice. *We* have no choice. Wouldn't you keep going?"

Thaddeus' head hung low. He didn't know what it was like to be beaten. His mother and father had never laid their hands on him. He couldn't fathom the feel of a whip on his skin, let alone by someone he trusted. But he *would* continue, wouldn't he? Because despite the threat of pain and death, he could still feel the pain of the Zoics, and he would never rest until they had peace. He knew Syrinthia felt the same. "Yes. I would."

Gripping the front of his shirt, she cried into his chest. "Please don't. Please don't. Don't come with me tonight."

Determination flooded his veins. "I have to. You're going to free them tonight. I promised you I'd help."

"No." Her fiery gaze met his. "I don't want you to. I want you to stop this. Stop before you go too deep and don't have anyone to save you like Rakland saved me."

His fingers dug into her arms. "Then you must stop too."

"No—" she started, but he gently shook her shoulders.

"I'm serious, Syrinthia. I promise I'll stop if you will. You can turn back now. But I can't walk away while you remain."

"I'm in too deep." She wrenched herself from him, staggering away as she hid her face. "You'll never understand. I can't walk away. Ever."

"Syrinthia!"

But she had run away, the echo of her sobs haunting Thaddeus as his hands balled into fists. His own tears joined hers as an empty chasm opened inside him.

He tried to convince himself he could put this behind him. His mother wanted him to stop so her family would be safe, his father wanted him to have a good education so he could obtain a powerful job, Thanatos wanted a good reputation so he could fight in the games, and Rakland wanted him to bring back old Duvarharia. Most of all, he thought of Syrinthia. Her intoxicating smile hid a dark and sinister secret she couldn't escape. The more he thought, the more he realized he could never escape either, not until he understood the darkness brewing around him and his entanglement in it.

If she was going to free the creatures tonight, then he would be where he knew he belonged.

CHAPTER 14

A CRAMP TIGHTENED in Thaddeus' leg. Wincing, he shifted his weight to alleviate the pain but only succeeded in worsening it. He didn't dare stand. Already, he sensed Syrinthia was aware of his presence, though he was surprised she did nothing about it. Crouched behind a corner, he could peer through a hole in the stone, perhaps where a prisoner's chains had once been secured. From here, he could see Syrinthia at the gates of the Zoics' cell.

With deft hands, she pulled out a set of lockpicks and threaded them into the metal lock. Nothing moved in the darkness beyond the gates, no green leafy hands reached out, not even a breath of air was released. The other cells had been full of whimpering, emaciated, tortured animals. So why was the Zoic cell so quiet?

Dread trailed up and down his spine. *Are the creatures dead? Are we too late?*

Finally, her efforts were rewarded with a *click* that echoed along the walls. His heart beat deafeningly in the following silence. Even the groans of dying animals had fallen away.

The gate swung open on screeching hinges. If no one knew they were here before, they certainly knew now. But no one came.

Turning, Syrinthia cast a glance over her shoulder. He ducked down, hoping she hadn't noticed him through the hole. Breath held in still lungs, he gently moved the edge of his cloak, hoping it hadn't been sticking into the walkway.

When she didn't come over or call out to him, he chanced a quick glance through hole once more, hoping he hadn't missed her entering the darkness. He hadn't. Instead of proceeding into the darkness, she simply stood still, hands open as if in offering.

After a few breathless moments, she sucked in a deep breath and exhaled. From her lips floated a beam of golden light, collecting in an orb above her outstretched palms. The light from the orb spread warmth through the cold dungeons, even to Thaddeus.

Like honey off a spoon, the light moved into the cell, bringing light to every corner.

He saw the blood first. It was splattered on the walls, crumbling off the ceiling, pooling on the ground. Much of it was old, but some of the pools glinted fresh in the light.

Resisting the urge to gag and ignoring every instinct telling him to run home to his mother's arms where he was safe, he moved from behind the corner as Syrinthia stepped into the cell.

I have to do this. Nowhere is safe for me or my mother. Her arms are only a fleeting glimpse of safety when our kin are being trapped and tortured like this.

Would she have understood why he needed to be here if he'd told her he was part Zoic? Or would she have seen him as another pitiful creature who needed saving?

When he reached the gate, he hesitated. Masses lay on the ground, clothed in the light of Syrinthia's magic, but they didn't move.

Last chance to turn away.

But he didn't.

Following her as quietly as he could, he covered his nose against the smell of blood and rotting plants. Soon, she would know he was here, and he would have to convince her to let him stay.

Syrinthia reached a dead-end wall. Disappointment and horror radiated off her as her tears filled the silent cell with a heart wrenching echo. Then she turned. With nowhere to hide, he could do nothing except meet her gaze.

Her eyes widened as her mouth dropped open. "Thaddeus—" The urgency in her voice caused his heart to skip.

"Syrinthia, please don't—" But before he could finish, something wrapped around his ankles. Stifling a scream, he clutched his head as a flood of images flashed through his mind.

A gathering of creatures danced through the fields. Plants were brought together for planting. Strange magic floated through the air, in the wind, in the songs that made the plants twist and grow. A new forest grew from intricate vines, flowers, and trees. Zoics of different plants banded together to do something no other tribe had done before: coexist. But then fear tainted the peace. Darkness spread. Screams tore the air. Their unity was too strange, too unfamiliar. It drew the killers like a moth to flame. Everything fell to ruin, to flame, to ash. They were being dragged in chains to the academy, to the dungeons where death would've been a mercy . . .

"Thaddeus!"

The images fled his mind as he woke to the present. Syrinthia's hands pressed against his temples; the warmth of her magic surrounded him, pushing aside the visions, thoughts, and horrors. Tears streaked down her face the same way they flowed down his.

"I saw them. I saw them."

"I know. I did too."

Slowly, they sank to the ground and cradled each other. No words could describe what he'd seen. Silence was an aching comfort.

The vines around his ankles loosened, but instead of shaking them off, he reached down to hold them with a loving hand. Tracing the vines to their source, he saw the same Zoic who'd twined flowers into his hair. The creature lay on the cold stone in a mess of flesh and vines. The face staring back at him was carved with anguish and sorrow. Tears gathered in its eyes as the vines weakly tightened around Thaddeus' hand.

Trying to still the sobs raking his chest, Thaddeus crawled to the creature and lay beside it. Cold, sticky blood seeped into his hair and clothes; the chill from the dungeon's floor overwhelmed the warmth of

Syrinthia's magic.

He didn't know what to say, didn't know what to do. *I'm sorry* were the only two words he could think. They weren't enough.

Slowly, the creature's eyes fluttered closed, and in their place, two dull flowers bloomed. The vines released his hand.

Syrinthia was pulling him away from the creature, saying something, trying to comfort him. But he didn't hear her, could hardly feel her.

This could be my mother. This could be me.

Finally, he let Syrinthia wrap her arms around him. He didn't know what he said to her, but eventually, she helped him to his feet. Together, leaning on each other for support, they made their way from the now lifeless dungeon. Her light withdrew from the cell, leaving it the cold darkness again.

"Thaddeus, you have to run." Though her words reached his ears, their weight didn't sink in. "Are you hearing me?"

She shook him roughly. The visions from the Zoic disappeared as he gazed into the golden light in her eyes. She was yelling at him, but her voice sounded so far away.

"They killed the Zoics because they knew someone was going to free them tonight. They know we're here." She shoved him away. He stumbled, trying to gain footing. The world came into sharp focus.

"Run!" Her scream echoed through the halls as he turned and obeyed. He slowed only for a moment, to hear her footsteps behind him. He heard nothing.

No.

Then the footsteps of a large group of people thundered through the corridors. Light from their torches and magic illuminated every possible hiding place. Worst of all, he heard them slaughtering the crying animals so they wouldn't hinder the search.

"Syrinthia." Turning, he raced back through the halls. But the gathering of hunters closed in. Even if he reached Syrinthia, they wouldn't make it out. But even knowing that, he couldn't abandon her.

When he reached the corner he'd hidden behind originally, his body froze.

Syrinthia stood in front of the gates, calm as if nothing was wrong. One of the hunters stood next to her, big muscly arms crossed over his chest, as he listened to her words. She pointed to the ground, and he scooped up the lockpicks she'd discarded. Quickly, he pocketed them, nodding at her explanation. He closed the gates and bowed to their leader.

Covering his mouth, Thaddeus pressed his face to the stone, peering through the hole. Panic twisted his heart. He waited for the moment Syrinthia was put in shackles and dragged away, but the moment never came. She knew them.

She spoke boldly with them, gesturing to the gates and corridors, saying something about having watched the culprit escape down a corridor. She pointed to the one farthest from Thaddeus, and a handful of the armed fighters rushed into the darkness, thirsty for death and blood.

Thaddeus' ears rang. Silent tears poured down his face. He couldn't watch any longer. Sliding down the wall, he curled in on himself, crushing under the weight of his emotion.

They're the Jen-Jibuź, *and Syrinthia is . . . He* couldn't bring himself to finish the thought, but deep down, he knew the truth.

Laughter and voices grew louder. They were coming toward him from the gate. If he stepped into the hallway now, he'd be spotted immediately. But his fate was the same if he stayed.

Icy terror froze his veins. His heart raced as if it would explode. *I'm helpless. Weak.*

Deciding he'd rather face them than be found hiding and slaughtered like prey, he scrambled to his feet. It was now or never. In a flood of adrenaline and panic, he threw himself into the hallway.

Three huge fighters towered over him, their drawn weapons dripping with blood. Syrinthia stood in the middle of them, leading them as if they answered to her.

Gulping, Thaddeus clenched his eyes shut, waiting for steel to rip through his body. Nothing happened. No one shouted out at him. No one even acknowledged him.

Instead, a familiar warmth hugged him, encasing him in muffled silence.

When he opened his eyes, the three men had walked around him as if he didn't exist. Syrinthia was standing in front of him, her eyes searching his face.

He wanted to lash out at her, to demand an explanation, to hate her for being in the cult. But when her hand cupped his face, he felt her emotions and understood her heart. She was trapped in a web of lies and hate. The wounds on her back were more than a warning. They were punishment for her betrayal.

Golden tears spilled down her cheeks.

"Please go home, Thaddeus, and never think of this again. Never try to fix this again. Promise me."

But he couldn't. Instead, he tried to reach for her, to hold her, to somehow save her from this waking nightmare, but his limbs failed him. Instead, he only croaked awkwardly. Sadly, she shook her head and turned to follow the hunters.

Though the torchlight faded, the warmth from her magic remained, protecting him.

"Syrinthia, wait!" When his body finally responded, he raced after them, trying to catch up. But when he came to the end of the dungeons, shoes caked in blood, they were gone. Then, as the last of her magic disappeared, he knew he was completely alone.

Drying the tears from his eyes and quelling the panic in his chest, he slunk through the halls, dodged the night guards, and pressed himself through the fence bars.

Desperation gripped his heart. He didn't have to be alone, and neither did she. Somehow, he would find a way to free her.

Chapter 15

"Thaddeus, I'm not very happy right now." Quinlan crossed his arms and narrowed his gaze.

A tight knot formed in Thaddeus' stomach. "No, you don't understand. This isn't just some rumor or made-up story. It's *real*. It's happening *right now*."

"So, you want me to believe you're skipping classes and breaking into professors' offices because you think a thousand-year-old cult is running the academy and trapping Zoics so the headmistress can use them for experiments and the games?"

It sounded ridiculous when his father said it. Face red with embarrassment and frustration, Thaddeus stuttered over his words, glancing at his mother for help. She sat demure on the couch next to his father, hands in her lap, face turned down.

"I know how it sounds, but it's true. I'm not skipping many classes and only because the teachers dismiss me for asking questions about the Shadows of Light or dragons and magic. They don't want to teach any of that because anyone smart enough to saddle their own horse would realize the academy is being run by a dark sect of the Shadows of Light."

Quinlan stood, eyes flashing. "Getting thrown out of class? Thaddeus, by the gods, I swear." He ran his fingers through his hair, the same platinum blond he'd passed to Thaddeus, and clenched his jaw. "Do you realize how much money I've paid for you to be in that academy? How much influence I had to pull so you could be in the higher classes? And now you're telling me you're getting thrown *out of them?*"

Thaddeus wrung his hands and took a step back. "No, I mean, yes, I do understand. But you've always said that we are our best teacher and that we should never immediately believe everything someone else tells us without proof."

Quinlan's eyes narrowed in warning, but Thaddeus continued.

"It's Thanatos' dream to be in the games, not mine. I want to learn about magic and dragons and the old ways. I don't want to go to the academy anymore." Tears filled his eyes. Somehow, talking about his feelings hurt more than the bullying. Not knowing how his father would react only added to his anxiety.

Naraina looked up, tears sparkling in her eyes. He thought he saw a warning in her gaze, but he didn't heed it. He had truths he needed to speak, a voice that needed to be heard.

Before Quinlan could speak, Thaddeus blurted out what he really wanted to say. "The cult is real. I've seen them. I've seen Zoics in the dungeon. Syrinthia and I went down there to free them, but someone had killed them first. Then the cult came and—and—" He found he couldn't push past the emotion choking his words.

"You did *what* with Syrinthia?" Quinlan's voice boomed through the room. Any chance of reconciliation was gone.

Every inch of his skin revolted as his father reached for him. His hands balled into fists as he screamed, "Don't touch me!"

Strong hands locked onto his shoulders and pulled him closer. "You are in so much trouble, Thaddeus. Do you even know what this means for me? For your mother, for Thanatos?"

Thaddeus couldn't look Quinlan in the eyes as he recoiled from him. His voice spoke on its own, ignoring every warning he screamed at himself. "Yes. It means death. Death for people like me who give an *ozi* about Duvarharia and the innocent Wyriders. And for Syrinthia and Mother, who can't escape the evil permeating this cursed land. It's all because worthless men of power like you only care about their trophy sons and looking good for the crowd."

A resounding crack filled the room. Thaddeus didn't comprehend what happened until the pain slowly started to tingle in his cheek then began to throb. He stared at his father in disbelief. The strike itself hadn't been very strong, but the damage to Thaddeus' soul was irreparable.

Tears filled his eyes. Anger filled his heart.

"Quinlan—" Naraina jumped to her feet and pulled Thaddeus from his father. Quinlan tried to justify his actions. Naraina pleaded for him to return. He shook his head to both.

"You can ignore me all you want," Thaddeus hissed back. "But I'm still your son, Quinlan, and I'm tired of being tossed aside like Eta filth." Wrenching the door open, he forced his heart to shut out his mother's crying. Right now, he had to take care of himself. "I don't care if you don't believe me, but I'm going to find and save Syrinthia."

"Thaddeus, get back—" Before Quinlan could finish his sentence, Thaddeus slammed the door behind him and ran into the forest.

Krystallos' roars filled the night as he took to the skies. Though Krystallos was an excellent hunter, it would be difficult for him to follow Thaddeus into the thick forest. He would be safe for now.

Not caring where he was going and unsure of where to start searching for Syrinthia, Thaddeus soon found himself wandering aimlessly through the streets of Upper Peace Haven.

The moons were full, giving him enough light to see the roads and laying dark shadows across the paths from the tall buildings.

Anger and hurt soon turned to tears, and, as much as he hated how often he cried, he couldn't stop the flow. His heart ached with the loss of the Zoics, Syrinthia's affiliation with the cult, then fear for her safety. He hated abandoning his mother, who'd done nothing to deserve his hateful words, but he hated his father more for striking him.

Then overwhelming disappointment drowned all other emotions as he stood alone in the streets, knowing Syrinthia was stuck in the clutches of evil people and he was powerless to help her.

Though the streets seemed empty and quiet, the shadows reminded him of the very real threat of kidnappers. *I was a fool to run after her.* He wanted to curl into a ball, cry until he slept, and then wake up to this being a nightmare. Instead, he took step after step. A quiet realization washed over him. *A fool I may be, but I couldn't have stayed in that house.*

Wrapping his arms around himself, he kicked a rock and watched it tumble down the road. Even if he couldn't save Syrinthia tonight, he was better off here than with a father who preferred one son over the other.

Eventually though, he would have to go home. His mother would worry, and perhaps his father would too, despite his anger. But someday, normality would return. He'd go to school, to the bullying and jeers. Even if he stopped searching for the truth, he would still be different, set apart. Rakland's first warning finally made sense. His very soul was different. Even if he convinced himself he loved the games and didn't care about magic and dragons, he knew he would never be happy without them. There would always be an empty hole in his heart, waiting to be filled. And Syrinthia . . . His nails dug into his palms. She would still be stuck in the cult, torn between two worlds like he was.

Eventually, the emotion and thoughts overwhelmed him, and the tears returned. Leaning against a fence post, he let himself slide to the ground and cry.

He didn't know how long he sat there or even if he dozed off a moment. But when he looked back up, he realized he was lost.

Worry gnawed at his stomach. Several rural houses stood nearby, more rural than he was used to. Large fields of land stretched between each other and the road. The open space invited an intrusive thought. *If something did happen to me and I screamed for help, no one would hear me.*

His skin prickled as he jumped to his feet. Knowing he'd come from the road to the left, he quickly turned and started back down it. Now seemed a good time for Krystallos to fly overhead.

With each step, dread settled deeper into his stomach. The feeling of being watched ran cold in his blood. Sweat beaded on his forehead. He broke into a jog, his heart drowning out the strikes of his feet against dirt.

The forest was just ahead now. Before he jumped over the fence and stepped into the trees' looming shadows, two figures moved from the darkness. Without hesitation, he whirled around to run back to the road. A third figure waited on the path.

Biting back tears, he wondered if he could outrun the first two figures. But they were already dangerously close and stood nearly a head and a half taller than him. He was trapped.

Then a hauntingly familiar voice rang out, and his blood ran cold. "What're you doing out here alone, Thaddeus? Don't you know this is when people like me come for little boys like you?"

Chapter 16

"Brina." Despite his dire situation, Thaddeus breathed a sigh of relief. Though her two brothers accompanied her, he'd rather face them than kidnappers. "If this is about the dress I ruined—"

Her venomous laughter cut the empty country air. "I just bought a new one. I wouldn't waste my time on you and something so trivial."

"Oh." He croaked a laugh, his jaw aching with nausea. "Then, I bid you a good rest of the night. I'm afraid I can't stay to chat; my mother wants me home." Then he kicked dirt into the face of the nearest brother and took off running toward the forest.

Jumping over the fence was harder for him than them, and they seemed only a breath away. The shadows of the forest stretched long and far. He'd misjudged how close it was. He had no chance of outrunning them. After all, he couldn't even outrun his own brother.

Thaddeus' lungs burned. His legs ached. Dirt skidded. His feet faltered and rocks dug into his hands as he fell. Scrambling against gravity and tired muscles, he struggled to his feet.

Then the wind disappeared from his lungs as a foot collided with his ribs.

Rocks cut his face as he slammed to the ground. The taste of dust and blood filled his cheeks. "Please—"

"Hold him up." Brina's scathing orders were immediately heeded.

Thaddeus gasped for breath. "Let me go. My father—"

Her punch, not as soft as he was hoping, collided with his stomach. The shooting pain started a throb in his head.

"Your father doesn't give a hatchling's *ue* about you. Thanatos is his favorite, and you know it. In fact, I'll bet he's just finished feeling up that *klushuuv sub*, Syrinthia, and your father won't even care he's home late."

"She's not his girlfriend!" Thaddeus threw himself at Brina, almost breaking free from her brothers. "Don't you dare talk about her like that." For a moment, he hardly noticed the pain of his arms being wrenched behind him to his shoulder blades.

"Oh my," she whispered slyly. He withered from her touch as she tucked a lock of hair behind his ears. "Do you have *feelings* for her?" Her smile turned to hateful scorn, and she spit in his face; her breath smelled of sour sugar. "Pathetic. As if she'd ever go for someone as worthless as you."

Her words struck a very painful chord in his heart. After all, she was right. He *was* pathetic. Though Syrinthia seemed happy to walk with him and share her study notes from the class they shared, he was nothing compared to his brother. That was made clear by the way her eyes lit up when Thanatos walked in a room. The hold his older brother had on her was the same she had on him.

"What do you want, Brina?" He wanted to spit the blood in his mouth into her face, but his swollen lips were already failing him.

"I'm so glad you asked." Before he could prepare himself, she pulled back her fist and launched it into his nose.

Unimaginable pain exploded throughout his face along with a maddening tingling. Blood poured from his nose and collected on his lips. She was saying something, but he couldn't hear over the ringing in his ears. One of the brothers shook him until his hearing cleared.

"That's for my boyfriend. Gordon. Who now has a disfigured nose because of your brother, thanks to you."

That's what this is about? Rage coursed through his veins but instead of giving him strength, it presented itself as a throbbing headache, racing heart, and more tears than he thought his body could produce.

"Someone wants you silenced, Thaddeus Valdera," she sneered. His blood turned to ice as she lifted a pouch of *femi*. "Someone very powerful." She pocketed the coins and crossed her arms. "I don't know who you crossed, but they aren't happy about what you've found." A long nail slid under his chin, forcing his gaze to meet hers. "Whatever it is you're doing, you're going to stop. Right now. Or else the next time you see me and my brothers, it'll be the last time you see anything."

The cult knew. Panic washed over him then numbness. The book he'd read said their eyes and ears were everywhere. He should've taken the warning to heart. The decision to seek out their secrets in one of their own strongholds had been foolish; it could end up being fatal.

But he refused to be silenced.

"Don't you get tired of this?" His words, hardly more than a croak on the wind, stunned Brina.

She stumbled over her words. "W–what?"

He gasped as his breath caught painfully on his ribs, then repeated himself. "Don't you get tired of this?"

"Of what? Taking advantage of your foolishness to fill my purse? Not one bit. Turns out, I have a taste for mercenar—"

"I'm not—" He snarled against the pain each breath brought. "I'm not talking to you." He nodded to her brothers. "I'm talking to them."

Their eyes widened. For a moment, he dared to hope for a shred of humanity in their cold hearts. Then their laughter filled the air.

They released him abruptly, and he fell. Every muscle in his body pleaded with him to lie down, to give up. *I have a chance. Get up. Run.* But with fresh wounds, fleeing was useless. Instead, he propped himself up and spoke his mind. If the cult paid them to silence him, they'd have to earn it.

"Just seems pathetic to me. That you two don't have anything better to do than beat up boys younger and smaller than you because you don't have the guts to say 'no' to your kid sister." The words felt so good as they escaped his lips, but the kick to his side and being dragged to the nearest abandoned farm building felt the exact opposite. He braced himself for his consequences.

Stars exploded across his vision as they threw him against the wall; sharp pain jolted from the back of his head down his spine as his head cracked against wood. Desperately, he swung against his attacker. His fists only met air.

Hands wrapped around his throat. Spots decorated his vision as he gasped for air. Tears trickled down his cheeks as his head felt like it would explode. The ringing in his ears returned.

"We don't do this just because she asks." Hate-filled eyes burned into his own. "We do it because we like it."

The hands loosened for a moment—long enough for a cold, deep breath. The air burned against his throat. Then a knee collided with his stomach.

Doubling over, he resisted the urge to retch. His tears darkened the dirt below him. Hot breath stuck to his neck as his attacker took a fistful of his hair and forced him to meet his gaze. Thaddeus hated those mocking eyes, hated how they reminded him of every hateful, belittling glance cast at him every day at the academy.

"You're worthless." Brina spat into his face, making him gag. "I brought my brothers because they enjoy the fight, but if I wanted, I could leave you bleeding and whimpering like a beat hatchling all on my own. You'll never amount to anything more than a bait dragon. I give you a year before you're kidnapped then only a few months before the arena contestants chew you to pieces."

Her fists struck his chest, his stomach, his head, over and over, until he slumped to the ground, unable to hold his arms up to protect him. *How much more of this can I take?* He didn't want to find out.

"You're lucky the one paying me simply wants you silenced. Next time they send me after you, I'll decorate Peace Haven with your blood and send your mother your head. Do you understand?"

A yelp escaped his lips as a brother stomped on his hand. Cradling it to his chest, he refused to answer as he was dragged to his feet.

"Do you understand?" Her voice shrieked across the night.

Mouth parting in a halfhearted croak, he started to agree, then stopped. The pain would end if he just told her what she wanted to hear. But the pain in his heart wouldn't. Every day, he'd have to live with himself, knowing he had picked the coward's way out. Slowly, he shook his head again.

"You have once last chance." Her voice was now dangerously quiet. "Will you stay silent? Will you stop searching for things that don't concern a *huula-shux* like you?"

"No," he whispered as hands tightened around his throat again. "Never."

Her screams filled the air.

Desperation flooded him. Syrinthia, his mother, his father, his brother, Krystallos—a vision of them pleading with him to stay awake, to fight back, to refuse this death flashed across his vision. *I can't die. I can't die. I won't die!*

His frantic, searching hands groped the wall. A splintered wooden handle found its place in his palm. The strength of desperation flooded his limbs as he swung the handle.

The sickening crack rang through the air, making his stomach roll. The hands dropped from his throat as the boy staggered backward, his hands clutching a gaping wound in his right arm. Blood seeped through his fingers and darkened his clothes.

For a long moment, no one moved.

Then realization set in.

Brina screamed the same moment the other boy lunged at Thaddeus. Relying only on the desperation to live, Thaddeus stepped aside and swung the handle again. This time, he spotted a glimpse of shining metal.

The blunt end of the weapon struck the boy in the back. As he staggered, he grasped something from the ground. When he whirled back around, he held a pickaxe, swinging like a berserk.

Blood throbbed in Thaddeus' ears as he dodged the ill-aimed attacks. He barely stayed on his feet as his legs wobbled, nerves screaming in pain. The pickaxe caught his shirt; he felt a tear as the pickaxe split the skin of his chest.

Brina's pathetic screams filled the night with chaos. The other brother staggered, taking a few wobbly steps, before straightening his shoulders. Rage in his eyes, he dragged his own weapon from the wall.

This is the end. Thaddeus shook his head against the thought, struggling to see past the darkness spotting his vision, mingling with tears. It took all his self-control not to bend over and lose the little bit of food left in his stomach.

No. It's not. Not yet. Time slowed as he dodged another swing from the pickaxe. The tool recklessly pierced the dirt; its wielder struggled to free it.

Before he fully understood what his body was doing, Thaddeus raised his weapon. The head of the large woodcutter's axe shone in the full moons before he brought it down on the closest appendage he saw.

Screams and blood erupted through the air. The boy threw himself away from the pickaxe, clutching his arm; it was hanging unnaturally from his elbow. Blood poured from the wound, pooling on the dirt as rage filled his eyes. With a scream, he lunged toward Thaddeus.

Taking one step back, Thaddeus swung his axe from where it had glanced off bone and aimed for the only place he knew would finally end the attacks.

A dull *thud* echoed.

Chunks of bone and flesh spattered the wall as a spray of thick liquid coated Thaddeus' face. The axe fell from his hands as he beheld the damage it caused.

The boy's jaw was torn from his face like his arm, hanging by only a few muscles and tendons. He blinked rapidly, confused. Turning to his sister, he staggered toward her, moaning as he tried to form words. Her bloodcurdling scream rent the night before she and her other brother dropped their weapons and fled.

Silence filled the air and the gaping hole in Thaddeus' stomach.

"No." Thaddeus stifled his own scream as the boy turned to him, shaking his head, tears rolling down his cheeks. He staggered over to Thaddeus, coming within only a few feet of him before he fell to his knees. His neck and chest were soaked with blood. All hate and anger had left his eyes. Now, Thaddeus saw only the fear of death he had felt only a few minutes before.

A guttural scream left his lips as he lurched to catch the boy as he collapsed. Cradling his bloody, mangled head in his arms, Thaddeus sobbed onto his chest.

"I'm so sorry. I'm so sorry. I didn't mean—If only you hadn't—" Words were not enough. He tried to mutter the healing spell he'd heard his teachers use, but his weak, transparent white magic only hovered over the wounds pathetically before dissipating.

Thaddeus rocked back and forth, his body rattling like the air in the boy's torn throat. "No, please don't die. Please don't die." But against every pitiful plea he screamed to the wind, the boy's blood slowed with his breath until his chest rose one last time then fell still.

"Wake up." Thaddeus shook the lifeless body, panic rising in his veins. "Wake up!" He beat against the boy's chest, hating how heavy the body had become, how unnaturally still.

"Oh, gods." He scrambled away from the body when the boy's glassy eyes locked onto his and the reality of the situation set in.

"I've killed someone. I've killed someone." Struggling to his feet, he tried to wipe the blood from his clothes. His efforts were futile, only spreading the blood.

He turned to flee, to never look back, to never think about this again. Then a chilling thought rooted him to the spot. *What if they're able to trace it back to me? What if they accuse me of cold-blooded murder? What if Brina and her brother turn me in? What will I say? Will they find my magic trace here?*

He couldn't leave. Not before he was sure not a shred of his magic trace would be left. Taking several deep breaths, he forced himself to concentrate on what his parents and tutors had instructed him about magic traces. The mental effort was almost more than he could bear. Just when he could feel the world of magic open around him, his chest pressed in on itself as panic raced his heart. Sinking to the ground, he hugged his knees to his chest.

"I can't do this," he whispered through salivating lips and sticky fingers covering his face. "I can't do it. I can't."

But you have to, his mind reminded him. *No one will believe you if you tell them the truth. Your father doesn't care about you enough to defend you. He'll most likely cave to Brina's father's influence so he doesn't lose his own job as an ambassador. No one will believe you. You cannot rely on the truth.*

Despite the hair he ripped out, the ditches in his skin dug by his nails, and the pieces of his clothes he tore apart, the voice in his head won over. Eventually, when the full moons hung high in the sky, his heart stopped racing and numbness washed over him.

Standing slowly, he turned to the body, gagging when he realized the eyes were still open, staring into a star-filled sky. Licking his lips, he forced his mind to seep into every crevice of the world around him. When he could feel the very rocks of the road and the wood of the shed, he searched for the magic traces.

Brina. One brother and . . . Nausea churned his stomach. The magic trace of the dead boy grew distorted. Only remnants of his life lingered, the rest tainted by death. The trace felt more like a void—an unimaginable darkness reaching out to Thaddeus from the shadows, tugging at his heart. He pushed it away from him as best he could, afraid of being driven mad by the way it tickled his legs and hissed in his ear.

Finally, his own trace came into focus. It pulsated with life, infinitely more powerful than the other three. *Was this what Rakland meant?* But he didn't ponder it any longer. Though he was sure his own trace would fade with the others, gone before morning, it had fused itself to a nearby object: the woodcutter's axe.

His eyes snapped open. The axe had been vibrant in his mind's eye, full of his magic trace. Now it was blended into the dirt, almost forgotten in dusty shadows.

"No, no, no. I don't want it." But he had no choice. If the elites found this weapon—oozing of his magic trace—by the bodies, he would be immediately convicted as a murderer.

It must look like a regular kidnapping. He took a step to the axe. *If the elites know a rusty farmer's axe was the murder weapon, they'll know it wasn't a kidnapping. Then they'll investigate the trace. They'll know it's you. They'll find you. You'll be executed the next day.*

Hardly aware of his actions, he knelt beside the axe. Everything inside him revolted against the blood and bone spattered weapon. He hated every inch of it, especially the way moonlight glinted off the death coating its blade. But as his fingers wrapped around the handle and he rose to his feet, he couldn't deny the instant connection he felt. An energy in it hummed as if it had been waiting for him and this moment.

Fixated on the blade, he hardly took one last look at the boy's body before walking down the road.

Nothing seemed real anymore. He felt removed from his body as if all this had happened to someone else. Time hung suspended. A dog barked once, and a dragon stirred in its sleep atop a roof, but then all fell silent. Thaddeus was nearly convinced he was the only living soul here, as if everyone but himself had died tonight.

Or maybe I am the one who died.

Somehow in his daze, he found his way home through the forest, the moons slinking into the second half of their journey.

As he hid the axe in a rotten, hollow tree trunk near his home, he vowed never to tell a single living soul what had happened.

He only hoped no one else would either.

Chapter 17

"**By the gods, Thaddeus!** Where have you been?" Naraina threw her arms around Thaddeus the moment he stepped through the door. Despite the pain her crushing embrace brought his battered body, he returned it just as fiercely.

I almost didn't make it home. The realization made him sick.

"Naraina." Quinlan's tone was dark.

As she followed his gaze, her eyes landing on Thaddeus' face, she gasped, taking a step back. "Oh my . . ." The rest of her words died on her lips.

An empty hole opened in Thaddeus' chest when she stepped away, horror shining in her eyes. He wanted her to hold him again, to rock him to sleep and promise that nothing like this would ever happen again. Words failed him as he whimpered and extended his hands, tears trailing down his cheeks.

"Oh, my *tyän*." All horror in her eyes immediately changed to worry as she crushed him to her again.

No pain could stop the warmth rushing into him. Sagging against her, he let the gut-wrenching sobs he'd been holding back escape his lips and lungs.

"Shh. It's alright now. You're home now. Don't worry. Everything's alright."

As she helped him to the couch, he wanted to believe her assurances, but he wasn't sure he could. *I've killed a man. His blood is on my hands.* The thought was overwhelming, and all he could do was hide in her arms and cry. Every time his father tried to ask what happened, Thaddeus felt her shake her head, and the silence would grow again. Just as exhaustion slowed the tears, pulling him to sleep, Thanatos' sleepy voice broke the stillness.

"Thaddeus? What's going on? Why are you home so late?"

Thaddeus looked up to see Thanatos' dark face pale as he moved into view of the carnage on his clothes.

"Gods of all. What happened?" He quickly sat next to Thaddeus. He reached out to touch him then hesitated, eyes fastened on the blood.

Quinlan stirred from the light slumber he'd fallen into and sat on the short table in front of the couch.

"Thaddeus, I know you don't want to talk about it, but we need to know what happened. And we need to get you to a healer."

Thaddeus nodded, but his mouth refused to speak. Tears collected in his eyes again.

"*Kinätyä segi.*" Naraina brushed back his hair, her fingers catching in the dried blood. She didn't seem bothered by the carnage anymore. "Can you please tell us what happened?"

Now was his chance—the chance to confess the horrific act he committed. The chance to get Brina and her brother convicted of illegal mercenary work and locked away so they couldn't hurt him again. The chance to show the other students he *was* strong, that he *could* protect himself. *But I can't. They'll lie and say I attacked them. They'll make me the villain.*

So instead, he lied. The words came from his mouth cold-hearted and detached, as if it had happened to someone else, not him.

He told them he'd ran into Brina and her brothers on the road, that they offered to walk home with him since he was alone and it was almost dark.

Thanatos scoffed but, after one look from Thaddeus, lowered his eyes and kept quiet.

Then he told them they'd been ambushed by kidnappers. The four of them had put up a fight, and once the kidnappers realized their prey wouldn't be easy, they'd fled. Thaddeus said he didn't know if any of the kidnappers had been seriously wounded, but he knew one of the brothers had an injury in his arm and the other was . . . dead.

Anything else he wanted to say dissolved into croaking sobs.

Quinlan and Thanatos pelted him with questions, but he only shook his head.

"I think that's enough for tonight." Naraina's tone conveyed finality, and immediately, his brother and father quieted. "Quinlan, I think you should call for a healer."

"Of course." Quinlan nodded, eyes dark with worry. He lingered a moment, looking as if he were going to say something. Thaddeus thought it difficult to believe that he was the same man who'd struck him only a few hours earlier. "I'll file a report after sending the healer. The elites need to know about this immediately." Then he disappeared outside. Krystallos' wings rattled the walls before fading away.

"By the gods, you stink." Thanatos wrinkled his nose, and Thaddeus couldn't help but chuckle through tears. "I wasn't going to say anything, but you do, *kinätyä segi*. Let's get you cleaned up?"

He let Thanatos support him as he limped to the bathing pool where Naraina began to run a steaming bath. After she poured a vial of oils and some herbal remedies into the pool, he was left alone to slide into the forgiving water. Closing his eyes, he tried to forget everything that had happened since school started; it was a nearly impossible task.

He wasn't sure how much time had gone by, but before long, a knock on the door followed by Quinlan's deep voice stirred him to wakefulness. "Son, the healer is here. Are you ready?"

He wanted to say no, but his entire body ached, and his nose seemed to be sitting at an odd angle. He had no choice but to say yes.

When he was dried and dressed in a soft robe, he stepped into the hall, coming face to face with a kind-eyed woman who looked hundreds of years old.

"Oh my. You've taken quiet the beating, haven't you, boy?"

He nodded and let her lead him to the living room.

"Do you want me to stay? If that's alright?" Naraina asked him first, then the healer.

The woman nodded as he whispered, "Please."

Gently, she pressed a kiss to his forehead before sitting. "I'll be right here if you need me."

With hands much softer than they first appeared, the woman perused his bruised skin, cuts, and fractures. Then muttering under her breath, she let magic seep from her fingertips into his skin. Gasping, he squirmed at the strangle tingles crawling across his skin and through muscle and bone. He'd never felt this type of healing magic before. It was so much gentler and painless than what he was accustomed to.

Finally, when the pain in his body had faded to a distant ache, she moved to his face. "Take a deep breath, and focus on my eyes," she whispered with a warm smile.

Nodding, he locked gazes with her, mesmerized by what he saw: a vast garden of blooming flowers and plants of exotic beauty. He hardly noticed when his nose cracked back into place and the blood disappeared from his skin.

"I know what you are." The words left his lips before he could stop them.

With a laugh that seemed it belonged to someone much younger, the woman cast a knowing glance to Naraina, who smiled and nodded, moving to stand by her son's side.

"Perhaps." Then she snatched his wrist, and a darkness fell over her face. "But perhaps that is why you got into trouble, eh? You shouldn't be risking yourself—"

Thaddeus shrank from her touch. "I don't understand—"

Naraina's narrowed gaze caused the woman to bow her head. "I apologize, boy. It is not my place to ask."

The sorrow in her eyes made Thaddeus wish he could tell her everything, including how hard he had tried to free their people.

But when he opened his mouth, Naraina cupped his face in her hands and pressed her warm lips to his forehead. "Shh. Not tonight. You need to rest."

Before he could protest or at least learn more about this strange woman who seemed to be a Zoic similar to his mother, Quinlan's cautious voice broke the moment. "May I come in?"

Naraina said he could, and immediately, the healer started counting out herbal remedies for him to take over the next few days.

When his father placed his hands on his shoulders, he did his best not to shrink away. Instead, he tried to find comfort in his father's words.

"I told the elites what happened. They found the other two kids who confirmed what you said. The boy's body was recovered, and the academy was kind enough to donate a considerable amount for his burial and memorial."

They confirmed my story. Why wouldn't they tell the truth? Then he realized if they did tell the truth, they would have to admit to being paid off, and then the academy and their secrets would get involved. The academy hadn't donated out of kindness; they were buying silence. The thought made his stomach churn. "Can I go to sleep now?" He hoped they would let him go without further question. Truthfully, he had no desire to rest. Rest would bring tomorrow, and with it, a confusing web of lies and danger he didn't feel ready to face.

Quinlan looked as if he had something else to say, but surprisingly, it was the healer who cleared her throat, placing a knowing hand on Thaddeus' shoulder. "The boy needs rest, otherwise my magic won't finish what it has started. Let him sleep. Tomorrow will handle the questions better than tonight."

Quinlan relented with a small smile. Something in his gaze looked almost like regret, like something was dancing on his tongue, waiting to be said. Instead, he only kissed Thaddeus' head and muttered, "Goodnight," before leaving the room.

Disappointment clawed at Thaddeus' stomach. *It was foolish of me to expect an apology.*

The healer left after refusing all payment, disappearing into the darkness of the night. But she remained in Thaddeus' mind.

"Mother?"

They paused outside his room. "Hm?"

"Who was that woman?"

A strange look crossed his mother's face. "Just . . . a friend I've known for a long time. Why?"

"Will I ever see her again?" The healer's magic was still working through his body, and the more he stood and talked, the more he felt it dragging him toward sleep.

A sweet smile on her tender face, she kissed his cheeks and rubbed her nose against his. "Maybe someday in a dream."

So, never? He could hear the finality behind her words. It was too dangerous for Zoics to meet regularly in Duvarharia. He would only see her again if he absolutely needed her.

"Get some rest. I love you."

"Love you too, Mother."

The door closed softly behind him. In the darkness that swallowed him whole, he could imagine the healer standing before him next to his mother. If he thought about it hard enough and could imagine the healer's face without the wrinkles, he was certain she'd look uncannily like Naraina. But before he could process this realization, Thanatos' impatient whisper broke the silence.

"What really happened, Thad?"

Nausea rose in his throat as the scene from only hours before repeated in his mind. He dragged himself to his bed and slid under the furs, turning his back to Thanatos. Though he knew better, he hoped Thanatos would drop the subject.

"Thad. Come on. You don't have to keep secrets from me. I know

Brina bullies you, and I just found out last week that she's Gordon's girlfriend. I should've known better than to let you walk home alone. I'm sorry."

Thaddeus bit back tears. He wanted so badly to tell *someone* what had really happened, but the more he compared the truth to his lie, the more he realized how preposterous the truth sounded. Even he almost didn't believe Brina and her brothers had been hired by the school to demand his silence. And if he told Thanatos, he'd have to tell him *everything*, and he wasn't sure if he could trust his brother that much.

The torrent of emotions rotted inside him, turning on themselves, growing deeper and darker. But eventually, he forced his tears aside long enough to whisper, "I said what happened. It was kidnappers. And you shouldn't apologize. It wasn't your fault."

Silence stretched until Thanatos shifted his bed and sighed. "Even so. I'm sorry."

Thaddeus couldn't still his quiet sobs enough to respond. Instead, he said nothing until the room slipped into the aching silence of sleep.

In the long moments that followed, Thaddeus came to a horrid realization. By lying to his family and by letting that lie be told to the elites, then to Brina's family, and to the academy, he had let them silence him. He had been faced with the opportunity to tell the truth about the school, and he had been a coward.

A pit opened inside him. The pain of it ached more than the beating his body had taken.

Never had he felt so alone, so ruined, so spineless. Not only had he already broken a promise he made to himself and to the Zoics, but no one knew how he truly felt. No one knew what had truly happened. No one knew how horrible it had been to feel the last breaths the boy took, or how his glassy eyes had bored holes into Thaddeus' soul, or the way his magic had left a void that thirsted for vengeance.

No one knew the price of his silence.

Silent sobs raked his body. The night had never felt so dark. The silence had never been so loud.

Even surrounded by the people who loved him, he was alone.

CHAPTER 18

THE SUNS ROSE, AND THE SUNS SET. Days passed Thaddeus by without him taking notice. He spent the majority of them in bed. On others, he let his mother convince him to help in the garden, clean the house, or make dinner. He hardly ate or drank or looked at Thanatos and Quinlan. Though he assumed his father deeply regretted how he'd treated him, Thaddeus remained inconsolable at the lack of a genuine apology. But even as much as it disturbed him, his father striking him seemed a mere drop in the sea of raging emotions boiling within him.

Nightmares haunted him every night, some of the boy he'd killed: dying eyes staring into his, warm blood seeping through his clothes, staining them, his hands, his soul. Others morphed into the captured Zoics and the horror they'd endured before their deaths. Then, when the nightmares stole away sleep, his imagination conjured a thousand ways the *Jen-Jibuź* and headmistress extorted and tormented Syrinthia and the Zoics. Sometimes, pure exhaustion drove him into restless sleep during the day, but his nights passed in painfully long darkness, every shadow startling him awake and setting his heart pounding.

Despite Quinlan's protests, Naraina convinced him to let Thaddeus leave the academy. Not surprisingly, the academy quietly approved their request without any consequences. They clearly didn't want Thaddeus digging around their secrets anymore.

Quinlan arranged for tutors to come to the house. For a few days, the excitement of academics sparked Thaddeus' mood, but the enthusiasm dissipated when he learned nothing about what he wanted to know—who was he as a Zoic, and dragon-less Duvarharian, and what his purpose was in a land thirsty for the blood of innocents and the arena's thrill.

Occasionally, Syrinthia came by, but she never stayed longer than necessary to speak with Naraina or drop off something she thought Thaddeus would like.

Time after time, Thaddeus begged his mother to ask Syrinthia to stay, to speak to him, to *look* at him, but the young woman only kept her eyes fastened to the ground as if ashamed for the fate she'd inadvertently brought upon him. Though she hadn't meant to drag him into the web of deceit with her, he'd rather be stuck *there* with her than *here* all alone with no one to truly understand what he'd been through or believe the horrors he'd seen.

On a quiet day sometime since becoming a killer, Thaddeus found himself sitting with his mother in her garden sanctuary. When the vibrant flowers twined around his ankles, coaxing him to sit between their stems, he released the tears he'd locked away after that horrible night.

Silently, patiently, Naraina sat beside him, letting him pour his emotions into the flowers, the dirt, and every plant in the garden that leaned a little closer.

Finally, the sobs slowed along with his heart, and the pain dulled for a moment. Finally, he mustered the courage to ask the questions he'd been biting back.

"Who am I? What am I even here for?"

Silence answered him, but he felt his mother thinking through the plants that connected their souls.

Then she spoke slowly, trying to find the right words. "We're all here for a purpose, Thaddeus. Even if we don't see it, even if it seems we don't belong. You're more important than you know, even if you are only the air beneath a dragon's wings. You may never know your importance, but there is always reason behind the way the world turns."

Emptiness filled his heart. Her words rang both wise and worthless. He wished she'd simply tell him what to do and how to feel so he wouldn't have to deal with the pain of figuring it out for himself.

"I'm sorry I don't have a better answer." Pain laced her voice, matching his heart. "I too have asked that question more than you know. We don't . . . belong in this world. Not like your father and Thanatos do. Your father has his magic and dragon, and Thanatos has the arena. But you and I, we have something else."

"What is it?"

"Longing."

"For what?"

Tears ran down her face as she gripped his hand in hers, letting him lean his head against her chest. "I don't know."

That night, when the house fell silent and still, Thaddeus gave up trying to sleep. Succumbing to insomnia, he pushed off the furs and let muscle memory guide him to his bedroom door. For a moment, he listened to Thanatos breathe in then out, processing what he planned to do. *Will he notice I'm missing, or will he be glad I'm no longer dragging him down?*

Biting his lip, Thaddeus opened the door and stepped into the hallway. The moons shone brightly through the glass tunnel to the creek below, sparkling eerily. Everything looked so lovely and ethereal. None of it seemed quite real, especially the thoughts and emotions guiding him.

A small noise caught his attention behind him. Whirling around, he expected to see his mother, perhaps in her soft black robe. But instead, an empty hallway greeted him.

A ball of emotion choked him as he thought of his mother, of what she would feel when she would wake to find her son missing. But he reassured himself he wouldn't really be missing. *I'm only going to find what we long for.* But a darker emotion swirled deeper in his heart.

Giving in to his comforting lies, he continued through the home, letting himself out into the cool midnight air.

Memories of the last time he'd stood under the moons crashed over him like the blood that'd splattered onto his face when his axe tore through the boy's face. Before the memories could overwhelm him, reduce him to lying in the dirt with knees to his chest, he pushed them away and focused only on running to the stables.

It'd been years since he'd ridden their old mare. Guilt washed over him for waking her at such a dark hour, but she seemed grateful for the attention and the opportunity to canter through the forest she and the boys used to explore so many years ago.

Part of him wished something would halt them, keep them from reaching their destination, but the roads remained straight and easy and the signs leading the way were unmistakable in the moonlight.

With each hoofbeat that pounded into the ground, his darkest thoughts surfaced, accompanied by every insult thrown at him. His mother was right. He didn't belong in this world. Her words drowned out the insults.

"What is it?"

"Longing."

Though he wasn't sure exactly what he and his mother longed for or even if they longed for the same thing, his heart knew, and he followed its calling.

When the night reached its darkest just before dawn, he slid off the exhausted and sweaty mare, his feet sinking into the muddy banks of the great Dragon Sea.

Tears collected in his eyes as he gazed across the watery expanse. It stretched on into the dark horizon, glinting magically under the moons. He'd heard hundreds of stories about this place, but none of them truly did it justice. Its beauty was incomparable.

The mare whined and stamped her hooves, nibbling at his shirt as if to pull him away from the water. He ignored her, moving forward step by step, entranced by the lapping waves on his feet. The darkness across the waters, assuring him of the Dragon Island's existence, was irresistible.

But he wasn't welcome here. No Duvarharian rider was. Not for fishing or for traveling. It remained a sanctuary for the dragons. Though right now, none of that mattered; what he longed for rested on the island at the center of the lake.

Tripping over his feet as he kicked off his shoes, he stumbled farther into the cold water, goosebumps rushing up his skin as he tore off his shirt, then his pants, and everything else until he stood bare before the world with nothing to weigh him down as he threw himself into the water.

The lake surrounded him, washing over his head. He let himself sink into the darkness. For a moment, he wondered what would happen if he took in a thick breath of the liquid and let himself fade into the water forever. He waited—for what he didn't know; perhaps for someone to jump in after him, pull him to safety, and remind him of the worth of life. But the warm hands never came. His own struggle for life, for the basic need for air brought him gasping to the surface, kicking the ever-encroaching water away from him.

With no reason or rhythm to his strokes, he pushed away from the shore and into the open expanse.

For what could've been seconds or hours, he swam and swam and swam until he couldn't see the land behind him any longer, until he was surrounded by nothing but sky and water.

Cold seeped into his muscles, his bones, his heart. The tears had started and stopped long ago, along with the cries of desperation and longing. Now only whispers to gods he wasn't sure existed remained.

"Please. If anyone is listening, please let me find the island. Please let me find a dragon to bond with. Please let me find somewhere to belong."

No one answered.

His muscles grew weary. His breath grew shallow through his numb and chattering lips. Each stroke barely kept his head above water.

Desperation throbbed in his heart as he realized something he hadn't been sure of the last month. *I don't want to die. I don't want to die. I want to live. I want to truly live!*

But the realization came too late. The waters wanted to claim him, and neither the gods nor the dragons had answered his plea.

As his limbs gave out, he cried for his mother, whose heart would be broken by morning. Then the waters closed over his head.

Darkness and silence entombed him.

He held his breath for as long as he could, struggled for as long as his muscles allowed. But inevitably, the air in his lungs escaped with the remaining strength in his muscles. With excruciating pain and panic, his desperate lips and lungs opened, letting in a flood of the lake.

Then the pain stopped, and a fog settled in his mind. Something brushed across his torso, a large fish perhaps—the last creature he would be near as life abandoned his body.

Before the darkness closed around his mind and heart with finality, he thought of Joad. Of the Shadows of Light. Of a world he'd wanted so desperately to be a part of but would never get the chance to be.

Then he felt nothing. All was dark. All was lost.

Chapter 19

In the darkness bloomed a beautiful dream of color and light. The sound of dragons roaring, scales moving against each other, and claws on rock echoed in the emptiness. But the dream felt very far away, as if it were a dream inside a dream. Vaguely, he wondered if he'd arrived in the Isles of Sankura spoken of the Shadows of Light book—the place the souls of Duvarharians went after death.

Then the sounds grew louder, and the images clarified. This wasn't a dream nor the afterlife.

Squinting against the light, he tried to sit up. Something heavy pressed against his chest, keeping him still.

"What—where—" Hoarse and quiet, his voice sounded unrecognizable. As his grogginess began to lift, the pain in his throat and lungs settled in viciously. Tears lined his eyes, but once his eyes focused on the creature standing over him, all thought of himself faded away.

A great eye blinked down at him. The massive head turned from side to side to peer at him with both eyes. They narrowed before the creature bent its head to press its hot snout against his forehead.

A dragon.

Unable to believe it he blinked several times and shook his head, trying to clear his thoughts.

Instead of a bed or the ground like he expected, he lay nestled in the bright red coils of a dragon's tail; the incredible warmth of the creature's body spread through him, chasing away the chill of the Dragon Sea. The tip of the dragon's tail kept him from sitting up.

Don't ... move ... little one.

The voice rang through Thaddeus' head softly, as if someone were whispering to him from across the room. The dragon was speaking to him, directly into his mind.

Too shocked to move, he watched with wide eyes as the dragon searched him, pressing its snout to his face, spreading glowing warmth from its chest into his body. Turning, the dragon rumbled deep in its throat, and another stepped from the darkness.

Emotion choked him. *Dragons. They're ... dragons.* Tears trickled down his cheeks, his hands shaking.

Are you in pain, little one? A deeper, more masculine voice rang in his head much louder than the first. The dragon had to repeat his question before Thaddeus shook his head.

Then why are you crying?

As delicately as a mother, the second, a Sun-Flash Dragon, brushed the tip of his feathered tail across Thaddeus' face, drying his tears.

An unexpected laugh bubbled from Thaddeus' sore throat. It quickly turned into a cough. Finally, he found his voice. "No. I'm not in pain. I'm only crying because ... because ..." He felt ridiculous for the words that came to his lips, but no others came to mind. "Because you are real."

The male dragon grumbled and blinked in amusement. *Of course, we are real. When have we not been?*

Thaddeus could only grin in response. *Of course they are real. Of course the island is real.*

The Sun-Flash Dragon rumbled to the Combustion Dragon who held him, and she moved her tail from his chest.

He says you're ready to stand. Be careful, though ... Please. Her voice grew stronger, surer in his mind as if speaking to a rider telepathically for the first time. He also wondered if she or the male had riders of their own.

With the help of the Combustion Dragon's tail, Thaddeus took to his feet, winded and dizzy by the small movement. He spotted his clothes in a pile by the dragon's claws. Slowly he donned them, trying to process this reality. "What happened? Where am I?" He knew the answers to both questions but felt he needed someone else to answer them, to make it more believable.

The Sun-Flash Dragon drew himself from the ground until he sat proudly, staring down at Thaddeus as if to remind the boy just how small he really was. *You drowned, little one. Not fatally, thanks to the Aqua Dragon who found you, but nonetheless, a few more minutes and you would've been beyond saving. I can only imagine what drove you to such a reckless swim. You knew you wouldn't make it.*

Shame dragged down Thaddeus' excitement. The dragon was right. He'd known the moment he stood at the water's edge that he wouldn't make it to the island. Many riders had tried, some even with boats, but none had been able to find the island. Many were never heard from again. Some said the water dragons either drowned the adventurers or turned their boats around.

So why? Why did they save me?

Having forgotten his thoughts were heard by the dragons, he was taken off guard when the Sun-Flash male answered. *Because you are special.*

"What?"

He breathed into Thaddeus' face and repeated himself. *Because you are special. Your soul is . . . different. Not many Duvarharians alive today have the soul of an old Dragon Rider. Not all Duvarharians are riders, but you are.*

His words were almost exactly like Rakland's. A shiver ran down his spine. How could he not believe either of them? The proof stood before him. Where every other adventurer had failed, he'd succeeded, or rather, the dragons had helped him succeed.

"But how?"

The Combustion Dragon shook her head and twined her tail around his feet, her excitement spilling into his veins. *I don't know. But your soul shines so much differently than any other's. You're a pure Dragon Rider. That is the only way I can describe it.*

Thaddeus frowned. "I don't understand, though. I'm only . . ." He paused, afraid if the dragons knew what blood flowed through his veins, they'd kick him off the island. But he'd grown tired of hiding, of lying, and the words tumbled from his mouth. "I'm only half Dragon Rider."

The male rumbled and gently beat his wings, creating a draft in the rocky cavern. *True Dragon Riders have never been measured by their physique, only by their souls. Your body may not come from pure-blooded Duvarharians, but your soul traces back to the first two-legged creatures the Creator placed on Rasa, and that is enough for the dragon bond to exist.*

A hum of vitality warmed his chest, as if something had awoken within him, offering him a strength he hadn't felt before. "Are you saying anyone can be a Dragon Rider? That not just Duvarharians can bond with dragons? Even Wyriders?"

Were they not all Duvarharians to begin with? Were they not made as one creature in the beginning?

The information overwhelmed him, but Thaddeus felt it to be true. He hadn't known how terrified he'd been over the possibility of being unable to bond with a dragon because he was only half Duvarharian. Without the fear weighing him down, he felt light enough to fly.

But now a yearning took its place. He wanted to fulfil this new truth that all dragons and riders were truly entitled to the blessings of the dragon bond. As that yearning took over his heart, he connected with another soul in this place who yearned for the same thing.

Eyes wide, Thaddeus stumbled over the female dragon's tail. His body responded to the calling before his mind had the chance to comprehend it. "I hear him," Thaddeus whispered. "I–I—" He choked on the emotion rising in his throat. "I *feel* him."

A growl of excitement from the dragons harmonized with each other as they followed his unsure footsteps through the dark cavern.

Light his path, brethren.

At the Sun-Flash's command, the cavern illuminated as the smallest dragons Thaddeus had ever seen began to glow and shine. They ranged from the size of eagles down to the size of hummingbirds. Each glowed a different color or scheme of colors. Their impossibly small roars filled the enormous cavern alongside their light, sounding like the music of windchimes or pan flutes. The sound rang so beautifully and the sight shone so otherworldly, Thaddeus couldn't help but cry.

The cavern extended much larger than he'd originally guessed, and the more the light spread and his eyes wandered, the bigger it became. More than just a tunnel with a few small dragons, it encompassed an expansive underground hatching ground. As far as Thaddeus could see, hatchlings, adults, dragonets, and dragons filled the cavern.

"By the gods." All other words failed him in his awe.

Shining crystals hummed with energy and light as Crystal Dragons breathed life into them. Rocks burning white from the Combustion Dragons' fire created heated nests lined with scales and brush. Clutches of eggs were stacked along the steep walls of the cave, extending into the distance. He realized he was walking along a suspended pathway that cut across the cavern. Beneath him, the magnificence continued until it came to a shining, sparkling rainbow river. It snaked through the rock below, stemming from a waterfall that poured from rock high above them.

More dragons appeared as they emerged from the tunnels: Nature Dragons, Cloud Dragons, Poison Dragons, Crystal Dragons, Peak and Stone Dragons, even Aqua Dragons. When he thought he saw a rainbow in the waterfall, a Rainbow Dragon emerged for a moment before disappearing back into the light-filled mist. He even spotted kinds of dragons he'd never heard of, kinds that were potentially crossbreeds with powers perhaps no one had seen before.

But despite all this, a single dragon held his full attention.

A connection new and exciting but that also felt as old as time itself pulled him through the cavern, across the elevated walkways, and up the huge staircase that the young dragons used before they were old enough to fly.

Up and up he climbed, the two dragons following him, until he stood at the mouth of a large cave, nothing but darkness before him.

The darkness wasn't empty, though. It hummed with life, with loneliness and bitterness, with longing—all emotions Thaddeus knew well. As he stood at the mouth of the darkness, he felt as though he was staring into a mirror that reflected him more clearly than any polished metal ever could.

Then a roar filled the air, echoing off the cave's walls, and a creature charged from the darkness.

In a flash of dark purple and a rancid acidic smell, Thaddeus crashed against the ground. He fought back, screaming at the creature, grappling with it.

His skin burned.

His eyes burned.

His breath burned.

Acid filled his lungs, his veins, his mind. Cuts in his skin oozed with the thick acid, the pain nearly unbearable. But what overwhelmed him was the pain that filled his heart when his skin met the creature's scales.

Agony. Rage. Sorrow. Loneliness. Passion. Power.

And life.

The dragon's strong tail wrapped around his neck, squeezing tighter and tighter.

Tears welled up in Thaddeus' eyes as stars spotted his vision. *I'm not ready to die. Not yet. Not anymore.*

His hands groped for something, anything he could use as a weapon. As his mind dropped into darkness, his fingers closed around a sharp rock. He brought it up with as much force as he could muster.

The dragon's roar echoed painfully. The tail loosened.

Thaddeus choked, scrambling to his feet. *Walk away. Find a different dragon to bond with. Walk away from this pain.* Brushing away dirt and blood from the side of his face, he gritted his teeth. If he walked away from this dragon and its pain, he'd be walking away from himself and his own.

Purple eyes glowed back in the darkness, waiting for rejection, waiting for the blow to land. But Thaddeus stayed. And he stood, unmoving, until the world fell away around them.

"I'm not afraid of you." Thaddeus took a shaking breath and stepped forward. The dragon snorted but didn't shy away. "I'm not afraid of what you are." He extended his hand but didn't bridge the final gap between their bodies. "I'm not afraid of your pain."

The dragon shook its head, throwing droplets of acid to Thaddeus' skin and the ground, filling the air with a sour stench. Thaddeus balled his fist and shook his head and whispered once more, "I'm not afraid of you."

With a snap of its jaws, the dragon roared and shied away, but only for a second.

Then, with a tenderness it'd hidden before, it pressed its head to Thaddeus' hand, bridging more than just the physical space between them.

Aches of anger faded into tears of sorrow, relief, and understanding.

Thaddeus staggered to the dragon, and they collapsed to the floor together, wings and arms wrapped around each other, holding the other up against the weight of the world and their pain.

He was the dragon, and the dragon was he. The dragon's name was Kyrell, the rider's Thaddeus, and at last they were one and the same.

Thaddeus gazed into Kyrell's purple eyes, past the grizzly exterior of sharp spines dripping with acid, past the pain shining in those eyes, past the anger residing in his heart, and into his soul, which shone with the same familiar longing. Now that he saw Kyrell's soul, a mirror of his own, he understood what the dragons and Rakland had seen in himself.

"I've been looking for you," Thaddeus whispered as he brushed his hand across acidic scales, which no longer burned him.

And I've been waiting for you.

Joy rushed through their veins as the pain of their pasts melted away into the promise of their future. No longer were they alone. No longer were they outcasts.

Jumping to their feet, the dragon and rider marveled at each other. Kyrell had never seen a rider before, having lived his whole life on the island, and he found Thaddeus' body to be rather strange, weak, and beautiful. *Your skin is so soft.*

Thaddeus laughed, for once not minding being called soft and weak. "Your claws are absolutely deadly." He ran a hand over one of the deeper cuts the dragonet had inflicted on him in their initial altercation driven by fear and confusion.

A flicker of guilt passed through Kyrell's mind, but Thaddeus quickly dismissed it. "There is no room for shame or guilt between us, and there never will be. Do you understand?"

I do.

With this understanding, Thaddeus mounted the base of the dragon's thick neck. The feeling of sitting astride the incredibly powerful beast came as natural as waking and sleeping. It felt neither strange nor uncomfortable to either of them. Instead, it felt like the fulfilment of a forgotten promise.

As they walked through the long halls of the cavern, Thaddeus listened closely to what the dragons and Kyrell had to say.

This hatching grounds is illegal according to the current Duvarharian laws, as you know. The walls shook dreadfully with the male's angry growls. Some of the smaller dragons fled at the sound while a few larger dragons slunk back into the shadows.

"I do. How is it able to exist without the elites knowing? Do other dragons not betray you?"

The female answered. *Some have tried, but dragons are harmed just as much as the riders by restricted breeding and hatching. Some dragon kinds are favored over others; the ones that don't fit into the standards of civilization are either killed or left to die. Some are even captured and shipped off to the* Xene'mraba.

Dread dropped into Thaddeus' stomach. "The Dragon games?"

Kyrell roared and shook his head. *It amazes me how little you riders know about your own culture.*

Kyrell, do not be so judgmental. Thaddeus is just as much a victim of this as you. The Combustion Dragon snapped her jaws at the dragonet, who shied away, but Thaddeus didn't miss the spark of rebellion in his eyes.

He didn't mind the tone of Kyrell's thoughts, though; he knew the fear and pain residing in his soulmate's heart. His bitterness was valid.

The Xene'mraba *are the true games of Duvarharia. The* benierku, *where riders fight each other, animals, or Zoics, are only the beginning. If a rider does well in the smaller games, he's promoted to the dark ring of what they call* Xeneluch-shuvub–*dragon tamers. Or as I like to call them,* Xeneluch-frasuub–*dragon slayers.* Kyrell's thoughts carried to the other dragons. Immediately, they fell silent, and the light of the crystals and small dragons dimmed.

"You mean they—" Thaddeus couldn't bring himself to finish his question. The very idea of Dragon Slayers made him physically ill.

The Sun-Flash Dragon nodded. *They capture, breed, and train dragons like field beasts.*

Bile filled Thaddeus' mouth. The fear and distress from Kyrell mixing with his own rage overwhelmed him; he had to close his eyes and focus on his breath to keep from vomiting.

The goal of the games is to subdue the dragon, but if that isn't possible, it's just as acceptable to kill the dragon. The riders are trained or tortured to resist the urge to bond with the dragons. If a pair should happen to bond, they're terminated immediately.

"How is this allowed to continue?" Numbness filled his heart. Tears weren't enough to grieve the loss and destruction the Duvarharians were allowing to happen. The games needed to be stopped and the blood of their leaders spilled.

The female dragon continued. *The games are notorious for obtaining gambling and sponsorships from the elites. It's easy for them to pay the military and government to turn a blind eye.*

We're here because we seek to preserve traditional Duvarharian ideals. Without us, some dragon kinds would be extinct. Like the Acid Dragon.

Thaddeus trailed his fingers across Kyrell's scales. He was an Acid Dragon. *Why is your type nearly extinct?*

Because we're considered a hazard to society. Instead of the world shaping itself to dragons, the dragons are forced to conform. If you happen to leave a trail of acid because the riders refuse to help you hone your skill, then you're ostracized for being dangerous. If you're unfortunate enough not to be terminated, you get taken for the games.

The amount of hurt and bitterness radiating from Kyrell was more than Thaddeus knew what to do with, but he understood it intimately. He too hid because of his Zoic heritage. He too risked being killed, used for the headmistress' disgusting experiments, or thrown into a game.

Appreciation overtook the bitterness, and Thaddeus knew how relieved Kyrell felt to find someone else who truly understood what he'd gone through.

Do you understand the consequences of bonding with a dragon like Kyrell?

Thaddeus paused, almost offended at the question, before answering the old male dragon. Truthfully, he *didn't* understand. Bonding with a dragon without a proper license was illegal in Peace Haven. Not only had he done just that, but with an Acid Dragon—a dragon kind marked dangerous and unfit for civilization.

Thaddeus gritted his teeth. The consequences were many, but none of it mattered. He'd bonded to Kyrell, and not only could he not undo it, but he wouldn't. Even if the world burned around him, he would never give up his dragon and the bond he shared with him. They were one creature now, and Thaddeus would rather die than be separated from him.

"I know I don't fully understand, but I am willing to accept the consequences whatever they are, however difficult, even if they result in death." His voice shook with emotion, and he didn't realize he was crying until he tasted salt on his lips. For a long moment, silence spread through the caverns.

I am pleased to hear you say this, Thaddeus, and I hope you will always feel this way.

Though he knew riders and dragons could fall away from each other, he couldn't imagine him and Kyrell doing so. Their bond, made long after the usual bonding period just after hatching, was made by choice, not base instinct. It would be a choice that would hold them together for eternity.

Silence stretched as they climbed higher into the caverns, the light growing brighter at the top. As his time on *Ulufakush* came to an end, he wondered if he would ever be able to return.

You will always be welcome here, Thaddeus, son of the old ways. Always.

Though he didn't know who said it, he had the feeling it came as a collective thought from all the dragons in the caverns below.

When they reached the surface and were standing on the edge of the lakeshore, the sand digging into Kyrell's claws, Thaddeus finally asked the question weighing on his mind since he woke up.

"What do I do now?" Even now, with his dragon at his side, his feet on the island he'd dreamed of visiting his whole life, he still felt as if this were all a wonderful dream.

The Sun-Flash male rumbled and turned to Thaddeus. *Now you go home. You fight for you and your dragon and the things you love. For magic, for your bloodline, for the old Duvarharian ways. And you do not stop fighting until you have brought back freedom, peace, and safety for all those who have been oppressed.*

Determination settled into Thaddeus' heart. "I think I can do that. At least I can try."

Trying is the only path to succeeding. May the suns smile upon your presence, little one.

Thaddeus hadn't heard the saying before, so Kyrell answered. *As do the stars sing upon yours.*

Crouching low, Kyrell sucked in a deep breath, spread his wings, and launched himself into the air.

For a breathtaking moment, they hung suspended, somewhere between flying and falling. Thaddeus thought perhaps he was too heavy and his dragon too young. But failure poisoned the mind, and he didn't want anything to stand between him and his dragon and success. So instead, he channeled all his strength and energy into Kyrell. With a rush of wind, Kyrell thrust down his wings, and they rocketed into the sky.

Cold morning air tore at Thaddeus' clothes and hair, biting into his skin and eyes. His legs already ached, but nothing could dampen the utter elation in Thaddeus' heart.

He was *flying*.

In only seconds, the earth stretched far beneath them, the trees small dots with rivers snaking through them like threads sewing the land together in a beautiful tapestry of life.

Tears rolled down Thaddeus' cheeks before the wind swept them away. His heart raced in time to his dragon's. He felt Kyrell's breath as if it were his own. They were one creature above the clouds, and Thaddeus knew in this moment, as long as they were together, they could take on anything the world threw at them no matter how difficult.

Have you ever flown this high before? Seamlessly, his thoughts mingled with Kyrell's.

I've never flown farther than the island. It's always been too dangerous. Though bitterness and sorrow were present in Kyrell's soul, so were relief and hope.

I will always protect you. I will never let them take you from me, and I will never let them take being a dragon away from you. Not as long as I live. I'm going to bring back a Duvarharia where no dragon will ever have to suffer as you have.

No words could describe the empathy and comfort shared between them. Their connection transcended all time, space, and matter.

All too soon, their flight had begun its end. Thaddeus could see his house in the distance. Kyrell started circling in a slow descent.

Anxiety fluttered in Thaddeus' gut. The consequences of bonding with a dragon were already piling up at his feet, and he wasn't sure how to face them. His mother would be worried sick, his father furious. Thanatos would resent all the attention being paid to his brother.

With a harsh jolt, Kyrell landed on the road, and Thaddeus dismounted. The morning suns were just luminating the garden, and the fresh smell of cold dew on the plants drifted toward them.

Time stood still. Birds trilled then stopped. The sound of a stream in the distance bubbled quietly as if in a dream, from somewhere peace never ended.

In this moment, everything remained beautiful and peaceful. But he knew the second he stepped forward into the world his family lived in, that Peace Haven existed in, nothing would be the same and this moment would disappear. But then again, had anything truly been the same since the night that cloaked figure came into his home?

Did he ever want it to be the same?

I want it to change. I want it to change beyond recognition. His dragon's thoughts held no doubt.

Thaddeus looked at him, staring deep into beautiful purple eyes. Running his hand down Kyrell's jaw, he smiled, peace settling into his soul. "So do I."

Together, with his hand on his dragon and Kyrell's wing around him, they walked to his home and toward a new age—one where he wasn't alone, where he had hope, where he'd finally found something worth fighting for.

PART 3
Forging of a Rider

PART 3

Forging of a Rider

CHAPTER 20

Peace Haven, Duvarharia
Year: Rumi 5310 Q.RJ.M

THADDEUS' FIST HOVERED before the door, unsure if he should knock or simply walk in, unsure if he was even still welcome. Inside, his parents' raised voices echoed. He wondered if they were talking about him. A gust of wind tousled his hair, and Kyrell growled defensively.

Krystallos alit on the roof, the windows barely rattling under his soft landing. His shining baby blue eyes sparkled in the morning rays as he eyed the Acid Dragon.

Kyrell bristled, his scales and spines rattling against each other. His dripping saliva burned small holes into the road.

Slowly, Krystallos snaked his head to the young dragon. About the size of a horse, Kyrell appeared miniscule to Krystallos. Sensing the older dragon's welcoming spirit, Kyrell edged forward until their noses touched.

A flash of magic sparked between them, and Kyrell stilled. A rush of joy and relief passed from him to Thaddeus. A grin swept his face. Even if his father would be upset, at least Krystallos was proud.

With newfound confidence, Thaddeus knocked on the door.

The voices on the other side silenced. For a long moment, Thaddeus wondered if he would have to knock again. Just before he did, the door flung open.

His eyes met the green of his mother's.

"Oh, Thaddeus," she whispered, and they fell into each other's arms. Their Zoic blood hummed in relief, no other words needing to be shared.

His father moved to their sides. Thaddeus kept his eyes closed, desperate to preserve this tender moment. But the yelling never came. Instead, Quinlan's strong warm arms wrapped around his wife and son.

Naraina gasped and loosened her hug. "Thaddeus . . ."

He quickly stepped away, bearing his dragon to the gaze of his parents.

"By the gods of Wyerland . . ." Naraina covered her mouth, her eyes wide.

Quinlan's jaw dropped, but no words escaped.

Biting his lip, Thaddeus dragged a line across the ground with his boot. "I . . . um . . . I went to the Dragon Sea, and . . . well, they saved me. The dragons, I mean." The pauses between his words filled with tense silence.

No one moved; not even Krystallos, who watched from the roof.

"And they—well, they took me to the island. Then I, uh, I heard a voice?" It sounded ridiculous when he tried to describe it. Embarrassment flushed his cheeks. "So I followed it, and it led me to *him*." He gestured to Kyrell. "His name is Kyrell, and we . . . we're bonded." He rubbed his hands together and stared at the ground, trying to bite back tears.

An arm he thought was his mother's wrapped around his shoulders, until it pulled him into a familiar side hug. With wide eyes, Thaddeus looked up to his father's face. Quinlan shook his head, his jaw working against itself. A million emotions and thoughts raced through his eyes. Then the man laughed, nervously at first then confidently until he brushed tears from his eyes.

"Are you mad at me?" The words jumped from Thaddeus' mouth before he could stop them.

Quinlan chuckled and shook Thaddeus lightly. "Yes, I am."

Thaddeus' stomach flopped. Pain filled Naraina's face. She opened her mouth, but Quinlan cut her off. "But what does it matter when I'm so much more *proud*?"

Thaddeus broke away from his father, frowning. "What do you mean?"

Quinlan looked from Kyrell then back to Thaddeus. "I'm mad at you for running away. I'm furious you risked going to *Ulufakush*. I'm a *little* upset you picked an illegal dragon, which will make getting you a bonding permit impossible, and gods know how this will look since you're the son of an ambassador." He shook his head. "But how can I be mad when my son has bonded? And with a dragonet, nonetheless. That's more difficult than you know, and as Krystallos tells me"—he nodded up to his dragon—"it's no small feat to be allowed on the island."

"So . . ." Thaddeus looked from his father to his mother; she seemed just as shocked. "You're not going to punish me or anything?"

A deep sigh left Quinlan's lips, and the sparkle in his eyes wavered. "No," he whispered almost inaudibly. "No punishment can undo what has been done. Enough trials await you and this dragon, and I don't want to have a part in making you struggle. You made a choice, and you will deal with its consequences—whatever those may be. I may be your father, but some things I cannot protect you from, this being one of them."

Thaddeus' heart dropped. Kyrell slunk closer and nudged his head under his arm. The empty fear he felt stung worse than being yelled at or punished. By the look on his mother's face, he knew she felt the same.

"One thing's for sure. You won't be going back to school."

Thaddeus couldn't help but whisper, "Thank the stars." A small smile curved his mother's lips, but she quickly suppressed it.

Quinlan frowned at the comment but didn't address it. "I still expect you to have an education, though. I'll arrange for the tutors to come back. But if I see you shirking your education because you're off riding your dragon, I swear there will be serious consequences, do you understand?"

Thaddeus tried not to roll his eyes. *You'd think by now he'd know I value my own education.* Then his heart soared with a sudden realization. "Will I be able to learn about magic and riding? I could have a tutor from the Dragon Palace!"

A dark shadow fell over Quinlan's face. "No," he snapped. "You'll do nothing of the sort. I refuse to have your education on science and the arts ruined by the fantasies of magic. Magic is hardly used in our age, and it's a waste of time. I don't want to hear you ask me again."

Thaddeus' eyes widened. "What—" He looked to his mother for support, but she dropped her gaze and shook her head. Though he clamped his mouth shut, protests boiled inside him. *This is ridiculous. I'm a rider now, legal or not. I have a dragon, and I have a right to magic. My father can't take that from me.*

But he can. Kyrell's dark voice rang though his mind, filling his blood with bitterness and truth. *He and the elites of Peace Haven can take away all your rights, just as they've taken away mine. You don't have a license to practice magic, and you won't find a teacher who will instruct you illegally; the penalty is too high. Our hands are tied.*

Thaddeus' fists balled. "Fine. No magic, then. And I promise I'll do my schoolwork. It's important to me too, you know."

Quinlan's eyes flashed as he opened his mouth, but Naraina's hand on his arm stopped him. Instead, he nodded and took a deep breath. "Good. Now get some rest. And maybe a bath too. Those cuts look deep."

Thaddeus' jaw ached from clenching his teeth. "Yes sir," he hissed.

With a smile that did nothing to warm Thaddeus' heart, Quinlan kissed Naraina's cheek. Just before he disappeared into the glass tunnel, he called over his shoulder, "Kyrell can never go into town. They'll take him from you if they find out he's an Acid Dragon and that you've bonded to him without a license. It's best you don't tell anyone about him for your own safety."

Thaddeus could hardly control his rage. *And for your reputation, you ñekol.* Even so, his father was right; that's what he hated most.

"I'm so proud of you, Thaddeus." Naraina's sweet voice dragged him from his thoughts. His heart softened when his mother tucked a lock of his hair behind his ear. "I'm sure your father is too, he just . . ." She looked to the now empty hall and shook her head. Emotion choked her words. "Well, he just hasn't been himself lately." She forced a sad smile onto her face, attempting to blink away the mist in her eyes. "I'm sure he'll snap out of it soon."

"Yeah." Thaddeus tried to smile back. "I'm sure he will." Neither of them truly believed it.

"Now." She nodded to Kyrell, who peeked out from behind Thaddeus. A low rumble vibrated through Thaddeus' back as Kyrell pressed himself against his rider. "Please introduce me properly."

Thaddeus couldn't help the silly grin on his face. "Mother, I'd like for you to meet Kyrell." Stepping aside, he pushed his suddenly bashful dragon in front of him.

If Naraina felt nervous or intimidated by the acid flecking off Kyrell's teeth and scales, she didn't show it. Bowing slightly, she pressed her fingertips to her forehead and whispered something in her native language.

Kyrell fidgeted before he carefully pressed his snout to the fingers on her forehead and rumbled. *Tell her she is the most beautiful Duvarharian I've ever seen. I am pleased to meet the mother of my soulmate.*

Thaddeus smiled and ran his hand down Kyrell's scales. The dragonet growled like a purr. Opening his memories, Thaddeus showed Kyrell his mother's origins. *No wonder she is so beautiful,* Kyrell grunted. *She reminds me of the fields on* Ulufakush.

Remembering she couldn't hear Kyrell, Thaddeus blushed. "He says you're the most beautiful creature he's seen, and you remind him of the fields on the island where he was born."

Her radiant smile lit up the room. Nodding, she laughed. "Thank you, Kyrell. That is rather sweet of you."

Kyrell growled low and blinked slowly, pleased to have made a good impression.

"And since you are soul-bound to my son, then know you are my son now, so if you ever need anything, even just a mother, then you come to me, alright?"

Tears laced with acid trickled from Kyrell's purple eyes. Though simple, her words carried everything Kyrell yearned to hear.

Before Thaddeus could warn her about the acid, she wrapped her arms around Kyrell's neck. For a moment, the dragonet froze. Then he melted into her arms, wrapping his head around her. The acid stopped flowing on Kyrell's scales, and not a drop touched her.

"Now," she stepped back, placing her hands on her hips. "You both must be starving."

Thaddeus grinned as his stomach growled and followed her into the kitchen. Kyrell snaked his head through the doorway before settling down out of the way. Thaddeus stepped down the cellar ladder to help his mother retrieve some vegetables.

"I think I have some meat in here from last night's dinner . . ." But while Naraina searched the ice chamber, something else was weighing on Thaddeus' mind. He wanted to apologize for leaving.

"Mother, I—" Before he could say any more, his stomach flipped uncomfortably and tears filled his eyes.

"What's that, Thaddeus?" When he didn't answer, she stood and turned. Her eyes landed on his teary face as his shoulders shook. "Oh, Thaddeus!" Taking him into her arms, she smoothed his hair, whispering endearments. "Why are you crying, my *tyän?*"

"Because—" He hiccupped and sniffed. "Because I left you, and I know you were worried, and I went into the lake, and I–I. . ." Sobs raked his body. "I wasn't sure if I wanted to—to keep going on."

Now her tears mingled with his. Though words couldn't patch the pain they shared, she tried anyway. "I'm so sorry, *tyän,*" she whispered.

Their tears began to slow. "I'm so sorry."

He could only nod. "Me too."

Smoothing his hair from his face, she searched his eyes. A thousand words swirled in the way her lips would part then close. Finally, she spoke, leaving the hard words unspoken in the dark. "Let's find that meat and get both your bellies full, shall we? Why don't you go wash up and take Kyrell to the hunting grounds. He seems old enough to feed himself."

Realizing how dirty he still was from the lake, he dried his eyes then climbed out of the cellar into the kitchen.

Kyrell waited for Thaddeus to open the front door. With a quick mental image, Thaddeus showed him the locations of their forest's best hunting spots and let him know Krystallos would show him the way if needed. Then he stumbled through the house to the bathroom.

Though the warm bath felt heavenly, it brought back memories of the cold water he'd almost surrendered to mere hours earlier. It didn't seem possible how much his life had changed in a day. As the images began overtaking his mind, loud banging on the bathroom door jarred him awake.

"Thaddeus, hurry up! I'm going to be late for school."

Relaxation burst like one of the bath's bubbles. Not everything had changed; Thanatos was still obnoxious. *Does he even know that I left?* Though he wanted to yell back, saying he should've woken up earlier if he didn't want to be late, he refrained. A more pressing question occupied his mind as he dried. *How do I tell him I have a dragon? Do I even want to?*

A towel wrapped around his waist, he opened the door, looking for Thanatos. Of course, he'd already left. Most likely he'd wait another ten minutes before bathing or would at least wait until Thaddeus needed to grab something from the washroom.

Rolling his eyes, Thaddeus crept down the hall. Thankfully, their room was empty; Thanatos must be eating breakfast. Thaddeus made sure to lock the door. Procrastinating seeing his brother, he took his time dressing.

When he stepped into the kitchen, he bit back a rude remark. Sure enough, Thanatos lounged at the island as if not as late as he'd insisted, sipping his *elush* at a snail's pace.

A small detail pushed away the bitterness and Thaddeus frowned. Thanatos never wore sleeveless shirts because they exposed his greatest insecurity—a peculiar birthmark that looked eerily like symbols of a forgotten language—yet he wore one now. Thaddeus immediately realized why: Thanatos had hidden the birthmark under a tattoo.

"What're you looking at?" Thanatos snapped.

"Nothing." Scowling, Thaddeus climbed onto the stool next to him. "I thought you needed the bath. Aren't you going to be late?"

Thanatos rolled his eyes and snarled around his piece of toast. His tangled bed hair made Thaddeus wonder how any girl found him attractive. "I have to eat, and you were taking too long."

"I wasn't in there more than five minutes."

"Someone's got attitude this morning."

Thaddeus opened his mouth just as Naraina stepped in from the garden. He swallowed everything he wanted to spit back at Thanatos. To put distance between them, he took the vegetables from his mother and washed them, adding them to the others they'd pulled from the cellar. Absently, he listened as Naraina mentioned something about a mole eating the roots of another tomato plant and asked what they thought about getting a domestic feline to manage the rodents. The boys only interjected when necessary, ignoring each other. Thaddeus took out his frustrations on the vegetables as he chopped them. Though Naraina insisted on helping, he finally convinced her to finish the gardening before the suns grew too hot.

As he lit the stove and poured oil in the pan, he turned to Thanatos, face emotionless. "I bonded with a dragon."

Silence filled the room.

The toast stopped halfway to Thanatos' mouth. A bird outside trilled a song, most likely mimicking Naraina. The clock on the wall ticked rhythmically.

Thanatos' eyes narrowed as if waiting for Thaddeus to laugh and say, "I got you!" That moment never came.

Thaddeus turned back to the skillet. The simmering oil popped, ready for the vegetables. He put them in the pan, and sizzling filled the tension, followed by the slow crunching of toast.

"Are you kidding me?"

A shiver ran down Thaddeus' spine. He stirred the food with a hand carved wooden spoon. "No. I'm not."

A mug hit the countertop, shattering the too still moment. "*Sulujnu*, Thaddeus. Do you even know how bad that is?"

Thaddeus' stomach roiled. His hands shook as he added the leftover cube steak. Words failed him. He *did* know. His dragon could be taken from him. He could be arrested, maybe even executed with his "dangerous" dragon. But Thanatos didn't care about any of that.

"If anyone at the academy even *thinks* they heard a rumor about you bonding illegally with a dragon, they'll *hate* me. I won't stand a chance at the end-of-year games. I'll lose all my supporters and have no chance of being picked by a good fighter league. Not to mention the shame you'll bring upon Father when everyone realizes his son is defying the very laws he works daily to uphold."

Thaddeus nearly dropped the pan, his hands shook so violently. He held it over a bowl and scraped the food out. A pregnant silence filled the kitchen as he put out the stove and gently set the pan back down, ignoring the urge to slam the thick, hot metal straight into Thanatos' face.

"You know what, Thanatos?" Thaddeus took a deep breath. "I don't really care." He turned around, fists balled, eyes flashing. For the first time, the usually transparent Shalnoa markings on his hand and arm flared with color, turning hot with the purple glow.

Shock and fear flashed in Thanatos' eyes as he glanced at the markings. He snarled. "You're nothing but a selfish little *ue*." Standing, he shoved his stool aside, taking a menacing step forward. "I won't have you ruining my life just because you're too weird to have your own."

"Don't come closer." The panic rising in Thaddeus wasn't accompanied by the usual urge to flee. This time, he wanted to fight.

Thanatos sneered. "Or what? You're going to do *what*, Thaddeus?" He lunged forward, grasping Thaddeus by his shirt, and shoved him against the stove.

Hate burned inside Thaddeus as his back dug into the hot metal grates. Thanatos had no right to treat him like this. No one did. And he done with letting them. Just as his hand wrapped around the handle of the hot pan, Kyrell roared, and the door to the garden opened.

Thanatos dropped his hold on Thaddeus and jumped back, but too late. Naraina stood in the doorway, a strange look on her face, lips parted, eyes misting. "Thanatos?"

He ran his fingers through his hair, unable to meet her gaze, full of shame.

"What—what's going on? What's . . ." A few herbs fell from her hands. She struggled to pick them up with shaking hands.

Thaddeus nearly buckled under the weight of the horror coursing through his veins. Though he wasn't in the wrong, the look in his mother's eyes shattered his heart. It took all his self-control not to throttle Thanatos. *At least I didn't take the pan to his head.* Though a part of him still wished he had.

"I was just, um, messing around with Thaddeus." With a nervous grin, Thanatos reached over to tussle Thaddeus' hair. He slid out of reach and shot him a dark look.

"Shut up, Thanatos. Just go to school already." His voice shook as he tried to keep Kyrell from blasting through the garden door and tearing Thanatos to shreds.

Thanatos searched his face, as if still hoping Thaddeus would agree they'd been messing around, but Thaddeus didn't flinch. *Just leave.*

Thanatos bowed his head, muttered a half-hearted apology to their mother, and quickly ducked out of the kitchen.

"Mother, I'm sorry you had to see that." Thaddeus quickly moved to Naraina. She stood still in the doorway, tears in her eyes, hands shaking and struggling to hold the herbs.

With tender hands, he took the clippings and placed them on the counter. Then he took her hands in his.

When their eyes met, he found himself looking into the face of a woman he wasn't sure he recognized. Her usual vibrance struggled to shine under a mask of sleepless worry and stress. Nausea flipped his stomach. *Did I do this to her by leaving?* He searched her eyes and noticed how her frown lines outnumbered her laugh lines. *No. Those are from years of deep-seated worry.* But the realization only made him more uncomfortable.

Guiding her to the bar, he pulled a stool out for her, and they sat together.

"I hate to see you two fighting." The words lurched in her throat as she dabbed her eyes with the corner of her apron. A smudge of dirt streaked across her cheek, but he didn't move to brush it away. It didn't seem right to comfort her when he felt responsible.

"I—" Words failed him. He hated it as much as her, but he didn't have a solution. Thinking back to the days when he and Thanatos had been inseparable, when he'd looked up to his older brother and wished to be like him, Thaddeus wondered what had changed. What had brought them to *this,* to a day when his brother had irritated him to the point of wanting to bash his head with a scalding pan? "I hate it too," he finally whispered.

Before he could say anything else, she shook her head and responded, "I hate that *all* of us fight."

Immediately, he remembered his parents' raised voices only a couple hours earlier. "All of us?"

She shook her head again and moved to leave. "I shouldn't worry you about this. It's not your responsibility."

Placing a hand on her arm, he swallowed. "I want to know. Please. I know . . . I know you don't have many friends here. I know you don't have anyone to talk to. Please, Mother. How can I help you?"

For a moment, she searched his face, and her lips parted. He thought she might tell him, but then a smile spread across her lips, and she brushed away the last of her tears. "No, it's nothing. Every marriage has its ups and downs. Ours is no different. Things have just been a little hard for me to get used to since you boys have been gone. But it's nothing, really, and you'll be home again now so I have nothing to worry about." She continued rambling but about nothing she really needed to say or what Thaddeus really needed to hear.

His heart ached. He could blame himself and try to fix it, but it wouldn't change anything. The fault wasn't his but a myriad of other things: the government, the games, the school, the cloaked man threatening his father, Nagaina's ancestry, his bond with a dragon, Thanatos' rebelliousness and how he came home stoned or drunk. Not one easily fixable problem existed in the mix.

But does that mean I have to sit back to watch the world burn and be a victim to the way things are? He didn't have an answer for that question. Neither did Kyrell.

Standing, Naraina gestured to the herbs on the counter. "Would you mind hanging those up to dry? I need to change my dress. I think I got some dirt on the hem." She quickly left the kitchen, her dress flowing behind her. He didn't see any dirt.

With darkness in his heart poisoning his appetite for the food he'd cooked, he fell to the task of tying twine around the herbs' stems and hanging them over the island bar. At least he had something to do with his hands other than smash them into the countertop. When he'd finished, he stood at the bar with his bowl of food, struggling to see it through the tears he so desperately wished would stop.

Come eat with me. Kyrell's voice gave him enough energy to pick up the bowl and slip through the front door. His dragon waited at the edge of the forest, a bloody yearling deer under his claws.

Dragging his feet, he joined Kyrell, and they shared their meal in quiet contentment. In the morning silence, when only the birds sang and dew still clung to the grass, he could almost pretend everything was alright, that they were still the perfect family they used to be, that everyone thought they were. The lie somehow made the truth more painful.

When Thanatos finally came outside, he stopped, gaze bouncing back and forth between Kyrell and Thaddeus. If he felt surprised, impressed, or even angry, he didn't show it. Nodding his head once, he started the walk to school.

"Mother and Father said they'd buy him a horse if he could go a month without coming home under the influence of something. So far, he's only ever lasted three days." The bitterness in Thaddeus' voice and heart echoed painfully.

Why don't they withdraw him if it's ruining his character?

Thaddeus set the bowl down and rested his head on his knees, legs to his chest. "I don't know. But I have a very bad feeling the *Jen-Jibuz* running the academy and the cloaked man have something to do with it."

Suddenly, he remembered why he'd run away in the first place.

"Syrinthia!" Jumping to his feet, he frantically mounted Kyrell. Dread settled in his heart. "We have to find her. We have to make sure she's alright."

Chapter 21

"**W**HERE IS SHE?" He struggled to keep his voice quiet. He and Kyrell had been waiting at the forest's edge just outside the academy gates for nearly a half hour, and they had yet to see Syrinthia. Thanatos loitered by the gates with his other friends, but even he seemed uneasy and kept glancing at the road, searching for her.

A large stick snapped behind Thaddeus, and he hissed in disapproval. *You've got to be quieter than that. All it takes is one glance toward us, and we're done for.*

Kyrell huffed his hot breath down Thaddeus' neck. *I can't sit still much longer. It's not in my nature.*

Thaddeus resisted rolling his eyes. *I've seen plenty of dragons sit more still for much longer.*

I'm not like most dragons.

Thaddeus couldn't disagree. Not wanting to argue with his soulmate, he dropped it, but not before he wished he knew some sort of camouflage spell. Kyrell growled low.

A moment of tense silence passed between them but then quickly dissipated. Neither desired to be at odds with one another. They were already at war with the world; it didn't make sense to be at war with each other as well.

I knew a Camouflage Dragon. Kyrell's thoughts wandered. *Back on the island. She preferred to be lime green most of the time, though.*

Thaddeus frowned. *An odd choice of color when one could choose anything.*

Kyrell's emotions reminded him of a shrug of dismissal. *I wondered the same thing until the other dragons told me it's rather common of Camouflage Dragons. Apparently, they spend so much time blending in that some of them forget how to take up space–how to be seen. Choosing a bright color reminds themselves and others of their existence.*

Chewing on his lip, Thaddeus wondered if he would choose a bright color or camouflage if given the chance. He had a disappointing feeling he knew what he'd choose. Even now he hid, cowering behind a bush rather than just waiting for Syrinthia. The realization made his skin prickle.

"It's almost time for the gates to close." Worry dropped into his stomach like thunder. "She's never been late." He could only imagine the worst.

What does she look like again?

Thaddeus closed his eyes and pictured her. Every detail of her face shone as clear to him as the forest around them and the cool breeze on their skin. The way her dark eyes shone gold in the light, or the way—

Alright, alright, I get it. Someone's obsessed.

Fire burned on Thaddeus' cheeks as his eyes snapped open. He turned to his dragon, ready to speak his mind, when Kyrell nodded to the road. *So, like her?*

Thaddeus whirled around.

It was Syrinthia. But . . . not exactly.

His throat constricted as his heart leaped into his mouth. "What did they do to her?"

She wore only the basic school uniform, lacking all her usual jewelry, hair braids, or makeup. Her head hung low and despite the warm weather, her shoulders were wrapped in a long cloak.

"She's not okay."

Obviously.

He ignored the attitude since Kyrell shared his worry.

How are you going to get her attention?

Each of her steps took her farther away from Thaddeus. His mind raced, searching for a solution. "I don't—" Then memories of a levitation spell from one of his father's books flashed through his mind. "Oh. Thank you."

You're welcome.

Thaddeus allowed himself only a moment to marvel at his dragon's ability to search his memories before muttering the spell's words, concentrating steady energy into a small rock next to his foot. When he'd first attempted the spell years ago, he'd only moved the rock a foot before his magic gave out. Expecting the same results, he overcompensated. Infused with energy, the rock flew into the air and smacked into his forehead.

Searing pain shot though Thaddeus' head as stars blotted his vision. A curse slipped from his lips.

"Thaddeus?"

Oh, ozi!

Not bothering to see who called, Thaddeus and Kyrell fell over each other, scrambling to run deeper into the forest. Kyrell's clumsy tail swept Thaddeus' feet out from under him, sending him face-first into another bush. Cursing, he flailed, trying to extract himself from the bristled plant. Kyrell's misguided help only tripped him even more. By the time he righted himself, they could hide no longer.

"Thaddeus, is that you?" This time the voice rang beautifully familiar.

Thaddeus raised his eyebrows at Kyrell before brushing himself off, tripping over vines to find her. "Syrinthia!"

As she stepped in front of him, he looked up from picking branches from his shirt and they collided.

Thaddeus looked down. Her bright eyes wide with surprise stared back. Relief cascaded over him like a waterfall. "Syrinthia, thank the gods you're alright. We've been so worried about you. I thought they were going to kill you, and it would be my fault—" He hated the tears collecting in his eyes, but he'd never been able to stop them before; this time was no different.

"Um, Thaddeus. That's really sweet of you, but could you maybe get off me before you say anything else?"

Only then did Thaddeus become embarrassingly aware of their position. He lay on top of her, hands on either side of her head, faces just inches apart. He wasn't sure his face had ever burned so bright red before.

In a flurry of arms and legs, he scrambled up and jumped away, distancing himself from her as far as possible without just running away. He could hear Kyrell's laughter in the back of his mind but he ignored it, just like he also ignored Syrinthia's gaze. Suddenly, the forest floor seemed very, very interesting.

"I'm sorry. I'm so sorry. I didn't see you there when we—and I was just so happy that—" His words were cut off as she threw her arms around him, pinning his arms to his side.

Eyes wide, he stared over her shoulder. "Um . . ." Nothing else came out.

"I'm okay, Thaddeus. I promise." She pulled away. "I was more worried about you when I stopped by your house this morning and you weren't there."

Relaxing slightly, he allowed himself a little smile. "You stopped by to see me? Why?"

"You're not the only one who gets worried, you know."

He flinched when her fingertips grazed his exposed arm. Sparks danced across his skin, but he forced himself to stand still. "What are you—" Then he understood. His Shalnoa glowed a vibrant purple—the same color as his dragon's eyes.

"You look different." A frown tugged her lips as she surveyed his face, and he did the same to her. Something like a bruise darkened her left jaw. Before he mentioned it, her gasp silenced him. "Thaddeus! Your eyes!"

Blinking rapidly, he froze. "What about them? What's wrong?" *Maybe I should carry around a little mirror like Thanatos . . . No, that's stupid.*

"They're purple!"

His jaw dropped. Words failed him until he repeated her. "They're purple?"

She nodded, marveling. "But that's impossible. The only way you could change your eye color is if you—" Her own eyes widened as she realized what she was saying. Just then, her gaze drifted over his shoulder, and a small squeak left her lips.

Thaddeus felt Kyrell move beside him. *You weren't supposed to be seen!*

Kyrell sneered. *I'm a part of you now, and you're basically in love with her. I have to make sure you aren't losing yourself to a* klushuub. *Besides, she figured it out on her own. Good thing she's smart. I wouldn't have liked her if she wasn't.*

Thaddeus' protests stopped abruptly as Syrinthia rushed toward Kyrell and bowed low, muttering a quick introduction of herself. Then she shamelessly admired the Acid Dragon.

"By the Creator! He's magnificent. I can tell he's male because of that thick ridge over his eyes, but I've never seen an Acid Dragon. Such incredible color in the scales, and no sun damage. Has he spent most of his life underground? That would explain how supple his scales are. You need to be careful with him and the sun. He's not used to the rays and will burn easily. I'd suggest going to a healer to find a salve for him . . ." She went on and on, touching more of Kyrell than Thaddeus even had.

Kyrell squirmed, both satisfied with her praises and uncomfortable with the violation of his space.

Is she always like this? Kyrell snapped his wing away as she tried to lift it and run her hand down his side. That didn't stop her, and moments later, Kyrell's claws were in her small, dark hands.

A laugh broke Thaddeus' lips, and he nodded. *Yes, but she seems particularly interested in you.*

When it seemed she'd finally satiated her curiosity, she finally stood back, hands on her hips, and nodded her approval. "He's perfect.

Wouldn't change a thing about him. I'm only a little jealous." Her wink caused Thaddeus to blush.

"Thank you. I'm rather proud of him."

And I of you.

"Let's walk for a bit." Syrinthia started off before she finished talking. "I don't want anyone to see him since you don't have a bonding license." She gestured for them to follow, and they quickly caught up.

Her comment about the license twisted his gut, and he avoided her gaze, choosing instead to pick his way over and around the extensive root systems of the trees. The scene looked like a forest in a room made of trees. Thaddeus was surprised Duvarharians weren't fond of walking through forests, but he supposed it had something to do with the Duvarharian instinct to be in the sky, like on mountains, plains, and clouds. After all, a forest was no place for a dragon to spread its wings.

"Does it bother you?" The words left his lips without his consent, and he wasn't sure if he was asking himself or her.

"What?"

"My not having a bonding license. Now that you know, you're perpetuating a crime. Which is one reason why I didn't know if I should tell you." He shot a scathing look to his dragon, who only grinned and blinked his secondary lids over his eyes in amusement.

"I'm glad you *did* tell me, or rather I'm glad . . ." She looked back, and Thaddeus realized he never formally introduced them.

"Kyrell."

"Lovely name. I'm glad *Kyrell* revealed himself. I wouldn't classify myself as a rebel, but the restricted bonding law is not one I will ever support. If that makes me a criminal, then I will proudly stand before the Creator to be judged as such."

Thaddeus' eyebrows rose. He'd heard her passionate opinions before but never with this conviction. "I'm glad."

She gave him a warm smile.

"At first I wasn't even sure I *could* bond with a dragon." A frown tugged his lips as emotion choked his throat. *Why am I saying this? Do I want to say it? How will she see me?*

She should know. She's a bit . . . different too, isn't she?

She is. Though Thaddeus didn't know as much about Syrinthia as he wanted, he knew she possessed a unique magic, different than anything he'd known Duvarharians to perform or be capable of. He remembered the way her soul felt when she let the power flow through her. It felt as if she were of the same thing stars were made of.

"What do you mean?" Her brows wrinkled in confusion. "He's older than the bonding age, sure, but it's not impossible to bond with grown dragons. It just takes both creatures choosing each other, which you seem to have had no problem with."

Thaddeus shook his head and took a deep breath, hands finding his pockets, eyes finding a tree far ahead. "I'm not . . . fully Duvarharian."

A long silence stretched between them. Thaddeus cursed himself. *I knew I shouldn't have said anything.* Sivgiv.

Patience. Give her time to think.

After what felt like an eternity, she took a deep breath and released it, nodding slowly. "You're half Zoic."

"How did you guess?"

She shot him a look that said, "*Really?*"

When he shrugged, she explained. "Your connection with the Zoics in the dungeons was inexplicable. No matter what kind of magic Duvarharians possess, even if they are bonded with a Nature Dragon, they lack any connection with Zoics, just like they lack connections with Centaurs, Fauns, or other Ventronovian Kinds. Besides, the only creatures in Ventronovia who can cross are Wyriders and Duvarharians. We used to be one Kind thousands of years ago, you know; though our magic has changed, our blood hasn't."

"So, you already knew?"

She frowned, stopping her walk. "Not really." Her voice softened as her eyes met his. "It was more of a feeling. I felt your soul move and breathe around me as if reaching out to be heard and understood. Something told me you were . . . different. I think I was drawn to that."

Fire raced across his cheeks. He hoped she didn't notice. "At first, I was afraid of who I am, of how the world sees me. I was scared I'd never bond with a dragon and use magic." He looked at the little threads of purple energy swirling around his hand. "But I think I can find a way to be both Duvarharian and Wyrider. Maybe I can be something old and new. A New Traditional."

Awe and respect shone in her eyes as he searched her face for a response. Though he could hardly hold the intensity of her gaze, he never wanted to look away from the way the darkness in her eyes danced with gold flecks—the unique magic flowing through her.

"You're also different." His body moving on its own, he reached for her hand. She didn't move away as he took it in his. The purple Shalnoa on his left hand lit up brilliantly, displaying his unique markings clearly. But his wasn't the only one with markings.

Instead of her Shalnoa being dull and skin-toned like any other non-bonded rider's, hers glowed a warm, brilliant gold and white. Her markings were unlike any Duvarharian markings he had ever seen before, even his own, which differed from traditional designs.

Tears trailed down her cheeks as she watched her markings move and shimmer as if with a life of their own. "Yes. I am."

They tightened their grip, drawing strength from each other. "What . . . who . . . ?"

Sniffing, she shook her head. "I don't know. I'm not sure I ever will."

The awe and wonder they had shared sank under the weight of grief, of knowing that she'd never belong anywhere so long as she didn't know who she was or where she came from.

"I have to admit"—her soft chuckle sounded pained—"I'm a little jealous. You have your dragon." She pulled her hand from his, wrapping her arms around herself in a lonely hug. "But I don't have anyone."

Thaddeus shook his head. "No. You have me." He poured all his compassion and empathy into his touch as he hugged her, hoping she would believe him and truly feel a part of something. Kyrell moved closer and wrapped his head around them, his tail curling around their legs and pulling them close.

"Maybe we can help each other." Thaddeus slowly released her from his arms and watched as she dried her eyes with her cloak. "Maybe we can learn more about who we are together, safe from anyone who might want to hurt us." His eyes flickered to the bruise on her cheek. Shame filled her eyes as she tried to cover the wound with her cloak.

"No," Thaddeus whispered, trying to stem his tears; he didn't want to appear weak. But as he pulled away her cloak and gently touched his fingers to her skin, he couldn't stop them from rolling down his cheeks, partly in sorrow, partly in anger. "Don't hide from me. Please."

Her own eyes filled with tears.

"Promise?"

She nodded.

"I don't know what I can do. I'm only one rider and one dragon. But I swear I will do everything I can to make sure you're not alone. To make sure that whatever happens to us, you will always have somewhere you belong, someone who cares."

A small smile lifted his lips as she nodded, trying to dry the tears that didn't stop.

"I'm sure you know, but Mother will always take you in. I think she's always wanted a daughter. She'd probably be happier to have you come home instead of Thanatos." He cracked a goofy grin, trying to lighten the mood.

Laughing through her tears, she smiled. "Thank you, Thaddeus. You don't know how much that means to me."

Kyrell nudged her as Thaddeus nodded. "I think I do, actually."

She hugged Kyrell's large face, and he closed his eyes, leaning into the embrace.

"Let's get you back to the academy. I'm sure they're worried about you."

Shaking her head, she started back. "I'm sure they are. Never been late before, but I guess there's a first for everything."

Thaddeus watched her a moment before Kyrell pushed him forward. "I guess so."

After a quick goodbye and her promising to stop by the house after school whenever she could so they could learn magic, she walked through the gates and disappeared.

The tenderness he'd felt gave way to fury. The bruise on her cheek continued to mock him, making him wonder what other injuries she hid. Balling his fists, he gritted his teeth and turned to follow Kyrell back into the forest. "I don't know who did that to her, but I swear to all the gods on Rasa: if I ever get the chance, I'll gut him throat to groin and make him pay for laying his hands on her."

Chapter 22

When Thaddeus returned home that evening, he skipped dinner and went straight to his room before slipping out his window to sit by their pond. Kyrell sat on one side of him, the Shadows of Light book on the other.

What do we do next?

Thaddeus let Kyrell's question simmer in his mind. He wouldn't have to worry about going to school anymore, but he still wasn't sure if whoever sent Brina would leave him alone. He couldn't keep Kyrell a secret forever; he didn't *want* to keep him a secret forever.

But though something had changed in his psyche and physiology since bonding with Kyrell—he'd grown taller, more muscular, and his mind sharper—he knew he couldn't fight the backlash he'd receive if the Peace Haven elites found out about Kyrell. Neither could he move somewhere more accepting like the Dragon Palace; he was still considered a child, and he was too scared to leave his mother behind in this corruption.

"I need to be able to protect myself. If something like . . ." Even over a month later, the memory of the boy he killed still brought a cascade of panic. "Like that one night happens again, I don't want to be helpless. I have you now, but if something should ever happen in broad daylight, I can't risk exposing you to protect me."

Broad daylight or not, if anyone raises a finger at you or even their voice, I'll tear their head from their body and swallow it whole.

Thaddeus chuckled, raising his brows at his dragon. "A little violent, don't you think?"

Not any more than what you wanted to do to whoever hurt Syrinthia. Kyrell fell to cleaning his claws with his snake-like tongue.

Thaddeus shrugged and turned back to the pond. "I guess you're right. But the point is, I need a weapon."

I thought you already had a blade.

He shook his head. "I have a blunt training sword my father bought three years ago, but only Thanatos has a real blade." Grabbing the book, he opened it to a marked page. "It says here, the Shadows of Light specialized in making Dragon Blades."

What's that?

Thaddeus skimmed the page, making sure he hadn't read it wrong. "They were blades made from special metals found throughout Duvarharia. Some say the metal came from the continent above Ventronovia—Chinoi—but others say it came from falling stars. Those are the two most probable origins."

What made them so special?

"They had the power to infuse with individual magic. The bond between the metal and its wielder's magic gave them the same special abilities a rider gained from their dragon. For instance, a Camouflage Dragon would pass their skin-altering abilities to their rider, and then on to the Dragon Blade. Some of those blades could simply camouflage with its wielder, but others were reported to possess the ability to change shape, turning it into a different weapon."

So, if you've gained my abilities, does that mean you can also produce and control acid?

Thaddeus ran his hand along Kyrell's scales. Usually just brushing up against the dragon caused burns. It was easy to see why Acid Dragons were considered too dangerous for society. But though Thaddeus' bare skin pressed firmly against Kyrell's scales, he wasn't harmed. His scales simply felt damp.

"I assume so. I know I'm at least immune to it. I can only hypothesize that if I were able to obtain a Dragon Blade, it would have acid in it much like your scales."

We'd be unstoppable.

Thaddeus agreed. "But that's only *if* I could get ahold of a Dragon Blade."

Why couldn't you?

Thaddeus snapped the book shut and tossed it aside, bitterness rising in his chest. "They were outlawed several hundred years ago in most Duvarharian cities because they were considered 'too powerful'. I asked Rakland about it as soon as I learned about them. He said he hadn't seen or heard of a Dragon Blade in all his life, even as a master swordsman. Even among the bonded, it seems Dragon Blades are obsolete."

Silence stretched between them. Neither knew anyone who could guide them in the direction of this forbidden knowledge. He'd been surprised that Rakland told him anything at all.

Then a thought occurred to him. But it was too farfetched, and he rejected it.

No. Kyrell latched on to the thought. *I see secrets hidden in his eyes. He might know more than you think. He seems like someone who wouldn't shy away from dangerous knowledge.*

"I'd have to get Syrinthia to smuggle me into the school. I doubt they'd let me walk in."

I don't think you'll have any trouble with that.

Standing, Thaddeus stretched and nodded to the house. "If we're going back to the academy, we'd better get a good night's rest."

Kyrell nodded and stretched his wings before curling up under the window.

After Thaddeus sneaked back into his room, thankful he didn't wake Thanatos who continued to snore annoyingly, he lay awake in bed for a long time.

His plan, though improbable, was his only shot. Hopefully, he'd find the answers he needed.

"**YOU WANT TO DO WHAT?**" Syrinthia furrowed her brows, trying to keep her voice low. Sunlight flickering through the academy forest's leaves danced across her dark skin.

Thaddeus took a deep breath. "I want you to smuggle me into the academy so I can talk to the upper student librarian. I don't know for sure, but I think he could help me learn more about the Dragon Blades and how I can get ahold of one."

She chewed on one of her fingernails before catching herself. "That's extremely risky. Since what happened to you and the Zoics, they've nearly doubled security. Why do you think he could help you?"

Again, he explained to her how the student librarian had made a few underhanded comments about knowing things he shouldn't and how he told Thaddeus to find him if he ever wanted anything strange.

"I'll admit, it sounds promising, but are you sure you want to risk it? Is a Dragon Blade really that important to you?"

Thaddeus pulled the Shadows of Light book from his satchel. "Every rider had one back in the Golden Age. It was a part of being a Dragon Rider. They were *everywhere*. Why would they disappear? They must be somewhere. If every rider had one, then they were important. I want to bring back the Golden Age, Syrinthia. An age where we are free to be ourselves, bond with dragons, and wield the weapons we deserve. A world where my people aren't hunted for sport, and you aren't trapped by a cult."

Her face softened as she searched his face.

"I'm going to do this with or without you. But I'd rather do it with."

"I know, I know." She placed her hands on her hips. "Alright. Let's go."

Kyrell protested to being forced to wait in the forest. *I promise I'll be* quiet.

It's not a matter of being quiet, Thaddeus argued, *it's a matter of how long Syrinthia can cloak me with her magic. We don't even know if she's strong enough to conceal me the entire time.*

Eventually, Thaddeus won, and Kyrell agreed to stay hidden until the task was complete. *But if anything goes wrong, you cannot stop me from reducing that ridiculous building to dust to find and protect you.*

"Deal."

With that decided, Syrinthia and Thaddeus stepped out of the forest. Thaddeus remained hidden from the world aside from an unusual gold sparkle—unnoticeable unless others knew what they were looking for.

Thaddeus' heart pounded in his chest. He knew Syrinthia felt nervous too by the way her hands shook and sweat beaded on her brow despite the cool breeze. He placed a reassuring hand on her shoulder, and she smiled, straightening her posture.

When they stepped through the gates, they were immediately beset by Thanatos and his friends.

Thaddeus snarled, repulsed by their raucous laughter, lewd jokes, and how most of them stumbled with last night's alcohol on their breath. Thanatos shouted excitedly when he spotted Syrinthia and quickly caught up to her, throwing his arm around her shoulder.

Thaddeus didn't miss the other female students' jealous glances, but he also didn't miss how Syrinthia's entire body tensed as she shrank from Thanatos' touch.

Blood boiling, he fixed his gaze on the ground, fists balled and teeth grinding. Though he struggled to tune out his brother's loud voice, he forced himself to lest he strike out.

Calm yourself. Don't do anything foolish. You'd only end up getting your blood spilled and Syrinthia exposed.

Thank you for that piece of encouragement, Kyrell. Sarcasm dripped in his thoughts as he rolled his eyes.

Anytime.

Though his dragon's snarky tone made Thaddeus want to throttle him, he found he missed it when his dragon's thoughts fell silent.

I'm still right here. Quit being so clingy.

I changed my mind. I liked it better when you were quiet. Thaddeus tried to maintain his annoyance but couldn't keep from smiling. The same amusement radiated from Kyrell.

As they entered the school, Syrinthia attempted to separate from Thanatos. "I need to go to the upper library. I'll meet you guys in class." She went to step away, but Thanatos' hold only tightened around her.

"Come on, Syrinthia." His eyes pleaded falsely as he pouted his lip. "You were so distant yesterday. Are you avoiding us?" He trailed a finger down her cheek, but she turned away.

She forced a smile, though it didn't reach the disgust in her eyes. "I'm not avoiding you, Thanatos. I wasn't feeling good yesterday, and I have a book that's due at noon. I don't want to forget later."

But Thanatos still didn't move his arm. "I don't believe you, but if you want to go, then go." He moved as if to kiss her cheek, but she pushed his arm off her shoulder and ducked under his hand.

Thanatos scowled.

"I'll be back as soon as I can! I promise!" Syrinthia nearly ran away, their roaring laughter chasing her down the hall.

For a moment, Thaddeus lingered, boring holes into Thanatos as his friends made fun of him for the unrequited kiss.

"Whatever. She'll come around when she knows what's good for her." Thanatos shoved one of his friends and cast a hungry glance after Syrinthia.

Move. Now. Kyrell's voice thundered in Thaddeus' thoughts, spurring him into a run. *You stupid fool. You let her get too far away. A few more feet, and her magic would've disappeared. You're too weak and stupid to face Thanatos yet. And despite the jealousy you feel over Syrinthia, she is not yours. You want to save her? Take down the cult that owns her. They're the real enemy.*

He didn't have to respond for Kyrell to know he understood. It wouldn't happen again. It *couldn't*. He had too much to lose now. Even if he didn't care about his own safety, he had his dragon, mother, and Syrinthia to think about now. Even though Thanatos' hungry gaze haunted him, taunted him, Kyrell was right. He had bigger problems to worry about.

Quickly, he caught up to Syrinthia. She seemed too distraught to worry that he'd almost been seen. She ducked behind a tall pillar in an empty hall, and he followed, the magic dissipating.

"That *sufax*!" In a fit of fury, she smashed her fist into the marble pillar.

Thaddeus' eyes widened. Her knuckles were unscathed, but a large crack marred the stone. It didn't feel like a good time to point it out though, so he turned his attention to her. "I'm sorry."

Drying her tears on her sleeve, she shook her head, teeth grinding. "It's not your fault."

"But he is my brother. And he brings shame to me and my family."

Syrinthia didn't answer, only shrugged. After a long silence, she took a deep breath and waved her hand over his body. The golden shimmer fell over him, and once again he disappeared from the world's gaze.

Without another word, she led the way up to the nearly abandoned halls of the upper classrooms. A few of the halls housed older students and some ongoing classes, but most of the others contained rows of sealed doors, only openable with magic.

What do you think they're doing in these rooms?

He felt Kyrell shift uncomfortably. *If it has anything to do with the stuffed Zoics you found downstairs, I'm not sure I want to know.*

Thaddeus agreed, but part of him wanted to see. He wanted the world to see. He wanted someone to pay for these wrongs.

Then they were standing at the library doors.

The magic fell away. Syrinthia hesitated before opening the door. "Are you sure you trust him? He's never been reputable. He's an outcast from the academy and a rebel against authority. No one's even sure how he's allowed to stay on staff. What if he tells on you?"

Doubt wormed its way into Thaddeus' mind. He took a deep breath, squared his shoulders, then pushed it away. He remembered how uncomfortable he'd been around the librarian. Yet he'd also felt as if he were one of the only real people he'd met since starting school. He couldn't explain why, but he knew the librarian wouldn't betray him. "I'm sure."

Syrinthia searched his face one last time before nodding and pushing the door open. "I'll be waiting out here," she muttered.

He stepped in; the closing door echoed behind him.

For a moment, he felt suspended in time, as if he were standing before a chasm, not sure if a path would appear for him. But the Shadows of Light book in his hand seemed to whisper promises he wanted desperately to believe.

Striding into the library, he walked straight to the desk, half expecting another librarian to be on shift. He wasn't disappointed.

Thaddeus cleared his throat. "Hello again."

The young man casually spun around in his chair, hand to his chin, one leg crossed over the other, a wildly smug grin on his pierced face. "I had a feeling I'd see you again." Leaning forward, he licked his lips. "What can I help you with, young rider?"

Thaddeus' face burned. *He can't possibly know–*

"It's written all over your face. Looked in a mirror lately?" Laughing, the librarian sprung from his chair. In a heartbeat, he had his hand wrapped in Thaddeus' hair, pulling him uncomfortably close.

Thaddeus froze as the young man caressed his ear. "Pointed tips." He poked at Thaddeus' cheek bones, just under his eyes. "Slitted pupils." He squeezed his biceps. "A sudden burst in muscular structure and"—he brushed his fingers across Thaddeus' lips as tenderly as if they were lovers—"sharp little fangs."

Breaking away, Thaddeus blinked, his heart racing, his cheeks burning, completely lost for words.

A bit forward. Kyrell laughed in his mind.

To say the least.

"Little flustered, aren't you? Poor thing."

The librarian stepped around the desk and pulled his glasses from his silvery hair, placing them on his sharp nose. "So, I ask again, rider. What can I help you with?"

Stepping as far away as he could without being rude, Thaddeus opened the book to the marked page on Dragon Blades and thrust it toward the librarian. "I'm looking for a Dragon Blade."

His eyes narrowed as he leaned against the desk and flipped through the book. Thaddeus could tell he was thinking rather than reading. "And why do you want such a blade? To gain power over the weak? To oppress those who cannot wield magic? To prove yourself to the elites that you are strong enough to be among them?" Venom laced his words as he snapped the book shut and stalked toward Thaddeus.

Though he desired as much space as possible between him and the librarian, Thaddeus stood his ground. "No. I want to bring back the old ways, the Golden Age of Duvarharia. Where everyone has a right to magic, to dragons, to the weapons of our people. Where we govern ourselves and are free to live with the dragons like we were created to."

The librarian stopped inches from him and tilted his head, their jaws almost touching. "Are you sure?"

Thaddeus felt a strange magic wash over him. A gentle fog drifted over his mind. He couldn't think of anything except the truth, but though his heart raced, he was not afraid. He had nothing to hide.

"I couldn't be more sure of anything in my life."

His demeanor relaxing, the librarian stepped back, a crooked grin spreading across his face. His eyes filled with tender authenticity. Sticking out his hand, he finally introduced himself. "Then the stars have led you to the right place. My name is Deimos Ovesen, and my family has been in the business of illegally smithing Dragon Blades for hundreds of years."

Chapter 23

Thaddeus couldn't believe what he'd heard. "You're jesting."

Deimos winked. "Not even a little, love. Here." He rolled up his sleeve to his bicep, exposing a sleeve of tattoos. "Take a look."

Thaddeus recognized one of the symbols immediately. "You're a Shadow of Light."

Eyes sparkling, Deimos covered his arm again. "From a long line of some of the last true followers. Many families before the fall were tasked with preserving traditional Duvarharian knowledge. They saw the path our beloved land was on and knew they'd enter a society that hated dragons and magic. This was the knowledge my family preserved." Pulling a knife from his belt, he held it in the light. Thaddeus gasped. The blade was engraved with symbols and veins that moved and glowed with an eerie light.

"A Dragon Blade."

Deimos nodded in pride. "Yes. One to call my own. It's not infused with my magic, though." A tinge of bitterness laced his voice.

"Why not?"

He pointed to his round ears. "No dragon."

Thaddeus' heart sank. "I'm sorry."

He shrugged. "Don't be. At least it's not for lack of trying." The sparkle of danger leaped back into his eyes. "I've jumped into the *Xeneluch-Rani* once or twice. Never made it, though. Always blacked out and woke up on the shore the next morning."

"The dragons saved you."

He nodded. "Good enough to save, not good enough to bond with. I don't think you realize how lucky you are to have not only made it to the island but to be allowed to bond. In fact, if it weren't for that, I would've killed you the second you asked about Dragon Blades."

With the way Deimos' eyes darkened and his hand strayed to his knife, Thaddeus knew he wasn't joking.

"I'll help you, Thaddeus, son of Quinlan, rider of a dragon. But you must bring me the metal."

"The metal?"

Deimos nodded and opened the book again, pointing to the bottom of a faded page. "Ossillite. The dragon ore. We'll forge the weapon but can't provide the material. You want it, you find it. If you're lucky, you'll find a tool or weapon the metal was unknowingly repurposed for."

Hope drained from Thaddeus. "But the Dragon Blades have been missing for hundreds, if not thousands, of years. How am I supposed to find ore or even enough tools that have trace ore in them?"

The librarian shrugged and settled back into his chair with an air of disapproval. He crossed his legs, propping them on the desk, hands behind his head, eyes shut. "I don't know. That's something you'll have to figure out on your own."

Frustrated, Thaddeus turned to storm from the library.

"But . . ." The dragged-out word forced Thaddeus to stop, turning just enough to see Deimos crack a crooked grin, his tongue absently playing with his labret piercing. "I'll give you a hint since you're kind of cute."

Thaddeus released an annoyed breath, though he couldn't deny his hunger for information. "What is it?"

"The Ossillite will infuse with your magic. Should only take a little touch." Deimos gestured as if sprinkling herbs into food and winked. "You'll know it when it happens. When you find it, love, I'll be waiting in the blacksmith shop two miles east from the old clock tower." Deimos blew him a kiss before he turned and opened the door. "I'll see you soon."

Thaddeus nodded and let the door close behind him. He'd only just opened his mouth to relay what he'd learned when Syrinthia placed a finger on his lips and shook her head. His skin grew hot with her touch, but he didn't move away.

"Don't tell me. The less information they can torture out of me, the better."

Bile rose into Thaddeus' throat, his mind flashing back to the bruise on her cheek, hidden with makeup today. What other marks couldn't he see?

"Understand?" Her finger still rested on his lips as if she could hold back his words until she felt certain he wouldn't speak.

Nodding, he felt an emptiness creep in when she moved away and cloaked him in magic.

The trip back proved uneventful since the students and teachers were in class—time that most guards considered break.

When they stopped by the gates, looking around to make sure a stray guard wasn't watching, Thaddeus searched his mind for something to say to make her smile, laugh, or at least not feel so alone. "Syrinthia—"

She cut him off. "Don't say anything. You don't need too." Hesitating as if unsure if she should, she reached out and squeezed his arm. "I'll be in touch. We'll teach each other magic sometime, alright?"

Thaddeus forced a small smile and nodded. "Yeah. Absolutely."

With a last glance, she turned and hurried back into the academy. Though he knew he'd be bullied, he desperately wished he could follow her.

Come, little one. Don't want you to be seen now.

Stepping from the gates, he made his way to Kyrell in the forest. The dragon had already heard the conversation with Deimos. They only had to make a plan to find the Ossillite.

A metal that infuses with your magic? What does that mean? Surely, you won't go around touching every piece of metal you find.

Thaddeus shrugged, an unwelcome thought nagging the back of his mind. He didn't want to admit it, didn't want to revisit the memory, so he tried to push it down. But he saw no other way.

Though he'd hoped he'd never have to see it again, he knew just where to find such a weapon.

THE RISING SUNS SHED their light once more upon the land of dragons. It trickled down between the thick, leafy canopy above Thaddeus and Kyrell. They were standing before a large, rotted tree trunk, neither moving, neither speaking. A whirlwind of emotions battered Thaddeus. Memories haunted him of hot blood on his hands, the weight of the dead boy in his arms, and the way his eyes glossed disturbingly fast as the life drained from him.

Swallowing, Thaddeus wished he'd taken just one more sip of water before coming outside, though he knew it wouldn't have helped. Contrarily, his hands were slick with sweat. He'd spoke with Deimos only yesterday. He'd spent every moment since searching for another way to get Ossillite. But unless he wanted to spend hundreds of years looking for a piece of random metal hidden anywhere across Duvarharia, only one option remained.

After he'd come to terms with his choice, he'd struggled with putting his plan into motion right away. But sleep had been restless that night and full of violent nightmares, which convinced him of his soul's inability for redemption.

In the small hours of the morning, he'd fallen asleep after praying he'd wake and it would all be a bad dream. But then he'd awoken, and nothing had changed. The librarian still waited for him to find the Ossillite, and he still only knew one place to find it.

Which brought him to the rotten tree trunk, wringing his hands and drawing lines in the sand with his boot.

We cannot wait here forever.

Thaddeus nodded. "I know, I know." But his words didn't match his actions, and he didn't move any closer to the tree.

Go, little one. It is your inheritance. Can't you hear it calling you?

How could he not? Its call was irresistible—undeniable. The tree hummed with magic, with recognition and remembrance. Tremors ran through his hands as if more eager than he to reach for his prize.

"I never wanted to see it again." He took a step forward, betraying himself. "I told myself I would never come back for it." But as his feet carried him forward, he knew he'd been lying to himself. It had become as much of him as he had of it. He hesitated no longer and stepped to the trunk, reaching into the darkness.

His hands grasped in the abyss. For a moment, he expected a woodland animal to snap its teeth around his fingers and draw the blood payment he felt he owed. Retribution never came. Instead, his hands found the worn handle of the tool, and he pulled it out.

A sigh of relief let his lips as his magic filled the weapon once again.

The axe shone in the morning light, catching the golden rays and shining brilliantly with purple energy and magic that wove itself into the metal's crevasse.

Flecks of dark crust lined the handle. He had to lie and tell himself it was sap from the tree, not blood.

It suits you.

Thaddeus nodded, turning it over. Somehow, he knew the metal wished to be free from the worn handle, free from the lowly material it had been lashed to for hundreds of years. It longed to be re-fastened to its former glory. It long to whistle through the air again, to taste blood.

Tears sprang into Thaddeus' eyes, and he sank to the forest floor, letting the axe drop in front of him as he drew his knees to his chest.

Suppressed memories flashed before him. Fear thundered through his chest, pumped through his veins, and gripped his mind. "I didn't want to kill him," he blubbered through tears, burying his face in his arms. "I'm not a murderer! I'm not a murderer!"

Kyrell wrapped his tail, wings, and neck around his rider, soaking in the pain, the anguish that had been hidden for so many months. *No. You're not. Let the gods take the blood from your hands. It was their fault you were forced into that position. Let them carry this weight. It is not one for you to bear.*

Thaddeus' shoulders shook as he tried and failed to speak.

You can move on from this. It doesn't have to define you.

Sniffing, Thaddeus wiped his nose on his sleeve. "N–no. But . . ." He took a deep breath. "If I turn this into a Dragon Blade, it will be with me forever. *He* will be with me forever."

Kyrell pressed his warm snout to Thaddeus' head. *That is true. But it doesn't need to be a burden. It can be your strength. Let it remind you that sometimes justice brings pain, but in the end, it's worth it. Sometimes lives must be lost before peace can settle. You fought for your right to knowledge, for your right to protect those you love. That is noble. That is just. Let his soul return to the gods but keep his memory with you. Remember that you must put down evil. And remember that every soul deserves a second chance.*

Thaddeus wasn't sure he was ready to take such deep words and apply them to himself. Too lost in his own darkness, he struggled to think of the light. But Kyrell was right. That night, he hadn't killed in cold blood. He'd fought for justice, for himself, for his mother, and for Syrinthia. If he wanted to change the world, if he truly wanted to take on this evil and banish it, he had to learn to face the gruesomeness of death and the truth of doing what must be done, even if it left scars.

I have to grow up. I have to desensitize myself to this. He pulled himself to his feet, taking the axe with him. *This may not be the person I wanted to be, but it's the person I must be. It's the person the gods made me to be. Maybe even the person Joad wished for me to be. I will fight for him. For the old ways and the Shadows of Light. Today we move forward.*

He mounted Kyrell, who let out a roar of triumph. *We do this together. Together.*

Then they set off to find Deimos.

THOUGH HE'D EASILY FOUND Deimos' blacksmith shop, its remoteness surprised him. All other buildings stood far enough away that Kyrell could join him from the sign at the road and down the long lane to the shop.

When they reached the second gate, a pack of dogs rushed to meet them, snarling and barking on the other side of the fence.

Kyrell roared, sending the dogs whimpering and scattering. *That'll teach them to mess with a dragon.* He bristled, eyeing the dogs as if he were going to eat them.

At the commotion, the front door of the modest dwelling opened, and an unfamiliar figure stepped out.

She stood taller and far more muscular than most women Thaddeus had seen. Her gaze burned into him across the grassy expanse, and his heart pounded, sweat beading on his brow.

We didn't pick the wrong house, did we? What if she realizes you're an illegal type and alerts the authorities?

I'd eat her before she could try.

Then the woman turned to yell into the house. Moments later, a familiar figure stepped beside her. Deimos whooped and waved, shouting into the house before jogging across the lawn.

"Hello, love." He winked as he unlocked the gate, letting it swing open. "I'll admit, I didn't expect to see you again for at least a few months."

Thaddeus chewed his lip. "I'm a bit surprised myself." They moved through the gate and Deimos shut it, making sure to lock it. Thaddeus would've been more worried about the locked gate if Kyrell hadn't been with him.

Deimos didn't seem fazed by Kyrell and hardly gave him a second glance as he strode past them, the chains on his belt clinking with every step. "So, you found some Ossillite?"

Thaddeus nodded. "I think so?"

Deimos shot him a skeptical look and tsked. "You *think* so? Did it bond with your magic?"

Thaddeus looked at the covered weapon strapped to Kyrell's back. He hadn't been able to stomach carrying it himself. *It'll be different once it's reforged,* he'd promised himself, but deep down, he wasn't sure if it would be. The hum from the axe still sounded like a plea for blood. "Yes," was his simple answer.

Deimos nodded, his crooked grin sweeping his face. "Then it's time you met my family." He gestured to the house, and Thaddeus' breath caught in his throat.

Deimos' mother was the woman who'd first stepped outside. Her silver hair, woven into thick braids, reached her ankles. Her shining gold eyes pierced his. A thin line of serious lips stretched under a hooked nose identical to Deimos'. She was one of the most beautiful and exotic Duvarharians Thaddeus had ever seen.

The father stood even taller, making him a giant compared to Thaddeus, whose skin prickled as he stood at the edge of the porch and looked into the man's eyes. His eyes were gold as well but swirled with magic that could only come from a bonded dragon. His features were angled and sharp. Ears with incredibly pointed tips poked from his long silver hair, which boasted the same braids and jewelry as his wife. Bulging muscles and rough hands bore testimony to hundreds of years of blacksmithing.

They were everything Thaddeus dreamed of Dragon Riders being.

Two other boys, both older than Deimos, and a younger girl came out as well, their faces considerably more youthful and less drawn. Their features were remarkably similar to each other's and their parents', though their eyes shone all different colors and their silver hair streaked with another color.

"Thaddeus, rider of the Acid Dragon, I present my family, the Ovesens, forgers of Dragon Blades for eight generations."

Thaddeus tried to keep his mouth from dropping. For the first time, he knew he stood among real Duvarharians. He couldn't help but wonder how much of the Duvarharian bloodline had been corrupted for the average Duvarharian to look so different than the ones standing before him.

Finally, he found his voice. "May the suns smile upon your presence." He planted his fist to his chest and bowed slightly. Kyrell growled and lowered his head.

"As do the stars sing upon yours." The man reached down and extended his forearm.

Thaddeus took hold of it, shocked at how gentle the man's touch felt and the warmth in his eyes.

"My son says you are in need of a Dragon Blade to be forged."

Thaddeus nodded, eyes flickering back and forth from the man to the rest of the family as they looked upon him curiously. "Y–yes, *Quse*, I am."

The man grunted then looked to Deimos, who seemed quite pleased with himself. "He also assures me you spoke the truth when you said you wished to bring back the old ways of Duvarharia."

Thaddeus' face burned as he remembered the magic Deimos placed upon him, forcing him to speak the truth.

"Oh, don't be so embarrassed." Deimos' sister jumped off the porch and pushed her brother.

"What'd I do?" But Deimos grinned ear to ear.

"That's his unique, lost magic: making others tell the truth," she explained. "Most purebloods have *something*."

"I knew it." The words escaped Thaddeus' lips before he could stop them. He scrambled for better words. "I'm sorry, I only mean you look so much different than everyone else."

That sounds even worse.

I'm aware.

"You're lovely people, I mean." *Awkward.*

Now they were laughing. He wanted to crawl inside his skin and die. But when Deimos slapped his back and gave him a friendly shake, he realized they were smiling and making fun of each other.

"I knew I liked you for a reason, love." Deimos winked before throwing an arm around Thaddeus' shoulder and steering him toward Kyrell. "Now, let's see that metal."

Without much success, Thaddeus tried to keep his hands from shaking as he undid the straps and unwrapped the axe. The whole family hovered around him, waiting with bated breath. It seemed this excited them much more than it did him. He had to remind himself they didn't know the grief he carried with this weapon.

When he presented the blade to them, his purple energy swirling around and through the metal, a collective gasp rang out.

Deimos' jaw dropped. Though his sister made fun of him for it, her wide eyes never left the weapon.

"Stars of old." The mother's eyes misted as she took a step forward. "That's King's metal."

"What's King's metal?" The Shadows of Light book hadn't mentioned variations of Dragon Blades.

"May I?" The father gestured to the weapon, and Thaddeus quickly handed it to him, feeling as if a huge emotional weight had been lifted from him.

"King's metal is a special type of Ossillite, purified in the age of Duvarharian Kings long before the Golden Age of the Lords and Council. It's potentially one of the oldest known strands of the Ossillite and the strongest. It's a miracle it survived this long. Most of it was unknowingly smelted into jewelry for the rich because of its lasting, tarnish-free shine. Others have brought King's metal to me before, but never in this quantity." He lifted the axe and admired it. In his hands, it no longer looked like a tool; it looked every bit like a Dragon Rider's weapon, even with the splintered handle.

For a moment, the man's eyes caught the dark crust at the conjunction of metal and wood. His eyes flickered to Thaddeus, who forced himself to meet his gaze. An understanding passed between them; the man said nothing about the blood before he swung the weapon a few times.

Whispers of what Thaddeus swore was an ancient language sang from the blade as it split the air. Though he didn't understand the whispers now, he knew from the way it called his soul and magic that one day he would learn.

The family passed the blade around, marveling, until the father took it back and heaved it onto his shoulder. Though a woodcutter's axe in Thaddeus' small hands, it looked more like a hatchet in his. "Come along, son. You didn't come for us to drool over an old tool. Let's turn this into a weapon you can be proud of, shall we?"

For the first time since he'd spoken to Deimos about the Dragon Blades, Thaddeus felt a thrill of excitement.

Following the father, daughter, and Deimos into the blacksmithing building, Thaddeus found himself in a completely different world. He'd expected a dark, sooty workshop like the ones that dotted the streets of Peace Haven. Impeccably clean and full of light from the skylights above, this looked nothing like that.

Every polished tool hung in a meticulous order. Several large kilns were scattered throughout the shop so more than one blacksmith could work at a time. One furnace stood out from the others in the center of the massive building; it stood nearly twice the size of the others and had metal pipes snaking to the roof. Thaddeus guessed this furnaced forged the Dragon Blades.

"*Ug, fursuu!*" The man's booming voice rattled the walls. Thaddeus wondered if such a powerful voice came from being bonded with a dragon and whether or not his voice would one day do the same.

A dragon landed on the shop, his giant gold and blue eye peering through one of the skylights. The man nodded as the dragon raised his head, a fire igniting deep in his throat. Fire exploded from his jaws, down the pipes, and into the furnace below, filling it with scorching blue flames Thaddeus felt from nearly thirty feet away. The fire also blazed unbearably bright, and he marveled as the family stared into it without blinking.

This is what we've lost. Thaddeus shook his head, a twinge of jealousy rising in him. *This is what Duvarharians should be doing. Not fighting and torturing animals in arenas.*

Kyrell couldn't have agreed more.

The three Duvarharians worked seamlessly together as they readied the anvils and drew large, colorful engraved tools from the walls.

"Dragon fire and Dragon Blade tools are the only way to properly forge Ossillite," Deimos explained as he laid out a series of hammers, each a slightly different shape. Holding a hammer about the size of his thumb, he winked, his pierced tongue playing with his lip piercing. "And remember, it's not the size that counts."

Thaddeus rolled his eyes, his face burning as he laughed and shook his head.

"Knock it off, Deimos." His sister smacked the back of his head with a thick glove. "You don't need to be so crude all the time."

"What?" Deimos shrugged and pouted. "What'd I do?"

She scowled then burst out laughing. "Whatever, Deimos."

Chuckling, he perfectly mimicked her tone. "Whatever, Frikka."

"Quit fooling around and make sure there's enough fuel in the fire. I don't want to see it burning low when I put in the filings to melt."

The siblings jumped back to work but only after Deimos shot Thaddeus a sultry look.

Thaddeus smiled as he watched them. *They seem so happy. I wish my family worked together like this.*

I think your family is too spoiled to work like this.

Thaddeus scowled, wanting to protest, but Kyrell was right. He and Thanatos had been pampered and spoiled. They'd had only the best food, home, education, and friends. He'd always thought of his father being different—*better*—than the other elites, but the more objectively he thought about it, the more he realized Quinlan wasn't so different. After all, no true Dragon Rider would deny his own son the ability to learn magic.

The family gathering around shook him from his thoughts.

"We're ready, Thaddeus, rider of the Acid Dragon. We only require one thing." The man wiped his hands on a rag and pulled out a curved knife. It looked remarkably similar to Deimos's.

Thaddeus' heart skipped. "Y–yes. What's that?"

"Your blood."

His jaw dropped.

"Gods of the stars!" Deimos smacked his father's arm. "You've got to stop saying it like that."

Frikka chuckled demonically as their father shrugged. "I don't know a better way to say it." Thaddeus thought he saw a flicker of amusement behind his stoic gaze.

"Like so." Deimos turned to Thaddeus, a broad grin spreading across his face as he batted his lashes. "Thaddeus, love, darling of mine that I love." He held out his hand.

Not sure if he should be amused or uncomfortable, Thaddeus placed his hand in Deimos', a small smile tugging the corners of his lips.

Deimos dropped to one knee, holding Thaddeus' hand above his bowed head. "In order to truly make the metal a part of you and your dragon, we require a small amount of your blood." He gazed with large eyes and brought Thaddeus' hand to his lips. "Please allow us to take just a portion of your life blood. You will not feel it one bit, I promise you, love. What say you?"

Thaddeus couldn't meet his gaze any longer without bursting out laughing. Soon the other two blacksmiths followed, but Deimos didn't seem embarrassed at all as he rose to his feet and dusted off his pants.

"Like so, father. Now, doesn't everyone feel a little better?"

"Mostly, though his face is red as a tomato." Frikka brushed tears from her eyes as she roared with laughter.

Thaddeus stumbled over his words when Deimos tossed his hair over his shoulder and said, "I have that effect on the boys."

"Oh, knock it off, Deimos. You're making it uncomfortable again." The father roared and pushed his son, who skipped around the table and grabbed a gold bowl.

"As you wish, Father." But the gleam didn't leave Deimos' eyes.

"What do I do?" Thaddeus' eyes widened at the knife hilt the father presented him with.

"Drag it across the underside of your arm. It shouldn't hurt. If it does, you're going too deep. Remember, we don't need very much."

Thaddeus nodded, gripping the knife until his knuckles turned white. His mouth dried and his ears rang. Positioning his arm over the bowl, he took several deep breaths.

I don't know if I can do this.

You can.

With the strength of his dragon behind him, Thaddeus drew the knife's sharp edge down his skin. A sliver of red followed the silver blade as blood trickled down his arm, dripping off his fingertips. Cringing, he waited for the pain or at least a sting; it never came.

"Bravo." Deimos clapped and took the bowl away while his father cleaned off the knife and Frikka bandaged his arm.

Within seconds, the family immersed themselves in the work, making molds for the ingots and filing down any impurities on the Ossillite. It seemed they'd forgotten about him. Even Deimos was hard at work, his brow slick with sweat, causing his silvery hair to stick to his face.

"What do I do now?" He felt powerless with nothing to do but watch and wait. *I wonder if the Dragon Blades were always forged by specialists, or if a time once existed when Dragon Riders made their own blades.*

Kyrell's lack of answer reminded him how much lost Duvarharian history begged to be found again.

The father wiped his brow on a rag. "This could take several days or weeks. You're the son of Quinlan the Ambassador, rider of Krystallos, correct?"

Thaddeus nodded, deciding not to ask how this man knew so much about his family. "I am."

The man grunted. "Then I will deliver the blade when it's finished." All joviality disappeared from his tone and eyes. "Until then, do not associate yourself with us and do not speak of your Dragon Blade."

Nodding, Thaddeus fell to messing with a loose string on his shirt. Being reminded of the severity of his actions wasn't pleasant. Not only had he risked his own family, now he risked Deimos' as well, even if they'd chosen this life themselves.

"Promise me, boy." His golden eyes burned as he narrowed them.

"I promise."

Then he turned to Deimos, who pretended to be too busy to notice the conversation. "That goes for you too, Deimos. Keep away from him, you hear? None of that flirting and fooling around. Lord knows you'll get yourself killed for it one day."

Deimos rolled his eyes then winked at Thaddeus. "Yes, Father, I promise." Though he joked, Thaddeus saw the steel in his eyes; as casual and foolish as Deimos seemed on the outside, he was just as serious as his father.

He'd kill you without thought if it meant keeping his family and their secrets safe.

Thaddeus nodded, a chill running down his spine. *I know.*

"How do I pay for this?" Shame fell over him; he'd rudely forgotten about payment and hadn't brought anything of value.

All three of them stopped, looked at each other, nodded once, then turned to Thaddeus. Their father smiled sadly.

"We ask for nothing other than freedom. Bring back the old Duvarharia, Thaddeus, rider of Kyrell, and set us free. That will be payment enough."

THE SUNS HAD ALREADY begun to set by the time Thaddeus walked down their road, Kyrell at his side. Both were dragging their feet, in no hurry to get home and be questioned about why he skipped lessons two days in a row. He'd already prepared himself for the lecture he knew his father would give. But one detail had been weighing on his mind since leaving the blacksmith shop.

"How did he know your name?" Despite racking his brain for any recollection of introducing Kyrell, Thaddeus was positive he'd never said his dragon's name to any of them, even Deimos.

He heard my thoughts.

Thaddeus stopped walking. "What do you mean?"

Kyrell turned, his large purple eyes searching Thaddeus' face. *I didn't have to project my thoughts into his. He could walk the mind realm as comfortably as any dragon I've ever met. He knew everything about me the moment his eyes laid on me for the first time. I assume he knew the same about you. He was in our minds without us even knowing. Without him even* trying.

Frikka's words rang in his mind again. *"That's his unique, lost magic: making others tell the truth. Most purebloods have* something." A chill ran down Thaddeus' spine. "Do you think that was his unique magic?"

Kyrell shook his head slowly. *No. He was hiding something else. His ability to walk through the mind realm was something Duvarharians should be inherently capable of.*

Thaddeus' heart skipped. *Inherently capable of? Walking through the mind realm, seeing the thoughts of others, and infiltrating memories? How is that even possible?*

Kyrell growled low. *It's almost unbelievable. But the dragons on the island used to tell stories of entire wars the Duvarharians fought in only their thoughts* and of Dragon Riders who would disappear for years, lost in their own minds and the minds of others. I thought they were only myths, but it would seem they aren't.

A laugh bubbled from Thaddeus' lips as he started walking again. "There's so much we don't know, Kyrell. So much we need to learn."

Indeed.

Thaddeus' hands balled into fists. "But ..." He stopped, the words heavy on his heart. Finally, he took a deep breath and let them out. "I don't think we're going to learn any of it from Peace Haven."

What do you propose?

Thaddeus looked to the stars then the mountains beyond. "We need to go to the Dragon Palace. We need to go where all of this started, where things are more like the past. Where everything isn't so corrupted."

Kyrell rumbled in agreement. *But I think you'll find that the corruption is just as deep there, only more hidden. Are we ready for such a trip?*

Thaddeus gritted his teeth, tightening his fists before relaxing them. "No," he whispered. "Not yet. But with Syrinthia's help, I will learn the magic of Duvarharians and Zoics, and I will train diligently until I am a rider worthy of the Ossillite. Then, once we are stronger, we'll strike out for the truth."

For freedom.

Thaddeus nodded. "For freedom."

Chapter 24

"No, you have to whisper the words with intention. You must feel them in your soul. Really *mean* them with everything that you are." Syrinthia bit her lip as she waited for some acknowledgment that he understood what she said.

"Alright." Thaddeus took a deep breath and closed his eyes. He straightened his spine, crossed his legs, and faced his palms up on his knees. *"Uvu,"* he whispered, pushing the power he felt from his heart and dragon into each word, thinking only about aging the apple in his hand from underripe, to ripe, to overripe. At first, he wasn't sure anything had changed. Then he felt the hard, taut apple skin in his hands grow larger and softer until he smelled the sourness of rotting fruit and felt juice running down his hand.

Syrinthia exclaimed and clapped. "That's it! Thaddeus, that's incredible."

But he wasn't finished; neither was the apple.

As juice dried and the apple shriveled, he became connected to the apple and the life inside it. Amazement filled him. Life didn't end with the apple's rotting. It simply became scattered, uncontained. It hovered around his hand, looking for somewhere to stay. He felt the urge to let the life seep into himself, to give him strength and vitality, but he also felt the apple's desire to do something else.

He leaned into the unfamiliar calling and let the life decide where it wanted to go. Only facilitating speed to the process, Thaddeus felt the rest of the apple disintegrate into compost, soil teaming with life ready to move to another plant or creature.

Syrinthia gasped, but he ignored the distraction. He let the dirt fall and gather above where he sensed a seed hid just under fallen leaves. The small fern plant seed held a fierce tenacity to live, to enter the circle of life.

"Nothing is ever destroyed," Thaddeus whispered in awe as he encouraged the fern's new roots and gave it all the nutrients it needed from his magic. In only a moment, a little sprout uncurled from the ground. "It's only redirected into something else."

He opened his eyes to see a beautiful fern plant by his side, almost the size of a mature plant. "Everything is in a constant circle of creation and destruction, and life, death, and rebirth is at the center of it all."

Syrinthia met his eyes, extending a shaking hand to the fern in disbelief. "How did you—" She shook her head.

Thaddeus shrugged. He didn't want to say, lest he be wrong, but he had an idea of why he'd resonated more with magic concerning plants than anything else they'd practiced the last few weeks.

Syrinthia ran her fingers across the fern, laughter escaping her lips as she admired it. "The Zoic blood," she whispered.

"I think so." Thaddeus' face burned red. He wasn't used to being open about his ancestry. Though he knew Naraina had noticed the changes in his body and mind, she hadn't talked to him about Zoics or magic since the day she welcomed him into her private garden. He sensed a growing fear in her, but when he confronted her, she only smiled through misty eyes and whispered how proud she was before retreating to the garden for the rest of the day. Thaddeus knew sometimes she went to places he could not follow.

"You *think* so? No, Thaddeus, there is no *thinking* about this. This is your Zoic magic, absolutely. No other Duvarharian I know has been able to complete a growth and decay cycle as effortlessly as you. The only ones I've seen come close have been training for tens of years. Most of them have dedicated their lives to the plants. They say you have to feel them." She took his hands in hers, her fierce stare making his stomach twist and flutter. "Tell me. Did you *feel* the plant?"

Thaddeus opened his mouth to say "no" but hesitated. He had felt the plant as if he'd *been* the plant, reaching for sunlight and soil. He still felt it—its leaves turning the light and soil into nutrients, its desire to propagate, and a small longing to be part of something greater, a part of the forest ecosystem around itself.

"Yes," Thaddeus whispered. "I did. I was the plant. I still am, somehow. I think I'll always be connected to it." His hand strayed to the plant, and it leaned toward him.

Syrinthia sat back, her eyes lighting up. "You're amazing, Thaddeus, rider of Kyrell. Truly amazing."

Don't praise him too much, little one. He's got a thing for attention and positive reinforcement. You'll make his ego too big for me to carry. Kyrell blew out a heavy breath and shifted his position on a thick growth of moss.

"I wish I could tap into my magic the way you can." Syrinthia's voice carried a note of bitter sorrow.

"I'm sure you can. We just have to keep working on it."

Shrugging, she tore at a piece of moss. Thaddeus had to bite his tongue to keep from saying the moss didn't appreciate that.

Not sure I'm not going to like my magic much if I hear plants complaining every time a deer steps on them.

Kyrell only growled in amusement.

"I think that's the problem, though." Eyes trained on the ground, Syrinthia let out a deep breath.

"What do you mean?"

"When I reach for my unique magic, I can't find it. Not like I can the Duvarharian magic. That's how I first realized I'm different. Do you feel a difference between your magic?"

Slowly, Thaddeus shook his head. "Not really. It feels different, but only like my right leg feels different than my left. It doesn't feel like someone's else's magic or like it's a different *Kind* of magic." A frown dipped his lips. He hadn't anticipated it being so hard to explain.

The elite have long fancy words to describe this, which I think is ridiculous anyway, Kyrell grumbled. *Do we describe the way we breathe and how it feels in our lungs?*

Sometimes.

Hardly. Kyrell huffed and narrowed his eyes.

"Well, mine is different. *Very* different." Syrinthia's voice cracked with emotion. Her eyes misted.

He wished he could hug her or make her laugh—anything to dispel her overwhelming sadness—but he knew it wouldn't fix anything, not really. But he wanted her to lean into him and find solace in his company the way he did in hers. His hands balled into fists.

"When I reach for it, it not only flees from me but disappears entirely, like a forgotten dream."

"I think I understand. Like how sometimes it's easier to see something at dusk if you're looking next to it rather than directly at it."

She nodded. "Something like that."

His brows furrowed. "There must be a way to tap into it. You can't be the only Duvarharian who has experienced this."

"What if I'm not Duvarharian?"

Their eyes met, and Thaddeus found he didn't have an answer. This was the second time she'd mentioned not being Duvarharian. But if she wasn't Duvarharian, what was she?

His lips opened then closed. "I don't know." It pained him how her shoulders fell, eyes fixed jealously on the fern he'd grown.

"Thaddeus!" Naraina's voice broke the tension. "Thaddeus, you have a delivery!"

Eyes wide, he turned to Kyrell, who'd leapt to his feet. "Do you think . . .?"

Syrinthia whooped and took off running. Kyrell chased after her, gliding above logs she jumped over.

"Wait up!" Laugher burst from his lips as he ran after them, struggling to catch up. Begrudgingly, he admitted Syrinthia was far more physically capable. He'd slacked in his physical training since leaving the academy. But if this delivery was what he hoped . . . it could change everything.

Breathless, he slowed to a jog as he approached the house. Kyrell, Syrinthia, and his mother were standing next to the wrapped object, which leaned against the house.

"The man specifically instructed no one to touch it before Thaddeus." A confused smile light up Naraina's eyes. "What is it?"

Words failed him as emotion rushed through his veins.

Syrinthia answered, a broad grin on her face. "Something very special."

Silence enveloped them as Thaddeus moved to the large object. Though he wasn't sure he could lift it, let alone wield it, he knew he would grow into it. If nothing else, it would motivate him to take training more seriously.

Heart racing, he dropped to his knees, overwhelmed by the moment. His mother's hand rested on his shoulder in reassurance. Syrinthia crouched next to him, whispering in his ear, "You deserve this. This is your destiny. Take hold of it and who you're meant to be."

When he looked into her eyes, she once again felt like something other, something *more*, than Duvarharian. Her eyes glowed gold, the certainty in her words sounding prophetic. Strength rushed through him, and he nodded.

"Thank you." He took the wrapped object into his arms. At first, the weight nearly crushed him. Then it shifted, making itself smaller and lighter. No longer did it dwarf him; instead, it matched him perfectly. Confused, he let the cloth fall away.

When his eyes landed on the black blade, little milky veins streaking through it, he lost himself in it. Without effort, magic rushed from his hands, twining in and around the handle. It infused itself into the weapon until the veins turned purple and pulsed with his heartbeat. Acid slipped down the handle and around his fingers then disappeared. The metal vibrated with energy, life, and the desire to defend, fight, and kill.

Purple tears blurred his vision. Kyrell threw back his head and roared. Thaddeus wished he could join him. After bonding with Kyrell, he hadn't thought it possible to feel any more whole; now he felt the same again.

"That's . . ." Naraina sucked in a deep breath as he looked up at her. She nodded, trying to maintain her smile. "That's a Dragon Blade, isn't it?"

Thaddeus' heart plummeted. If she knew it was a Dragon Blade, then she also knew how illegal and dangerous they were. With the back of his hand, he dried his eyes. He tripped over his own words, trying to explain, but she shook her head, tears glinting in her eyes.

"No. It's alright, it's better I don't know." She pressed her soft lips to the top of his head. "I'm so proud of you, Thaddeus. So proud." Though her voice and eyes shone with pride as she went back inside, he couldn't help but wonder if her fear outweighed the joy.

"I'm no better than my brother," Thaddeus whispered. The realization struck him like a tidal wave, threatening to dislodge him from the confidence and personal growth he'd obtained by embracing his ancestry. He had engaged in illegal activities, same as Thanatos. They were both bringing disgrace and danger to their families and themselves.

"No, Thaddeus. You're—"

"Yes, I am." His tone sounded harsher than he meant, but he didn't back down. "In fact, I'm worse. At least Thanatos' drugs and drinking won't bring harm upon the rest of them family like my choices could."

She didn't have an answer.

They sat in silence, seconds stretching to minutes. As much as he wanted to cast away the weapon, it was as much a part of him as his arm. If the fear of danger forced him to relinquish it, wouldn't he also have to give up Kyrell? He'd made his decisions, and, for better or worse, he was stuck with their consequences.

"You're not the same," Syrinthia finally whispered. "Thanatos is selfish. He breaks the law because he's self-centered, attention seeking, and lost. He doesn't know who he is or what he wants to be. The things he participates in—the drugs, drinking, gambling—they all perpetuate the society surrounding the games that would steal your mother and torture her in an arena. Do you understand? In a way, he kills your mother every day. But you are trying to save her." Thaddeus didn't realize she was crying until he turned to her. "So don't ever say you're anything like your brother, Thaddeus, rider of Kyrell. Because I'm betting my freedom, my *life*, that you're not. Understand?"

Now he cried too. Kyrell moved closer to wrap them in his wings. "I understand. I am not my brother."

Syrinthia nodded, trying to dry her eyes. "Good. Thank you. Are you hungry?"

Thaddeus' eyes widened at the sudden change of topic, but then he noticed how his stomach grumbled. Laughing through tears, he jumped to his feet, holding out a hand to help her up. "Yes, I think I am."

She brushed herself off and sniffed. "Good. I am too. And I'm tired of thinking and feeling and practicing magic. Let's get food and eat in on the bridge so we can watch the *Qeźujeluch*."

Thaddeus grinned. "I think that's a wonderful idea."

THE SUNS HAD ONLY just set by the time he and Kyrell returned home. While he and Syrinthia ate their meal of fried cabbage rolls at the bridge, Kyrell had flown back to *Ulufakush* to visit and hunt. Both were full and content as they approached the house. For a moment before they entered, Thaddeus appreciated the peace and calm.

Hopefully, your mother didn't tell Quinlan about the blade.

Thaddeus shook his head. *I think she knows it's enough for my father* to deal with us being Zoic and having a dragon. I think he can only tolerate so much.

Just as he reached for the doorknob, an angry voice shouted inside, "Do not interrupt me, Quinlan, Duvarharia's disappointment!"

Thaddeus' blood ran cold. He knew that voice. Memories of the cloaked man raced through his mind. His stomach turned. "That *dasuun qevab*," he hissed. He wanted to burst inside and cut him to pieces; his Dragon Blade hummed, eager for bloodshed.

No! Kyrell's voice froze his body. *You must not kill without cause. Your parents can protect themselves. And frankly, the cloaked man isn't wrong. Quinlan is a fool.*

Thaddeus tore at his lips with his sharp teeth. Kyrell was right, of course. But burning hatred flared in his chest; the urge to defend his mother and stop the torment of his family remained impossible to ignore. *What if he attacks? Quinlan may be a fool, but he's still my father. I will not stand idle if things grow violent.*

That goes without saying, but you've much to learn from being silent and unseen. You've no idea how strong that creature is nor whether he is armed or has powerful magic. Learn first, then decide if you should fight.

Thaddeus' body relaxed slightly; the hand hovering over his blade fell to his side. For a moment, he stared down the door, hands flexing then balling. "Okay." Some of the rage eased from his veins as he released a deep breath. "I'll crawl in my window, pray Thanatos isn't home, and find a way to eavesdrop again."

I'll stay in the forest to observe him when he leaves.

Do you know where Krystallos is?

He was at Ulufakush *when I was, feasting with the elders and speaking in their Council. I doubt he'll be home for a while.*

Thaddeus nodded before skirting around the house, choosing to go through the garden rather than by the pond in front of the windows. Krystallos being gone was both a relief and a concern. Without time to dwell on it, he focused on the trip through the garden, out the gate, across slippery rocks in the creek, around the other side of their house, and to his window. Praying his wet boots wouldn't damage the wood floors once inside, he used magic to unlock the window and pushed it open, standing on large planter rocks to reach.

Hoping he hadn't missed too much of the conversation, he slipped through the window. Taking off his boots but leaving his stockings, he sneaked down the hall, across the glass walkway, and to the cracked-open hallway door.

Rage filled his blood again as their conversation came into focus.

His mother was crying, his father sounding on the verge of tears. "He's just a boy," Naraina pleaded.

Nausea washed over Thaddeus as he looked through the crack; she sat on her knees at the man's feet, clinging to his robe.

The man didn't spare her even a glance. "Just a boy? How foolish. Neither of them are *just boys*. They're deadly to Duvarharia. You knew they would be before they were born, yet you went through with it anyway. And don't tell me again that you aren't at fault because you're a Zoic, Naraina. That's the most pathetic excuse I've heard. Anyone with any intelligence knows Duvarharians have been breeding with Wyriders for thousands of years since the Golden Age. Why do you think weak riders like your husband are dominating the outer cities of Duvarharia? Our blood is poisoned with yours. None of us are pure anymore, not even me!"

That eshisifoz džou. Thaddeus reached for his axe, but Kyrell stopped him again.

Don't be rash and let this opportunity pass.

If he touches her...

Then rip his head from his body and crush his heart under your foot. Until then, wait.

Thaddeus turned his attention back to them.

"But that's just it!" Naraina took to her feet, hands pressed together as she begged. "He's leaning into being Zoic! He's embracing being a

Terrestrial. He helps in the garden and is learning how to listen to the plants and coax disease from them. He sits with me in the flowers of our ancestors and lets the magic flow through him. Quinlan hasn't let him learn any Duvarharian magic, absolutely forbids it. Right, Quinlan?"

She turned to her husband. His face seemed paler than Thaddeus had ever seen. For a moment, he expected his father to betray him. Then he whispered, "That's true. I've done my best to keep him from anything Duvarharian. He may not like the games, but he hates the Duvarharians because of them and wants nothing to do with them. He believes the Shadows of Light are the faction running the games and that Joad facilitated them. He'd much rather run off to Wyerland and find his mother's tribe than live here."

Thaddeus' heart skipped. *He believes what he's saying. Why? How does he know I've learned about the Shadows of Light?*

When he looked back to Naraina and saw the shining relief in her eyes, he knew. Whatever he'd told her, she'd relayed to Quinlan in a way that twisted Thaddeus' words and protected him from the creature. His father only truly lied about Kyrell.

The cloaked figure pushed Naraina aside and moved to Quinlan. "Are you speaking the truth?"

Quinlan didn't move away, standing his ground against the disfigured form. "Yes. I am."

Darkness swirled from the man's cloak and gripped Quinlan's legs. "You better be, Quinlan, fool of an ambassador. I have eyes and ears everywhere. If I catch even whispers that anything you've said isn't true, that you've been hiding something from me . . ." A bony hand reached out, clawing dangerously close to Quinlan's throat. "I won't hesitate to gut you throat to groin, but only after I've done the same to both your cursed sons and the *shekkamubs*. Do you understand?"

Thaddeus' hand found his axe. Before he could burst through the door, the cloaked man turned toward the hall, a hiss escaping his lips. Then a loud crack resounded around the room, and he disappeared.

Heart thundering, Thaddeus staggered. *He's gone. He's gone. He's gone.* Panic clawed at his throat and mind.

Thaddeus.

He's gone. He disappeared. He's gone!

Thaddeus!

Thaddeus snapped out of the shock. The chaos of his father yelling and his mother crying crashed down on him like a wall of fire. His tears mirrored his mother's as he gasped for air, struggling to force his shaking legs to carry him into the seclusion of his room.

He's gone through Dasejuba, *which means he's extremely powerful and most likely bonded. If you'd jumped out a second earlier, he would've killed you immediately. Do you understand the severity of this?*

Thaddeus couldn't answer. The severity was clear: the cloaked man was most likely the *Jen-Jibuz's* leader, which meant his enemy was infinitely more powerful than he.

His Dragon Blade axe suddenly felt small. The magic he'd performed earlier now seemed weak, useless. He rushed back to his room, slipped out the window, and clung to Kyrell pitifully, wrapped in leathery wings.

Deep breaths, Thaddeus. Deep breaths. I'll never let anything hurt you. You are safe.

But they knew it was a lie. They could make thousands of promises, but in the end, their enemy would easily desecrate them in each other's arms.

Thaddeus' nails dug into Kyrell's thick, scaly leg. With broken breath, he forced his thoughts into words. "Kyrell?"

The dragon rumbled low.

"We have to leave." Fresh tears spilled down his face as a new emotion overcame him. "We can't—" His voice caught on emotion as he squeezed his eyes shut. "We can't stay here."

Kyrell pressed his warm head to Thaddeus' back and pushed him closer. For a moment, they were silent, feeling the weight of the other's emotions. *No,* Kyrell finally whispered, *we cannot. If we do, we won't survive long enough to gain freedom for anyone, including ourselves.*

The thought of leaving his mother, the only home he'd ever known, the woods he found solace in, Syrinthia, and all the progress they'd made with magic terrified him. So did the realization of how little he knew about Duvarharia. He'd never been outside their city, besides the small countryside nearby. To reach the Dragon Palace would be at *least* a two-day journey. He didn't even know where to start. Should they try to bypass the mountains? Was that possible? Or would they have to fly high above them in the freezing, low oxygen altitude? They hadn't flown together for more than an hour at a time. Were they capable of making the journey?

You worry too much.

Thaddeus shook violently; he was freezing despite being pressed against warm dragon scales. Tears pooled in his eyes despite his curses against them. *I'm weak,* he thought to himself.

No. You're a child.

That did nothing to console Thaddeus. How could he combat being a child? He couldn't grow up faster. If he waited to grow up, he'd be stuck trying to survive in a city that seemed to grow smaller and more dangerous each day.

There's no shame in being weak or a child, Thaddeus. More people in the world should be childlike and soft. You were born to be someone soft, someone full of life, love, and opportunity, but you were forced to become someone else. You must give yourself grace as you make your transformation.

But will we survive long enough to make it?

Kyrell didn't have an answer. They sat in dark silence until the moons had noticeably shifted in the sky.

How will we make money? I've no savings, and I've never worked a job. How does one go about doing all that?

I don't know.

Thaddeus' heart dropped, but he couldn't expect a dragon who grew up on an isolated island to know how the world of riders functioned.

But I know we'll find out. We're resilient. You're intelligent, and I'm strong. I'm sure the Dragon Palace has many jobs for young riders like yourself.

Thaddeus nodded. Their conversation felt so overwhelming and distant, as if they weren't really planning on leaving.

But we are. We have to.

I know. Thaddeus squeezed his eyes against the thought and gripped Kyrell's leg harder. *I know.*

Thaddeus almost dozed off in the silence that followed until Kyrell moved his leg. *Wake up, little one.*

Eyes snapping open, Thaddeus shook his head, trying to blink away the drowsiness.

Thaddeus . . .

He wasn't sure he liked Kyrell's tone.

I think we need to leave tonight.

Chapter 25

Thaddeus' heart raced. "Tonight?" His voice sounded as small and unsure as he felt.

Kyrell rumbled. *We cannot fly during the day if we want to stay hidden. Your skills and strength won't grow overnight, but the danger we face from the Jen-Jibuź can and will. We leave tonight, or we risk not leaving at all. I'm not strong enough to properly sense our surroundings, but a strange magical presence lingers here as if we're being watched.*

Thaddeus scanned their yard and pond. Little white and pink lily flowers shone eerily in the moonlight; water shimmered and reflected the stars. Beyond the pond stretched a manicured lawn and terraces before the forest. A shiver ran down his spine; the darkness of the forest could effortlessly hide any number of monstrosities. By traveling through *Dasejuba*, the cloaked man proved he didn't need doors or windows to violate their safety. Worse, Krystallos still remained at the dragon island.

"Do you think the creature will come back tonight?"

Do you want to find out?

He didn't.

"Okay, okay." Thaddeus took several deep breaths to calm himself. None of them succeeded. *We can do this. We have to.*

Standing on unsure feet, his stomach threatening to reject the food he and Syrinthia had shared, he grasped the windowsill and pulled himself through. He made a mental list of what he'd need. *Shirts, shoes, a cloak, pants, undergarments, wool in case we fly over the mountains . . .*

He didn't even own a travel pack big enough to fit it all. Kyrell constantly reminded him to leave useless items behind. He found a tattered old pack buried in his closet, but it fit even less than expected. In the end, he settled for one set of clothes besides what he wore, the wool cloak, and one extra pair of boots. All memorabilia would stay. An empty hole opened in his chest.

I'll have nothing.

You'll have freedom.

Thaddeus now knew why Naraina chose to live in fear rather than try to move somewhere safer.

We need food.

I sense Thanatos coming home. Try not to bump into him in the living room. He seems to be under a drug's influence and in a wretched mood.

Thaddeus rushed to the kitchen as quickly and quietly as possible. He'd just pulled the door nearly closed when Thanatos opened the front door. The *bang* of the door hitting the wall made Thaddeus' skin crawl.

Thanatos barely managed to shut the door as he stumbled into the living room, singing under his breath as he made his way to the hallway. He didn't even try to be courteous to his sleeping family. Thaddeus listened to him stumble drunkenly until their door shut behind him. Shoving down his anger, Thaddeus turned back to the difficult task of packing food.

Nothing that needs to be chilled, Kyrell reminded. *No meat, no milk, no cheese. Nothing in glass jars because they might break in flight.*

Few options remained. Exasperation rose in his chest, threatening to paralyze him. He attempted to push away the panic for now. He'd have plenty of time to think of all the reasons this was a bad idea on their way to the Dragon Palace.

In his concentration, he didn't notice the garden door open.

"Thaddeus?"

He jumped, clamping a hand over his mouth to stifle his gasp. "Mother."

She stepped inside and hurried to him, cupping his face in her hands. "Thaddeus, what are you doing? Why are you packing?" The panic in her voice broke him.

"Mother, I . . ." Collapsing in her arms, he let the panic, sadness, and fear overcome him. Heavy sobs shook his shoulders.

"Oh, *kinätyä segi*." She cried with him as she crushed him in her arms, stroking his hair.

"I have to go," he whispered as she drew away to look at his face. "I have to."

The pain in her eyes overwhelmed him. She only nodded. "I know. I know." Pressing a firm, quick kiss to his forehead, she started gathering a small supply of dried food. The portions sat in soft magic-made-glass containers and sealed against decay.

"I make these for your father's trips. Take plenty. And this as well." She passed him a collapsible strainer with a funnel at the bottom, explaining, "It's for filtering unclean water if you can't use magic. It's not perfect, but it's good in a pinch."

Thaddeus' eyes widened as he gathered the supplies; he hadn't known half of them existed. He got the uncomfortable impression she'd made these in preparation for something like this, either for him or for herself. His skin prickled. *Had she ever wanted to run away?*

"You'll want to go south, almost to the Lota Woods but not quite. They probably wouldn't let you cross the border anyway, but that's alright. It's going to take you almost three days with how small Kyrell is. And then—"

"Mother?" He hardly heard what she was saying. The thought of leaving her consumed him. "*Mother.*"

She finally stopped talking. "Thaddeus?"

All resolve in him shattered when their gazes met. "I don't want to go." The words spilled from his lips followed by a strangled sob. Everything he'd ever known, he'd be leaving behind. *I'm just a kid. I don't want to leave. I don't want to do this alone.*

"I don't want you to either."

They collapsed into each other's arms, wishing for the moment to never end.

"I don't want to fight to survive, I just . . ." He couldn't put words around the longing inside him.

"I know, *tyän*, I know. But you must."

I must.

We must.

They drew apart. "I don't want to see either of my boys grow up. I want you to stay small and easy to protect, but—" She shook her head, trying to dry her tears. "But I can't wish that. You've already grown up. I fear what may happen to you out there alone, traveling across the wilderness or in the big city of the Dragon Palace, but Thaddeus . . ." She cupped his face in her hands, forcing him to focus only on her. "I fear more what may happen to you if you stay. Do you understand?"

He nodded. "I'm trying to."

She crushed him in her arms again, hand behind his head, and rocked back and forth. "Alright," she whispered. "Let's finish packing."

Before dread, uncertainty, and fear set into their limbs and paralyzed them forever, they moved into the living room, clothes in his arms, food and a small pouch of *femi* in hers.

Outside, Kyrell paced nervously. *The strength of that presence draws near. We don't have much time left.*

"The forest is nervous. It fears something." Naraina tightened the straps on Kyrell's neck, unease in her voice. The ominous presence weighed on them all.

"Take this." She pulled a salve from her pocket. "It's good for riding sores. I wish we could get you a saddle, but ..."

Smiling as best he could, he secured the salve in a satchel pocket. A rider required a bonding license and their dragon's measurements to get a saddle made. Obtaining a saddle for Kyrell would be impossible without an illegal saddle maker—an occupation punished by death.

Before he mounted Kyrell, he rested a hand on Naraina's shoulder. "Tell Syrinthia why I'm leaving." The words dragged across his lips, tasting like poison. Their dinner together felt like years ago, not hours. He didn't even feel like the same person. When did everything change so much?

Naraina nodded. "Of course. I will. But Thaddeus?"

"Yes?"

"Don't you think she already knows why?"

A dark silence stretched between them. Memories of things Syrinthia had said—the conversation between her, Rakland, and the cloaked man—rushed through his mind. She knew. She had to. This struggle encompassed them both. Only she was stuck inside the *Jen-Jibuź* while he was stuck looking in. They fought together, but alone. "I think so." His heart plunged into a sea of dread and regret.

Time slipped through his fingers, but he couldn't bring himself to leave.

We have to go, Thaddeus. Soft pity hung in Kyrell's thoughts though his tone was stern.

"Do you think . . ." The words tumbled from Thaddeus' lips as he tasted the salt of his own tears. "Do you think she could go with me?" He already knew the answer, but it drove a knife into his heart regardless.

"No, she can't."

He tried to protest, but she interrupted him. "She's too deep in the cult. They won't let her leave, not without tracking her down and fighting for her. If she goes, you won't stand a chance at finding what you seek. You have to let her go."

His heart broke all over again. Biting his lip against his grief, he shook his head, watching his tears collect on the dirt.

"You're not strong enough to protect her. Not yet." She squeezed his hand in hers. "Promise me you won't go after her."

Part of him wanted to curse her for her doubt, but part of him knew she was right. "I promise," he finally whispered, and his heart hated him for it.

Naraina pulled him into her embrace one last time; her arms felt like a warp in time, providing one last place he felt safe, loved, and understood. He clung to the feeling.

When she released him and he mounted Kyrell, his house no longer looked like a home. It looked like a prison. For the first time in his life, he finally felt free. "I'll come back. I promise."

She nodded as Kyrell crouched to the ground. "I'll be here. I always will be."

"I love you."

"I love you, my *zinligil-shätshgugi*."

With a powerful shove, Kyrell launched himself into the air, faltering only a moment before his strong wings carried them higher. In only a few minutes, his mother appeared as a mere speck next to one of many houses dotting the land below.

Kyrell circled, finding an air current traveling south, and before Thaddeus could even believe it, they were on their way to the Dragon Palace.

THEY STOPPED TO REST early in the morning after successfully passing Peace Haven's border patrol—a much smaller battalion of warriors than the government let on. *Does the reduced protection have anything to do with the prevalence of the games? And why are the elites and council members responsible for border patrol turning a blind eye?*

The questions put a bad taste in Thaddeus' mouth, and despite finding a soft patch of moss to lie in, he couldn't sleep more than a few minutes at a time.

Exhausted, Kyrell fell asleep almost as soon as he touched the ground. He didn't wake until the suns dipped low, boasting a monstrously bad attitude and complaints of aching wings and sores from Thaddeus' boots.

Thaddeus sagged under the crushing doubt and dread that their less-than-pleasant start brought.

After an hour of arguing and complaining, they finally took to the skies again.

At least the moons are full and the clouds sparse.

Kyrell snarled. *At least.*

But Kyrell wasn't the only one hurt and tired. The lack of a saddle forced Thaddeus to use unfamiliar muscles to keep from sliding off Kyrell's smooth scales. Angry blisters opened on his inner thighs, and though his mother's salve provided some comfort, he knew the fiery pain would return tomorrow.

Around midnight, they descended and pitched camp in open valley plains under a starry sky. Lacking an appetite, Thaddeus snacked on dehydrated food he hadn't the energy to rehydrate. Despite his grumbling stomach, Kyrell quickly fell asleep, oblivious to the world.

Though they'd spent all day arguing and grumbling or giving one another the silent treatment, Thaddeus' eyes misted when he looked at his soulmate. Scooting closer, he lifted Kyrell's wing and slipped underneath, feeling the dragon's warmth on his skin. Acid crawled across Kyrell's scales as if with a life of its own.

As he laid his head on Kyrell's leg, every inch of his body protesting any movement, he felt Kyrell's breathing slow and his heart slip into a steady, restful beat.

Tomorrow will be better, Thaddeus promised. His eyes slipped shut and his tangled, windblown hair fell into his face. A rock dug into his side, but it paled compared to the rest of his pain. *It has to be better.*

WITH THE ARRIVAL of the morning suns, they woke to a deer standing at the edge of their camp. The doe's eyes widened, and she paused before bounding away. Thaddeus made Kyrell promise he wouldn't eat her. Though Kyrell didn't eat that doe, he did follow her to the herd and snatched another for his meal.

Thaddeus found the energy to heat water for the food. The small meal satisfied his hunger and offered humble comfort before they took to the skies again.

Do you think we'll arrive by nightfall?

Kyrell shook his head. Banking his wings, he caught a new air current. *It's possible. The wind is strong today. Can you see the border from here?*

Thaddeus squinted into the horizon. A strange blue shimmer flickered in the light miles away. *I think so. Is it the blue shimmer?*

It's much more colorful than blue.

Not to me.

Then look through my eyes.

Thaddeus frowned, completely unprepared as his consciousness completely merged with his dragon's body.

Confusion exploded through them, knocking them from the sky. They plummeted until Kyrell managed to steady himself. *Gods of all, you don't have to possess my entire body, little one. Just my eyes. And don't forget about your own body. I'd hate to race the ground to catch you.*

He apologized but refused to be discouraged. The experience of seeing through a dragon's eyes consumed his attention, more incredible than anything he could've dreamed. Every color shone more vibrant and intense, and the distance Kyrell could see seemed limitless.

Thaddeus focused on the horizon where he'd seen the blue shimmer and saw Kyrell was right. The border contained more than a blue shimmer; thousands of colors wove together, even ones he'd never seen before nor could describe. It wavered and moved like wind through grass or water against a shore and extended into the sky as far as he could see, forming what looked like a giant dome over them.

Does it go all the way around Duvarharia?

According to legend.

How is that possible? Thaddeus drew back into his own body, the border reduced to a simple shimmer again.

I don't know. Most magic fades after the caster dies. For this to have lasted so long is a testament to the skills we've lost as Duvarharians. That kind of power is unfathomable these days. Replicating the border's magic has been attempted and failed for hundreds of years. No one's come remotely close to the expanse of such a shield. With what we know, it's impossible.

Thaddeus shook his head, unable to tear his eyes from the border and his memory of its colors and brilliance. *Somehow, we'll find a way to bring back that power.* He clung to that hope, trying not to let the doubt brewing inside him surface.

As they soared above it, Thaddeus couldn't comprehend Duvarharia's vastness. Throughout the day, Thaddeus spotted more and more townships and cities scattered across the lush landscape, the population growing denser the farther south they flew before turning west. Even the steep mountains seemed to burst with life, lacking the miles of snow he'd expected.

The border creates a greenhouse effect that keeps everything warm and lush all year, despite Duvarharia's more northern position in Ventronovia.

That makes sense. After all, dragons are cold-blooded, right?

Yes, but a few Kinds like the Peak Dragons are an exception. They're why most of the mountains still have snow and ice at their peaks.

They watched other dragons dive through the clouds; some flew as high as them—presumably traveling as well—but most flew much farther below, closer to the cities they lived in. Thaddeus' heart swelled as the dragons chased each other. A couple riders jumped into the sky, freefalling until their dragons swooped under them.

The suns slipped behind clouds, scattering brilliant colors across the sky and lighting everything with gold and pink. All problems and worries faded with the vanishing day.

Have you ever seen such a beautiful sight?

Awe stirred in Kyrell's heart. *No. I don't think I have. But I imagine the Dragon Palace is even more magnificent.*

Thaddeus squeezed his eyes shut, hands tightening on Kyrell's spines. *If it is, I don't think I'll be able to handle it.*

You'll have to. Kyrell roared in laughter. *I refuse to carry your limp body while I explore on my own.*

The wind stole away the sound of Thaddeus' own laughter. *Alright, then I'll only partially faint from joy.*

That's a start. And don't you have need to make a Qumokuhe *or* Suźuheb *for that woman?*

The last conversation between him and Anrid rushed through his mind. *Yes, I want to make her a* Suźuheb. He made a mental note not to forget again. *That way she can feel how amazing this place is, not just see a picture of it.*

As the suns began their nightly descent, a small rise of mountains grew just ahead. Thaddeus wanted to fly over them before stopping for the night, though Kyrell feared he would collapse in exhaustion before they made it.

I just want to see what's on the other side.

Kyrell groaned. *I do too, but you're not the one who's been carrying us both and keeping us aloft for hours.*

Desperation filled Thaddeus' heart. "Please, Kyrell. *Please.* I just want to see if the Dragon Palace is there, just to see it before the suns set. We don't have to finish the journey tonight. I just want to *see.*"

Though he cursed, Kyrell's thoughts swelled with anticipation. After an extra burst of energy from them both, they rose higher into the sky, mountains rushing away beneath them.

Thaddeus kept his fingers crossed, daring to hope he would see the Palace, dragons, *freedom*. When they crested over the tip of the small mountain, the sight stole his breath away.

The mountains around them descended sharply into a huge valley full of giant rock formations towering into the skies, nearly as high as the mountains themselves. The faces and bodies of gigantic carved statues of dragons and riders faced the mountains and border as if guarding the heart of Duvarharia. Entire ecosystems spilled down from large plateaus on the rocks, each miniature mountain entirely different from the next. Some shimmered with color—towering trees with pink and blue leaves and rivers as red as fire. Others appeared ice cold—trees with black leaves and water as clear as glass.

Below, the colossal structures and statues plains sprawled across the terrain. Rolling hills and smaller mountains dotted with livestock, farms, and towns sped under Kyrell and Thaddeus. Strange hills interrupted the plains as they rose steeply into the sky then immediately plummeted back down.

Massive steps, cliffs, and ledges had been carved from the steep mountains, and each individual hill boasted its own town. Thaddeus marveled at how perfect an environment the steep cities created for the hundreds of dragons flying to and from the many ledges and hills. Not an inch of the landscape went wasted.

Kyrell began to circle lower, but before they passed below the height of the sharp hills, Thaddeus saw the suns sparkle on a towering structure far in the distance.

Kyrell, it's . . . All words and thoughts abandoned his mind.

The Dragon Palace.

PART 4
The Dragon Palace

PART 4

The Dragon Palace

Chapter 26

Dragon Palace, Duvarharia
Year: Rumi 5310 Q.RJ.M

Set on a massive stone plateau miles away stood the largest city sprawl Thaddeus had ever seen. It overtook the plateau like a mass of crawling vines, and at its center rose the steeples of the Dragon Palace itself.

The palace, primarily constructed of white granite, defied all the laws of gravity and architecture his mother had spoken so much about. The structure extended into the clouds, giving the illusion that it was built from the clouds themselves. The spaces towering between the expanses of granite and some of the smaller buildings looked to be made of pure, shining magic.

Then it disappeared behind a hill as they continued their descent. Thaddeus' lungs were tight. A lump lodged in his throat as he committed the beautiful image to memory. He never wanted to forget how the suns' light sparkled on the city.

Silence fell over them as they processed a flood of emotion. Thaddeus felt foolish for worrying that the Dragon Palace wouldn't be as incredible as he'd dreamed or that he wouldn't be welcome. An overwhelming sense of belonging settled into his heart.

Finally, Kyrell broke the silence as they glided between the hills. *I can find us a secluded place in the trees below if you'd like. Unless you want to find an inn.*

An inn? He wasn't sure what he'd been planning—certainly not that they'd be sleeping on rocks and exposed to the weather—but the possibility of them staying in the cities or even on the plateau itself seemed overwhelming. *I don't know if we have the money for it.*

I don't think we should let money stop us from enjoying this. We can beg at the Palace later if we must. Let's get some good rest tonight.

Heart racing, Thaddeus nodded and gestured to a particularly quaint city on one of the smaller hills. *Let's try there.*

Uncertainty filled their hearts. Thaddeus almost expected a patrol dragon to arrest them for flying and bonding without a permit. The attack never came.

Instead, they were greeted by steep cobblestone streets snaking around the small hill. Decorated buildings were carved into the rock above and below the roads. Skylights lit the dark, cavernous rooms. Plants grew abundantly from cracks in the old roads; flowering vines snaked up buildings and around clotheslines that stretched high across the roads, dotted with tunics of styles and colors Thaddeus wasn't used to seeing.

Finally, they found a landing pad carved from rock and lined with wooden railings. Decorative posts held warm energy lights and colorful flags to lead the way.

When Kyrell's claws clicked against the ground and they jerked to a halt, Thaddeus felt as if he'd arrived home.

Before he dismounted, a rider with long, sharp ears, feminine features, and a strong body sauntered over to him. A dragonet followed close behind. Thaddeus tilted his head, unsure if the rider was male or female, before deciding he looked more masculine. The rider pulled out a clipboard and conjured a very active *juufu*.

Thaddeus' heart lurched. *Is he going to fine us? Did we–*

His fears subsided when the rider swept his incredibly long hair over his shoulders and beamed, his dual-colored eyes sparkling. "Hello, rider," he drawled in a thick, unfamiliar accent. "Are you a *susengube* or resident?"

Blinking back his surprise, Thaddeus slowly slid off Kyrell's neck. "Oh, um, a visitor, actually."

The rider's brows furrowed with confusion.

Thaddeus' face burned when he realized the rider didn't understand him. "Oh! Um, a visitor? I'm not from here. I'm from Peace Haven."

His face brightened as his *juufu*—a magic-conjured pen—scribbled faster. "Peace Haven!" The city sounded very different on his tongue. "You're a *susengube*. I'm Bo. Follow me." Bo gestured excitedly as his dragonet stumbled in front of him, nearly tripping them both.

Should we follow?

Kyrell shrugged. *I don't see why not. I sense no malicious intent, and I doubt that little dragonet could best me in a fight should anything take foul.*

Agreeing, Thaddeus jogged to catch up with Bo as they stepped onto the bustling, brightly lit streets. Energy lights hung low over their heads, giving a warm, welcoming glow to the quaint brick and stone buildings, flowering vines, colorful window shades, and stained glass.

Their guide spoke rapidly as he gestured to random oddities like a bakery, an old statue of two dragons and a rider, a blacksmith shop, and even more shops and buildings that Thaddeus couldn't understand.

I had no idea the language would be so different.

I didn't either. He's speaking in an almost seamless mix of common tongue and Ancient Duvarharian. Additionally, the mix of accents is impressive.

Thaddeus thought maybe only Bo spoke that way, but as he caught snippets of the laughter and conversation around him, he quickly realized he and Kyrell were the abnormalities. *Fascinating.*

They even act so differently. Kyrell nodded to two Duvarharians standing in front of a shop. One held a woven blanket of a dragon, the other held a bag of money; their dragons played on the roof of the building next to them. The riders stood inches apart—despite a height difference of two feet—yelling boisterously. Only seconds later, they exchanged money and a blanket and hugged, laughing like old friends.

Indeed, they do. But they didn't find the strangeness alienating; somehow, it felt comforting.

Thaddeus turned his attention to the buildings, realizing they stood larger and farther apart than at first impression. Nearly everything accommodated small to medium dragons. Streets and alleys stretched wide. Extra-large doors on the second or third floors boasted landing pads. Thaddeus marveled at the infrastructure. By sinking their buildings into the ground and cliffsides, the Duvarharians had found a way to make exorbitantly large buildings without using copious amounts of building material.

Thaddeus snapped back from his thoughts when their guide gestured to a grand building, announcing something that included "inn."

Thaddeus bowed to thank Bo, but to his surprise, the Duvarharian wasn't finished.

"Best inn in the city . . . two thousand years old . . . hosted the Lord and Lady of the . . ."

Two thousand years? Thaddeus' eyes widened as he surveyed the building. Carved entirely out of rock, the inn stood apart from the other structures of cobblestone, brick, or granite. Huge pillars stood outside holding up a landing pad nearly fifty feet above them.

It seems far-fetched, but the style and construction look *vastly different from the rest of the city.*

Thaddeus agreed.

"Hello, *susengube*?" Bo waved his hand in front of Thaddeus' face, his blue and green eyes darting back and forth between Thaddeus and Kyrell.

"Sorry, what was that?"

With naturally long green nails matching the color of his dragonet, Bo poked Thaddeus in the stomach. "Hungry?"

"Oh! Yes. Very." His mother's dehydrated food, while suitable for traveling, left Thaddeus desperately wishing for fresh meat and vegetables. "Do you know a place with good meat?"

Bo's eyes widened. "Meat?"

Thaddeus' face burned. "Yes? Meat please. I'd like a steak or—"

Bo clapped excitedly. "We have the best meat!" Grasping Thaddeus' hand, his touch colder than he expected, he pulled him into the inn.

Decorated more elaborately than the outside, the interior boasted of polished rock in which Thaddeus could faintly see his reflection. Huge pillars circled the room. Two massive staircases curved around the grand entrance hall and up to the second floor. Couches, chairs, lounges, and an abundance of potted plants tastefully embellished the room, giving each sitting space a sense of privacy. Retractable doors in the ceiling opened to an indoor landing pad on the second floor. Paths crossed overhead to the outdoor landing pad. Dragons and riders came and went as they pleased. Though the aura bordered on frantic, a sense of peace resonated through the air; these Duvarharians were busy but not stressed.

"Come! Dinner has begun." His hand still gripping Thaddeus' wrist, Bo weaved his way through the crowd. Many riders and dragons called out, "Hello, Bo!" in their strange accents.

Before he could process the chaos, Thaddeus found himself seated at one of many sectioned tables in a large restaurant. Different sizes of tables sat at ground height; seating sank into the floor, large enough for a rider and their dragon. Thaddeus had never felt so small before. Clearly, dragons' convenience presided over their riders'.

"They take your order, I make it. Only the best meat in all Duvarharia!" Without another word, their self-imposed guide sprinted off to the kitchen, leaving Thaddeus stunned with no idea what to expect.

"How are you today?" A young rider dismounted her dragon, pulled out a paper, and conjured a *juufu*.

"Wonderful, actually." Thaddeus sighed in relief when her clear pronunciation made her Duvarharian accent less noticeable.

Pointing to the drink menu, she encouraged him to try the *lurujmu fuju*. When he bashfully stated he wasn't old enough for the liquor, she dismissed him with wave. "You are a rider. Duvarharia is yours to enjoy."

Thaddeus' heart raced as emotion rose into his throat. *We're accepted here, Kyrell.* But Kyrell was far too busy flirting with the server's dragon to respond.

A lovely dragon. Says her mother is a Seduction Dragon and her father an Acid Dragon like me.

Thaddeus smirked at his dragon's giddiness. "Stricken, aren't you?"

Kyrell snarled. *No.* But the twitch in his tail gave him away.

After only a few minutes, his drink arrived. He marveled at the richness of the first stip. Full of wood tones and caramel vanilla, the drink slipped smoothly down his throat. He welcomed the warmth and relaxation it created.

By the time his food arrived, his appetite had been properly whetted by the drink and tantalizing aromas. As soon as his teeth sank into the tender steak, he knew he'd found his new favorite meat.

What if it's dragon meat?

Thaddeus rolled his eyes as he savored another forkful. *I seriously doubt it is.*

You never know. Kyrell's rumbling laugh vibrated through the floor. *See how they bring in fresh kills for the dragons? If we stay here tonight, I want to have breakfast tomorrow.*

Thaddeus followed Kyrell's gaze as a delivery dragon lowered a limp deer onto the table in front of a white dragon who reminded Thaddeus of a swan: beautiful and graceful, but dangerous.

"As long as this meal doesn't take all our money, then we'll do that."

Lucky. You get food, and I don't.

"You ate an entire deer last night."

Kyrell grumbled.

After picking the crumbs off his plate and downing the last of the *lurujmu fuju*, refusing multiple offers for refills, he sat back against the cushions, feeling very full and sleepy.

"Did you enjoy?" Bo returned, his nearly white hair now half tied up, a small stick stuck through it to hold the knot in place.

With drowsy eyes, Thaddeus took his hand and allowed himself to be helped to his feet. His head spun. When he looked at Bo, he couldn't decide if he looked more beautiful or handsome. Before he could stop himself, he patted his shoulder. "Your food is as magnificent as you are stunning."

Bo beamed and bowed back. "I have been serving guests . . . my inn . . . three hundred years. It never ceases to please . . . give visitors the most authentic Duvarharian experience."

Thaddeus' eyebrows rose. "Three hundred years," he whispered as he placed his arm around Kyrell for balance.

Bo nodded, his own dragonet chirping and clumsily prancing around Kyrell's legs. ". . . show you to your room." He waved another dragon over.

Digging his hand into his pocket, Thaddeus pulled out a few gold *femi*; it seemed an offering too small. How could any amount be enough to compensate being welcomed into the Dragon Palace valley as a free rider? Tears rose into his eyes.

Bo closed his fist around the money and kissed his hand. "No, rider. Simply enjoy. You have no worries in my home."

Before Thaddeus could properly thank the strange rider, the other dragon quickly ushered him and Kyrell into the grand hall, up the stairs, down stretching halls, and to a grand door that opened into a cavernous room big enough for Kyrell to fly in. A skylight above let in a stream of moonlight. Thaddeus thought the stars shone brighter over this side of Duvarharia. *Although that could just be the lurujmu fuju.*

Without hesitation, the Acid Dragon jumped onto the properly sized bed and flopped down, rolling in the soft furs.

Barely taking time to shut the huge door that swung easily on greased hinges, Thaddeus stripped of his travel-weary clothes. A hot spring bathtub, cut straight into the rock floor on the other side of the room, steamed with fresh water; vine-covered lattice surrounded it for privacy. Though the sight tempted him, his weary body begged for sleep.

He slid under a fur on the bed and curled between the legs and wings of his dragon.

Then a wave of homesickness washed over him. This was his first night spent in a bed not his own, his first dinner alone in a restaurant, and one of many nights he wouldn't get to kiss his mother's cheeks and wish her goodnight. Thinking about his mother brought tears to his eyes as he gripped Kyrell's claws.

I miss her too, little one. The emptiness Kyrell felt mirrored his own. They comforted each other. Eventually, the tears slowed then stopped.

His mother wanted him here where he was free—where his bond with an Acid Dragon and lack of a bonding license didn't matter. Where no one gave a second thought to the axe he carried. A place where the buildings still remembered the Golden Age and their owners remembered old traditions.

His heart swelled as he processed this moment—a moment when all his dreams had come true.

Eventually, his mind filled with wonderful dreams in which he learned all the ways of the old Dragon Riders, traveled Duvarharia to free the Zoics, and helped them and Duvarharians bond with dragons and learn magic. The sleep that encompassed him was the first fulfilling rest he'd had in over a year.

CHAPTER 27

THADDEUS WOKE TO A trumpeting dragon and was thrown into a fit of confusion. Kyrell's wing stirred over him, and Thaddeus frowned. *Kyrell, how are you inside?* Then he bolted upright. *The Dragon Palace!*

With a loud holler, Thaddeus leapt out of bed and danced, spinning until his head throbbed and he couldn't keep himself upright. Collapsing back onto the bed in a fit of laughter, he shoved against Kyrell; he woke with a groan.

Can't you be excited later? What happened to sleeping in and enjoying this room?

"Kyrell, you lazy lump of meat. We're in the capital of Duvarharia. Anything that is worth seeing is out *there*, not here in bed. Besides, I thought you wanted to have breakfast served to you at one of those fancy tables? I think they had *rusadabe*."

Now Kyrell pranced about the room, roaring in excitement. *Well, when you put it like that . . . I'm ready right now. Let's go.*

Kyrell hopped from foot to foot in anticipation, but Thaddeus only laughed as he dipped a toe into the hot spring bath. "If we go down covered in dirt and with tangled, greasy hair, we'll be frowned upon." Deciding the bath wasn't too hot, Thaddeus quickly stripped and stepped into the natural rock basin. He marveled at how the water circulated through the basin then filtered out through pipes leading into the wall. "I suggest you clean up too. You look a sight."

Kyrell stood straighter, licking his claws. *I do not. A dragon never looks messy.* But doubt laced his thoughts.

Slapping the water, Thaddeus gestured to the large pool. "They set us in a room that fits you. Come enjoy it a moment, and then we'll feast on breakfast until our purse runs out."

Though he grumbled, it only took one dip of his tail for Kyrell to realize how much he wanted a long hot soak. Growling low in satisfaction, he lowered himself into the deep end, leaving only his snout and eyes above water. *It feels incredibly good on my muscles.*

Thaddeus agreed.

After soaking far longer than intended, they quickly dried, dressed, and made their way downstairs. Now that he was well rested and could fully take in his surroundings, he felt underdressed. All the riders wore bright, flamboyant clothes; many had furs with exotic colors and armor that sparkled in the morning light streaming through the landing pad. Looking down at his plain black pants and green shirt, he promised himself the moment he found a way to make money, he'd buy real Duvarharian clothes.

Minutes later, they sat before a freshly killed *rusadabe*, which Kyrell devoured in less time than it took for Thaddeus to order a steeped fruit drink.

They made their way to the front desk, explaining how they hadn't checked in because someone named Bo had given them a room and food.

The receptionist smiled and nodded, unfazed. The receipt she handed them only listed their breakfast. When he insisted on paying for the room, she waved her hand and said something that clearly meant he wasn't to argue.

Feeling extremely grateful, though wishing he could thank Bo somehow, they strode into the morning suns, pockets still full of *femi* and hearts of new beginnings.

"Where shall we go first, Kyrell?" But Thaddeus already knew the answer they shared in their heart.

The Dragon Palace!

THE FLIGHT LEAVING the small island-like hill was extraordinarily pleasant. The morning air, crisp and cool, carried many other riders and dragons. Some flew in patterned formations, others carried huge slings of materials and goods. The vastness of the culture and lifestyles was overwhelming.

And I used to think Peace Haven was big.

Traveling will certainly change your perspective on life.

Indeed.

They saw many other Acid Dragons, a couple Poison Dragons, and other "dangerous" types. Peace slowly replaced their familiar unease. They were accepted here.

As they continued their flight to the Dragon Palace's main city on the Stone Plateau, Thaddeus realized how much he'd underestimated the size of it. No matter how long they flew, it seemed the city stayed the same size, like a far-off mountain.

Thaddeus. Look up.

Thaddeus turned his gaze to the clouds above. His heart skipped a beat. *By the stars. Is that . . . ?* A city built out of clouds seemed too absurd.

It is. The Cloud Dragons, or Imagination Dragons as they're often called, have built their homes into their element. I know many Kinds do this, like Crystal, Stone, and Peak Dragons, but I had no idea they could fashion solid buildings out of clouds.

Thaddeus shook his head as he watched very solid riders and dragons walk across vapor bridges extending between cloud islands. Plants grew from pots and planters, and even granite statues stood on the fluffy white condensation.

"Unbelievable," he whispered.

After navigating thick air traffic, they descended to the Stone Plateau's landing zone. Just before they landed, Thaddeus took in all he could of the Plateau's polished surface and the thousands of years old intricate carvings and symbols etched into it. Though he felt the ground too sacred to walk upon, in minutes they'd landed, and his feet hit stone.

With no particular plan in mind except wanting to see all they could, they set off into the city. After getting separated more than once, Thaddeus ended up riding upon Kyrell's neck, only dismounting when he saw something particularly interesting.

Vendors selling a variety of wares lined the streets, many extending into shops behind them. Thaddeus found a tradesman offering Duvarharian clothes he liked and walked away with a significantly lighter purse.

In testament to how important the Duvarharians thought the sky, thousands of kites fluttered high in the wind. Some, though crude, danced proudly in the air in an array of colors, ducking and dodging each other as they fought for the highest altitude. Others were lavishly decorated, strung one after the other on a single string over a hundred kites long. Fairy Dragons mischievously ducked and weaved through the kite strings, using the wind from their wings to either change the kites' direction or lift them higher.

When lunchtime came, the vendors stopped, and the restaurants filled. Thaddeus found himself in a particularly long line in front of a food stand, but when he smelled the delicacies ahead, he didn't bother moving.

When his turn to order came, he found himself faced with an enormous list of street fried rolls. Because many of the options contained ingredients with which he wasn't familiar, he asked for their most popular roll and was quickly handed a steaming roll stuffed with crab, an unusual vegetable, and cabbage. Spicy sauce dripped down his fingers as he bit into it with a satisfied sigh.

The afternoon suns had just begun to dip behind the Palace, shedding shade upon the city, when Thaddeus finally mustered the courage to march straight toward the inner city and Palace.

The farther into the city they ventured, the larger the streets and buildings became. Houses with perfect lawns replaced market booths. The homes, no longer made of white granite or polished stone, appeared crystalline, but Thaddeus felt the hum of energy only magic possessed.

"How're they able to manifest their magic into something so solid and tangible?"

Kyrell brushed his wing against a wall, watching as red magic sparks scattered to the ground before disappearing. *I think it has something to do with all energy being matter and all matter being energy. When you have power over one, you have power over the other, and they are interchangeable. The energy in the world is what makes the Duvarharian mastery of matter possible. The matter exists apart from you until you access the energy tying everything together. Then it is child's play to make something like this.*

Thaddeus' eyes widened. "How do you know so much about Duvarharian magic?"

Kyrell shrugged and licked his lips as a horse and cart passed by. *I spent a lot of time in the caves of Ulufakush. I didn't have much else to do but learn and simmer in bitterness.*

Thaddeus nodded. "Understandable."

Their attention turned to the looming Palace, still a ways before them but overwhelming with its size and complexity.

Each layer was connected to other towers and buildings by intricate suspension bridges. Waterfalls fell from balconies into artificial rivers, ponds, and swimming pools before spilling over again. The waters' spray caught the suns' light, scattering rainbows across the clouds and white granite. Flowering vines and bushes engulfed portions of the Palace and filled the air with intoxicating perfumes, attracting small pollinating dragons, hummingbirds, butterflies, bees, and other unfamiliar and exotic creatures. One section of the Palace burned in endless flames and coals that never spread. The very top of the Palace spilled into the cloud land above.

When they reached the thick wall surrounding the palace, separating it from the inner city, Thaddeus expected to find the gold gates shut.

They stood open and guardless.

Skeptical, Thaddeus maneuvered toward them. As they stepped across the threshold, not a single alarm sounded nor an eye batted in their direction.

Releasing a deep breath, Thaddeus skipped and playfully punched his dragon. Though Kyrell pretended to be unimpressed that they made it through, Thaddeus knew otherwise.

The scale of the palace grounds inside the wall put the inner city to shame. Thaddeus couldn't fathom the size of the dragon who would warrant the gargantuan scale of the streets, buildings, and doorways.

"Do you feel very small?"

Kyrell's tail swished as he rotated his head, trying to see everything at once. *Very much so.*

Each step they took felt like drops in an ocean as they moved through the courtyard. Time seemed to move incredibly slow, as if they were ants in a rider's home and not a rider in their own city.

Other dragons and their riders milled around the gardens at a similarly lazy pace. It seemed the best activity in the Palace was simply relaxing.

Many of the waterfalls, fountains, and waterways snaked into the intricate garden, collecting into a lake in its center. Exotic animals swam in the water. Some seemed familiar, like the swans, until they beat their not two but *four* wings. Some of the birds changed from white to blue to pink then back to white so subtly, he wondered if it was a trick of the light.

When they reached the edge of the lake, he gazed into its depths, expecting to see his murky reflection staring back. Instead, he was staring hundreds of feet into a chasm full of crystal-clear water teaming with life. Little *Qežujeluch* lizards darted in and out of the lily pads and clumps of colorful algae.

"Kyrell!" Thaddeus jumped, unable to contain his excitement as a creature raced toward the surface. "An Aqua Dragon!"

The Aqua Dragon leaped out of the water; its scales and water droplets filled the air with a cool breeze and a thousand little rainbows. For a moment, the creature seemed suspended, as if defying time and gravity. In place of legs and wings grew four fin-like appendages and a myriad of smaller fins along its body. Their eyes locked. Thaddeus' heart skipped before the moment shattered as the dragon dove back into the lake. It disappeared with nothing more than a ripple in the glass-like water; Thaddeus wondered if he had seen it at all.

Not caring that he and the new clothes he bought were now damp, Thaddeus took one last look into the seemingly bottomless lake, imagining what other wonders it hid.

Past the courtyard, they came to another long street weaving through the Palace toward what Thaddeus assumed to be the main building—the one that vanished into clouds. He wanted to go inside and explore, but his eye caught a sign. He turned to see if he had read it right.

"Tell me you're seeing what I'm seeing."

Kyrell turned to the old sign hanging above massive carved wooden doors. *Library of the Golden Age.* He nodded. *So it is.*

All thoughts of the Palace's majesty dissipated as Thaddeus rushed to the library doors, praying they were unlocked. When he pulled on the handle, the door swung with a long, loud groan. He instantly recognized the scent of old paper and tablets.

"Hello?" The word echoed in the darkness. No one answered. "Hello? Is anyone here? May I come in?" Silence. Shrugging, he stepped inside. Kyrell followed close behind.

The bright suns streaming behind them lit up the dust particles in the air before illuminating a circular desk about thirty feet inside. Everything else remained in darkness. What appeared to be lantern light dotted the vast room, but he wasn't sure until he shut the large door.

Heart pounding, Thaddeus waited, motionless, until his eyes adjusted. Sure enough, lanterns on each of the enormous shelves did offer weak lighting along with rows of dirty skylights. A stained-glass dome arched over the center of the library, but so much dust and grime covered it that he couldn't even decipher what art the colored glass depicted.

"Hello?" His whisper echoed as loudly as a shout. This time, something farther in the room moved.

I sense a presence here.

What is it?

Kyrell shook his head, stepped forward, and took a deep breath. *A dragon, I think. But their presence is weak.*

Are they dying?

Kyrell shook his head.

Sleeping?

Again no.

Should we find them?

Kyrell looked to the extensive floor-to-ceiling bookcases. Platforms on the second and third floors extended across the bookcases and held rolling ladders.

Must be a million books here. I doubt we'd find what we're looking for, even if we searched for a hundred years.

Kyrell was right. As much as Thaddeus wanted to sit in this library and never leave, to learn all he could from the ancient tomes, he would need help if he wanted to find anything specific about the Shadows of Light.

Do you know where the dragon is?

Kyrell shrugged his wings. *We can find out.*

Each step they took echoed like hooves on stone despite how quiet they tried to be. *I couldn't imagine trying to study or read in here without the librarian getting mad every time you breathe.*

Kyrell rumbled in amusement.

There.

Kyrell followed Thaddeus' finger. At the end of the long center aisle, past study tables and between the curved stairs to the second story, rested a gigantic dragon tail. It snaked under the second story balcony into pitch darkness. Despite the library's unfathomable size—big enough for several adult dragons to move about—this dragon's tail made it all look small.

Toying with his damp shirt hem, unsure what he should say or even if the dragon would help them, Thaddeus attempted to swallow his fear and crept closer. When they were near enough to touch its tail, he paused, unwilling to step any closer.

What should I do?

Ask for help. Politely.

Mouth dry, Thaddeus licked his lips and cleared his throat. "Um . . ." His voice sounded so small. "Excuse me?"

Silence.

Maybe louder.

Maybe they're dead. Maybe they're not even the librarian.

Kyrell rolled his eyes, tail waving impatiently. *Louder, Thaddeus. I'm sure they're just sleeping. Probably an old crotchety dragon who won't help unless you show determination.*

Thaddeus cleared his throat again. "*Ahem.* Hello? Are you the librarian?"

Nothing.

Oh, for the gods' sake! Kyrell stood on his back legs, stretched out his wings, and released the loudest screeching roar Thaddeus ever heard from him. Though he plugged his ears, the ringing didn't stop. His eyes watered from the pain.

Dust fell from the books. A few of the tables behind them shuddered.

Kyrell stamped his claws and shook his head. *There.*

I don't think—

A vicious growl rumbled the walls; a few dozen books fell from their shelves, and Thaddeus thought the glass dome would collapse. The tail snaked into darkness. The sound of scrapping claws filled the hall before a long hiss mingled with it. *Who dares wake me? You cannot take me away! I am the books' guardian, and I will fight till death to protect them!* The dragon's head came from the darkness. Her jaw hanging open, displaying shining rows of fangs. Her white eyes darted from side to side.

She's blind. Thaddeus's heart melted. Old as this dragon was, she was still determined to protect the knowledge of the past from radicals who would rather watch it burn. "Dragon, we are not here to take your library or you. We seek to make use of it, to learn of the old ways, traditions, and magic."

Though the dragon stilled, a constant tremor gently shook her head and wings. Turning, she focused dead eyes on him and Kyrell. Her voice effortlessly penetrated their minds, shoving aside what little mental protection they had. *Is this true? Or have you come to trick me? I will not hesitate to eat you if you're lying.* A large blue tongue snaked out of her mouth. Thaddeus took a few steps back.

"I promise. Look." Then he did something he'd only ever done with Kyrell. Closing his eyes, he opened his thoughts and memories, exposing everything: him learning about the Shadows of Light, wanting everyone to be free again, and wanting himself, Kyrell, Syrinthia, and Naraina to be safe.

The dragon's body relaxed as she felt Thaddeus' true intentions. *I see.* Her deep sigh washed over Thaddeus as a cold breeze. *Thaddeus, rider of Kyrell, I'm honored to meet you. I've been waiting for you for a very, very long time.*

Chapter 28

Thaddeus' skin prickled as his stomach flipped. "Waiting for me?"

The dragon nodded and groaned as she pulled herself from the small nook she'd wedged into. First her neck snaked out—longer than most dragons Thaddeus had seen—then her lanky legs, one wing, then another, then two more, before finally her back two legs and tail spilled into the hall. When the dragon rose on her hind legs and tried to stretch her four wings, the walls groaned from being pushed against. The dragon snarled, unsatisfied. *Ridiculous room is too small for a good stretch. They should've made it larger.*

Thaddeus wasn't sure how they could've. Just one of this dragon's claws was as tall as Thaddeus. Even Kyrell was only the size of the dragon's head.

With a loud string of cracks, she extended her back before hunching like a stretching cat. When the dragon finally adjusted to the new space, shamelessly smashing tables and chairs in the process and forcing Thaddeus and Kyrell to move far away, she finally answered his question.

Yes, Thaddeus. I have been waiting for you.

"Why? How?"

The dragon sniffed, looking for Thaddeus and Kyrell; her face stopped only a few feet away. Thin, opaque eyelids blinked. Though her eyes were colorless and sightless, when Thaddeus looked into them, he felt as if he were staring into the dragon's very soul. It wasn't hard to imagine a day when she'd been small enough to fly through the library, assisting other Duvarharians in their search for knowledge.

A man claiming to be the speaker of the Dragon Prophecy visited me nearly eighty years ago. He told me the prophesized savior would come seeking knowledge of the Shadows of Light. When I asked what they looked like, he said he was still trying to uncover the rest of the prophecy, which the elites had hidden. But he'd spoken to Centaurs and learned from their star readings of the predicted locations where the rest of the Dragon Prophecy would be revealed to Quinlan the prophet. That's where he learned that someone wanting to bring back the old ways would come here.

Thaddeus' heart raced as fast as his limitless questions. Countless myths and rumors regarding the Dragon Prophecy circulated Duvarharia, but not many truly believed them. "Quinlan? My father? He's the prophet of the Dragon Prophecy? It's *real*?"

The dragon scoffed. *Is it real? Of course, it's real. The Great Lord himself came to us one hundred years ago to predict the renewal of Duvarharia. He said a traitor would bring evil from the north, but a savior would be born to stop them–someone who would bring back the old magic–and a helper would arrive for them. Quinlan the scribe was the prophet it was revealed to. He was only a boy at the time, apprenticed to Tabor the Master Scientific Recorder.*

But after the prophecy, the Palace elites promoted him to Ambassador to keep watch on him and all the prophecies that followed. They've kept the prophecy a secret from everyone; they don't even keep a known written record of it. Until the Speaker, no one knew anything about it. But he spread the news throughout the land, hoping to raise followers to bring the full prophecy to light and free Duvarharia from bondage.

Thaddeus stumbled into a chair. The old wood creaked under the stress. "My own father. The prophet of the Dragon Prophecy."

I thought it was a child's tale. Kyrell pressed his snout to Thaddeus' legs, comforting his rider as best he could.

"So did I. But that means—" A flurry of memories came rushing back. The cloaked man and Quinlan's conversations finally made sense.

He was more sure than ever that the cloaked man was the *Jen-Jibuź's* leader. Hot tears rose in Thaddeus' eyes. "They know I'm the savior of the prophecy, that I'm to bring back the old Duvarharia. That's why they didn't want me learning magic or bonding with a dragon. That's why my parents are being threatened by the *Jen-Jibuź*. The sect and schools like the Peace Haven academy are profiting from the games. They must know the evil of the prophecy is the games which originated in Wyerland in the north."

His fists balled until his knuckles turned white. Rage coursed through him. He was more involved in this conspiracy than he ever imagined; he wasn't just a victim, he was a plaything to them. "*Señekol!*"

Kyrell snarled. *If I could, I'd rip them apart limb from limb. The cloaked man and Quinlan both. They had no right to lie to you. Not only have they denied you your freedom, but they've kept you from your destiny!*

The old dragon bowed her head in sorrow. *I am sorry this breaks your spirit and heart so much. It was not my intention to tear apart your life. I only want to see Duvarharia be free like it was when this library was built, when I was young.*

Heavy sorrow replaced anger. "I cannot be full of rage. Rage causes one to do things he doesn't mean. I don't want to tear my father limb from limb. He's not all bad. He's protected me from the *Jen-Jibuź* and their leader—the cloaked man—and though I'm angry at him for keeping the prophecy from me, I don't know the full story. I don't know what the Great Lord said to him. I've only heard from the mouths of others who haven't heard the full prophecy."

The dragon lifted her head. *You speak with the wisdom of a rider from a hundred years ago and the heart of a child. You are more than I expected you to be.*

Thaddeus wiped away his tears and stood. "I want to do what's right. I've seen the devastation this confusion has brought. Yes, the evil must've come from the Wyriders; yes, they hate Duvarharians, but I'm living testament that not all Wyriders are bad. No matter what they've done in the past, no one should be slaughtered in cages for entertainment."

Kyrell drew closer, his hot breath filling Thaddeus with strength.

"But even then, I can't be mad at the Duvarharians. They're told Zoics are abominations or animals with nothing to contradict that. It's the same with the *Jen-Jibuź*; they may have come from the Shadows of Light but that doesn't make the original religion evil. It means we don't know enough about our history and the people around us to make proper moral decisions. Syrinthia is in the sect, and she isn't evil. I must assume she's not the only one. I have to think differently if I want true change."

The two dragons trumpeted in agreement.

But despite their support, he didn't know where to begin. What had started as a simple task to expose the academy's corruption and secrets was now something much bigger.

Your mind may not know where to begin, Thaddeus, rider of Kyrell, but your heart knows. You seek the power of love, the power of Shushequmok, *the Pure Ancient Magic. The only one who can truly teach you that is Joad himself, the keeper of the Pure Magic.*

A shiver ran down Thaddeus' back. "Joad . . . Isn't he the rider who founded the Shadows of Light?"

Some say he is more, some less, but yes. He is one and the same.

"How do I learn about him? How do I learn about the Shadows of Light?"

A small smile spread across her fangs. *By opening your heart and mind. I've already alerted the Shadows of your presence. Soon, they will come to you.*

Thaddeus looked to Kyrell, who nodded. *Let's do this without fear.*

Smiling, Thaddeus kissed his snout. *I agree.*

Now, shine your light into the darkness.

Gathering his magic, Thaddeus concentrated it into a shining orb of light and sent it to where the dragon had been sleeping. The light revealed hundreds of bookstacks the dragon had been lying among, guarding.

Until the Shadows find you, take these books. Gold energy wrapped around a small pile of books, lifting them into the air and carrying them to Thaddeus. They were so old and dusty that he couldn't read their titles, but the weight of their importance and knowledge was unmistakable.

Keep them safe. They're the very books the Jen-Jibuź *has been trying to destroy since they heard of the prophecy. I have kept them safe this long, but now it's up to you.*

Tears filled Thaddeus' eyes. "Thank you."

The dragon shook her head. *No, thank you, Thaddeus. Thank you for not giving up on us, on magic, the dragons, and the old ways. I long for the day when my library isn't attacked by new age radicals, I long for the day it is once again filled with magic, young dragons and riders like yourself, and hope. I believe you are our savior, even if we don't know the whole prophecy. I believe you will bring the renewal of the land.* She touched her snout to Thaddeus' head. *Please make it so.*

Thaddeus hugged the dragon and planted a kiss to her scales. "I will. I will."

Now depart and ready yourself for the Shadows.

Thaddeus mounted Kyrell, using magic to keep the books stacked in his lap. With their prize in hand and the mystery of the library uncovered, the walk was considerably shorter.

And, Thaddeus? Kyrell?

They turned back as the dragon lay down among the tables and chairs. *May the suns smile upon your presence.*

As do the stars sing upon yours, he and Kyrell responded in unison.

I'll see you on the other side.

Nodding, Thaddeus watched as the dragon's eyes slipped shut. Then they opened the doors and stepped back into the light.

The doors shut behind them with a definitive slam.

You don't think she– He quickly wiped away the tears gathering in his eyes.

Kyrell laid his head back against Thaddeus's leg. *Maybe. But be happy for her. She fulfilled what she wanted: to pass their knowledge to someone who cared. I think we came at just the right time.*

Thaddeus nodded. "You're right." He wasn't sure why he was crying over the passing of a creature he'd just met. But an undeniable, gaping hole opened inside him where he'd once felt the dragon's presence. He felt as if the fabric of reality itself had torn and he'd been charged with holding the weight of it shut.

Let's enjoy this day and celebrate in honor of her life.

"I didn't ask for her name."

I think she was too old to remember.

A solemn silence settled over them as they backtracked through the gardens, taking one last glance at the infinite lake. Thaddeus no longer desired to visit the main building of the Palace. Its illusion of grandeur had faded now that he knew it only held power hungry elites who didn't want the Duvarharians knowing the truth. The real magic was in the world, in the dragons and riders themselves, not in a stuck-up Palace, no matter how beautiful it was on the outside.

After a few long, quiet minutes, they exited the gates and were looking down the hills of buildings to the Stone Plateau far below. The streets and skies were full of riders, dragons, and the shimmer of their magic. This is what he wanted to remember most about Duvarharia, not a building.

Closing his eyes, hands held out and palms up, he began whispering his intentions in ancient Duvarharia. He'd convinced Syrinthia to teach him the spell just a few weeks ago and worked tirelessly to perfect it.

Slowly, his magic pulled particles from the air, the ground beneath him, the gold of the gates, and the plants decorating the gardens and shaped them into a thin tablet. There, they formed into colors, shapes, and emotions. It was full of longing and awe, fear and power, freedom and persecution, and beauty. This was Duvarharia—a country of new and old traditions, fighters and artists, and a people doing the best they could in an age that wanted to snuff them out.

When he opened his eyes, the tablet lay finished in his hands. Aesthetically, it was the exact likeness of what stretched before him, but as he turned it in the light, other images came forth: the suns setting over hilled cities, a kind innkeeper and his young dragonet, an Aqua Dragon leaping from a lake, the chaos of the market, and an old light blue dragon among dusty pages of a library. Each image radiated a different emotion; anyone who touched and looked at it would feel it. The only image missing was the Dragon Palace itself.

Ironic, isn't it.

"What?"

That you should come all this way to see the Palace, to make this image for Anrid, and then leave out the very thing that had once been so important to you both.

Thaddeus traced his fingers over the image, thinking back to the other *Qumokuheb* and *Suźuheb* he'd seen in the marketplace. The magic was so simple, anyone could master it—so simple, they shouldn't be worth anything. But here the marketplaces sold thousands a day to Duvarharians from cities like Peace Haven where most magic was illegal. He gripped the *Suźuheb* close to his chest. Being free to make his own *Suźuheb* and *Qumokuheb* was what made the Dragon Palace so special.

"I've learned a few things since then."

Kyrell nudged him playfully. *Thank goodness. You were such an ignorant little* daufa *back then.* He easily dodged Thaddeus' lazy punch.

"You weren't much better."

Perhaps not.

"Are you hungry?"

Kyrell rolled his eyes. *You know I'm not. But since you clearly are, let's find somewhere to eat.*

They descended into the city and found a restaurant that was large enough for Kyrell to enter but not nearly as grand as the one back at the inn. However, the food was just as delicious, though Thaddeus quickly found most authentic Duvarharian food was far spicier than he was used to.

After downing his second glass of *Fuse* milk, he dabbed at his eyes, ignoring Kyrell's rolling growls as he laughed.

"Don't make fun, Kyrell. You couldn't stand it either." Thaddeus took off his cloak, suddenly feeling much too warm, and wished he could take his boots off. His mouth still burned from saturating an entire mouthful of meat in the spicy sauce he'd been served.

"Are you alright?" Their server returned, worry in his eyes as he set down another glass of milk, which Thaddeus quickly started drinking.

Nodding, his upper lip coated in white, Thaddeus pointed to the sauce. "You should warn people before giving them the spiciest sauce you have."

The server frowned. "Spiciest?"

Thinking he wasn't understood because of his accent, Thaddeus started to explain. "Yes, the spic—"

"That's not our spiciest. That's our regular sauce."

They stared at each other, waiting for one to laugh and say he was joking. The moment never came.

"Are you alright?" the server asked again, brushing his orange hair from his eyes as he looked around, presumably for help.

Then Thaddeus burst out laughing, only worrying the server more.

You weakling! Kyrell rolled on his side growling with amusement. *You couldn't even stand the regular sauce!*

Tears streamed down Thaddeus' face as he clutched his stomach. "I'm fine, thank you," he finally managed to wheeze between laughs. "Just not as tough as I thought I was."

The server didn't look convinced that Thaddeus was indeed well but seemed relieved he could leave their table.

When Thaddeus paid for the meal, still chuckling with embarrassment, he made a mental promise to increase his spice tolerance.

They then searched for an inn. They were forced to pass a few because of their nearly empty purse, but one innkeeper directed them to the home of a family looking to make extra money. The family was incredibly hospitable and insisted on Thaddeus eating something. Not wanting to offend them and after seeing other tenants join the small meal, he slipped into a chair at the large table.

They asked him questions about Peace Haven. Though he didn't understand much because of their accents, he gathered that Peace Haven was considered an outcast city due to its extreme restrictions and geographical relation to the border. Though some of his answers dampened the mood of the gathering, they assured him they weren't upset but rather solemn for the life he was forced to live. They were livid when he mentioned how some dragon kinds were labeled as too dangerous and forbidden.

After the heartwarming gathering and a few delicious citrus pastries for dessert, the woman showed him to his room, talking nonstop and pointing out everything he could use and where the bathing room was. She had to explain several times that Kyrell could sleep on the balcony or roof before Thaddeus understood her, but she didn't seem annoyed in the slightest.

After changing into the loose, comfortable Duvarharian clothing he'd bought, he settled down on the balcony with Kyrell. The full moons combined with the warm street lanterns and small lights strung across the roads provided just enough light to read by.

He picked up one of the books the dragon librarian had given him and opened it to the first page. The aged spine crunched and creaked.

"I feel I'm violating it just by opening it. What if the pages fall out? I'd hate myself if I damaged these books in any way."

Kyrell licked his claws while eyeing the book. *Books are made to be read. The only real damage you could do to them is let them rot on a shelf.* He shrugged his wings. *They've lasted this long; I'm sure they'll last a little longer. The dragon gave them to you to read, not hide.*

"I know. You're right." He still hesitated before turning the pages.

Though the symbols appeared almost familiar, the message remained foreign. The book was almost entirely written in Ancient Duvarharian—

far more words than his limited vocabulary. Deciding it was useless until he'd studied the old language more, he chose another. This one was in the common tongue.

Though he only wanted to glance over the pages, the words captivated him. He ended up reading a chapter from the middle of the book before anything else. From what he understood, this was written by a firsthand witness. Most likely, this had been referenced for his book back home.

Time flew by as he let the book drag him in.

He learned the Dragon Palace had once been a hub of trade for all the surrounding countries like Ravenwood, Wyerland, the Human Domain, and even the northern country of Chinoi. Not only that, but it was also the leader in advanced science and technology. The book spoke of wonders Thaddeus couldn't even wrap his mind around like telescopes powerful enough to see the landscape of faraway planets and devices that built pathways through *Dasejuba* across time and space, making it possible for unskilled magic wielders to teleport themselves and objects. They'd even had powerful forms of communication that allowed someone in Duvarharia to speak directly to someone in the Human Domain.

But it also spoke of the events that led to the Golden Age's downfall: power, greed, and corruption. The rest, Thaddeus knew well. But he wanted to know what brought the Golden Age, so he turned to page one.

One of many accounts, this record spoke specifically of Joad, the harnesser of Pure Magic, the embodiment of the Creator, and the first Great Lord of the Golden Age. He'd been worshipped as a god and loved by his people. But the elites coveted his power and followers. Their attempt to kill him resulted in him and his followers using the Pure Magic to overtake the elites and establish the line of Lords—a bloodline supposedly still strong today.

His eyelids grew heavy as he tried to take in all the information. Picking up another book, he compared the accounts. Some of the information was the same, some of it wasn't. The second book stated the elites had succeeded in killing Joad and someone else had started the line of

Lords. He picked up a third book, only to find that it spoke nothing of the Creator or the Pure Magic, only that Joad had been the first Lord in the Golden Age.

Dismayed when the rest of the books were entirely in Ancient Duvarharia, Thaddeus pushed aside the pile, his head spinning.

"How am I supposed to bring back the Golden Age if I don't even know how it really started?" He leaned against his dragon, a deep sigh escaping his lips.

Kyrell wrapped his wing around his rider and curled his head next to him. *I don't know. But one thing they all have in common is the rider Joad. Whoever or whatever he was, he did establish the Shadows of Light, and we at least know they were the embodiment of the Golden Age. At least, before they were corrupted. If what the dragon said is correct, we may find our answers very soon.*

Thaddeus barely heard his dragon's thoughts as his mind drifted to dreamland. "I hope so," he murmured before sleep finally overtook him. His dreams were full of different men claiming to be Joad and fighting each other for the right to be called the *real* one.

CHAPTER 29

THADDEUS.

Groaning, he rolled over and pulled the soft furs over his head, blocking the light he'd suddenly become painfully aware of.

Thaddeus. Wake up.

Shaking his head, he tried to recapture the dream he'd been having of himself and his mother in a soft field of sunset-colored flowers. It smelled like home as they waited for Syrinthia to join them.

Thaddeus!

He jolted awake as Kyrell pushed him off the bed, letting him hit the ground with a dull *thud*. Thaddeus staggered to his feet, head reeling, arms flailing. "What in Susahu was that for? I'm absolutely exhausted, can't you see that?"

The Shadows of Light were here.

The words didn't sink into Thaddeus' mind as he tried to detangle his hair with his fingers. Stumbling around furs that had fallen around his ankles, he sat back on the bed, heart pounding as he tried to gain a grasp of his surroundings. "What do you mean?"

Kyrell nodded to the side table. A note rested on the mahogany wood.

Frowning, Thaddeus reached for it and squinted at the small parchment. He stared at the words for a long time until they made sense. It read: *Thaddeus, rider of Kyrell, we heard you have arrived and are looking for* us. *If you are who you say to be, meet us at this address at three in the afternoon, no later, or we will leave.* It was signed *the Shadows of Light* with a small note instructing him to burn it.

"How am I to remember the address if I burn it?" Growling, he tossed the note to the bed, still upset with Kyrell for the rude awakening.

I've memorized it. Besides, you don't have to burn it right away. Maybe get some clothes on first.

"Just give me a moment." Thaddeus hung his head in his hands. Nausea rolled into his throat. For a moment, he wondered if it was from last night's food, but had it been, his sleep would've been restless. This was something else.

You're homesick.

"No. I just—" The words stopped at the lump in his throat. Instead, he cried into his hands. Kyrell curled at his feet and rested his head on the bed beside him. Between breaths, Thaddeus managed to whisper, "Yes, I suppose I am. I miss my family, Syrinthia, and my home. I never realized how much it all meant to me."

Kyrell growled softly. *I'm sorry. Sometimes it takes moving away from something to truly see it. If it's any consolation, all will still be there when you return. You've only moved away for a little while.*

Thaddeus nodded, taking deep breaths to slow his heart. In this moment, he felt very small again, as if everything that'd happened to him in the last few months hadn't really happened at all and he was still just a young boy who wasn't sure where he belonged in the world.

I'm a little older now, a little more mature, but I still don't know where I belong.

But you are learning. You cannot discount that. You know you are Zoic, you know you are Duvarharian, and now you want to learn what it means to be a Shadow of Light. Kyrell gently nipped the note between his lips and placed it on Thaddeus' lap. *You may long for home, but home can wait. This cannot. It is almost noon, and you cannot be late. This is what we've been waiting for. A way out. A way forward.*

Drying his eyes, Thaddeus took the parchment and repeated the address until confident he'd never forget it. Then he held it over a match's flame, watching as it licked up toward his fingers until all that was left was the corner he held and a breath of ash. Then he dressed and packed, knowing he wouldn't be back tonight. He'd either join the Shadows of Light or go home.

On the way out of the home, he kissed the woman on her cheeks and gripped the man's forearm respectfully, thanking them for their overwhelming hospitality. They told him to come back and visit. He wished he could but didn't think it likely.

As he set off into the city once more, purpose hastened his step. When he stood in front of the tavern at the address he'd memorized, he paused only for a second to feel the weight of this moment upon his shoulders. Then he stepped inside.

The door shut behind him just as a city dragon trumpeted three times.

The tavern was larger than he'd expected and appeared to be more of a gathering place than just an eatery. A few families and their small children congregated in the space. Full bookshelves lined the walls. Other smaller rooms branched off the main room. The atmosphere was light, happy, and free. Any trepidation he'd felt before entering disappeared.

Thaddeus felt as if he'd stepped into a different world than the one bustling outside with loud street vendors and eccentric Duvarharians.

A young boy skipped over to him.

"Welcome to the Shadow Tavern. Are you here to meet with someone, or would you like a drink?"

"Um . . ." Thaddeus stared down into the boy's eyes, wondering what looked so familiar about them. "I think I'm here to meet someone, though I wouldn't oppose a water, if you don't mind."

The boy beamed and nodded before taking off to the bar, motioning for Thaddeus to follow.

Taking a seat on one of the stools that reminded him strongly of the ones in the kitchen back home, Thaddeus wrapped his fingers around the cold glass. "Thank you." Thaddeus took a long drink then stared at the boy when he realized he hadn't moved after handing him the glass.

"Is there something I can help you with?" Thaddeus looked around, expecting the boy's mother or father to come get him. No one seemed worried.

Instead, the little boy giggled and stepped up on what Thaddeus assumed was a shelf on the other side of the bar. "You're like me." The boy reached to touch Thaddeus' face. He surprised himself by letting the boy touch his hair.

"What do you mean?"

Kyrell moved closer, growling low to warn the boy that he wouldn't hesitate to rip his arm off should the need arise. The boy, however, didn't seem phased.

Don't be so violent, Kyrell.

I can't help it.

"You're . . ." The boy leaned in, glancing around as if about to share a dark secret. "You're a Zoic!"

Thaddeus' eye shot open along with his mouth. "I—what—how do you know?"

The boy smiled and closed his eyes, pulling gently on Thaddeus' hair. His little fingers grew small blooming flowers that he left in his tangles. The sweet fragrance of the flowers brought tears to Thaddeus' eyes. Now he knew why the boy's eyes were familiar.

"We always know. We're brothers!" Then his eyes darted to Kyrell. Instead of being afraid, he giggled, ran around the counter, and climbed onto Kyrell's back.

Kyrell's eyes widened as he stood very, very still.

Thaddeus ...

A laugh escaped Thaddeus' lips as he watched the little boy twine flowery vines around Kyrell's purple scales.

Why is it—he—on me?

Under his dragon's awkward uncertainty, Thaddeus sensed amusement. "I think he likes you."

The boy muttered something in a language that sounded like Naraina's before sliding off Kyrell's neck and standing in front of him. He reached for the dragon's face. Kyrell lowered his snout, eyes wide, as the boy planted his small hands on either side of Kyrell's jaw and stared very seriously into his eyes. "I'm going to bond with a beautiful dragon like you someday."

"But, if you're a Zoic, then—" Thaddeus stood behind the boy, his gaze locked onto Kyrell's. He couldn't bring himself to tell the boy pure-blooded Zoics couldn't bond with dragons.

"I know what you're going to say." The boy turned and scowled deeply. "And you're wrong." He turned back to Kyrell and threw himself against his large snout, tears running down his cheeks. "They say Joad stopped all that. They said he brings us back to the old dragon magic. They told me he'll bridge our souls, and I'll bond with a dragon."

Thaddeus knelt beside the boy, utterly confused.

"The Great Lord said Wyriders could bond with dragons?"

It was the boy's turn to be confused as he wiped tears from his shining green eyes. "Not the Great Lord. Joad."

"Is he not one and the same?"

"No." The boy looked at him as if he was crazy. Then he smiled. "You're new, aren't you?"

Thaddeus felt his face flush as he nodded.

Then the boy took his hands, his face bright again. "You're the rider they told me about! They're waiting for you."

Heart racing, Thaddeus let the small boy lead him toward the two families sitting with the playing children.

What's going on?

I know as much as you.

"Mommy! Daddy! The savior is here!"

Thaddeus felt as if he were in a dream.

As two of the parents stood, a shimmery image fell from them, scattering the illusion that they were just regular Duvarharians; they were anything but. Immediately, Thaddeus realized they were not only Zoics, but Zoics who had bonded with their respective plants. The male was a flower type—like Naraina—but the woman seemed to be bonded with a trapping plant of some sort. Their skin was green and leafy, their hair of vines and leaves. Small snapper plants grew from the woman's head like hair; they moved on their own, snapping at a fly that buzzed by. The magic faded from their children as well; they were just like their parents, only the plants on their fingertips and hair hadn't fully bloomed yet.

The other couple didn't change as they stood, but they were just as breathtaking. They stood nearly eight feet tall and had dramatically pointed ears, slitted pupils, skin like small dragon scales, and long clawlike nails. Their children, however, looked like regular Duvarharians despite them both having sapphire-blue hair like their parents.

Thaddeus' jaw dropped as the little Zoic boy ran to his father. The man swooped him up, speaking rapidly in the Wyrider language.

The Duvarharian man stepped forward and extended his forearm, a warmth in his eyes that contradicted the fierceness of his stance. "Hello, Thaddeus, rider of Kyrell." He nodded respectfully to Kyrell, who blew out a sigh of acknowledgement. "I am Hoyt, rider of Ingrida, and a Shadow of Light. May the suns smile upon your presence."

Swallowing past the dryness in his mouth, he forced himself to focus on his words rather than the creatures' strange beauty. Nodding, he managed to whisper, "As do the stars sing upon yours."

The Duvarharian woman introduced herself as Brunhild before ushering her children away, announcing that it was nap time. They protested ruthlessly, trying desperately to get a closer look at Kyrell. The Zoic male introduced himself as Arlan, rider of Fusa, and shuffled his children along with Brunhild's. The female Zoic introduced herself as Koa, rider of Pipere.

"Now, Thaddeus." Koa smiled brightly. "Why don't you tell us why you've come to the Dragon Palace?"

Moments later, Thaddeus found himself on the couch across from Koa and Hoyt, telling them of the last year and explaining that he'd come in search of the Shadows of Light, of a place to belong.

When he finished, silence fell over the room.

It seemed other guests had been listening as well. Thaddeus' face reddened as he curled in on himself, wishing the couch would swallow him whole. *Are they going to make fun of me?* The scathing laughter of the academy students rang in his ears and turned his stomach. His breath hooked in his lungs as he focused on one of the little toy dragons the children left behind.

Then a hand rested on his shoulder—warm, comforting, inviting. Looking up, he met Koa's gaze. Her snake-like hair moved gently around her head; the little mouths at the end of each vine reached out as if offering comfort. "May I sit next to you?"

Though he nodded and moved over, he wasn't sure he was fully comfortable with her being so near. Kyrell moved closer to make sure his presence hadn't been forgotten. Arlan motioned for the dragonet to move closer. "Come, dragon. You are just as much a part of this as he."

Kyrell tilted his head, eyes narrowing, before he moved in front of the couch and laid his head beside Thaddeus. Thaddeus touched his scales for comfort.

Koa smiled softly, her bright green eyes shimmering with the same red hue decorating the inside of the snappers' mouths. "You know what I am, correct? I know you're one of us too; I see it in your eyes."

Thaddeus nodded curtly, unable to tear his eyes away from the plant mouths and the small spines designed for trapping insects.

"So you know how unsafe it is for me to be here in the Dragon Palace."

He nodded again, subduing a laugh when the plants snapped at each other and nibbled on his shoulder. "You're a Zoic."

"And you remember how I introduced myself?"

A flutter of excitement flipped his stomach. "Koa, rider of Pipere.

You're bonded. With a dragon."

"Yes." She looked back at Hoyt, grinning. "I am."

Thaddeus tried to make sense of it all. "But how is that possible? You're a full-blooded Zoic, aren't you?"

"Correct. I moved here from the tribes of Wyerland. But it's possible because of Joad, because of the Shadows of Light. Hoyt came to Wyerland to teach Arlan and myself about Joad, to free us from the bondage we had been subjugated to, not just by the Duvarharians, but also by the Wyriders—the Aristocrat Wyriders." A strange look softened her eyes, one almost like awe. "You're an incredible person, Thaddeus. You understand the hardships of both Duvarharia and Wyerland, and yet your heart has turned to love, compassion, and knowledge rather than bitterness. That's an incredible feat for someone so young."

He was surprised to see tears in her eyes, mirroring his own. "Yes, but what can I do? I'm constantly reminded that I'm one small rider and that I'm not strong enough to protect myself, even with that." He pointed to his axe, which he'd leaned against the couch. "I'm not allowed to be seen in public with my dragon. I can't find anyone to teach me magic, so I have to practice in secret to protect myself against the *Jen-Jibuź*. Even now I'm afraid. What if you're part of them?"

Emotion choked his throat. He took deep breaths to release the fear, grateful to be rid of it, even for a moment. "The only reason I'm telling you all this now is because—because I don't know how much longer I can survive like this." Burying his face in his hands, he cried out his pain— all the nights he'd wished he wouldn't wake up, the days he'd wanted to run away and never come back, and the rage he felt when he'd seen Syrinthia's bruised body and the fear in his mother's eyes.

Koa's arms wrapped around him. The plants nibbled at his ear and gently wrapped around his head in little hugs of their own.

"Thaddeus, thank you for trusting us with this information and the thoughts of your heart." Hoyt knelt in front of him. "I know we're strangers, and you don't know who to trust, but I don't want you to feel that way anymore. We're your family by blood and soul. You've been led to us by all the people in your life who love you: your dragon, your mother, this girl Syrinthia, the forgers of your Dragon Blade, Rakland, the librarian you met just yesterday—none of it is coincidence. This is you being taken care of. Do you understand that?"

Thaddeus looked up, ashamed of his tears until he saw tears in the man's golden red eyes. "I don't understand."

"The librarian told you she thinks you're the savior of the prophecy, correct?"

Thaddeus shrugged. He didn't feel like a savior.

"We believe that too." Hoyt nodded at Koa, who agreed.

"We've been waiting a long time for a Dragon Rider who wants to bring back the Golden Age. We may not know the whole prophecy, so maybe we're wrong, but Thaddeus—" She searched his face in a way that reminded him so much of his mother. "You're everything we've been searching for. Your goal is to bring back the Golden Age of the Great Lord, but your heart tells you there's more. What you're searching for is the Golden Age of Adriva, the first dragon country before Duvarharia, before Ventronovia, before Wyerland—a time when Wyriders and Duvarharians were one and the same, where all of us were bound together under the Ancient Magic and living in beautiful peace. You've bonded with a dragon, have a dragon blade, and felt the magic of dragons in you, but you also have the free compassion and tolerance of the Wyriders and Rasa's soil in your veins. You have everything you need to complete what you've set out to do. We will support you—teach you the old magic, the old traditions, myths, legends, how to ride a dragon, and even master the terrestrial Zoic in your veins—if you'll let us."

Thaddeus looked deep into her eyes, trying to find a hint of a lie, then he searched Hoyt's face. "But how do I know I can trust you?" His mother wanted him here, wanted him to find his people, his home. Had she dreamed of empty hope? Now that everything he'd hoped for stood in front of him, he wasn't sure if he was ready to take hold of it.

You don't have to make a decision right now. If they truly care about you, they'll wait. They'll want you to make the right decision for you, not them.

Thaddeus nodded. "Can I take some time to think about it?"

The two Shadows of Light exchanged a nod.

"Of course." Hoyt stood and offered his hand to Thaddeus, who took it and stood. "I would never pressure you into a decision like this. I know you've dealt with a dark sect before, and I don't want you to associate us with them. Think it over. Read the books the dragon gave you. If you decide to let us help you, train you, feed you, protect you, and show you a different way to live in these strange times, then come to *Rabur-Fechamu*. It's the mountain fortress just northeast of the Dragon Palace that contains something having to do with Shadows of Light and Joad. I think you'll find it incredibly fascinating."

Thaddeus sighed with relief. "Thank you."

Koa kissed his hand, the plants in her hair nipping at his fingers. "No, Thaddeus. Thank you for showing us hope is still alive, that maybe someday people like you, me, and your mother will live alongside our Duvarharian brothers in harmony once again."

Unable to speak lest he start crying again, Thaddeus only smiled before turning to leave.

"Are you leaving?" a small voice piped up from the hall.

When Thaddeus turned, he caught sight of the little Zoic boy peeking around a corner, eyes filling up with tears.

"I am," he muttered, suddenly sad to be leaving this place that felt so comforting and safe. "I think so," he corrected.

"No!" The boy ran, arms open, full force against Thaddeus' legs, sobbing and gripping him as tight as he could. "Don't leave, *kinätyä gudi*. I want to play with you. I want to make flowers with you, ride your dragon, and learn magic. Please stay."

"Oh, my stars!" Arlan came running down the hall, trying to pry his son from Thaddeus' legs. "Let Thaddeus go, Zara! He needs to think it over. What on earth will he think of us if you keep him trapped here?"

The little boy finally let go and allowed himself to be held on his father's hip. He stuck a thumb in his mouth while tears ran down his face, blooming into flowers when they hit the ground. "But he's like me," he mumbled. "He should stay. We're friends."

Thaddeus' heart softened as he brushed the boy's green hair from his face. "I think I'm going to come back." Though he was surprised by his words, they felt right. This was his chance to belong somewhere, to have the support he needed to grow and free the people loved. If he walked away from this, he'd have to live his whole life fearful of Kyrell being taken away, his mother being taken for the games, Syrinthia being exploited by the school, and so many other horrible things. Yes, he faced risk. These people could be a cult, a church laden with conspiracy, corruption, and power-hungry individuals. But he faced the same risk if he walked out the doors, refused their help, and went back home.

So as he looked into Zara's eyes, he meant the words with all his heart. "I'm not leaving."

Then he turned to Koa, Hoyt, and Brunhild, who'd stepped out of the hall. "I want to accept your offer. Please. Teach me everything you know about the Shadows of Light and Joad."

The families gathered around him, rejoicing in their native tongues and the common language and promising they would take care of him and protect him. Thaddeus was quickly overcome with little children as they rushed from the hall.

"Yay! *Kinätyä gudi* is staying!" Zara planted a kiss to Kyrell's snout and then to Thaddeus' cheek before weaving little flowers through his long blond hair.

"Now!" Hoyt clapped his hands. "Let us rejoice with the others in *Rabur-Fechamu!*"

The tavern came to life as other families came out of the private rooms, bustling to get ready for the celebration. Brunhild gave Thaddeus a satchel to put the books in and even taught him a spell of protection for them. Then he followed them all outside and mounted Kyrell, amused as the children were strapped into small saddles on the backs of their parents' dragons. A tender warmth spread through his chest.

Do you think we made the right decision?

Kyrell rumbled low and stretched his wings. His scales caught the sunlight, casting purple light rays all around them. *I truly do, Thaddeus. I think this is the beginning of a very beautiful time for us.*

Thaddeus brushed the tears from his eyes as they took to the skies. Hoyt's dragon, Ingrida, trumpeted, calling tens of other families and riders from their homes to join them.

"I think so too."

CHAPTER 30

THEY FLEW OVER A LARGE LAKE, river, small forest, and the first low mountains. Koa flew close by, explaining where they were headed.

"The mountain is one of the largest in the Dragon Palace valley. For the last hundred years, the Council has been carving a fortress out of part of it."

Thaddeus tried to process the words he heard before the wind took the rest away. "A fortress? But isn't Duvarharia in a time of peace?"

She shook her head. "Not since the prophecy. Since Quinlan took it to the Council, declaring an evil was coming from the north to destroy Duvarharia, they changed the spending plans, moving priority from culture, magic, and intelligence to military forces. The military, especially in the Dragon Palace, is the strongest it's been for a thousand years."

Then why didn't we see forces on the streets like other military-forward cities?

Koa's dragon answered Kyrell, who relayed the message to Thaddeus.

She says the military is all around us. More and more children are being raised to fight; the schools have shifted to defense and offense spells rather than using magic to further science and sustainability. It's subtle, but it's strong.

"What about Peace Haven? Why haven't we heard of any of this there?"

"Peace Haven and some of the other outlying cities like Gorlon and River-Pass are considered outcasts from Duvarharia even though they're officially under Dragon Palace command. They're small and far away; the Dragon Palace would rather not bother with them. Their reputations of participating in the black markets and games would tarnish the Council and take far too much time and money to fix."

Then why did my father move there? Especially as a Dragon Palace ambassador?

Kyrell snarled. *Because he knows the prophecy. He knows if he lived anywhere else, you'd become a traditional Duvarharian and become the savior of the prophecy.*

But what if I'm not? What if that's just a misunderstanding? I can't imagine my father opposing me saving Duvarharia from evil. Why would anyone try to stop the savior?

Koa's dragon, Pipere, hearing some of the conversation, spoke her thoughts to Kyrell who passed them to Thaddeus. *If we're right about the evil being the games and the corruption of the Aristocrat Wyriders, it's possible your father has wealth in the games. Perhaps he gets paid to hide the severity of the Peace Haven games.*

Thaddeus shook his head. "I don't appreciate the things my father's done to me the last year or so, but I still don't see him as someone who profits from greed. If anything, he'd want the games to free my mother from her fear and oppression."

"That's just it, though," Koa interjected. "You said a cloaked man went to your home, threatening your parents. He made sure you were in the academy and said your father should've never married and had children. He was upset when your parents said they didn't think they could have children. Obviously, he and whatever cult he leads knows your mother is a Terrestrial Zoic. That's blackmail enough to get you, your mother, and your brother killed and ruin Quinlan's career."

Dread settled in Thaddeus' stomach. "Perhaps my father *did* know they could have kids. Perhaps he knew one of us would become the savior of the prophecy. But the cult found out."

"Perhaps."

I find myself more disappointed in my father than angry, but I resent that he didn't do better to protect us.

What more could he have done, though? The only place Naraina's lack of Duvarharian magic wouldn't be abnormal is a place like Peace Haven where magic is restricted. Koa and her family may be able to live here in the Dragon Palace, but look at her.

Sneaking a glance to the Zoic woman, Thaddeus saw what his dragon meant. She was pouring an insane amount of magic into the shimmer hanging around her and her children, hiding their green skin, hair, and plant-like similarities so they'd appear Duvarharian.

The Dragon Palace may be free for Duvarharians, but it's certain death for Wyriders. I'm sure the only way she and her mate have been able to survive here for so long is because of the Shadows of Light protecting them and teaching them magic. The Council would've never allowed his affiliation to them or to your mother. Even her lack of a dragon would've been dangerous.

But Brunhild doesn't have a dragon.

A flicker of sorrow passed from Kyrell to Thaddeus. *Her dragon was killed smuggling a group of Zoics into the Dragon Palace a few years ago. Brunhild had to assume a different name after faking her death so the Council wouldn't execute her too.*

Thaddeus' stomach turned. *How do you know?*

I asked. Fusa told me.

I'm beginning to think the Dragon Palace is not as wonderful as I originally believed.

I agree.

The *Suzuheb* in his satchel weighed on his mind. How could he take it back knowing it was of a place that would shun Anrid because she was too short to properly ride a dragon?

Maybe they wouldn't shun her. Maybe they'd accept her.

No. Thaddeus balled his fists. *Look around, Kyrell. Do you see anywhere that can be accessed by horse and carriage?*

Silence stretched between them. A surprising lack of roads snaked across the ground far below them; many of the hill cities didn't have any ground access roads. The Stone Plateau itself only had a few small, steep roads leading up to it. Thaddeus figured it'd take an entire day to traverse them on horse, let alone a clunky carriage. Their hearts sank.

Peace Haven may discriminate against Anrid for being an elus-ugu, but the Dragon Palace's very infrastructure offers no place for her. And what about other disabilities? Are all the disabled left to fend for themselves or never leave the thresholds of their own homes? What about other Duvarharian cities?

Kyrell didn't have an answer.

"If I may say something." Koa waved at them. "Sorry, your dragon had his thoughts open to Pipere, and I couldn't help but hear what you were saying."

Oops.

Thaddeus chuckled. "Of course."

Koa's smile faded. "That's one of the reasons the Shadows of Light have struggled so much to make a difference the last thousand years. We used to be the most well-respected group of thought, but after the corruption and the *Jen-Jibuź*, we lost our reputation. Since then, it's been a dark downward spiral. Most Duvarharians still believe in the Great Lord, but many don't know the truth about him and Joad. They follow the Great Lord as if he is a god or born to the Creator, but in doing so, they take their Duvarharian passion and wrongfully apply it to aspects of our lives that end up oppressing minorities instead of celebrating them." She gestured to the hills below them. "As you've already seen, the infrastructure is radical. It no longer suits those with disabilities or even foreigners. Do you know how hard it is to trade with Centaurs when they can't reach the Palace without a day's hard climb?

"And illegal game arenas fill the mountains. The Council won't acknowledge their existence because it puts money in their pockets. But now they've endorsed their own games in the large arena on the other side of the Palace, calling it a peace compromise. We've been doing our best to teach riders a different way to live, but it's almost impossible to convince anyone when it would mean complete transformation of all current infrastructure."

"Are you saying the only way to really change anything is to start over?"

She frowned, starting her answer several times before she got the words right. "I don't know, to be honest. Sometimes yes, it seems that's the best way. But to do that would mean destroying everything that currently stands. Everything would have to be destroyed then built again, and it would destroy millions of lives. It's impossible. The only hope we have is to keep spreading our message of freedom and acceptance and teaching the old ways. That's why you're so important, Thaddeus; you have influence in a stronghold like Peace Haven. If you could convince your father to join us rather than the cult, to follow the prophecy rather than fight it, we'd have an ambassador on our side, which is more than we've had in a long time."

"I see what you're saying." But Thaddeus wasn't sure he completely agreed.

Kyrell banked, following the lead of Hoyt and Ingrida as they began descending toward the intimidating mountain before them. Even from here, Thaddeus could see the massive amounts of construction being done, excavating thousands of loads of rock and taking them to other places on the mountain where Rock Dragons bent and shaped them into other uses like landing pads, balconies, huge statues, or pillars. Some of the rock was re-worked and taken back into the mountain or flown to the rest of the Dragon Palace valley.

"You said the Duvarharians don't know the truth about the Great Lord."

Koa nodded.

"What is the truth?"

She pointed to a section of the mountain where construction hadn't yet reached. "It all starts there." A bright smile spread across her face. "Hoyt loves to tell the story. I'll let him do the honors."

Anticipation building, Thaddeus pushed aside his worries of the future and tried to let himself enjoy the moment. Even if the Dragon Palace wasn't what he'd hoped it would be, he was riding his own dragon, his own Dragon Blade on his back, through the heartland of Duvarharia; that alone was a dream come true. And now he finally had the chance to learn more about Joad, the Great Lord, and the lost ways and magic of Duvarharia.

They alit on a large landing pad decorated and painted with designs, pictographs, and symbols nearly faded from the suns. He could make out some of the pictures, but most of them didn't make sense.

Dismounting quickly, they moved toward two gigantic doors, making room for the other riders and dragons to join them. As soon as the dragons had folded their wings and the straps loosed from the children, the landing pad swarmed with young Zoics, riders, and hatchlings chasing each other. Thaddeus was surprised to see a child as young as three years old bonded with a young dragon the size of a dog.

Were you that small when you hatched?

Kyrell turned up his snout as the children raced under him. The little hatchling accidentally stumbled against his legs before scampering off with a frightened squeak. *Of course not. My parent dragons were much larger when my mother laid her clutch, thus the eggs were bigger, and so was I.*

I didn't know that had anything to do with the size of hatchlings.

It has everything to do with it. That's why dragons are encouraged not to mate and lay clutches when they're young. The hatchlings end up being too weak to survive long unless they're born in a hatching ground with the protection of other adult dragons.

What happened to your siblings? If you hatched from a clutch like you said.

Kyrell shifted his wings and shook his head, popping his neck. *My acid was the strongest when I hatched. The others were burned badly by it and didn't survive.*

Thaddeus' eyebrows shot up as he stared at his dragon, waiting for him to say he was kidding.

He wasn't.

That's . . . lovely.

That's life.

"Come, Shadows! Let's feast and celebrate tonight. We have a new brother among us!" Hoyt raised his hands to the doors as the riders and dragons cheered. With a burst of powerful magic, he shoved the doors opened. The Shadows of Light began to pour in.

"Well? Shall we?"

Kyrell nodded, and they fell into line.

Half pillars carved into the mountain's stone framed the massive doors. The entrance was plain compared to the detail of the landing pad, but when they stepped inside, Thaddeus was amazed.

Before them stretched a gargantuan bridge, big enough for several dragons the size of Krystallos to walk side by side. Decorative carved stone railings lined both sides of the walkway. Under and beside the bridge was a huge cavern. Energy lights lit the space, amplified and directed by large mirrors. From the central platform, smaller staircases branched, leading to other hallways and caverns lining the walls up and down the cavern. Dragons flew to and from the smaller halls and caves.

The more riders and dragons who joined from the hidden halls, the more Thaddeus realized the Shadows he met in the city only lived there because they blended in. Nearly all the mountain-dwelling Shadows looked entirely different. Some had the same color skin as their dragons' scales. A few even had wings, tails, claws, and fangs. One rider had four eyes of four different colors that moved in different directions, just like their dragon's.

He was alerted to a tremendous underground river and lake system far below when an Aqua Dragon flew onto one of the platforms. Water cascaded from its body and disappeared into the air like an endless waterfall. The rider was shirtless, displaying two sets of gills under her breasts. Fins protruded from her arms, legs, and back, and on her hair grew beautiful strings of algae and coral.

A Camouflage Dragon changed colors and shapes rapidly in excitement as its rider greeted old friends. Their entire body shape, appearance, and gender changed at the blink of an eye.

He could've watched the Duvarharians all day, but once he caught sight of Zoics descending from the mountain homes, he saw nothing else.

He'd never seen a Bestial Zoic before, but he knew them the moment he laid eyes on them. They were half beast, half Wyrider, and shared characteristics of the animals they'd bonded their souls with. One family had huge feathered wings, talons, and legs like eagles, and nearly Duvarharian faces with feathers and large, curved beaks. Others had tails of big cats or canines, large ears pertaining to their soul animal, and either fur or scales covering their bodies. Most didn't wear clothes. The feline Zoics were alone while the canines moved in large packs. Some of the bird Zoics walked hand in hand with their mates, while others remained solitary.

Though the plant Zoics were more familiar, he hadn't anticipated their diversity. It seemed like a whole forest and meadow walked through the cavern. Flowers and vines grew where the Terrestrial Zoics stepped. None of them tried to hide their branch-like limbs. One had a bird's nest in her hair.

Thaddeus, come along. They're leaving without us.

But tearing his gaze away from the diversity around him proved impossible. It was overwhelming. It was beautiful. It made his soul sing.

A lump of emotion rose in his throat. This wasn't a wild dream. The Shadows of Light really were who they'd claimed. He forced himself to follow Kyrell through the crowd to the middle of the cavern. A colossal platform, big enough for most of the Shadows to gather on, stretched before them, a single table at its center.

What do you think that's for? It was only big enough for about fifteen riders and lacked chairs.

I'm not sure, but I'm sure we're about to find out.

Hoyt and Brunhild stood by the table, their children and Ingrida nearby. Fusa, Koa, her mate Arlan, and their children stood on the other side. They gestured to Thaddeus as the crowd parted, falling quiet besides a child's occasional giggle.

Knowing his face was bright red, Thaddeus bashfully made his way to them.

"I apologize for all the watching eyes. We hide nothing from each other, and the news that you may be the savior of the prophecy travels fast. They're only curious and hopeful." Koa's reassuring smile eased some of the tension in his gut.

"We don't know if I am or not, though."

Hoyt nodded. "You're right, we don't. But that's no matter. If you are, the path toward being the savior will come naturally without force or unnecessary pressure. And if you are not, today is still a day of celebrating someone who is willing to learn."

Thaddeus smiled. He wasn't sure he hoped he was the savior or not, but he felt peace regardless.

"Now, I'm assume you want to know the truth about Joad, the Great Lord, the Ancient Magic, and the Shadows of Light?"

He cast a quick glance at his dragon. Kyrell nodded. "I do. Very much."

"It all started thousands of years ago in these very caverns with a young Duvarharian named Joad."

CHAPTER 31

THE CONGREGATION SETTLED DOWN, eyes glowing in anticipation. Even the children quieted. Thaddeus quickly realized why Koa had been so adamant Hoyt tell the story. His forgotten pure-blood magic was being an *urku-qurkoźo*—a master storyteller.

With a wave of his hand, magic gathered in the air, turning different colors and shapes until Thaddeus was looking at an image exactly like the caverns they were in, though smaller, void of the energy light, and without the table.

By the gods. Have you ever seen something so incredible? Kyrell moved closer. The magic's reflection danced in his eyes.

Thaddeus shook his head, equally entranced. *Never.*

"Joad was from the outskirts of Duvarharia in a little city now lost to time. No one is sure if he was a pure blood or half Wyrider, but all agreed he was the most traditional Dragon Rider born in a thousand years. When he was around one hundred years old, he discovered this cavern—a spawning ground of wild Shadow Dragons."

The magic shifted and changed, telling the story with Hoyt's words. Shadows clawed up the platform where the image of Joad stood, his hands outstretched to the darkness—a stunning contrast to the golden light pouring from his skin.

"Unlike the other Duvarharians, Joad knew that Shadow Dragons were not of Raythuz as many believed. No dragon ever created is of the fallen warrior. It's not the Creator's will to ban any rider from any dragon, dangerous and strange as they may sometimes seem."

The shadows formed into a dragon. It bent its head to Joad's hand, and in a whirlwind of shadow and light, they were bonded. Out of the shadows rose hundreds of dragons before they poured from the cavern and into the skies of Duvarharia—freed.

"Some believe those Shadow Dragons had been locked into the mountain by the Creator himself to preserve them. Whether or not that was true, we do know they were the only dragons not under the government's control at that time.

"Then Joad's message of love, forgiveness, acceptance, and freedom began to spread. His followers, who'd once been denied dragons, bonded freely with the Shadow Dragons. They followed Joad and his dragon, Falkner, the same way dragons follow their riders—the same way Joad's Shadow Dragon followed him and his light. The name the Shadows of Light quickly grew from that."

Thaddeus watched as hundreds of riders were lifted from horrific slums and the dirt-ridden, magicless poverty they'd been forced into by the elites. The scene was far too familiar, as if Thaddeus were watching what Duvarharia was becoming again.

"The officials who'd once controlled Duvarharia with an iron fist, powered by their twisted religions and ideals of the Creator and the Dragon Priests, were losing power. And they were enraged.

"City-destroying fires set by elites were blamed on the Shadows of Light. Thousands of young dragons were slaughtered when illegal hatching grounds were discovered. Children were executed if they were suspected of using illegal magic or bonding without a license."

Thaddeus blanched at the bloodshed, wishing he could turn away, but he couldn't. He had to see the destruction awaiting himself and his family if he didn't try to make a change.

"But even through the hardships, Joad taught love and peace; he taught that all hate and revenge, even of the religious kind, fueled the Corrupt Magic. He claimed to be the vessel that would bring back natural Duvarharian connection to the Pure Ancient Magic over which he was Lord. Instead of fighting the elites, he used his power to build. When the slums burned, he used the Pure Magic of Creation to raise up hatching grounds and new infrastructure. He and the Shadows of Light gained wins, shaping a new Duvarharia out of the ashes with love and hope. That is why some believed he was the son of the Creator himself or the Creator incarnate. Until Joad and Falkner, no one could wield the Creation Magic but the Creator Himself."

How is it possible for one man to do all those things? Do you think he was really a god? Kyrell shook his head as Hoyt's magic displayed an entire city rising from stone with a wave of Joad's hand. Where ashes had once been, dragons and riders populated the city, turning into a thriving economy with freedom and acceptance.

I don't know. But I want to learn. I want to know about the Pure Magic he wielded. I want the Shadows of Light to teach us.

"But the elites were not to be slighted. The worst persecution came when Joad pronounced Duvarharians were to love all creatures, including Wyriders. He began teaching magic to Wyriders and letting them bond with dragons. That was blasphemy according to the elites—an offense that went directly against the old religious texts. Finally, they had a reason to put Joad and Falkner on trial."

Tears rose in Thaddeus' eyes. Hoyt's magic showed Joad being captured and, despite the power in his veins, letting himself be dragged away. Instead of slaying the elites, he agreed to submit if his followers would be spared.

"Knowing the Shadows of Light would be powerless to lead themselves or resurrect their cities if Joad died, the elites and priests agreed to his terms. The following days were some of Duvarharia's darkest. The skies were choked with black clouds. The stars fell silent, even to the Centaurs. Ventronovia itself, which had benefited from Joad's teachings, hoped Joad would destroy the elites and priests."

Hoyt paused, searching the eager faces of the creatures around him. Thaddeus thought he would die from the suspense. *This is his chance to kill them all and be done with them once and for all. I would slaughter them mercilessly if it were me.*

I agree. Kyrell licked his lips, tail twitching in anticipation.

But the image forming in the magic above wasn't anything that Thaddeus and Kyrell had hoped. Instead, Joad and his dragon, Falkner, were led, shackled with magic-suppressing chains, through the streets of the Dragon Palace.

Thaddeus' fists balled. *That's ridiculous. He could use the Pure Magic to break the chains, magic-suppressing or not; the Ancient Magic was more powerful than any other magic, and his dragon could turn to shadow. They're just giving up!*

Kyrell, equally frustrated, looked as if he were going to pounce into the image and free Joad himself.

"After his trial, which none of the Shadows showed up to for fear of their own lives, Joad and Falkner were led to the Stone Plateau for Duvarharia's harshest execution."

Hot tears spilled down Thaddeus' cheeks. Joad and Falkner were secured to posts, wings drawn out, feet chained to stone, arms and legs stretched out, heads held high.

Weak. Thaddeus couldn't tell if it was his own thought or Kyrell's.

"Magic is carried in blood, which is why spell-weavers are infamous for draining the blood of magical creatures to obtain temporary power. But the Duvarharians also believed that magic carried the soul, and if your magic spilled from your body, your soul would be left to wander Rasa, unable to pass on into Sankura. To be executed in such a fashion was called *rubuź Xeneluch*—blooded dragon."

Rage rose as nausea. He couldn't imagine doing such a horrible thing to *anyone*—denying them passage into the next realm.

"That is the death that Joad and his dragon, Falkner, were sentenced to."

A scream lodged itself in Thaddeus' throat. He watched helplessly as the priests and elites dug their Dragon Blades and magic into his wrists, arms, legs, torso, face, neck; his dragon suffered the same. The dragon and rider become unrecognizable as blood saturated their bodies, pooling across the once white stone.

Faintly, he heard members of the crowd weeping.

This is disgusting. I can't believe this is what they base all their beliefs upon and show this to their children.

Thaddeus stood, ready to mount Kyrell and fly far, far away. This was no worse than the games.

"But that is not the end." Hoyt's gaze locked onto Thaddeus.

Thaddeus narrowed his gaze, arms across his chest.

Give us a chance, little one. Pipere projected his thoughts into Thaddeus' mind.

I will try, he answered then blocked his mind to the dragon.

Hoyt continued. "As blood and magic left Joad's body, so did his soul, spreading across Rasa, unable to pass into Sankura as planned. But the elites and priests never foresaw what happened next."

White light lifted from the pooled blood. Though the elites and priests seemed unaware of the light, many of those who witnessed Joad's death did see it.

"The Pure Magic once held in Joad and Falkner's blood escaped back into Rasa, into the souls and magic of the Duvarharians. Bound with it was his will and soul so that anyone who listened to his wisdom and followed his teachings of love, peace, and acceptance would have command over the Pure Magic of Creation."

Thaddeus' heart swelled as he watched riders and their dragons learn to command the Pure Magic and use it to spread Joad's message to not only Duvarharians but also Wyriders, Centaurs, and humans. The country was united under a new law: all creatures were created equal by the Creator. Out of the ashes of a land the elites destroyed rose a new Duvarharia. One with trade routes to the rest of Ventronovia and even places for Centaurs, Fauns, and humans to live. The forests in Duvarharia became alive with forest nymphs and spirits. Then, as the elites lost power, the Duvarharians themselves formed a new government.

"Some believe Joad and Falkner rose from the dead and became the first Great Lord of the Golden Age. But we know he lives on in the Pure Magic around and in us. It was one of his loyal followers, one whom he called a brother, who was nominated to lead Duvarharia. He was the one who led the Duvarharians in the final battle against the shapeshifting demon Etas and wiped them out once and for all, ushering in a new age. It was during his thousand-year reign that Ventronovia experienced the most peace and prosperity it ever had."

The magical images faded. All eyes turned to Hoyt. The crowd's excited energy spread to Thaddeus, and his heart began to race.

"This is the history we, the Shadows of Light, have passed down for thousands of years. No matter what corruption grips Duvarharia, Joad's message is the same—no matter who you are, what your Kind or Race is, who you love or mate to, whether or not you're bonded or can wield magic, or even what kind of magic you use, Joad's love and acceptance extends to all Dragon Riders and Wyriders alike."

Thaddeus' eyes locked onto Hoyt's; for a moment, he thought he saw the expanse of the stars in them. "That is who we are: bearers of Joad's Light, Shadows of Himself, wielders of the Pure Magic, and a source of love, freedom, and acceptance for everyone. If Joad changed the world with love, then we can too."

Thaddeus nodded as the crowd cheered. *I think I understand now,* Kyrell's voice rang in his mind, and Thaddeus agreed. Everything made sense: why the academy kept the Shadows of Light hidden, why the school trained up arena champions instead of intellects, why men like Quinlan who loved their family still made choices that harmed them, why people like Syrinthia were stuck doing bad things for bad people. They were chained by the lies and hatred Duvarharians imposed upon themselves, blind to power available to them in Joad's words and the Pure Magic.

Truly, no one is all evil. I think we're just used to living in a world without goodness and love. If only they were given a chance, taught a different way to live, they'd be free from themselves and each other–free to love and live the way we were intended to.

Kyrell roared in agreement. *We must learn and teach others. We must become strong to protect ourselves but even stronger to face evil without violence. It is the only way.*

His decision was made. Thaddeus stepped to Hoyt and Koa. "I want to learn more. I want to follow in Joad's footsteps and shape Duvarharia into the great country I know it can be, that the people deserve and long for it to be. I want to see justice and equality for all Duvarharians and Wyriders. I want . . ." He paused, letting the weight of his words settle on him, to feel the gravity of the choice he was making. He didn't have anyone to consult before making this choice, only his dragon and inner heart. But when the words left his lips, he knew he'd made the right one. "I want to become a Shadow of Light."

The crowd roared in celebration.

Tears filled Hoyt and Koa's eyes as they knelt before him, fists to their hearts. "Welcome, Thaddeus and Kyrell, to the Shadows of Light, to the beginning of your freedom, ours, and all Duvarharia."

Thaddeus bowed before them, unable to stop the tears spilling down his cheeks. No longer would he be powerless. No longer was he insignificant. No longer would he have to stand back and watch people hurt each other and the ones he loved. This was the answer he'd been searching for.

Extending her hand, Koa smiled and gestured to the table. "Come place your mark on the table to remember your promise and for others to see and be inspired by."

Taking her hand, he let her lead him to the table. When he was next to it, he could see thousands of Shalnoa marks layered in the table, each a promise to love all creation and to spread love and freedom rather than hate and oppression. Some shone brighter than others; some were dull, but even next to faded marks, the others shone warmly, enveloping Thaddeus in an aura of safety and opportunity.

Holding his hand over the table, he closed his eyes, drawing upon Kyrell's magic. Then as he whispered his promise, purple magic twined from his skin, etching his Shalnoa markings onto the table forever. "I vow to love all creatures on Rasa equally, to uphold them rather than oppress them, to teach with love and patience, to impress Joad's message upon them, and never to turn someone away because of my own resentment or prejudice. I vow to be a diligent Shadow of Light for as long as I live."

As the last of his markings left themselves on the glimmering table, the cavern erupted into cheers. The multitude of diverse creatures swarmed around him, congratulating him and welcoming him into their family. Koa embraced him as Hoyt shook his hand. Koa's little boy climbed up his leg and weaved a crown of flowers around his blond hair, declaring him his official big brother.

Thaddeus mounted Kyrell as the crowd hurried to the feasting halls. Their hearts, souls, and minds were more one ever before.

Welcome home, Thaddeus. Kyrell's thoughts swirled with thick emotion. He too was accepted rather than feared for what he was.

Thaddeus laughed around his tears. He wished Syrinthia and his mother were here to feel the same, but knew he was making a world where someday they would. *Welcome home, Kyrell.*

Finally, they had somewhere to belong.

PART 5
Desecration

Chapter 32

Dragon Palace, Duvarharia
Year: Rumi 5313 Q.RJ.M
Nearly Three Years Later

Morning sunlight streamed through open patio doors. Thaddeus' eyes flickered open to a moment of calm just before a dragon's roar woke up the rest of the mountain. Kyrell was curled just inside the doors, soaking up the warmth through his glimmering purple scales.

They'd woken like this many times, but this morning felt different. For the first time since they'd joined the Shadows of Light, Thaddeus realized just how long they'd been away from home.

Time had changed them. Kyrell was now triple his size, and Thaddeus had never seen him so strong and healthy.

Thaddeus stood before his mirror and took a moment to meet the eyes of the face staring back. His pupils were now slit, and his ears almost an inch longer and pointed. His canine teeth had grown into fangs. Corded muscle wrapped his bones, providing endurance and flexibility. His skin was golden, and hair bleached white from hours spent in the sun. Fingers traced along his sharper cheek bones and the slowly growing patches of stubble.

I suppose parts of me have yet to catch up.

Just don't let anyone hear that embarrassing squeak in your voice. Kyrell snaked behind Thaddeus and sneered when his rider cringed.

"You're jealous I'm so much handsomer than you."

Kyrell rolled his wings, the spines along his back clicking together like music, and shook his head. *You wish.*

Chuckling, Thaddeus slipped a shirt over his head and glanced at the mirror again. The shirt covered the strong body he didn't recognize but exposed the boy buried beneath—the one who'd run from home out of fear, weakness, and pain.

Is he still there, inside of me? His hand strayed to his chest as a knot tightened in his stomach. It'd been months since he'd last cried about home. He should've been glad. Instead, he felt empty. Did he leave a part of himself behind every day he stepped into rigorous training and missions to spread Joad's message? Each day had been a new adventure, joy, and excitement. But in all its shiny newness, had he forgotten to feel . . . something else? The Duvarharians were loud and boisterous, and he missed quieter pleasures like his mother's garden and the breeze through the forest around his home.

I think so. Kyrell pressed his head against Thaddeus' back, letting him lean against him and draw on his strength. *I think he's just . . . smaller than he used to be under the confidence and strength you have now.*

Does that mean I'm not myself anymore?

Kyrell peered over his shoulder, eyes surveying every inch of Thaddeus though he knew his rider deeper than any eye could see. *I think we're all made up of different paths, different possibilities of ourselves. Our inner soul, the eternal part of us, never changes, but perhaps it manifests in different forms and ways throughout our lives.*

That's terrifying.

It's comforting.

Thaddeus supposed it was both. Freedom to change and grow was comforting, but the thought of losing himself felt frightening and uncertain.

Taking a deep breath, he calmed his mind and thought of his mother's face, Syrinthia's bright magic, and Anrid back at the academy, waiting for a *Sužuheb* or *Qumokuhe*.

"How long have we been here, Kyrell?"

Kyrell hummed as he thought back. *Three years. Three years, two months, and four days, I think.*

Tying his long hair up, Thaddeus made his way to the door, hands resting on the stone frame a moment longer than usual. "I've loved every moment of this. I think I could stay here forever."

But something troubles you.

Thaddeus sighed. "I came here to escape, to learn, to grow, to find a different way to live so I can free myself and my loved ones from oppression. But I fear if I continue as I have for the last few years, I'll be merely prolonging what I originally set out to do—running from my problems, not facing them"

You want to go back.

Thaddeus nodded. The great doors to the room he'd called home for the last few years shut definitively behind them. Though his mind was made up, tears still fell down his cheeks. But with the tears' return came a reconciliation between the boy he'd once been and the rider he'd become.

He knew he'd made the right choice.

ANNOUNCING HIS DECISION to his found family proved much harder than he'd anticipated.

Koa didn't think he was ready; she wanted him to train longer. But Hoyt and the others understood that if he stayed now, he'd never face his destiny and the path Joad laid out for him.

They assured him they'd always be there for him, only a dragon's flight away. They even told him of Shadows living in the Peace Haven region. But though they tried their best to prepare him with dignity, the meeting ended in tears shed and desperate, crushing hugs.

That night, the Shadows threw a huge celebration commemorating his work as a Shadow, his devotion to Joad, and the new life awaiting him. They reminded him that he'd be tempted to turn to violence to face the trails ahead, but they promised him the Pure Magic was stronger than any strength or other magic he'd grown the last year, and the Pure Magic would only respond to a soul of love and acceptance.

"You're going to be alright, Thaddeus," Koa whispered as she embraced him. "You're stronger than you think, but you're also caring and sensitive. Don't let anyone take advantage of it, and don't suppress it in yourself. It'll be what gets you through dark times."

Thaddeus nodded and hugged her tighter, blinking back tears. "Thank you, Koa, for everything." Her hands twined little flowers around his wrists.

"You don't have to thank me, Thaddeus." She cupped his face in her hands. "You're a part of us now, forever. And should we never meet again on Rasa, we'll see you again in Sankura."

Confidence filled Thaddeus as he smiled through his tears. "Of course."

"Kinätyä gudi!" Zara barreled into Thaddeus' legs, squeezing them fiercely. "Why are you leaving? I thought you were staying forever!"

Thaddeus lifted the heavy boy onto his hip, poked his button nose, and tucked a vine of hair and flowers behind a green ear. "Do you remember when I told you about my mother with eyes like yours?"

Zara nodded as he sucked on a flower, tears brimming in his wide, adoring eyes.

"And do you remember the friend I told you about? Syrinthia?"

His eyes lit up. "The one you're going to marry?"

Thaddeus shook his head, a pit opening in his stomach. "I doubt that." A memory of Syrinthia laughing and threading her arm through Thanatos' flashed through his mind. "She . . ." Was she committed to Thanatos? Did she still like him, or had he mistreated her? What changed in the years he was gone? He'd never said goodbye to her. Did she hate him for it? Dread tainted this moment between him and the little boy he'd considered his brother. *Joad, take these thoughts from me, if only for a few hours, so I can enjoy the family you gave me without thinking of the family I was born with.* Turning back to Zara, he smiled. "She's young, like me. I don't think either of us will marry anyone for a long time."

"Then you should stay here." Zara burst into tears again. All Thaddeus could do was hug him and let him release his sadness on his shoulder in the form of salty tears and sap-like boogers he knew he'd have to wash out later.

"Now listen, *kinätyä segi*." Zara calmed enough for Thaddeus to set him down and kneel to his level. "I'm only leaving for a little while. Do you know how long Duvarharians and Wyriders live?"

Little eyebrows furrowed as Zara sucked on the flower at the end of his thumb. He shook his head.

"Hundreds of years!"

Zara's face lit up. "Hundreds?"

Thaddeus stretched his arms out to emphasize the number. "Hundreds." He nodded. "Which means you and I will have *hundreds* of years to ride dragons together and play swords and go exploring in caves and hunting for Cave Dragons. But first, I need to go home to my mama and my friend for a few years, alright?"

Zara stood, eyes downcast, brows furrowed, weighing his options. Eventually, he looked up and planted his hand on Thaddeus' jaw. "You promise?"

Thaddeus held his small hand to his cheek. "I promise. And then after this life, we'll have eternity together in Sankura."

"Eternity," Zara whispered then nodded. "Leave so you can come back quicker." With a small push against Thaddeus, he ran off to play with the other children.

Shaking his head, Thaddeus stood and laughed with Koa. "Do you think he'll remember me?"

Koa nodded. "I know he will. You're not easy to forget, Thaddeus, rider of Kyrell."

Then Thaddeus was swept back into the celebration, enthralled by the beautiful, loud, free culture of Duvarharia.

Kyrell beat his tail against one of the massive drums set up along the main walkway. The deep beats of the towering dragon drums shook the walkways and dislodged small rocks from the ceilings. The sound mingled with the giant horns the dragons blew into, creating wild, untamed music that was both intoxicating and terrifying.

Brunhild said the Duvarharians once marched into battle with the enormous drums and horns. Thaddeus couldn't imagine the terror their enemies must've felt at the sound. He prayed he'd never be on the receiving end of it.

In a circle at the center of the platform, Shadows performed great feats of magic, swordsmanship, dance, or art. Thaddeus joined in with the reality-manipulating magic he'd mastered, bending the stone around him and creating duplicates of himself and Kyrell, which fooled many in the audience. Someone called for him to sing a song, and after more than a few pleas, he asked Arlan to accompany him with a lute. He chose a song his mother used to sing while they gardened.

Many moons ago I passed
A forest made of springtime.
I met a woman made of leaves,
A thousand secrets past.

I could not help my weary soul,
And how it whispered with her breeze.
Against the fates and what I know
I fell in love, a fool.

I know I should know better,

To trust and love the woman
Who lies and dies in winter,
And leaves for warmer springs.

I tasted her upon my lips,
Nectar sweet and addicting.
I gave my soul and heart to her,
To feel the forest's bliss.

I asked the forest for her name,
And listened as it whispered.
It spoke to me, such secret fates,
But nothing I could claim.

I know I should know better,
To trust and love the woman
Who lies and dies in winter,
And leaves for warmer springs.

She warned me of the turning times,
And how the winds were changing.
A ring she gave to me to wear,
Then left me, such a crime.

She'd swore she'd come to me next spring,
Unchanged by winter's death.
So I waited by that wooded edge,
And wore her golden ring.

I know I should know better,

To trust and love the woman
Who lies and dies in winter,
And leaves for warmer springs.

Just like her heart was fleeting,
The seasons come and then they go.
A drop of rain, a falling leaf,
And I've been left waiting,
And I've been left alone.

I know I should know better,
To trust and love the woman
Who lies and dies in winter,
And leaves for warmer springs.

When the song ended, tears streamed down Thaddeus' face. Years ago, when he listened to his mother sing it while they gardened, he thought it was nothing more than a simple folk song. Now that he knew what it was like to love something that could be ravaged and changed by time, he understood its deeper meaning.

When he returned to Peace Haven, would it be like the lover in the song, completely changed by the winter of evil? Would he even recognize the woman of his own affections? Or would she too turn away from him like the woman made of leaves?

Impatience and dread settled deep into his stomach, and he couldn't seem to leave fast enough.

After expressing his gratitude to the Shadows and promising to follow Joad's teaching and bring peace to eastern Duvarharia, he excused himself from the celebration and made his way back to his room.

Sleep was fickle that night. Peace Haven preoccupied his thoughts—the place he longed to return to but didn't want to call home.

What if your worries are unfounded? What if nothing has changed? Kyrell moved to the side of the bed when Thaddeus cast aside the furs, which were suddenly too hot.

But what if everything has changed?

Neither knew which was more terrifying.

Thaddeus crawled out of bed and curled beside his dragon on the floor. Despite the cold stone beneath him, with his dragon's wing over him and his strong heartbeat against his back, his heart and mind finally calmed.

I suppose we'll find out in a few days.

I suppose we shall.

Then Kyrell breathed a sigh of heavy magic over his rider, and together, they fell into deep slumber.

CHAPTER 33

Peace Haven, Duvarharia

A Few Days Later

After leaving the Dragon Palace, Thaddeus and Kyrell experienced intervals of excitement and loss. But as they neared the city he'd worked so hard to escape, gaping numbness opened inside him. Time felt suspended, as if the boy he'd once been never left Peace Haven. But that boy was no longer; now he didn't fear being seen with his dragon. As a citizen of the Dragon Palace, he was entitled to his dragon, axe, and magic.

He only hoped Peace Haven would agree.

The city's silhouette brightened as morning sunrays scattered pink hues across the hills and buildings. The landscape rolled beneath them, a contrast to the sharp inclines of the Dragon Palace valley. Thaddeus could see how inhospitable for dragons this land was. It offered no place for dragons to take off from, lay their eggs, or build their cities. This was a land for creatures who crawled on the ground, not took to the skies.

Will this be the place I live out my life?

Kyrell didn't answer.

The Dragon Palace had been wonderful, but Thaddeus was sure Syrinthia and his mother couldn't live there; the Duvarharians there were too unforgiving of differences. A small smile curved his lips as he touched one of his satchels. He couldn't wait to see Syrinthia's face light up when she saw the gift—a *Suźuheb* of her favorite dragon kind: the Aqua Dragon.

At least it will show her the beauty of the Dragon Palace instead of its corruption.

Thaddeus nodded, then emotion choked his throat. What if she didn't want anything to do with him? He'd left her without saying goodbye or even writing a note explaining himself. A knot tightened in his chest. Would she understand? Would she forgive him?

The city passed under them now, the same as it had been three years ago. Artificial lights flickered. Dull buildings squatted low to the ground, only a few of them strong enough to hold a dragon. The once impressive Council Hall now looked like a pompous joke compared to the Dragon Palace's architecture.

Do you sense the darkness over this land?

Thaddeus closed his eyes and tilted his head back, extending his mind into the air, the wind, the trees, the grass, and anything flowing with life. Only, life *wasn't* flowing; it was stagnant, like an old pond without a drain.

He fixed his gaze on the academy. It towered above the other buildings, its gates more prison-like than he remembered. The magic in his heart told him it was blocking most of the life flow.

I do. Is it a new darkness, or do you think we're only now capable of sensing it?

I'm not sure, but I want to find out. Kyrell descended to a small, private road, knowing Thaddeus wanted time to process and adjust to being home before arriving at the front door.

I don't think it'll ever have been enough time.

Likely not, but some time is better than none. You're capable of this, no matter how impossible it may seem. Think of it as done, then the task will not loom ahead of you.

Nodding, Thaddeus slid from his dragon's back. As soon as his boots hit the ground, a wave of inferiority crashed upon him. His knees weakened under him. He felt as if all his former mindsets and beliefs were reaching out to him, yearning to haunt him and fight his new confidence and power.

Grounding himself, Thaddeus repeated a few Shadows of Light mantras, remembering what they'd taught him about meditating during overwhelming circumstances. Then he took Kyrell's advice and resolved himself to the inevitability of this meeting. One after the other, his feet moved him down the familiar road, returning him to all the people and places he loved and hated.

Is Mother alright? Is Thanatos home? Will Quinlan be proud or furious? A thousand worries rushed through his mind. Knowing he'd soon have answers was almost as horrible as the questions themselves.

Eventually, he reached the door.

Welcome home, little ones. Krystallos stirred on the roof, scales shining in the early morning light. He was exactly as Thaddeus remembered. The comfort of familiarity washed over him, easing some of the knot in his stomach.

Thank you, Krystallos, they answered.

Then before they could say anything else, Krystallos answered some of Thaddeus' worries. *Your father is in the kitchen waiting for your mother to come in from the garden. Thanatos is not home. He's not been home for several weeks.*

Thaddeus' heart twisted. *When did everything change so much?* It seemed only yesterday he and Thanatos had raced home, excited to see what their mother had cooked, excited to see their father waiting in the kitchen with fantastic tales. Nothing but love and joy had filled their lives. *How could a family once so perfect have fallen this far?*

Perhaps they were not so perfect to begin with. Krystallos was right, but Thaddeus didn't want to agree.

To avoid his father, he walked around the house to the garden.

With practiced movements, Naraina harvested ripe fruit from a flowering vine, filling the wicker basket beside her. Though she was as beautiful as always, time hadn't left her untouched. Her hair was longer now and tinged with grey. Her eyes didn't shine so brightly, and her hands tremored as she moved from vine to vine. But regardless of the changes, she was his mother and everything he'd missed and loved.

Undoing the latch with shaking fingers, he opened the gate, making sure to shut it again as she'd always instructed. His footsteps were quiet, unlike his pounding heart. Part of him felt like a spirit watching her, waiting for her to notice him, unsure if she ever would.

The suspense in time broke when he cleared his throat. "Mother?"

"Thaddeus?" Slowly, she turned, and their eyes met. For a moment, neither moved.

Then a laugh broke through his tears. "Mother, I came back."

Tears filled her eyes as she whispered, "I know."

The distance between them disappeared as they embraced. Her fingers brushed over his hair as she planted kisses all along his forehead. "Oh, my *kinätyä segi*." Her eyes searched his face, memorizing his changed features. "You've grown up so handsomely. By the gods."

He too noticed the smaller details time etched into her face. Her skin was much paler; a few new wrinkles lined her eyes and mouth; her collarbones were more pronounced. Mostly, he noticed the fatigue in her eyes.

"Did I do this to you?" His stomach rolled as he touched her worn face. *How could I forgive myself if her suffering is my fault?*

Her smile wavered. "No, Thaddeus. Not you. I wondered about you traveling the world to learn, grow, and find yourself, but I never worried. I knew the gods would take care of you. But Thanatos—" She chewed on her lip to hide back a raspy sob.

Rage burned deep in his heart as he drew her back into his arms. His hands were gentle on her, afraid of how fragile she'd become. *I'm going to kill him.*

Not if I don't first.

But the anger lasted only a moment as her heart beat next to his. The world softened around them. Today was only for those who loved him in return. "I'm not ready to see Father."

Though her eyes were sad, he knew she understood. They drew apart. His hands made hers look so small in his grasp.

"Alright," she whispered, nodding. "Just—" A deep breath rose her chest. "Just be home for dinner?"

"I promise." Leaning down, he kissed her cheek. "I promise to be here for many more dinners to come. I don't plan to leave again for very long time."

"That's good." A smile brightened her face as she bent to pick up her basket. It seemed too large in her small hands. Had she always been so petite, or had he really grown that much? What else had changed?

"Mother?"

"Hm?"

Heat rushed into his blood with unwelcome dread. He swallowed. "Where's Syrinthia?"

A distant look passed over Naraina's face. "Krystallos said she was looking for something by *Xeneluch-Rani* earlier."

He didn't ask for what before running from the garden and mounting Kyrell's back.

He'd once searched for something there too. Something no one should go looking for.

CHAPTER 34

"Syrinthia!"

She stood in the shallow of the lake, the water moving around her waist like an old friend dragging her into an embrace. Her white dress trailed behind her, sticking to her dark skin, clinging to her like life does to things that are dying. She neither turned back nor moved farther into the water.

"No, no, no." Thaddeus jumped into the lake before Kyrell fully landed. "Syrinthia?" He inched closer, heart thundering in his chest.

"Thaddeus? Is that you?" She turned slightly, her voice so quiet he wasn't sure she even spoke.

Thaddeus held out a hand, nodding quickly. "It's me. What are you doing out here?"

She looked to the waves that the dragon island lay beyond then back to him. Pain and longing filled her eyes.

He remembered that feeling too well.

Step by step he crept closer until the water was at his chest. A strange current pulled him in, coaxing him to the depths that had once nearly claimed him.

"I don't—" Her eyes locked onto his and flooded with tears. "I don't know."

"Syrinthia—"

Pushing the water away, she rushed to him and threw her arms tightly around his neck. "I didn't know where you went," she choked out, her voice raspy as if she'd been crying for hours. "or what happened to you. I was devastated when Naraina told me. I was worried sick."

Thaddeus' heart sank. "I know." The words were pointless, empty, but he didn't know what else to say. He'd known what he'd chosen, and this was the consequence. He'd made the best decision for him. *But it hadn't been for her.*

"Did you find what you were looking for?"

"What do you mean?" He knew what she was asking. He just wasn't sure how to answer.

"Did you find what you were looking for?" She pulled away, searching him just like his mother had.

He tried not to let his eyes wander, but he couldn't help noticing the cuts and bruises on her skin. He nodded. "Yes. I found the Shadows of Light and joined them. I learned about Joad, his teachings, and the magic he commands. I found a new way to live, one of peace and acceptance where all Duvarharians and Wyriders are free. I found—" He almost said, *I found a world where you'll be safe,* but he couldn't promise that. Not before he had a chance to prove he could fulfill that promise. "I found everything I was looking for."

"I'm glad." A deep sigh escaped her lips as she stepped back; the distance felt like miles. Her arms wrapped to hug herself, as if her own embrace was more comforting than his.

Hopelessness washed over him. *But I came back because I didn't find you there.* The words sat on the tip of his tongue, threatening to spill over; instead, he swallowed them back with guilt and uncertainty. "But I'm sorry I left."

A flicker of hope sparked in her gaze.

"I'm sorry I left you without saying goodbye. That was extremely *chue* of me, and it was wrong. I had to do it for me, but"—his hands flexed then closed, refraining from cupping her cheek and caressing her skin gently across the bruise under her eye that made his stomach roil—

"I'd hoped you'd find a way out somehow."

He hadn't wanted to talk about the *Jen-Jibuż*, but how couldn't he? It was the center of their lives—everything she was living through, that he was afraid of, that tied them together. Would they even be friends without it? Though he shoved the cursed thought deep inside him, acid rose in his throat at its remnants.

"No." Something between a laugh and a sob parted her lips. "No, I couldn't. But I've tried so *hard*." Soft hands hid her face as she shook her head.

He stood uncomfortably before her, feeling worthless and disconnected. Her pain ran oceans deep, and he'd added to that. How could he expect to comfort her?

"I'm so tired, Thaddeus." She hiccupped. "I just don't know how much more of this I can take." Her gaze moved back to where the suns rose over the *Xeneluch-Rani*. The sky was bluer now; a gentle breeze over the water brought a hint of morning warmth.

His heart lurched. "I don't want you to mean that."

She shook her head.

"I don't want you to mean that," he repeated, eyes trained to his reflection in front of him, shivering though the water around them really wasn't cold enough for his body to react that way. "But I understand." His eyes finally met hers. "A few years ago, I stood here wondering the same thing." Tears rushed down his cheeks, but he didn't suppress them; they fell into the Dragon Sea, its waters more willing to accept his suffering than anyone else.

"I didn't know." She made no move to touch him or bridge the gap between them now, but regardless, a deeper connection formed between them.

"No one's ever cared enough to know."

"I care."

"I know."

For a moment, neither moved. A million words hung between them.

Thaddeus reached for her hand but hesitated then awkwardly pointed to the shore. Without a word, they pushed away from the greedy water. Though the lake's pull didn't fully disappear, it was easier to ignore when the water wasn't so close to their hearts.

Kyrell moved by his side, providing some warmth in the cold atmosphere.

"I have to stop this." He whispered so quietly, he wasn't sure he'd spoken until she shook her head.

"You can't."

His hands balled as he ground his teeth. Years of suppressed rage bubbled to the surface again—rage at Thanatos for shaming his family and stressing his mother; rage at the *Jen-Jibuź* for controlling Syrinthia and abusing her; rage at the world that worked so hard to deny him happiness, safety, and success; rage at being helpless.

"I can." Trying to bury the rage, he focused on what the Shadows taught about anger fueling the darkness, about finding peace in all situations. "I have a power they don't—the Pure Magic of Joad. Once they hear his story, they'll realize all Duvarharians and Wyriders should be free." His voice rose. "And they'll realize the pain they've caused so many people like us. I can change this. I can save you."

Before he could stop himself, he took her hands in his and drew her close. His eyes begged her to trust him. But instead of excitement, he saw only tears and defeat in her eyes.

"No, Thaddeus." She turned away, avoiding his gaze. "You cannot save me."

The air left his lungs as his chest constricted, his throat stinging. "Yes, I can." Reaching for her hand again, he blanched when she shrank away.

"No, you *can't*." Her voice was suddenly stern, definitive. "You can't just expect everything to magically get better because you've seen enlightenment. Not everyone has had the same experience as you. Not everyone gets the chance to run away to the Dragon Palace and be free." Fire burned in her eyes as she stepped forward, and he stepped backward. The water reached for his ankles.

"No, that's—" It felt as if his heart were shattering into a million little pieces.

"You think you can wave your magic over everything and fix it. That just because everything has fallen into place for you because of providence, that it'll do the same for everyone else who believes." Her teeth tore at her lips.

"Syrinthia, I didn't—"

"Well, I believe, Thaddeus!" Tears poured down her face as she snapped. Sobs escaped her lips as her hands balled into fists at her sides; bruises and cuts lined her knuckles. "So, where are my miracles?" Her voice, quiet and dark, drew shivers down his spine.

"I don't know," he whispered, biting back his own tears.

"Where is my escape? Where is my dragon to sweep me off my feet and carry me to better lands?"

Kyrell hung his head.

She gestured to the axe on his back. "Where is my all-powerful Dragon Blade to protect me when they do *this?*" With shaking fingers, she tore her tattered wet dress from her shoulders, baring her chest to him.

Thaddeus choked when his eyes fell on the swollen red, tears, cuts, and rips on her chest. Each bruised, bloody line drew the shape of the Shadows of Light symbol upside down.

"They've cut this into me over, and over, and over, Thaddeus." Her body quivered as she stood before him, soul more exposed than flesh could ever be. "And for what? To remind me of my place. To remind me never to speak out, to never run away, to never question or disobey." Her arms fell to her sides, her shoulders caving on themselves. "They use me in the games, Thaddeus."

"No . . ." He shook his head, wishing it wasn't true, but her silvery scars and red lashes stained his mind. *Maybe this is just a nightmare, and I'll wake up soon.* The nightmare continued.

"When they discovered my unique magic, they locked me away,

tested me, tormented me for answers." Her arms couldn't wrap tighter around herself. "And one day, I transformed."

"Trans . . . transformed?" The words hesitated on his tongue. "Into what?"

She shook her head, a sob escaping her lips. "I don't know. Something powerful. Something they found worthy of the games. Thaddeus . . . they made me . . ." Hysteria rose in her voice. "They made me kill dragons." She staggered from his touch. "I can still feel their blood on my hands, hear their cries . . . They haunt me. They want my soul."

What sick ñekol would torture her to the point of murder? Kyrell's thoughts were full of anger and repulsion.

Thaddeus was still struggling to wrap his mind around what she'd said. What did she transform into that was capable of slaying dragons in a blood lust not even she could control? Anytime she'd used her magic, it had been kind, pure, beautiful, and healing. "Th–they can't do that." He stumbled over the words, dread chewing his heart. "You're Duvarharian! You're Rakland's charge, for stars' sake!"

"Not anymore." Her nails dug into her skin. "I was put on trial and deemed non-Duvarharian. The academy owns me now. I have no rights."

Thaddeus covered his face. *This isn't real. This can't be real.*

This is the most real thing that's ever happened in your life, Thaddeus, in either of our lives. Now is not the time to break down or cry or give up. Pull yourself together.

Thaddeus clenched his jaw. He didn't know how to answer his dragon, didn't know how to answer Syrinthia.

"Do you understand now? You can't fix this. Reasoning with them, teaching them about Joad—none of it will work. No matter how much I've cried out to Joad, to the Creator, or any other gods, none of them have saved me, and they won't. Duvarharia will. The prophecy wills it. It's in the stars."

Thaddeus' heart lurched. *The Dragon Prophecy.* Again, the prophecy was at the center of it all, yet he still didn't know its entirety. *The Shadows believe I'm the savior.* Kyrell was right. Now was not the time to back down or flee.

"Are you listening, Thaddeus? You can't stop this. It's inevitable."

"You're wrong."

She cried in exasperation and kicked the water. "Thaddeus, you just don't get it! You've been *gone*. You don't know what you're up against, and just because the Shadows of Light trained you for a few years doesn't mean you're strong enough to save everyone! Why don't you understand?"

Thaddeus straightened his shoulders. "Because I'm following Joad, and he knows all things. His judgement through the Pure Magic will lead me and give me the strength to do whatever needs to be done."

"No, no, no!" She pulled at her hair. "*Please*, Thaddeus, listen to me." She took his hands in hers, desperate to make him see her way. "Let's go somewhere else. Right now. We can fly south to Ravenwood, away from the corruption. The Igentis Artigal is accepting of Dragon Riders. I'm sure he'll let us find refuge there."

Lips pursed, he shook his head. "Fleeing won't make it go away."

"No, but you and I can't fix this. We'll only die trying. Don't you want to save me?"

"More than anything. You know that."

"Then get me out of here. *That* is the only way."

He wanted to cave to her pleads, to leave the danger and this wretched life far behind. But he couldn't. Steely determination settled in his heart. "And what about my mother?" His hands grasped her in an iron clutch. "Are you asking me to leave her behind and pray the *Jen-Jibuź* don't torment her as well? Would you wish all you've been through on her? Or on thousands of other Wyriders? Is *that* what you want?"

"Thaddeus, please stop this." She tried to tug her hands from his, but he pulled her closer.

"No, Syrinthia, *you* stop this. All of it. I already ran away once, and look where it left you." Tenderly, he touched the side of her face and caressed her neck where dark, broken skin was discolored red and blue. She leaned into his touch, eyes fluttering shut against the pain. "I worried so much about what awaited me coming home. I never could've imagined this nightmare. And"—he bit his lip—"I hate myself for leaving you behind to save myself. I'll never forgive myself for it. I'd rather us die fighting than living in hiding on ground stained with the blood of the thousands we left behind."

She didn't answer, only clenched her eyes shut. Silent tears trickled down her cheeks.

"I'm driven mad seeing you like this. It makes me want to rip the world apart to patch the tears in your skin." Finally, he had the courage to say the words he'd aways wanted. "You mean more to me than you know. I think about you endlessly, especially at the Dragon Palace. Every time I saw the Aqua Dragons or tried a new food, I thought of you, of how much I wanted to experience it with you. But I can't do that if we run away. Syrinthia, you are my inspiration, my muse; you make me believe the world can be a better place."

Rubbing his thumbs across her knuckles, he took a deep breath. "For once, let *me* save *you*. Just once." Then his fingers twined in her hair as she moved into his arms, melting against his touch as she cried.

When her tears quieted, he sought the courage to ask the question burning in his and Kyrell's minds. "Will you tell me about my brother?"

Silence answered.

Gently, he brushed a lock of hair from her face. The tears rushed down her face again; she hid her face and shook her head.

Thaddeus quelled the anger in his chest. "Tell me what he has done."

"I can't." Panic laced her words as she tore away from him, digging her nails into her goose-bumped skin.

"Yes, you can." He pulled her close again, showering her with calming magic the Shadows taught him. "I have to know what he's done to you." Carefully, he titled her chin up to meet his gaze.

Biting back rage, he listened. Thanatos became unbearable the moment he'd realized Thaddeus left. He never let Syrinthia out of his sight if he could help it, and he pressed to make their relationship official. When he refused him, he called upon the *Jen-Jibuź* for help.

"He used me. For my body, my magic, my mind, and especially for good standing with the *Jen-Jibuź*. They progressed him in the games by providing weapons and sponsors. He's . . . wicked and unstoppable."

Over and over his mind repeated the abuse, his body trembling with suppressed hatred. Kyrell's tail lashed the water, claws digging into the sand, a low growl in his throat. Nausea tainted Thaddeus' mouth as he wondered how many times Thanatos' unwelcome hands roved over her body and how many of the lashes and bruises resulted from her refusal.

"Why haven't you left him?"

Blood beaded on her lips where her teeth tore them apart. "I can't. The *Jen-Jibuź* . . . their leader, the cloaked one, won't let me. They think—" She buried her face in her hands, hiding herself and her shame.

"What do they think, Syrinthia? You have to tell me. I can't be in the dark anymore."

Sucking in a deep breath, she cried. "I know, I know." Sniffing, she wiped her nose on her wrist, stalling as long as she could. Several breaths later, she spoke, her words almost too quiet to hear. "The *Jen-Jibuź* wanted me to become friends with him, with you, because the prophecy said the traitor would be one of the prophet's sons."

The blood drained from his face. He wanted to stop her from saying what he already knew.

"Quinlan, your father, was the prophet. And Thanatos is his firstborn. The *Jen-Jibuź* believes he's the prophesied traitor. They said he'd bring Duvarharia's destruction if he grew up to be a traditional Dragon Rider."

Her words gutted him. In that moment, everything made sense. The conversations between his parents and the cloaked man, between Syrinthia and Rakland. Everything circled back to him, Thanatos, his father, and Syrinthia. The *Jen-Jibuź* had never been the focus; it had been him, Thanatos, and the prophecy.

Cold realization washed over him. "You helped him become an arena warrior."

"Yes." Shame poured off her, filling the lake.

"You encouraged him to join the games, to forsake magic, the dragons, *everything*."

"Yes."

"Why not just kill him?" His jaw ground against itself. "Why not spare the hundreds of lives he's ruined by just ending his?" Though he couldn't believe the words leaping from his throat, he also couldn't deny the validation they brought. Kyrell rumbled in agreement.

Syrinthia choked back a sob. "Because your mother loves him, just as she loves you. But, Thaddeus, it's *working*. The stars have told the Centaurs he's not the prophecy's fulfillment. If what we've done will save Duvarharia, then it'll have been worth it. All of it."

Thaddeus wanted to throttle her. "Don't you hear what you're saying? No matter who they think the traitor is, the prophesized evil is still in Duvarharia. It's tearing us apart from the inside out. It's the very games he's participating in and the lashes on your skin!" He pressed his hands to his head. "*Loizi* the prophecy! So many lives have been ruined by it, and no one even knows all the words. You should've never agreed to watch over him or commit to him. It'll *never* be worth what you've endured."

Flinching at his tone, she turned away. "But it was either his two hands on me or the hundreds of the *Jen-Jibuź*." He almost didn't hear her whisper. "Besides, I think—" She clenched her eyes shut, arms hugging tight around her torso. "I think he loves me, in some small way. It's not always bad. Some nights he's sweet and dresses my wounds—"

"No," Thaddeus growled. "That's not love." Blood pooled in his fists where his sharp nails dug into his palms. "I'll kill him." Red clouded his sight as he drew her close. "I'll feed him his own bloodstained hands and gut him like the pig he is, but only after I return every bruise and cut he's ever left on your body."

Syrinthia clung to his shirt, shaking her head. She looked so fragile in his arms. No matter what words came from her mouth, betraying how she felt on the inside, he saw the fear and defeat in her eyes.

"No, Thaddeus." She shook her head quickly. "You can't kill him. They did something to him, something horrible, something that changed him."

"Then I'll kill them too."

A cry of exasperation escaped her lips. "And what about Joad? I thought you didn't seek violence."

Thaddeus' heart warred against itself.

Evil can only be reckoned with so far. Sometimes, it just needs to be squashed. Kyrell's voice echoed in his mind.

He took a deep breath. "They'll get one chance. Only one. If they choose violence, so will I."

Though she begged him not to go, he felt her soul screaming for the nightmare to end, for the pain to be over. Since he didn't want her to end it all under the Dragon Sea, he'd find a way to end it himself, even if that meant staining his hands with his own brother's blood.

"Where is Thanatos?"

She clamped her lips shut as he gently shook her.

"Syrinthia, please, tell me. Where. Is. My. Brother?"

"The games." The words slipped from her lips like poison. "He's waiting for me tonight, for me to support him."

A new rage flooded through him as Kyrell reared back on his legs, growling low in his throat.

"To support him how?"

"In the *Xene'mraba*." She held back a sob. "He's Peace Haven's most beloved *Xeneluch-shuvub*—dragon 'tamer'."

Kyrell threw back his head and screamed, beating the waters with his wings. Vengeance clamped around his heart. *I'll tear the* dasuun qevab *limb from limb and make him pay for every dragon he's slayed!*

Blood clouded Thaddeus' vision as he moved to mount Kyrell.

"Thaddeus, they'll kill us!"

He whirled around, his face inches from hers. "That's why you're staying here."

Her lips parted in protest as her hands reached for him. The brief desire to kiss her flashed through his mind. Immediately, he destroyed the notion; he refused to be like his brother who'd forced his desires upon her. She wished to be free, and right now, that was the only desire he intended to satisfy.

Hissing through his teeth, he shut out her cries and tore her pleading hands from his body. Then he mounted his dragon, and they took to the skies.

CHAPTER 35

KYRELL, I DON'T KNOW *how I'll focus on the Shadow's teachings when you're filling my thoughts with blood and vengeance.*

Kyrell growled low, and the images of the *Jen-Jibuź* members and academy professors lying dead ceased. But in their absence, Thaddeus couldn't ignore the thirst for vengeance that poured from Kyrell's heart. Or maybe . . . maybe it seeped from his own heart.

We have to start with love, like the Shadows taught. I know we're not strong enough to defeat them alone, but I have to trust Joad's magic will rise to my aid if needed. It must.

Kyrell banked to the left, facing the academy. Now that the city was bathed in bright morning light, Thaddeus realized the academy hadn't stayed the same. They'd expanded into the surrounding forest and improved the arena by adding a new dome-like cage; it was fit for the *Xene'mraba*—the dragon games.

Rage poured through Kyrell's blood and into Thaddeus' thoughts. The dragon stopped withholding his thoughts as painful memories surfaced. Every time he'd wanted to leave the island, he'd been constantly reminded that the games sought dragons of his kind to slaughter for entertainment.

I'm so much more than that. Kyrell roared. *We are so much more.*

Thaddeus' fist tightened around his axe. The weapon no longer brought back nightmares of the boy he'd killed. Now it was an extension of his soul, an instrument of justice and protection. Confident Joad's message could change the corrupted Duvarharians, he didn't plan on spilling blood today. But even so . . . the axe pulsed with his magic and emotions. If any of them dared attack those he loved or continue in their evil ways, he wouldn't hesitate to fill the void with their blood and corpses.

I almost hope Thanatos will defy me. Let him bully me once more. I'll show him.

And if he doesn't? If he chooses Joad?

A knot constricted in Thaddeus' gut. A year ago, while deep in his studies of Shadows of Light's teachings, he would've said he wanted to see his brother and father freed by Joad's love and kindness. But now, he struggled to desire anything but vengeance for Syrinthia's torment.

Gritting his teeth, he answered, *Then I'll let Joad judge him. I hope all Duvarharians turn to Joad. I trust in Joad's power.*

Silence stretched between them as they neared the school. The crowd's cheers and dragons' roars reached their ears.

Then Kyrell voiced the doubt that already swirled in Thaddeus' heart. *Do you truly believe what you're saying? Would you be able to let the abuser of the woman you love walk free after all he has done? Do you truly believe you'd be able to forgive him?*

Thaddeus' teeth worried his lips. *If Joad can forgive him, then I must try.*

Before he felt ready, they landed at the academy gates. A throng of Duvarharians stood elbow to elbow in line to see the games. The cacophony of wounded dragon roars and the occasional rider's scream made Thaddeus' stomach turn.

The sounds of death awoke buried memories of the boy he'd killed. The confidence he'd felt about shedding blood, even for justice, wavered. Even though he'd been protecting himself, he'd hated the way killing someone felt; how much worse would this be? Would he have the strength to do what he must if they rejected Joad? Would the Pure Magic lend him the courage he needed to display Joad's power?

I suppose we will find out.

Thaddeus swallowed acid and nodded, handing two silver *femi* to the ticket master.

The grisly, one-eyed man jerked his head to Kyrell. "I thought their type belonged in the cages, not out," he jeered through yellowed teeth.

Thaddeus' blood boiled. Kyrell snapped his jaws inches from the man's face. He screamed, throwing himself backward.

"If you want to put him there yourself, you're more than welcome to try, but I don't recommend it if you like the way your skin stays on your bones." Thaddeus snapped his ticket from the booth, eyes boring into the ticket master's.

The man scrubbed his face as flecks of acid burned his skin. Incoherent words tumbled from his mouth as he shook his head violently. With one last glare, Thaddeus pushed through the gates.

A twinge of guilt flashed through him as he thought of the Shadows. They wouldn't have approved of his hateful words. But how could he show kindness to someone who'd rather his dragon be dead? His heart continued to war against itself. *Joad, forgive me.*

Moving with the jostling crowd, Thaddeus found himself among the most depraved citizens of Peace Haven; these were Duvarharians denied magic, historical teachings, and dragons. They needed Joad's message the most; they needed his courage and power to stand up to the government. But as he listened to them, he realized they hated magic and dragons as much as their leaders. A few even said dragons should be put to work as slaves and beasts of burden. Another said magic was too unfair and should be outlawed altogether.

They have no idea they're just as capable of wielding magic and bonding with dragons as the elites. If only they would rise to claim their rights and inheritance. Kyrell hissed at a woman jeering at him. She dropped all the food she'd bought and bolted.

How do we even speak to them? For generations they've been brainwashed and lied to. What could we even say to change their minds?

Beg the Pure Magic to guide your words. I'd rather eat the ignorant fools than speak to them.

Thaddeus ignored Kyrell as he licked his lips.

They entered the tall stadium archway and were guided up long ramps and out onto the seating which looked like large steps. Each row of seats was barely large enough for dragons to join their riders.

However, the top of the arena cage in the center of the seating held nearly fifteen of the elites' dragons. They napped and preened themselves as if another dragon wasn't being torn to pieces with magic just below them.

Thaddeus wished he could look away, but he couldn't. This was reality, and he had to face it. The Poison Dragon blew a black cloud of poison to the *Xeneluch-shuvub*. It encased the fighter as the dragon limped to the other side of the arena. A trail of blood decorated the sand as its back right leg dragged lifelessly behind it, hamstrung.

The crowd hushed as they waited to see if the dragon tamer was dead. A shimmer of gold magic swirled the poison around her before blowing away. She was unharmed.

The crowd cheered. Thaddeus bit back tears.

We have to do something.

And what do you suggest? Kyrell's raging eyes burned into his. *We can't do anything from up here, and that dragon's as good as gone anyway. Death is a mercy for them at this point. We have to focus on stopping this completely, not just saving one dragon.*

Kyrell was right, but Thaddeus hated it.

The *Xeneluch-shuvub* threw back her head and screamed to the sky. The sound was unlike anything Thaddeus had ever heard. It wasn't a battle cry; it wasn't a cry of victory. It was manic, bestial. A dark shiver ran down his spine into his soul.

Slicing her hands through the air, she released magic in the form of gold knives. The conjured weapons streaked toward the dragon, cutting into their underbelly and severing scales from their back. A keen cry pierced the air as splatters of blood decorated the sands and stained the wall. The tamer stalked the dragon, coming within feet of it with a cruel smile on her face, before unleashing all her magic and hate upon it.

This wasn't a fight.

It was a slaughter.

The crowd fell silent. The air now rang with the dragon's screams and the magic's whistling death.

Everything fell still.

The tamer stood, shoulders heaving from labored breaths, hands glowing with magic, and eyes ablaze with fury as the dragon sagged to its knees.

Whatever color the dragon and tamer had been was now cloaked by blood. Thick, hot rivers flowed from hundreds of lacerations down the dragon's body.

Staggering to its claws, the dragon coughed a cloud of poison. It dissipated before even reaching the tamer. She stepped forward, tore off her helmet, and spat in the dragon's face. "Just die already, you worthless *Xeneluch ue*."

With dull, hopeless eyes, the dragon gave up and fell to the sand, shuddering in pain. Its chest heaved once, then twice, before falling still. Its gaze clouded in death.

The *Xeneluch-shuvub* crawled to the top of the dragon's body and conjured a golden sword before sinking it deep into the underside of the dragon's neck—the strike of merciless victory.

Turning away, Thaddeus choked back sobs. Kyrell's claws dug into the polished rock, every muscle in his body shaking, aching to pounce and rip the fighter to shreds.

Calm yourself, Kyrell, before you hurt someone innocent.

None of them are innocent. Kyrell's low snarl turned heads. *Not one of them.*

Thaddeus could barely watch as riders with whips forced their chained mounts to retrieve the dead dragon. Maniacal reins of magic snaked to the dragons' mouths, drawing blood at even the smallest movement. Limp and lifeless, the slain dragon appeared even smaller than it had in life. Cold realization washed over Thaddeus; the dragon hadn't been much older than Kyrell when they'd bonded. What little food he had left in his stomach, he lost into a nearby bucket.

"First game?" A hand slapped his shoulder as he set the bucket down.

Rage seethed in him. Nodding, he shrugged his shoulder from the man's drunk hold.

"That's alright. Good thing they have those buckets, eh? It gets easier, though. You'll get used to it."

Thaddeus wiped acid from his lips and sneered. "No. I'll never get used to it." In a moment's impulse, he grabbed the man's shirt and brought him close, blanching at the rotten smell of his breath. "This place is full of vile, filthy excuses of Duvarharians. You should be working *with* the dragons, not *killing* them. It's as bad as if women and children were being slain. Don't you see? We are as much the dragons as they are us. We are all one Kind. So, I'm sorry if it's not easy for me to watch my brothers and sisters be gutted and slain. I hope and pray to all the gods, Joad, and the Creator himself that I *never* get used to it."

The man's eyes widened, his mouth hanging open, his hands shaking. Thaddeus dropped him and turned away, shaking his head.

"Come, Kyrell. I think I know what we must do now."

Without another word, Kyrell followed him down the steps to the other side of the arena.

From the pits, *Vuk Quseb*—game masters—dragged another dragon. Larger and feral, the new dragon dwarfed the victorious fighter. Even if he didn't survive the rest of the night, Thaddeus hoped he'd at least take several of the dragon-slaying *Xeneluch-shuvub* down with him.

Ahead, he spotted the box where the elites sat. The academy headmistress stood in the middle of them, a crown of silver dragon scales on her brow. Thaddeus ached to send an arrow of magic through her heart, but he pushed aside vengeance in favor of Joad's message.

Imagine the good she could accomplish with this academy. Instead, she runs games and uses children as arena bait.

That's why we must convert them. Their influence on Peace Haven alone would spark incredible change. In fact, all these Duvarharians' lives could make a difference if only they had the chance to change.

Thaddeus ducked behind a wall separating a stairwell and the seating; here, he'd be able to melt into the shadows while creating his diversion.

Raising his hand, Thaddeus focused on his intent and whispered it in the ancient language to solidify it. His plan would take considerable magic and energy; he couldn't afford to mess it up. A hand on Kyrell's leg to draw strength and energy, he closed his eyes and imagined the arena, the people, the battle ensuing below, and the metal cage.

The metal cage. The metal cage. He hissed the words in the ancient language as the Shadows had taught him. *The metal cage bending, straining, weakening, collapsing.* With a deep breath, he released the magic.

The air tore apart with the dissonance of bending and snapping metal.

Panic swept the stadiums.

The dragon launched himself against the chains around his body, straining for freedom. With one more whispered phrase and burst of magic, Thaddeus weakened the chains; they bent tremendously before shattering. The dragon slammed into the metal cage, his roars mingling with the screaming crowd as they stampeded toward the exits.

Thaddeus climbed up the wall he'd hidden behind and slipped through the crowd. Though he wanted to take advantage of the chaos and slay a few of the elites, he turned his focus to the magic-enhanced megaphone behind and above the box. In moments, he'd taken over the megaphone's magic. Sensing a magic more powerful than his own, the announcer fled.

They're so weak. I can't believe I used to admire them!

Kyrell's tail flicked in agreement.

"Kill it! Don't let it escape!" The headmistress' shrieks somehow managed to carry over the chaos.

The elites' dragons, who'd scattered from the cage, quickly encircled the arena, creating a barricade. A row of elite guards scrambled to the arena walls and materialized bows with ten-foot arrows.

With an ear-piercing roar, the dragon broke through the damaged metal, stood on his back legs, and stretched his wings.

Time slowed.

Despite old wounds, tears in his wings, and stiffness in his joints, the dragon appeared magnificent to Thaddeus. Despair faded from the creature's eyes as he looked skyward to the stars, to the clouds where he belonged.

Then forty magic arrows embedded in his chest.

As his eyes glossed with death, something jerked on Thaddeus' soul.

Kyrell...

I felt it too.

The tug came again as a powerful wave of magic crashed into them. Where the dragon's body lay, Thaddeus sensed a swirling pit—a void where the dragon's soul had once been. With black tendrils, it reached out for him, for anyone, to fill the emptiness. Irresistibly, it pulled him in deeper and deeper and deeper...

Thaddeus!

Hard ground collided into him, shoving breath from his lungs. When he looked up, past the stars blotting his vision, Kyrell was standing over him, tail poised to strike him again.

Snap out of it, Thaddeus. That's a soul vortex.

A hand to his throbbing head, Thaddeus used Kyrell's tail to stand. *What in Susahu does that mean?*

A rip in the spiritual, magical realm opens when a dragon is killed violently. It's a gaping wound that'll fill itself with anything and everything, even if you're not the murderer. Look over there. You almost joined them.

Thaddeus' blood ran cold. Just to their right, an entire row of riders lay strewn across the seats. Dark blood trickled from every orifice, their eyes sunken and black. Only then did he realize how much his own eyes hurt and the drip of blood oozing from his nose. He tore his gaze from them, a shiver racing down his spine as he wiped the blood away.

With shaking legs, he followed Kyrell as they moved away from the cage, from the body, from the lingering death.

Laughter pierced the air as the headmistress mocked the hysterical audience. "So you came to see blood but cower when it lands in your laps. *Dasunab!* Did you really think I'd let one accident end my games?" As the elites taunted, a nervous chuckle rippled through the crowd. Slowly, they made their way back to their seats as the dragon's body was dragged away, the arena sand raked, and metal magic casters mended the cage. In only minutes, the "accident" was erased.

Thaddeus shook his head. The headmistress' skill at manipulation was unmatched. But what disturbed him most of all was how no one seemed interested in *why* the cage was ripped apart.

Why don't they care?

Kyrell shook his head. *Maybe this has happened before.*

I doubt it. Don't you think they'd want to seek out the offender and punish them to make a statement? Unease slithered in his stomach.

Kyrell didn't have an answer.

A dark cloud settled over the arena. Everything grew muted, distant, and quiet, as if in a dream.

Another chained dragon staggered into the arena. The headmistress announced the next tamer, a magicless fighter. The crowd swooned; this was clearly one of their favorites.

The smaller gates below opened. The *Xeneluch-shuvub* stepped out.

Thaddeus staggered against Kyrell. "No."

"Thanatos! Thanatos! Thanatos!" The crowd's screaming churned his stomach.

With a few quick steps, Thaddeus descended the staircase, axe in hand and ready to throw himself at his brother. Then as the crowd stirred, eyes full of fear landing on him, Kyrell's tail wrapped around his waist and dragged him back up the steps.

Dasun. *You must keep your wits.* Kyrell's voice boomed in his mind, driving all other thoughts away. *You cannot let your anger and vengeful thirst consume you. You have a bigger plan to end all of this once and for all. Don't compromise it by acting like a child.*

But I can't watch him kill a dragon.

Then don't.

Thanatos lifted his sword above his head, soaking in the cheers, oblivious to the pain of the dragon pulling against the chains, crying to be free, to the life he'd snuff out, to the lives he'd already ruined.

Syrinthia was right. The *Jen-Jibuź* had changed him. He was taller, stronger, older. He reeked with the dark magic the Shadows warned him against—a magic that granted strength and power beyond natural gain.

Doubt grew. *Will the Pure Magic be enough?* Thaddeus was hanging all his trust in a magic he hadn't even channeled yet. His heart skipped. Then Koa's voice rang in his memory. *"Doubt is the fuel of the Corrupt Magic. You must banish doubt to make room for Joad."* Straightening his shoulders and taking a deep breath, he connected his voice to the megaphone and spoke.

"Stop," his voice boomed across the arena.

The crowd felt silent. The dragon ceased struggling. Thanatos stopped gloating.

"This is wrong. All of it. The games, the fighting, the senseless bloodshed. You're all better than this."

A few bystanders jeered and screamed for the games to resume. Guardsman rushed around the megaphone, searching for the culprit. A magic wielder placed his hands upon it and scowled. It would take more than one rider to take it back.

"You may not know another way to live. You've been taught that dragons are animals, that only the elites can bond, that only some can use magic, but none of that is true. Believe me, I used to think the same thing, but then I realized this is no way to live. Look at the person next to you. Do they look happy, healthy? Is this the best you can do with your lives?"

To his surprise, many of the riders turned to each other, eyes wide as recognition dawned. One woman broke down sobbing.

Confidence fueled Thaddeus' words. "This is not what the Duvarharians were created for. Before the Golden Age, the world was just like this. Dragons were hunted, and hatching grounds were controlled by religious officials. Their twisted religious control was as detrimental then as our government is now."

Someone cheered. A few more joined in.

The headmistress screamed at her guards, threatening to kill them if they didn't find the intruder. Three more magic wielders stepped up to the megaphone. Time was almost up.

Joad, put your message in their hearts.

"But a Duvarharian named Joad and his dragon, Falkner, taught differently. He showed that all dragons and riders were equal and heirs of the Pure Magic—a creation magic empowered by peace, love, and acceptance. Pure Magic created Rasa and has the strength to recreate *everything*. And it's accessible to you because Joad's spilled blood released it back into Rasa. We're not isolated in our bodies. We're connected to each other, to the dragons, to the land, and to magic. We don't have to be slaves any longer!"

Nearly half the crowd roared in agreement.

A man jumped up onto a border and screamed, "Down with the government and the elites!" Others quickly followed.

Thaddeus' heart raced as Kyrell's wing wrapped around him. *It's working. Syrinthia was wrong. Change is possible. Nothing is stronger than the Pure Magic and Joad.*

The crowd surged toward the elites as they clung to each other, cursing the crowd, panicking as their own audience turned against them.

Thaddeus's eyes landed on a young woman as she closed her eyes, attempting to tap into her magic. A spark danced between her hands as she struggled to concentrate.

"That's it," Thaddeus whispered. He pushed a tendril of energy to her, encouraging her to release the magic she'd kept oppressed.

The white magic crackled to life as her Shalnoa glowed. Eyes shining, she faced her palms to the elite's box. A mass of energy streaked toward them, smashing a corner of the granite wall to dust. Dozens of other riders followed her lead, tapping into parts of their souls and minds they'd been told didn't exist. Many of them cried when the magic appeared. Some threw masses of energy into the elites' box, crumbling it piece by piece. Many were so awestruck, they simply watched the magic dance around their hands.

Incredible. Kyrell's tail flicked, his eyes sparkling.

"It is." Tears filled Thaddeus' eyes as the riders came to life, waking up from a very long, very bad dream. They were free, and with Joad's message, they could change the world.

"Time to free the dragons."

CHAPTER 36

If he could release the dragons, they'd have a chance to bond with the riders in the audience. The wonder of seeing Duvarharians bond freely stood a chance to change the headmistress' heart. Then freedom would spread like wildfire as the newly bonded pairs carried Joad's message across Peace Haven. Miracles could happen.

Excitement hot in his blood, Thaddeus turned to make his exit. His eyes glanced over Thanatos in the arena. Their gazes locked.

Dread opened like a gaping maw in his stomach as the fury in his brother's blue eyes burned into his. Thaddeus broke their connection and raced through the doors and into the dark halls. Thaddeus leaned against the shut doors, grateful the darkness covered him like a cloak.

"He saw me. He'll tell them it was me. Oh, gods, what do I do?"

Kyrell stalked down the hall past him. *We're going to get down to the pits before they find us, and we're going to free those dragons or die trying. You gave your fellow riders hope, now let me give my kin the same.*

Steeling himself, Thaddeus caught up to Kyrell then mounted. His heart beat so loud, he was sure the elites would hear it.

When they reached the bottom levels, they turned left instead of right and used magic to blast down a locked door. When the smell of blood and feces burned their noses, they knew they were on the right path. Thaddeus covered their faces with purifying magic so disease wouldn't set in their lungs.

Down a flight of stairs and through another tunnel, they entered the dungeons he and Syrinthia had been in three years ago. He paused to look at the very gate the Zoics had been locked behind. Familiar fear and failure rose into his heart as he remembered that day. *Today won't end like that.* It couldn't.

A flicker of life moved beyond the gate. He rushed to it, feeling the presence of more Zoics. This time, he didn't wait for them to come to him. Instead, he used magic to unlock the door and cast it open. Though he didn't have time to coax them into the light, he sent a stream of his magic into the darkness so they could know they were free and would have energy to escape.

Heart breaking, he forced himself to pass the animals howling in their cells. He tried and failed to drown out their pitiful cries.

I'll come back. He wasn't sure it was a promise he could keep, but he wanted to try.

The halls widened into newer construction. With one last blast of magic, the final door opened, and they stepped into the dragon dungeons.

The floor-to-ceiling cells were far too small to be crammed with so many and bloodied dragons. Many of them were restrained around their necks, legs, and wings by hefty metal bands, which chains could easily be attached to. The center of the cavern's ceiling boasted a trap door and elevator system leading to where the dragons were chained and released in the arena. In a dark corner lay a motionless pile of limbs and wings.

Thaddeus' legs nearly buckled under him as he moved closer to the youngest dragon, even smaller than Kyrell had been when they'd bonded.

"What use do they have for a dragon so small and helpless?" His fingers wrapped around the cold bars, heart sinking as the dragon scrambled to the back of the cell, hissing as it tried to hide in the shadows. Thaddeus didn't sense much intelligence in the dragon, as if its will had been destroyed by its captors.

Bait, Kyrell whispered, pressing his snout to the gates. *She's a bait* dragon. *They're sometimes used to lure the other dragons out or enrage them. If they're lucky, they get killed by the fighter dragons their first time out.*

"If they're lucky?" Thaddeus' eyes roved over the little dragon's scarred and mangled body. One of her wings hung lifelessly by her side.

Being mauled and thrown back into a cell over and over is a much worse fate than death.

Thaddeus wanted to do the same to the elites. A few deeps breaths did little to calm his anger. "That won't happen to her again." The metal glowed as the acid from his hands dissolved it. Puddles of liquified metal gathered on the ground.

The little dragon's eyes widened as she chirped fearfully.

"Talk to her if you can. Show her what's happening. I don't think she's strong enough to fly out, so tell her how to get out the way we came."

Only a few minutes later, the cramped space was full of dragons shrugging their wings and stretching their stiff limbs, some for the first time in months. Between his and Kyrell's acid, only cooling puddles of metal remained of the cages and collars. If the *Vuk Quseb* wanted to harbor dragons here again, they'd have to spend thousands of *femi* in repairs.

Now to find our escape.

Closing his eyes, Thaddeus calmed his mind and opened his consciousness to the Pure Magic. *Joad, show me what is above. Show me who will oppose us and make our path clear.*

For a moment, nothing happened. But when Thaddeus opened his eyes, his vision had changed. All inanimate objects bled together, seemingly unimportant, while all living creatures shone brightly with life. When he looked up, he saw through the ceiling, revealing two Dragon Riders operating the elevator. Though their magic traces were strong, they wouldn't stand a chance against twenty dragons at once. When he stressed the importance of finding a way out, the path lit up in gold. Above them were two doors. One led to the arena sands, the other outside—freedom.

Thaddeus' heart thundered in excitement as he opened his physical gaze and thanked Joad.

Kyrell rumbled in satisfaction. *Let's go.*

With Kyrell by his side, Thaddeus drew on both of their strength and imagined pulling down the ceiling. Purple magic twined from his hands, fastening to the elevator in the form of two chains. A screaming groan filled the air as the wood and metal strained against the guards' protection seals.

"I don't know if I'm strong enough." Sweat poured down his face, drenching his clothes. Even with Kyrell's energy, he could feel himself failing.

When he nearly collapsed, a tail touched his leg, then a snout to his back. Every dragon either touched him, Kyrell, or each other, lending him their strength and magic. The flood of power that surged through him was nearly uncontainable. With one last pull, the seals were broken, and the elevator fell with a crash. A gaping hole awaited them.

The guards above yelled in surprise and anger, but before they readied their magic, a small dragon flew up to meet them. A spray of blood decorated Thaddeus' face as he mounted Kyrell. They flew up next, the other dragons close behind.

With a single breath, Kyrell melted a hole in the doors' hinges. Before he could finish melting them, the largest dragon threw himself against them, wrenching the doors away from the wall before jumping outside and into the air. The others couldn't follow fast enough.

Thaddeus hollered in excitement as the dragons roared and took to the skies. The audience screamed, half in horror and half in awe.

We did it! Kyrell charged outside, beating his wings. *Now hopefully some of the dragons and riders bond and perhaps change the headmistress' heart. But if that doesn't work, we'll have enough on our side to tear her down.*

Anticipation flooded his veins. "I have one thing to finish before the guards find us."

Kyrell nodded. *Of course.*

Not wasting another moment, they flew back into the pits.

When they arrived at the familiar cell, a group of about thirty or forty confused Wyriders wandered the halls. Some were Terrestrial, and others were Bestials, but all were his family. Frightened when Thaddeus and Kyrell drew near, they huddled together and wept.

"Hey, hey." Hands held out, he kept his voice low and soft. "It's alright. I'm one of you. I'm here to save you."

A young feline Bestial stalked toward him, hissing. After hesitating, she sniffed the tips of his fingers. When she looked into his eyes, he knew she understood what he was. In only a second, she was lying at his feet and purring, her puma tail flicking from side to side.

Only moments later, the other Zoics surrounded him, clinging to him, weaving flowers into his hair or pressing their heads against his hand. None were older than ten or twelve years old; Thaddeus wondered how long it'd been since they'd seen their parents or been properly cared for. Their innocence reminded him of Zara. Thinking of the Duvarharians who hunted such beautiful and gentle creatures, sold them, performed experiments on them, or forced them to face death in the arenas, Thaddeus couldn't help the growing thirst for vengeance in his heart.

Do monsters like that even deserve to be saved by Joad's message? Or should justice come at the end of a blade? Kyrell wondered.

Thaddeus didn't want to answer.

Taking a deep breath, he smiled, knowing these Zoics' lives wouldn't end like that. But first, they had to get them into the forest while the chaos caused by the freed the dragons kept the guards' eyes off the trees.

"Come on, we have to hurry. We're going outside." They cheered. "But we can't let them see you, so as soon as you see the forest, run for it as fast as you can. Stay hidden close to the fence until I come for you."

What will your mother think when you bring home a small army of Zoics?

Thaddeus chuckled nervously. *I'm more worried about my father.*

But at that moment, they were most worried about the guards. Already, dozens of footsteps and angry voices echoed through the dungeons.

After a few narrow misses and one wrong turn, they reached the last door. Cautiously, Thaddeus pushed it open, scouting for guards. The chaos above seemed to have grown more violent.

But when he looked up, he saw a rider sitting astride a freed dragon. She called the others to rise and be free. A grin swept across Thaddeus' face. The world was changing, and he was proud to be a part of it.

This is only the beginning, Kyrell reminded him as a knot of emotion tightened in his chest.

Thaddeus waved at the Zoics in the tunnels as he held the door open. "It's clear. Remember what I said. Run to the forest and wait for me by the fence."

The Zoics pushed past him in a whirlwind of wings, tails, branches, and leaves as they rushed for the trees. With as much magic as they could spare, Thaddeus and Kyrell fueled their flight. But in his concentration, he'd forgotten his own surroundings.

A footstep behind him alerted him to another's presence. He moved in time for a blade to nick the back of his neck. A hot line of blood slipped down his back. In a heart's beat, he drew his axe. He knew who it was even before he turned.

Kyrell growled low, muscles tense, ready to pounce. *I didn't feel him sneak up. Something's wrong with him; dark magic hides his intentions.*

"Thanatos." His vision clouded red as he stared deep into his brother's bright blue eyes. *The* Jen-Jibuź *is giving the riders an unfair advantage; that's why so many more dragons die.*

Thanatos grinned, but the gesture didn't travel to his eyes. "Thaddeus. So thoughtful of you to show up to my game." His voice was deeper, richer, than Thaddeus remembered. His hair was longer, his face chiseled. Dark olive skin was bronzed from the suns. If the hate on his face didn't make him so ugly, Thaddeus' might've been jealous.

"Did you like how I made sure to ruin your fight first?" Though the timing had been a coincidence, Thaddeus loved how Thanatos' nostrils flared and eye twitched.

"Yes. How thoughtful."

"Are you here to kill me?" The words jumped from Thaddeus' lips before he could stop them. Any brotherly love he used to feel for Thanatos melted into determination and disgust.

"I don't know. Are you going to surrender for the headmistress to decide your fate, or are you going to be the *umu qucha esh num* you've always been?"

Thaddeus wanted to rip his tongue out, but he held back. *Joad, give me strength to give him the same chance you gave me.* Deep down, though, he didn't believe Thanatos deserved that chance; Kyrell agreed.

"I plan on doing neither. I'm here to bring peace and freedom. Even to you. You don't have to live this life, Thanatos. If you want, you could bond with a dragon, learn magic—"

Thanatos threw back his head and laughed, eyes sparkling cruelly. "Do you really think I don't want this?" He pointed to the stadiums. "They *love* me. They bend the world to my whim. All the adults who patronized us now quiver at my feet because of the money I bring them. In a year's time, I'll be one of the richest *Xeneluch-shuvub* in Duvarharia, and someday, I'll travel to Wyerland to fight there too."

Thaddeus bit his lip and lowered his weapon. His teeth ground against each other as his heart warred with itself. "I *don't* think you want this. I think you take out your self-hatred on the dragons you fight. I think you've narrowly escaped so many soul vortexes that sometimes you wish one would swallow you whole. I think the prizes make you desire more, but nothing satisfies you. I think you crave love, so you force it from Syrinthia. I think you hate this life."

Thanatos sneered and swung his sword in large circles, stalking closer. "Oh, by all means, tell me who I am. You'd know more than anyone else after you abandoned us for three years."

His words bit like cold metal, but Thaddeus pushed on. "I *do* know you, Thanatos, and I know you're not a monster. As much as I hate you for the things you've done to the people I love"—his fist tightened around his axe—"I want to believe none of that was truly you. With Joad's message, you'd be free to walk away from this life, back to the light, to the things that make you truly happy."

For a moment, Thaddeus thought he saw remorse flash in Thanatos' eyes.

"And I didn't abandon you," he whispered against his tears. "I went to find us hope."

The look in Thanatos' eyes disappeared. "The only one of us who ever needed hope was you, Thaddeus. You've been pathetic and helpless since you were born. You've always been weaker, stupider, more sensitive, a crybaby. If success stared you in the face, you wouldn't have the *vukko* to take hold of it. Of course you'd choose some flimsy ancient religion to cling to. It's the best you can do."

Humiliation burned in Thaddeus. His teeth drew blood from the inside of his mouth as he kept himself from throwing his axe at Thanatos' head. "It's not some 'flimsy religion'. It's truth and it's freedom. It has the power to change the world."

"Alright, then prove it."

Thaddeus wanted to crawl into his own skin. "I can't. Joad has to—"

"That's what I thought." Thanatos sneered as he lifted his sword. "Because if you could prove it was real, then why aren't we living in paradise *right now*? Why do people like me have to put up with insufferable *huladaub* like you?"

Tears streamed down Thaddeus' face. His lips opened, then shut against his resentment and hatred; fear held them back. Fear came because he'd never been strong enough to stand up to his brother. Fear stayed because he had to believe a better life existed. Fear won because he wanted to be worthy of Joad's saving. Otherwise, what hope did he have? Even he was a murderer.

"I've already alerted the headmistress. I told her I'd leave you to be made an example of, but now"—he drew a hand down his blade—"I don't think I want to wait." Then he lunged.

Sparks flew as Thaddeus' axe met Thanatos' sword. Though acid burned into the ordinary blade, Thanatos didn't stop advancing. With rapid, trained combinations, Thanatos had both Thaddeus and Kyrell slinking away, unable to do anything but defend.

I'm not good enough. I've never been good enough. Why did I think I'd changed?

Kyrell screamed. *No! We're better than this! You're letting your old self cloud your mind. You've trained for this. You have magic, and you have Joad! Fight like the Shadow you are!*

Kyrell's energy and strength poured into Thaddeus, and their minds melded even deeper. Thaddeus let all the training and instinct push aside the childhood insecurities and sibling rivalry holding him back. *I am good enough.*

Kyrell roared triumphantly.

Step by step, slice and dodge, they shifted from defense to offense. Thanatos' eyes widened as his younger brother pressed him with techniques far beyond what was taught in the academy.

The righteous voice in Thaddeus told him to stop, to pull back, to show mercy. But the bitter child of revenge whispered that this was his chance to end the pain once and for all.

Thaddeus hooked his axe around Thanatos' sword and cast it aside, leaving him unprotected. With a deft movement, he spun his axe toward his neck, the image of his brother's head apart from his body filling his mind with satisfaction. But the memory of a boy's jaw parting from his face replaced gratification with horror.

His axe mere inches from skin, Thaddeus' locked eyes with his brother's; fear shone in them. He pulled back the attack.

The edge of the axe caught Thanatos' chin, taking a slice of skin and blood with it. His scream filling the air made Thaddeus' stomach roll.

Breath and muscles burned. He became acutely aware of his own body as the intimate connection with Kyrell faded. But instead of exhaustion, he felt elation. He'd not only beaten his brother but also his own lust for revenge in showing him mercy.

"Get up." Thaddeus held his axe to Thanatos' face. He was kneeling, hand dripping with blood as he clutched his wound. Kyrell moved to keep him cornered.

When he finally staggered to his feet, Thaddeus expected to see defeat in his eyes. Instead, he smirked. "You should've killed me when you had the chance, you soft *nesa*."

Kyrell roared in warning but too late. Thaddeus only had time to whirl around before the headmistress released her magic.

Everything in both his mind and Kyrell's went dark.

Chapter 37

The metallic smell and taste of blood rudely brought Thaddeus to his senses. Flickering lights blinded him. Someone nearby cried, pleading. Pain around his wrists, waist, chest, and ankles alluded to his bondage. The ground he lay on was cold and unforgiving as it dug into his bare skin, his clothes having been stripped away. When he tried to speak to Kyrell, he sensed only vast darkness. Horror and the smell of vomit beside him churned his stomach.

When he opened his eyes again, the throbbing in his head grew worse. Chaos hummed dangerously in the air. Bars encircled him. A constant light shone ahead of him. The crowd screamed, some in fear, some excitement, others in horror.

"Thaddeus!" The crying voice washed over him, fraught with emotion. Warm hands touched his face, his shoulders, his hair, his chest. "Are you alright? How do you feel? Can you sit up?"

Groaning in response, he realized how scratched his throat was. Had he been screaming? A vague memory and nightmarish visions washed over him. Clenching his eyes shut, he tried to roll over, away from her, away from the light, from reality.

"No! Thaddeus, listen to me." Her hands pulled him close, struggling to lift him. "You have to sit up right now." With shaking fingers, she undid his bindings.

Pain exploded through his face as her soft palm struck his jaw. The shock sent a shiver of energy through his veins as he sat up. His heart raced fervently, erratically, as if no longer sure how to function. Foreign magic snapped in his cells like a virus.

"Can you see me?" Her hands cupped his face, turning it to face her.

"Syrinthia?" Her name fell unappealingly from his lips, his face uncomfortable and swollen. Vision clearing, he took in her dark skin lined with cuts. Gold metallic lingerie hung from her slumped body. Tied up in intricate knots and braids, her thick hair shimmered with gold dust. Strapped around her feet were delicate golden sandals and laces that twined up to her thighs to a short white skirt. "Why are you dressed like that?"

A strange laugh parted her lips. "They want me to look like a goddess."

"But you already do. Every day," he rasped. A small blush decorated her cheeks beneath the dark circles under her eyes. "Why are you down here? With me? You deserve . . . better." The weight in his heart pulled his head and shoulders down.

"No. This is where I'm supposed to be." Tears filled her eyes as she pulled him to her chest and held him, resting her cheek on his tangled hair. "I don't want to be anywhere else."

Leaning into her touch, he tried to make sense of the spinning world, tried to remember what happened before the darkness descended upon him. Kyrell's mind stirred from unconsciousness, and a wave of clarity flooded him. "I thought . . ." He tried gazing up at her. "I thought you were safe. I left you . . . so you'd . . . safe."

She shook her head and tripped over her words. "I–I'm never safe. Not–not from them."

Panic stirred in his stomach; nausea pushed bile to his throat. "No, you have to be safe. I have to save you. I have to—"

"Oh. Thaddeus." She gently rocked him, cradling his head. "It's too late."

"It can't be too late," he whispered. "There was so much more—"

The cell gate swung open with a crash. Two bulky guards tore Syrinthia away. Thaddeus screamed, clinging to her touch, raging against them, begging for mercy, for them to take him instead. Two more guards grabbed him and jerked him to his feet. But as much as he struggled, Syrinthia didn't. She walked submissively to the waiting crowd. Looking back one last time, she smiled, tears falling down her cheeks, before the guards pulled her into the light.

"Syrinthia!" He thrashed against his captors. They responded by driving their gauntleted fists against his bare flesh. Distantly, he was aware of Kyrell straining against his own chains and tormentors.

The headmistress' voice rang above the others as her sickly green magic washed over every inch of the arena and dungeons.

"You do not want to follow Joad and the boy who speaks of him! He is nothing but a myth, a made-up legend to instigate bloodshed and civil war. You are free under the guidance of the elites and the Council. You work for them, and they care for you. What more do you want?"

The crowd's unintelligible cheers shifted into a singular chant. "Blood! Blood! Blood!"

Thaddeus cried. His heart constricted, feeling as if it were giving up. *What new realm of Susahu is this?*

The guards dragged him into the light. It burned his eyes, and he threw up. Spitting up acid, he tried to shield his eyes from the flickering lights. The guards didn't let him; his shoulder popped under the strain. Kyrell's muffled scream rang out somewhere behind them as painful shocks of magic prodded him onward. When he came into view, Thaddeus choked against his own screams.

Long streaks of red had been whipped into his once flawless purple scales. Metal cuffs bound his wings and tail to his body. An iron muzzle clamped his jaws shut and cut into the flesh around his eyes.

Kyrell . . .

No worse than you.

Thaddeus wanted to protest until he saw his own torn, beaten body through Kyrell's eyes. The small comfort they shared lasted only a moment when their eyes fell on the arena.

They'd captured them.

Every. Last. One.

Every freed dragon, Zoic, and rider knelt in the arena's sand, arms, wings, and legs bound with magic, heads bent in shame and fear. The headmistress, elites, and even the Council looked down upon them with hate and disgust.

"No." Thaddeus strained against the guards, screaming and spitting at the headmistress. They didn't turn an eye. The pain in his own flesh eventually quieted him. *This is all my fault. I shouldn't have come here. I shouldn't have given them a chance.*

"Quiet!" The headmistress shouted, and the crowd immediately fell silent, lips sealed and minds numbed under her magic.

"This is the traitor! This is the boy who sought to disrupt everything we've worked so hard to create! Have we not taken care of you, Peace Haven? Look at your beautiful homes. Have the games not paid for them? Have we not made Peace Haven a city of power and prestige? We did, not the Dragon Palace! They only see worth in magic and dragons, but we see *you*. We've given you the opportunity to rise to power *without* magic or dragons. We've taught you to hold your own in a world that wants to see you fail. Haven't we?"

The crowd found their voices as they chanted in agreement. With venomous words, they threw rotten food into the arena, many of it striking the already beaten Duvarharians and Wyriders.

"But this *child* and his dragon want to take that away from you! What say you to that?"

"Kill them! Make them pay! Kill them! Make them pay!"

Thaddeus tried to call upon his magic, but shame and pain blocked him from it. Instead, he curled in on himself as hundreds of eyes turned to him. The ravenous bloodlust in their gazes tore into his soul, exposing him more than the lack of clothing ever could. He was hated, humiliated, unwanted. He wasn't enough.

I should've sunk under the waves of the Xeneluch-Rani. Then none of this would've happened. Who was I to think I could change the world?

Kyrell whimpered as he collapsed to the sand, scales stinging from the fire of the whips. *I'm glad you didn't succumb to the water. I'm honored to have bonded with you. Perhaps this is alright. Perhaps someone will carry on our message after we die, like they did with Joad, and change will still come.*

Thaddeus' stomach flopped. He didn't *want* to die. Not now. Not like this. But Joad had given up his life, seemingly pointlessly, and the world had still changed after it. Maybe Kyrell was right. Maybe he should accept the end with dignity. Maybe Syrinthia was right. Maybe it *was* too late.

"Let your bloodlust be satiated by something else." The headmistress' words sparked a ripple of confusion. "Killing them will only make them martyrs. I say we teach them a lesson they won't forget, shall we?"

No. Thaddeus' eyes locked with the headmistress'. A dark smile narrowed her gaunt lips as she raised her hands. *Joad, please help us! Please!*

The guards lining the arena lifted their arms and conjured their bows of magic.

The little feline Zoic looked at Thaddeus, tears streaming down her face. She opened her mouth, first in a plea, then in pain and shock. A fiery red arrow protruded from her chest.

"No!"

The world slowed. The Zoics, dragons, and riders stood still, suspended in time as their bodies filled with arrows. Then the air echoed with the dull *thuds* of their bodies dropping lifeless.

Magic burst from Thaddeus' body. Acid poured from his skin, eating into the hands of his captors. Kyrell's bonds fell away as they rushed to each other. In a heart's beat, Thaddeus was on his back, flying toward the headmistress, ready to burn her body into a pile of blood and bone.

But chains of gold magic shot up toward them, wrapping around their waists and legs. With unexpected power, they were wrenched to the sand. Choking as he breathed in more sand than air, Thaddeus slipped as he and Kyrell struggled to their feet. He forced himself to ignore the red liquid pooling around the lifeless captives only mere feet away.

"Give him his axe! I want to see how pathetic a traditional rider really is!"

Someone from the elite's box threw out his axe. It embedded into the sand inches from Kyrell's tail. Thaddeus raced to grab it. With a shaking arm, he held it weakly in front of him while scrubbing sweat and sand from his eyes.

Their attacker drew close.

The blood drained from his face.

"Syrinthia?"

But she wasn't who he remembered. This Syrinthia loomed nearly twelve feet tall. Her once dark hair burned fiery gold and moved about her head and shoulders as if underwater. Huge golden dragon wings spread from her back, and a long tail snaked around her in the sand. Instead of two beautiful dark eyes, four golden eyes burned in their place. A spear stood tall in her hand, the other held the magic chain.

She hesitated. Her eyes flickered between gold and dark brown. "Thaddeus . . ." she whispered. Then her back arched as she fell to her knees screaming, black veins spreading through her wings. When she staggered to her feet, her eyes were dull and lifeless under the pain. This is what she'd meant when she'd said she transformed, when she'd said they'd taken her beautiful power and turned it into something worthy of the games.

Thaddeus wanted to rip out his own heart to stop the pain inside it.

"Fight her and show us your might, Dragon Rider! Show us how powerful the ancient Duvarharians are!"

No, I can't! Hysteria clawed at his mind.

But it wasn't a choice.

Her spear stabbed at him in rapid succession, cutting through the air so fast, it screamed. He and Kyrell struggled to dodge her attacks; they had no chance of getting their own in. With no armor to protect them and their already present wounds slowing them down, they didn't stand a chance.

He haphazardly threw himself onto Kyrell's back as they stumbled away. Kyrell's foot caught on the tail of one of the dead dragons, and he staggered. The split second was all the opening she needed. Kyrell's piercing scream reverberated off the arena walls as her spear penetrated through his wing. Searing pain laced through Thaddeus' shoulder, and he nearly fell from Kyrell's back.

But even as Kyrell's blood trailed behind them, overwhelming pain blinding them, they refused to turn and fight.

The crowd roared in disappointment.

They breathed for a moment. Syrinthia hadn't followed them; the pile of bodies stood between her and them. She staggered back, tears rolling down her face. Her lips parted in protest, and for a moment, Thaddeus saw her grip on the spear slacken. Then the headmistress clenched her fist. Syrinthia clawed at her head, screaming in pain and madness as the magic flooded her body.

With renewed rage and pain that demanded reprieve, she opened her wings and took to the air. Nothing stood between them and her.

Kyrell, we have to move. But when Kyrell dodged a whip of her golden chain, Thaddeus fell from his back. He tried to stand, but his legs buckled under him. His limbs felt like lead against the sand.

With a low groan, Kyrell dragged himself to stand over him.

"Kyrell, move." Thaddeus saw the headmistress grin. She knew the pain Kyrell's death would bring him. He choked on his tears. "Kyrell!"

Kyrell didn't move. Thaddeus willed his body to.

Syrinthia raised her spear.

The crowd waited, silent in anticipation.

"Syrinthia! Don't!" To save his dragon, Thaddeus pulled himself through the sand and into the path of the spear.

The tip of the blade scratched his head before halting. Blood trickled through his scalp and into his eyes. "Don't do this. Please," he cried.

"This isn't you. They've done something to you, and I don't know what but—" Sobs raked his chest as he stumbled toward her. "But I know you love Aqua Dragons and the bridge with the *Qeźujeluch*."

The spear lowered as she landed.

"I know you've wanted to use your power to take other's pain away. I know you want to be free."

Her eyes widened and flickered between black and gold.

"Syrinthia, I know *you*." Her wings flickered and dropped, drawing back into her back as her frame grew smaller.

The headmistress screamed orders, trying to conjure the magic she tormented Syrinthia with.

They were inches apart now. "You've taken so much pain from me," he whispered. "Now let me take yours." When he touched her face, he opened to her pain.

Every muscle, bone, fiber, thought, and memory inside him burned with a thousand fires. He fought back screams. He wanted to tear apart his own flesh until the pain stopped. But he refused to take his hand from her face. Kyrell's warmth and strength flooded through him as he pressed against his back and took some of the pain himself.

It was only them, surrounded by her glowing, warm magic. The rest of the world faded away.

"I have a *Suźuheb* of an Aqua Dragon I made for you at the Palace. I want to give it to you. I want to tell you everything I saw and show you the life I dreamed of for me, for you, for *us*. Joad will make a way. He'll save us. He and the Pure Magic will keep us safe."

"Thaddeus, what are you saying?" Small tears of blood leaked from the corners of her eyes. Her hands found his.

Cupping her cheeks, he pressed a soft kiss to her forehead and choked back a sob. "I'm saying I love—"

Her body jolted, and she gasped. Confusion filled her eyes as blood trickled from her lips. The tip of his brother's sword extended farther from between her breasts.

"No, no, no." He caught her as the sword withdrew and she collapsed.

They fell together, his body shielding hers from the fall. With shaking hands, he cradled her head and brushed back her hair.

"Syrinthia!"

Her eyes dulled as she struggled to make them meet his. Bubbling blood frothed at her lips as she struggled to speak.

"Joad, help us!" Thaddeus begged to the god he'd given his entire life to, sworn his soul to. Hands over her chest, he screamed the healing spells over and over as Kyrell poured his energy into him. But despite all his faith, all his desperation, despite crying to Joad, the Creator, and the Pure Magic, the wound refused to heal.

Her breath slowed with the flow of blood, stark against his pale skin and the sand.

"Why isn't it working? Joad, where are you?" Tears fell to her face as he pressed his lips to her forehead, her cheeks, her nose, waiting, searching, desperate for the Pure Magic.

With one final breath, her chest rose, then stilled. Her eyes stared off, clouded. He buried his face in her neck and screamed.

Everything around him—the crowd's cheers, Thanatos' mocking words, the headmistress' confident speech—all of it faded away.

He didn't come. Thaddeus' body quaked with rage, with grief. His fingers clawed at her limp body with fain, false confidence his god would save her, would save them all. *We gave everything to him, and he didn't come.*

Kyrell spoke the words lurking in their hearts. *Everything the Shadows taught us–love, forgiveness, second chances, acceptance, hope, peace–all of it was Xeneluch ue.*

He failed us. They all did.

When Thaddeus closed her eyes, he stopped holding back. Hate, resentment, trauma, bitterness, every emotion he'd shoved deep inside him for the sake of the Shadows and Joad he finally unleashed. Placing her gently on the ground, he took to his feet, axe clenched tightly in his hands.

"Look what you made me do, Thaddeus. Is this what you wanted? To get Syrinthia killed?" Thanatos hid a laugh as he brushed away fake tears.

"Take her name off your lips, you *żebu quhuesu dasuunab*."

No longer held back by fear, by morals, by religion or love, a deep power came loose inside Thaddeus. Instead of fighting it, shunning it, hiding it, he embraced it.

Magic rushed from Thaddeus' hands and wrapped around Thanatos, lifting him into the air in a deadly embrace. All confidence drained from his face, replaced with fear and a half-spoken plea for mercy. Thaddeus didn't wait to hear the rest of it. With a wave of his hand, he threw his brother against the arena wall. His body hit the unmoving granite with a hollow *smack*. Limp, he fell to the sands and lay motionless.

Chaos broke loose.

On Kyrell's back, Thaddeus took to the air. With one wrench of Kyrell's acid-laced teeth, the arena metal gave way. In seconds, five of the elites lay dead, their heads either separated from their bodies by his axe or their bodies melted by acid. Though the fresh blood was hot and slick on his skin, he took one of the dead man's clothes and armor and donned it. Then he saw his target: the headmistress.

The hate and rage inside them gave strength like nothing the Shadows had taught, though they'd warned him against it. Now he knew why.

We're unstoppable.

This is what we were made for.

Cutting through the crowd and anyone who dared oppose them, Thaddeus left a trail of blood-slicked steps. The headmistress stood ahead of him, screaming at her guards for protection. The power inside him easily batted away her magic as if she were a child waving a stick.

When he reached her, he ignored her pleas and wrapped his hand around her neck, squeezing tightly. Her green eyes bulged as her face turned a dark shade of red.

Kyrell tore the guards to pieces if they dared come close to save her. Most quickly chose their own lives and fled. Thaddeus cast a glance at the arena; it stood nearly empty. The few spectators who remained stood in frozen shock next to motionless, bloody masses.

Amazing how they no longer desire bloodshed when it's from their own flesh.

"Do you see the lives you've ruined?" Thaddeus didn't loosen his grip.

The headmistress croaked an answer.

"You've taken someone I love." Tears of acid slid down his face, filling his vision with a purple haze. "I think it's time I return the favor."

He spat in her face. At first, she blinked in confusion. Then her eyes widened as the burning started. Small holes dotted her skin, her eyes, and her mouth as the acid in his saliva melted into her body. Her silent screams rasped through the air as she thrashed against him. Her burned eyes rolled into the back of her head.

When the acid reached her throat and made her skin slick, he dropped her, letting her thrash out the last moments of her life in pathetic agony. Only after her body lay still did he kick her lifeless form and walk away. She would never harm another student or Zoic again.

Eyes roving over the blood bath before him, he felt no empathy, no remorse. They hadn't shown him mercy; he'd only returned the favor. But that wouldn't bring back who he'd lost.

Taking a deep breath, he reached to Kyrell for support as they picked their way around the bodies. Burning flesh and acid stung their nostrils and permeated the night air. The air was still—far too still—under the darkening evening sky.

Landing on the sand below, Thaddeus balked before approaching Syrinthia's body. A small piece of him had almost hoped he'd come back to find Joad had healed her. He didn't even know why he'd chanced to hope. Collapsing to his knees, he pulled her lifeless form into his arms and cradled her, holding her head to his heart.

"I think we could've been happy together," he whispered through his sobs. "I think we could've changed the world, you and me."

Tucking a braid behind her ear, he rocked her back and forth, biting his lip against the sobs and screams clawing at his throat. "I dreamed of us having a family. Little part Zoics, Dragon Riders, and whatever beautiful creature you were. I dreamed we'd teach them about love and beauty and acceptance. I dreamed of a world we'd be safe and happy together."

Kyrell let out a keen roar and bent his head beside Thaddeus. He pressed his snout to her head as great tears formed in his eyes. Thaddeus had never seen a dragon cry. The sight broke his heart all over again.

A deep breath rattled in his chest. "But what I dreamed for us could've only existed in a perfect world. I see that now." He pressed his lips to her forehead one last time, lingering as he breathed in a mix of metallic blood and floral perfume. "I'm sorry I realized it too late."

He placed his hands on her chest, gathered his magic, and whispered his intentions. *"Nuben ehash vul. vul ehash nuben. Lisu nuflu żufaż e."* Shining light encased her body, transforming it into pure energy. The energy condensed as he envisioned the Aqua Dragons she'd loved so much and the beautiful gold of her magic. The blue and gold stone that remained in his hands contained everything good and beautiful about her. Now her body would be safe with him instead of those who'd abused her.

Pressing the amulet to his chest, he made a vow upon it. "Never again will I let the weakness of my own heart stop me from doing what must be done. Never again will I let mercy prohibit true justice. Never again will I let a hollow faith stop me from saving the people I love."

Turning, he took one last look at his brother's motionless, twisted body by the wall and mounted Kyrell.

"Duvarharia cannot be recreated until it has been purified of the rancid evil inside it. I will make sure it pays for its sins. And if I must decimate it down to the very dirt to do so, then so be it."

With a roar of approval, Kyrell pushed off from the ground and took to the skies.

Nufa *Joad and the Shadows of Light. I will make my own way.*

PART 6
Reign of a Traitor

PART 6
Reign of a Traitor

Chapter 38

Southern Duvarharia

A Few Weeks Later

THADDEUS SET DOWN his empty mug and leaned forward, wiping yeasty froth from his lips as he waved over the bartender. He'd spent the last few weeks traveling to outskirts of Duvarharia, searching for anything pertaining to the power that the Shadows of Light warned about—the Corrupt Magic. Finding even whispers of it had been harder than he'd anticipated; most Duvarharians already possessed a deep fear of magic, let alone of one that held the power of complete annihilation.

But his persistence had begun to pay off. Rumors had surfaced of a recent catastrophe caused by Corrupt Magic.

Sliding three gold *femi* to the bartender along with a silver for his drink, Thaddeus whispered, "Tell me what you know about the Sleeping."

The bartender's eyes narrowed as she rolled her sleeves up her tattooed arms and firmly planted her hands on the bar top. "I don't know anything."

Thaddeus shrugged and reached to retrieve the currency, but her long nails gently tapped his hand.

"Well, maybe I know something."

Smirking, Thaddeus pulled another gold *femi* from his pocket and held it up. "All four for everything you know and a little more."

Nodding, she turned away. After filling another customer's drink, she glanced around to make sure no one else needed her before leaning over the counter. With her nails she drew circles on the old wood. "The Sleeping . . . You ask about a *very* dark magic." Her eyes searched his. "Aren't you a little too handsome to be thinking about things like this? Surely you have a pretty girl at home you'd rather spend time with."

Thaddeus' stomach turned and contemplated rejecting the alcohol he'd just drank. "She's dead." He answered curtly. "Tell me what you know."

Eyebrows raised, she released a deep breath. "Whatever I say, it didn't come from me."

He nodded.

"A little over a hundred years ago, the forests in Ventronovia were alive, full of nymphs, tree spirits, water spirits, and Fauns all living under the Centaur government in Ravenwood. They were called the Sházuk. But a little-known cult that worshipped the stars rose to oppose the beliefs and government of the Centaurs. They insisted they could take control of Ventronovia if they followed the stars themselves rather than the Great Emperor who supposedly controls them. They were cast out, but in secret their practices grew. Somehow, they obtained a relic—"

Thaddeus's eyes widened as he leaned forward.

She scoffed. "Don't get your hopes up, boy. The relics, or artifacts as they're sometimes called, are hardly more than legends barely worth passing down from generation to generation. Most are just over-glorified family trinkets sold for obscene amounts of money."

Narrowing his eyes, Thaddeus pulled the *femi* back. "I didn't ask for your opinion, only information."

Growling, she rolled her eyes and continued. "Somehow, they *supposedly* obtained a relic, a staff of some kind I think, or perhaps a lyre. I can never remember. Anyway, they apparently created a bridge between Rasa and Hanluurasa—something that *supposedly* hasn't happened for thousands and thousands of years. In doing so, they unleashed a star entity who spread dark magic over the land. The leader of the cult realized what she'd done and used the relic to banish the being back to Hanluurasa. But inadvertently, the relic amplified the creature's power, and the entire living forest fell under what they call the Sleeping. Whatever happened, they're as good as dead now."

"Can they be wakened? Can the magic be reversed?"

She shrugged. "If anyone knows anything about it, it'd be that pompous Centaur Igentis Artigal." She hissed his name with sing-song contempt.

A small grin spread across Thaddeus' lips. *You hear that, Kyrell? A relic that harnesses Corrupt Magic and amplifies it. It may hold the power we need to begin Duvarharia's renewal.*

Indeed.

Vaguely, Thaddeus became aware of Kyrell snarling at a few mercenaries who eyed his shining scales. A second later, one lay dead and the other ran down the street smelling of fear and urine.

The woman's voice snapped him from Kyrell's thoughts. "And one more thing, if it's of any worth to you." Her teeth tugged her lips as she debated whether to share her information or not. "I've heard rumors of a similar relic."

Narrowing his eyes, Thaddeus leaned forward. "What do you mean, 'similar'?"

She shrugged, shaking her head. "I'm not sure. But that staff, or whatever it is, isn't the only object floating around Ventronovia with that kind of power. Southern Duvarharian legend speaks of another relic that made its way to the Cavos Desert and caused some problems before disappearing."

"Anything else you can tell me about it? That's a little vague." Frustration welled up in him, but he bit it back.

A shiver ran across her skin. "No. And I'm done answering your questions." The hard darkness in her eyes told him pressing her would be fruitless.

"Thank you." Thaddeus pushed her the gold *femi*, surprised when she didn't take them.

"I don't know what you're after, but I see the look in your eyes. I've seen it many times on more faces than you've lived years. You won't find what you're looking for."

Annoyance twisted Thaddeus' heart as he stood from the tall stool. "And what do you think I'm looking for?"

Shaking her head, she hesitantly swept the gold *femi* into her apron before wiping her hands, as if she were wiping them clean of guilt and responsibility. "Revenge."

WHAT YOU'RE PROPOSING *is nearly impossible. You can't just walk up to the Igentis. It took your own father, an ambassador, years before he was given clearance.*

I know. Thaddeus ripped off a piece of stale tavern bread and shoved it down his throat, using acid to break it down. *But I know Artigal is a religious dasun. The Shadows spoke highly of him and alluded to his support of their cause. As long as I can keep that "look" out of my eyes, I'm sure I can convince him I'm still with the Shadows long enough to get the information I need.*

Kyrell rumbled in anticipation. *I've always wanted to hunt in their forests. The other dragons say they have the largest deer and elk in all Ventronovia. Hopefully, you won't blow our cover too quickly and I'll get my chance.*

Thaddeus laughed and tossed the last of the bread to the wind, watching it fall to the forests below until the darkness of night swallowed it whole. *I promise I'll do my best. But even as religious as he is, Artigal is one of Ventronovia's most powerful and intelligent creatures. He's no stranger to spies, assassins, and traitors. It'll take all our wit and magic to deceive him.*

Trans-Falls, Ravenwood
A Week Later

STRAIGHTENING HIS SHOULDERS, Thaddeus adjusted the dark, flowing garb of the Shadows of Light. Standing before the great *Gauyuyáwa* was more surreal than he'd ever imagined. A spark of pride lifted his lips. His father had worked tirelessly for years to stand here; all he'd done was show a guard the Shadow of Light symbol in his Shalnoa.

Without another question asked, they'd led him through their thriving forest city straight to the *Gauyuyáwa*. To his surprise, the expanse of buildings stretched far through the branches of the trees. Though his father had explained many times that the Centaurs lived in trees, Thaddeus had never been able to picture it until now. With how effortlessly the Centaurs traversed the large steps and swinging bridges, Thaddeus was convinced they used some sort of strange magic.

It was quickly obvious that their city, as extensive as it was, had not been built for the comfort of dragons. Though their doorways and roads were big enough to accommodate the Centaurs who towered high above him, they were still too small to accommodate most dragons. It irked him that Kyrell couldn't join him in the *Gauyuyáwa*. But if anything went wrong, he was confident Kyrell would tear the tree apart, regardless of its importance to the Centaurs.

He'd been instructed to wait outside while the guard spoke to Artigal. A heated conversation has risen on the other side of the great doors. Thaddeus prayed to his mother's gods that they'd let him in. Then the door swung open.

The guard shook his head, clearly in disagreement with the Igentis. "The Igentis Artigal has agreed to meet with you."

Smiling graciously, Thaddeus bowed and spoke with the honeyed sweetness that used to come so naturally but now felt like poison. "Thank you very much. This is truly a matter of extreme importance."

Hopeful dasunab, Kyrell scoffed. *Religion is such a weakness.*

Thaddeus couldn't have agreed more.

The Centaur stepped aside and motioned for Thaddeus to enter. After he did, the door shut heavily behind him—a reminder of the distance between him and Kyrell.

Nothing will go wrong. I'm here to find a way to awaken the forest. I've been sent by the Shadows themselves. The messenger for my arrival must've been late. He'd repeated the story so many times, he almost believed it. Almost.

As he moved farther into the tree, he was amazed at how much bigger it seemed on the inside than the outside. It was big enough to host a good number of Centaurs, and the staircase circling up to higher floors would accommodate them comfortably.

Then Thaddeus shifted his attention to the center of the room. There stood the Centaur he'd once been positive he'd never see.

"Igentis Artigal." Thaddeus bowed low as the entirely white Centaur turned to face him.

"Welcome, Thaddeus, rider of Kyrell. I've heard a great many things about you."

His heart skipped a beat. When he looked up, awe filled him. The swirling colors in Artigal's eyes were mesmerizing and unreal. He felt as though he were peering into something more than just another creature's eyes. "Only good things, I hope."

Artigal didn't crack a smile. "Only the best. The Shadows of Light spoke very highly of you. They said they believe you're the savior of the Dragon Prophecy." His eyes narrowed, clearly skeptical of their judgement. Thaddeus wondered if he knew the full prophecy or not, if he knew something the Shadows didn't.

Maintaining his lie despite his doubt, Thaddeus shrugged and smiled. "I know not either way, but regardless, I've strived to make my life worthy of Joad's praise."

Though his comment seemed to relax Artigal's shoulders, he quickly understood why Artigal had such a harsh reputation. Not a hint of amusement or leniency existed in his eyes or face.

"Which is what brings me here."

Artigal crossed his arms. Though he wasn't as tall as most of the other Centaurs Thaddeus passed, his presence held overwhelming power and authority.

"I heard from the Shadow of Light that the forest is under the influence of the Corrupt Magic and has been subdued in what you call the Sleeping."

Something of emotion flashed across the Igentis' deathly white face, but he remained silent.

"The Shadows of Light taught me about Joad and the Pure Magic, and I'm aware Pure Magic holds power over the Corrupt. I don't know if I can be of assistance, but I'm looking to make a change in Duvarharia, to prove to the riders and dragons that Joad's authority is unwavering. I think if I could help wake the forest, it would be a huge example for their faith."

Silence stretched between them. Artigal's eyes never left his. Thaddeus found it almost impossible to maintain the eye contact for so long, feeling he would be lost or his secrets exposed if he did. But though he wanted to look away, he trusted that Kyrell's hold on his memories and unwelcome thoughts would be enough to shield him. Though Artigal was the most powerful Centaur in Ventronovia, his magic was still weak compared to most Duvarharians, at least in theory.

"Usually, I wouldn't trust someone I haven't spent an inordinate amount of time with. Especially with a project so sensitive. I'm surprised the Shadows of Light even told you about the Sleeping. It's something we've tried to keep under Rasa's whispers."

Thaddeus remembered how fearful the bartender had been, and he inwardly scoffed. *I wonder how many creatures Artigal has killed to keep this quiet.* "I understand; however—"

Artigal held up his hand. "I gather from what you've said that you haven't heard the Dragon Prophecy."

"That's correct." Thaddeus' stomach rolled.

"Then you must not know the prophecy stated the traitor to Duvarharia would be Quinlan's son."

Thaddeus' face drained of blood as he bowed his head. He had to think fast. "I do know, actually," he whispered very quietly.

Artigal's presence grew darker. "I know who you are, Thaddeus, Quinlan's son."

Panic wrapped its icy hands around his heart. *Just how much does he know?* "Igentis, I understand how this looks, but I have a brother, as I'm sure you know. Thanatos, he's the oldest. He . . ." Thaddeus let the tears collect in his eyes. "He's lost his way. He hates Duvarharia, the dragons, riders, everything. He's determined to rise to the top of the games and spread his influence across Duvarharia and even to Wyerland."

Shaking his head, Thaddeus wrung his hands and continued. "I fear what that means for Duvarharia. Wyerland is to the north, and the Wyriders hate the Duvarharians. If he gains enough power and convinces them to seek revenge . . ." Thaddeus gritted his teeth, turning to face Artigal with determination. "I may not know the full prophecy. I may not know who the traitor is, but I *do* know I love my country, I love Joad, and I love dragons and magic. I want to see my country and people thrive, not be destroyed."

Artigal stroked his beard as his gaze roved across Thaddeus. Just as he opened his mouth, the door behind them flew open, crashing against the wall with force that shook the tree.

"Artigal! Don't let this boy deceive you!"

Hardly able to conceal his snarl, Thaddeus whirled around. In the doorway stood the most strange and frightening Centaur he'd ever faced. Her skin was the color of diluted blood while her horse body was nearly black; pink hair grew from a mane down her back and nearly trailed the ground. A belt hung around her waist, holding potion bottles and herbs. But the most horrifying sight was the mangled skin of her body. Thick scar tissue created a monstrosity of disfigurement across her horsehair.

When his eyes met hers, he gasped. White and sightless, they darted around the room until somehow her gaze landed on him.

In her hand stood a twisted, dark staff that exuded power. Immediately, Thaddeus realized it was the relic that put the forest under the Sleeping.

Artigal himself is harboring the relic and has put it into the hands of a mangled, blind Centaur? He's more corrupt and foolish than I thought.

Indeed. But she was screaming something about the stars and your destiny from far down the road. She sees through you. Either convince them both, or kill her and take the staff. Our time here is running out.

"Artigal, this boy is not who you think he is."

The Igentis moved to Thaddeus' side. Claustrophobia closed in on him. Though his hands ached to hold his axe, he'd lose all chance of negotiation if he drew it. "I'm Thaddeus, son of Quinlan, rider of Kyrell. I can't be anyone else."

She spat and slammed her staff against the floor. "Yes, of course you are." She pointed with a long finger, the tip and nail stained black. "But that's precisely the problem, isn't it, Thaddeus? You have blood on your hands. I see it!"

Thaddeus would've laughed and mocked her lack of sight. But she *knew*. The rumors of the Peace Haven massacre hadn't even reached the small taverns yet, and no one knew who'd done it. *So how does she know?*

Eyes narrowing, Thaddeus sucked in a deep breath through his teeth. "I don't know what you're talking about. I've never taken a life."

She laughed darkly and stepped closer. "You're on a war path, a path for death and revenge. The prophecy spoke of *you*, not your brother. *You* are the traitor of Duvarharia. *You* wish for its destruction, and *you* have come here to find a power great enough to do what you seek."

Thaddeus hated her with all his soul.

"And you will not have it."

In a split second, Thaddeus drew his axe and leaped toward her. A roar of fury escaped his throat as he aimed for hers.

But to his surprise, she side-stepped the attack and jammed the top of her staff into his side, knocking him to the ground. In a flurry of attacks, she descended upon him with unbelievable accuracy and skill. Only twice, he found an opening and nicked her skin. But her muttered words of healing and the potions on her belt stopped his acid.

A shout as loud as thunder shook his muscles, rendering them useless. For just a moment, a powerful magic raced through Thaddeus; he reached for it, tried to contain it, but it escaped his grasp. Recognition dawned on him. This was the Pure Magic. Hatred flooded his veins.

With a snarl, he lunged at Artigal.

Blinding white magic streaked toward him. Searing pain flooded his face, streaked down his neck, and throbbed in his head. Hot blood splattered against his skin. Then the vision in his left eye went dark.

He clutched his eye, screaming against the unbearable pain. Blood seeped through his fingers. The Pure Magic tore through him, burning the parts of him that wished for hate, destruction, and revenge. Outside, Kyrell roared with the shared pain and staggered as he clawed at his face, trying to free himself of the anguish.

Dragging himself to his feet, Thaddeus held his axe in front of him. Tears blinded his good eye. Any second, he expected either the staff to beat the life from him or for the Pure Magic to tear apart his soul. Instead, the female Centaur roared with anger.

Artigal held her back. "Esmeray, control yourself! The Great Emperor won't let me kill him." Frustration and helpless anger burned in his fiery red eyes. "It's not in His will, not now." To prove his words, he attempted to unleash the magic again. It sparked at his fingertips, then died.

A flicker of cold victory passed between Thaddeus and Kyrell. *So, we're not the only creatures the faithless Pure Magic has failed.*

No matter, Artigal can keep it. We'll find the much more reliable Corrupt Magic and never be abandoned again.

As he staggered to the door, an image flashed before his mind.

Artigal, small and old, full of color, was lying on a soft bed. He was no longer in power, no longer full of the Pure Magic. He was dying. Through the vision came a message.

Smirking, Thaddeus turned to face Artigal one last time, their eyes burning into each other's with unrestrained disdain. "You will not live to the Great Emperor's return, Igentis Artigal. You will die a slow, pitiful death before seeing what you so passionately desire."

The Igentis' eyes flashed from red to blue, the anger in his face dissipating into disbelief and horror. Then the emotion vanished under a practiced mask. "The Great Emperor may not wish you dead yet, Thaddeus, traitor of the Dragon Palace, but the next time we meet, you will not be so lucky."

Laughing, Thaddeus hissed through the pain, "We shall see, *ñekol guxo*."

Before his luck ran out, he fled the tree and mounted Kyrell. They were in the sky and far away from Trans-Falls before anyone could retaliate.

Thaddeus drew strength from Kyrell and muttered a strong enough healing spell to stop the bleeding in his eye and numb the pain. But no magic he was capable of could return his sight. Inwardly, he cursed Artigal and promised his revenge.

The Centaur woman, Esmeray, may have ruined his first plan, but the Sleeping hadn't been the only rumor he'd heard. Another older legend spoke of a great power hidden in Ventronovia, one supposedly strong enough to give the wielder almost unlimited connection to the Ancient Magic.

Where to next, little one?

To the Cavos Desert and the once great dragon city of Yazkuza.

Chapter 39

Cavos Desert, Ventronovia
A Week Later

A WEEK PASSED BEFORE Thaddeus had amassed enough supplies to last in the barren desert. By then, rumors of the massacre had spread like dragon fire. Some of the stories he'd overheard in taverns replayed in his mind as he and Kyrell glided over desert sands.

"I hear nearly forty Duvarharians were killed at an academy. In cold blood. They say one of the dragon tamers snapped."

"No, I heard it happened at a Xene'mraba. A Dragon Rider protested and started a mob. Then the mob was killed for 'excessive violence'."

"You've got it wrong. An illegal rider and his dangerous dragon murdered a bunch of innocents at an academy because of mental illness and resentment."

Each account was different, some with more truth than others. But one theme stayed the same: fear that the perpetrator had yet to be captured and no one quite knew what he looked like.

Thaddeus twitched a smile. This wasn't how he'd imagined creating change in Duvarharia, but it was far more effective. Awareness of the dragon games grew and with it came protests against corrupt officials and the illegal dragon markets. Thaddeus hoped the movement would gain momentum.

Thaddeus, do you see that?

Thaddeus let his mind meld into Kyrell's as he gazed through his dragon's eyes. Miles away, an anomaly in the desert caught their attention. Rocks jutted from the sea of sand and dipped down into canyons.

Do you think those're the ruins?

Drawing back into his own body, Thaddeus nodded. *Most likely. We'll be there by midnight I expect.* Among rumors of himself, he'd also heard of great sand creatures that hunted at night through vibrations in the sand. Most didn't believe them, but Thaddeus was certain he didn't want to chance Rasa opening to swallow him while walking through old desert ruins at night. *Then we'll make camp and wait until morning to explore.*

Rocky cliffs drew closer, and Thaddeus knew they'd found the old city. What little still rose from desert sands alluded to a once incredible city potentially larger than even the Dragon Palace.

From what the dragons told me, the entire city was originally occupied by dragons alone. They built everything with their own magic and for their own convenience. It remained like that for thousands of years until riders discovered it.

The idea seemed unbelievable.

When they landed, Kyrell rumbled happily and dug his claws deep into the ground. As soon as Thaddeus removed their supplies from his back, Kyrell tossed and turned in the sand, marveling at how it scratched and exfoliated his scales.

I wish we had something like this in Peace Haven.

You have the sands of the Xeneluch-Rani.

Kyrell scoffed. *It's not the same. I could live here.*

Rolling his eyes, Thaddeus proceeded to make camp. Wanting to spend as much time sleeping as possible, he ate only a loaf of bread and a tuberous root he'd snatched from unsupervised farmland. With a wave of magic, he renewed the cooling spell around their small supply of meat, propped his head up with rolled furs, and gazed at the stars. The sand was soft and warm, and he almost agreed with Kyrell.

Itches all scratched and scales soft and shiny, Kyrell finally curled up beside his rider.

The stars seem bigger here somehow.

Thaddeus agreed. He wondered how long it'd been since he truly looked at them. One by one, he picked out familiar constellations. Memories of his father and mother teaching him and Thanatos those constellations while lying on their lawn floated into his mind.

Angrily, he wiped away his gathering tears. How could he shed tears for his father and brother when they'd spared no love or mercy for him? But despite chastising himself, the tears broke through anyway and were soon followed by heart wrenching sobs, which landed heavily on the desert night air.

Kyrell wrapped his wing around his rider, his own heart aching for the times and people now lost.

Dozens of soul voids stared back at him when he tried to close his eyes, just as they had every night since the massacre. When he'd finally fall into fitful sleep, he'd awake screaming and sweating, the vortexes hovering at the fringes of his mind. The terrors left him crazed and shivering, seeking anything to keep them at bay. At first, he'd used *ui-mufak*, but when it wasn't strong enough to banish the night terrors, he turned to dark solutions—sometimes dragging cuts into his arm, sometimes consuming powerful herbs bought from dealers in shady inns.

But out here, nothing stood between him and the gaping darkness and loneliness. Not even the blade of his axe brought relief. In the vast openness of the desert, everything was larger and more consuming, not just the stars.

The moons moved slowly. Each shaky breath Thaddeus sucked in and out drove deeper the pain in his heart—a clawing, aching, screaming pain. With the pain came memories: Syrinthia's bloodstained lips and the hole in her chest. They arose, and he relived them, too afraid of forgetting her entirely to bury them again.

You cannot keep dwelling on her death. She was so much more than that.

Thaddeus dug his nails into the thick scales on Kyrell's legs. *How can I not? It was my fault she was killed. It was my fault Thanatos hated me so much he was willing to drive a sword through her to punish me. I should've waited until after his fight. I shouldn't have yelled at him when we were young. I should've been kinder, more patient.*

He was a brute, Thaddeus. Nothing you could've done would've changed that. He was the one yelling at *you. He* ostracized *you from the academy and his friends. It was never your fault. None of this was, least of all his hate, pride, and anger. Those are his emotions to own–his responsibility, not yours.*

But Syrinthia told me she wanted to leave. She knew how powerful the Jen-Jibuź were. She tried to warn me, and I didn't trust her. And if I didn't trust her, then did I really . . . Though he didn't have the strength to finish, Kyrell heard the words in his heart.

You did trust her, and that was why you went anyway. Because you knew that even if you ran away, they would've found her; running away only prolongs the inevitable. Just because you wished to prove her wrong doesn't mean you didn't love her. I've never seen a rider love another so purely and truly as you did. You cannot take that away from yourself, not for anything. You tried. That's what matters.

Thaddeus shook his head. *Do you think she knew?*

Kyrell took a deep breath. Thaddeus' memories of her flashed through his mind: her laughing, pulling him along to someplace in the school, standing up to bullies for him, learning magic with him, and confiding in him about her powers. *I know she did. More than anyone else.*

Instead of comforting Thaddeus, Kyrell's words brought up a new grief inside him. Fresh tears dripped to the sand. *Do you think she could've loved me the same?*

I don't know.

Though true, Kyrell's answer drove a stake through his heart. Thaddeus grieved the loss of his truest friend, but even more, he grieved the loss of possibility. "I don't think I'll ever love another. I don't think I'll ever find another like her." Sniffing, he wiped his nose on the already damp corner of his cloak.

Kyrell sighed and laid down his head. *I don't think so either.*

Clinging to his dragon, Thaddeus pleaded with any god who'd listen to chase the nightmares away. Finally, darkness swept over him, and he fell into a dreamless sleep.

AT THE FIRST LIGHT of morning, Thaddeus already had their camp packed. In sunlight rather than moonlight, the canyons appeared much larger than he'd initially anticipated. Impatience crawled its way up his throat. With nothing more than a few vague words from the rumor-passing bartender to lead them, their search could take months, maybe even years. Even if he searched the sand for magic, the sheer expanse of the ruins would make it as difficult as finding a diamond in the desert.

"We certainly have our work cut out for us." His voice was considerably cheerier than he felt.

Kyrell snarled, just as impatient and less eager to mask it.

Deciding to work in a grid pattern, they marked their starting point with a streak of purple magic and landed on a small ledge below. At one time, it'd been a small landing pad; now it was weathered stone and jagged edges. Beyond the landing pad was what might've been an entrance if it wasn't caved in with rubble.

Already frustrated, Thaddeus stilled the impatient tremor in his hands and planted his palms on the rock. Inhaling deeply, he pushed his mind beyond his body, through the rocks, and into the passageways beyond. Faintly, he sensed great halls, caverns, rooms, stairs, and ledges. Bitter nostalgia of *Rabur-Fechamu* in the Dragon Palace valley washed over him. But nothing inside possessed the power he was searching for.

Opening his eyes, he stepped back. "This place is so old, most of the magic traces have been dissipated by nature. Even if what we're looking for *does* exist, who's to say its magic trace hasn't faded as well?"

Kyrell shook out his wings and dragged his claws across the stone. *Your negativity is driving me insane. What if we just rip it apart stone by stone or melt it with acid until we've found the relic?*

Thaddeus would've been more amused if Kyrell wasn't so serious. Part of him wished they could, but they treaded on sacred ground. Old tomes and scrolls remained hidden deep in the caverns, preserving rich history. He wanted every ruin to be intact when he finished what he'd started in Duvarharia, not only to restore its ancient knowledge and history, but to allow dragons to inhabit Yazkuza once again.

Kyrell agreed grudgingly. *But promise me one thing: if this search takes longer than three days, we'll look for something else. If we spend too much time chasing myths and paying barkeepers and secret traders, someone is bound to take notice. If that means moving on to something besides whatever is here, then so be it.*

Seeing the wisdom in Kyrell's words, Thaddeus promised. They marked the ledge, then flew to the next.

A cave-like opening extended a few dozen feet into the cliff side but ended again in rubble. Any books he found along the way were either faded beyond legibility or of menial topics like cooking and the reuse of hatched dragon shells.

Every cavern they explored presented more of the same. Some went far into the rock; others were no more than piles of debris. Some held priceless artifacts like mosaics, pottery, weapons, or fabrics; none were what he wanted. He left them undisturbed, to be collected later when Duvarharia was rebuilt and he could ensure their preservation.

When they reached the bottom of the canyon, they took a moment to rest in the shade of a nearby hatching spire. Though he promised Kyrell three days, Thaddeus was already willing to quit. It felt foolish to be running around Ventronovia searching for mythical relics. Clearly some were more than myth, but not every rumor could be based in truth. Either the relic they were looking for didn't exist, or the desert had beaten the power from it.

I didn't expect you to give up so easily.

Thaddeus tilted his head back, squinting against the relentless suns.

Downing a swig of water from the canteen after cooling it with magic, he shrugged. "I'm just tired is all. I haven't given up. Not yet."

Kyrell didn't press the matter. They both knew Thaddeus wouldn't rest until he'd saved Duvarharia from itself. Time moved slowly as they rested. Kyrell's eyes slipped shut as he descended into slumber.

"Wait." Thaddeus jumped to his feet, eyes wide.

Kyrell scrambled to his feet, Thaddeus' realization flooding his thoughts. *The magic. It's all around us!*

"Precisely." Heart pounding, Thaddeus abandoned his supplies and ran into the desert. The magic would have to originate somewhere. They just had to follow the intensity of its frequencies. "At first I just thought it was the life around us, but there aren't nearly enough creatures in the desert for it to be so powerful."

Is it the sand itself?

Thaddeus shook his head, stumbling over the sand and rocks as he rushed toward the growing frequencies. The pulses grew stronger until they started to fade. He moved back a few paces and stomped his feet. A hollow echo answered. Dropping to his knees, he frantically brushed away the sand. "Help me, Kyrell. It has to be under here."

Kyrell reared back his head, sucking in a deep breath. Then, with Thaddeus' help, he concentrated his breath into a powerful wind. A stretch of old wood appeared.

I'm amazed you didn't break it by stomping on it, Kyrell sneered.

Ignoring him, Thaddeus called upon his magic and pushed it into the wood. Wiggling huge metal stakes from the wood, he stacked them to the side and levitated the planks. A gaping hole lay before them.

The darkness below swallowed all light, even with the suns at high noon. Dizziness washing over him, Thaddeus peered over the edge. Magic pulsed from the cavern in droves so powerful, his eyes watered.

"This is a very powerful place. The relic must be here. I know it is."

Sharing his rider's confidence, Kyrell waited for Thaddeus to mount before he dropped gently into the darkness. As soon as they cleared the opening, he spread his wings. Even with their caution, they crashed into the rocks below with entirely more force than expected.

An avalanche echoed through the cavern as the rocks beneath them gave way. Kyrell managed to scramble onto a rocky ledge before plummeting with them. They waited to hear how far down the rocks landed.

Silence.

A chill ran down Thaddeus' spine. "I'm hoping they just hit the sand that quietly."

You don't think this is a bottomless pit from the old legends, do you?

Thaddeus nearly responded, saying he didn't believe in such absurd legends, but why not? All the others had been true so far.

Ears ringing, Thaddeus held onto Kyrell's tail for support and stretched out his foot. He stepped down onto another ledge. Just a foot down was another. He stepped onto it and then another. "Kyrell, these are stairs."

Hopeful, they took one step at a time until the slightly curved staircase leveled out to sand. They shared a sigh of relief.

Realizing his magic wouldn't sufficiently light the ravenous darkness, Thaddeus instead reached his magic to the shining sands above them. Channeling the sunlight, he bent its rays and fought against the darkness as he pulled the light around them. It glowed dully, but as his eyes adjusted, he could start to make out some details.

The entire room was circular in shape. A perfectly preserved mural decorated the smooth wall. Breath caught in Thaddeus' lungs as marveled at it.

The image had no true beginning, middle, or end; each image flowed naturally into the next. From the desert the dragons raised a thriving civilization. The dragons commanded magic in a way he'd thought only riders could. Their power was awe-inspiring, unquestionable, and terrifying—everything Thaddeus dreamed them to be. The murals also depicted the final extinction level battle against the Etas.

A cold shiver rushed through Thaddeus' and Kyrell's bodies. He almost expected the painted Etas' demonically red eyes to blink back. Their bodies took the shapes of mangled mutations of ordinary creatures, each different from the last.

Then his eyes fell on a massive metal door—not a painted one, a *real* one.

"Kyrell . . ."

Some of the designs are Shadows of Light runes.

"Do you think . . . ?"

It must be.

Tripping over hidden debris, Thaddeus pushed through the thick darkness, feeling it was more fog than shadow. Collapsing to his knees, he pressed his hands to the door. Immense power radiated from it and whatever lay beyond. This was everything he had been looking for and more.

Anticipation hummed in his veins as he rose to his feet, hands suddenly sweaty. *This is why I was destined to become a Shadows of Light. This door has been waiting for a Shadow for thousands of years. It was waiting for me.*

With tender familiarity, he read the engravings—the same spells, chants, and mantras he'd fastened into his heart during his time at the Dragon Palace. Taking a deep breath, he extended his magic into the door; purple energy flooded the grooves and veins in the dark iron.

"This is it," he whispered.

His magic filled the rest of the door. He waited for it to open. And waited. And waited.

Worry creased his brow as he pushed more of his magic into it. But instead of it opening, the door rejected his magic. Slowly, the purple energy receded from the metal and snaked back into his hands and fingers.

Growling, Thaddeus fought against it. "I am a Shadow of Light, and I command you to open!" With one last shove, he thrust his magic against the door. It shuddered, then returned it to him. In a blast of pain and blinding purple light, it threw him back on the sand. His blood burned from the force of the magic, and air escaped his lungs as the back of his collided with a rock.

When his vision stopped spinning, he clambered to his feet and charged the door, striking it, pleading with it, cursing it. It wouldn't react. It wouldn't accept even a spark of his magic.

Collapsing before it, Thaddeus slammed his fist into it before his shoulders sagged helplessly. Acid tears scorched the sand beneath him. "I don't understand. I'm a Shadow of Light. I have their mark in my Shalnoa. I pledged my life to them, and I did nothing but follow their teachings. I called to Joad, pleaded with him, bargained with him. And for what?" A sob tore from his throat. "Nothing."

Burying his face in his hands, he wept. He wept for the betrayal he'd endured and for his wounded eye, which burned from the salt of his tears. He wept for Syrinthia, whose death seemed impossible to avenge, and for his mother he'd left to grieve alone. He wept because he could do nothing else.

When his tears slowed, Kyrell gently tapped his leg with his tail.

"What do you want?"

He pressed his warm snout to Thaddeus' face, breathing comfort upon him. *I know you feel abandoned, that none of this is working out. But I found something you'll will want to see, if for nothing else but to find comfort in the knowledge you once cherished.*

Begrudgingly, Thaddeus dragged himself to his feet with the help of Kyrell's tail and followed him into the darkness. On the opposite side of the cavern, Kyrell nodded to another door.

The door was void of Shadows of Light markings and already cracked ajar. A twinge of shame shot through him. He'd acted with the immaturity of a child, throwing a fit while Kyrell had moved on to find something else of use.

I apologize.

And I accept.

Leaning against the door, they worked together to open it. When it swung wide enough for Kyrell to slip through, they stepped inside.

The sight took his breath away.

A library bigger than the one at the Dragon Palace stretched before them. Two colossal dragon statues carved from single slabs of marble towered over the walkway before the enormous floor-to-ceiling bookcases on either side. Just like the library at the Dragon Palace, suspended walkways stretched along different levels of the bookcases.

As they moved past the giant statues, he spotted a few benches and even a lamp; they looked like children's toys compared to the scale of everything else. Even the books were nearly twice or thrice the size Thaddeus was used to, some even larger.

"I don't know what to look for or even where to start."

Neither do I. But this was the last place the Duvarharians fought against the Etas, wiping them from the face of Rasa for good. Perhaps they accomplished it by means other than that sealed door.

Nodding, Thaddeus moved to a stack of books under a nearby bench. It appeared as though someone had stuffed them there in a hurry. Taking the top book off the stack, he blew a thick layer of dust off it. As expected, the title was in the ancient language. Grateful for some of the Shadows' teachings, he opened the book. It was a battle log dating thousands of years ago, just before the Golden Age.

Hands trembling, he turned to the first year of the Golden Age, the year the Great Lord ascended the throne and the last fight against the Etas was won.

The log read as expected. The battle took place in the desert, and all remnants of the Etas were exterminated. Nothing spoke of a relic, power, or even a certain Dragon Rider with unnatural skill or power. Their win had been organic and fair.

But when he turned the page to learn more, a blank page stared back. Thaddeus scowled. *Why was this detailed log shoved under an abandoned bench, and why was the rest of it blank?*

"How old is Yazkuza?"

Kyrell shook his head, eyeing the log over Thaddeus' shoulder as he scanned every blank page for something they missed. *No one truly knows. But it officially ended when Ventronovia united under the Dragon Riders' first reign long before the Golden Age. After that, some cities or townships cropped up, but none lasted more than a couple generations. I think a stronghold was built for desert crossers, but it was abandoned after the Etas were killed. Then the Cavos Hatching Grounds thrived among the ruins for a couple hundred years until they fell into worse disrepair and were never used again. Nothing here is under five thousand years old, of that I am certain.*

"Surely, whoever left this here didn't anticipate the entire city being abandoned. But why didn't they come back?"

Perhaps he wanted it to remain hidden. Or perhaps you are not the first to find them.

Thaddeus set the tome on the bench and picked up the others. A couple were logs from other captains, also with blank pages after the start of the Golden Age; others detailed Etas, their strategies, the way they reproduced, and even their anatomy and intelligence.

None of it surprised Thaddeus; he expected a captain to record and collect information on the enemy. But why were they all together? Why were they shoved under a bench? Was Kyrell right? Had someone else found them first? If so, who?

As he scoured the books for information, Thaddeus noticed a tear on the edge of the first log's back cover. Frowning, he prodded it. The fabric woven tightly around the wood cover had either peeled away or had been ripped. On a moment's whim, he stuck his fingers into the tear.

His fingers brushed another paper. Heart thundering, he worked it out of the cover. It was as small as his hand and had hastily torn edges. A date, nearly missing from the top tear, read the very day after the last battle against the Etas was fought.

The ink was dark and spotted. An image drifted through Thaddeus' mind of someone hunched over a desk in the dark, writing so fast ink splattered on the page, smearing under his hands before he mercilessly tore the paper from a pad and shoved it in the torn cover.

Why write down something so secretive? Kyrell's tail flicked with impatience.

As Thaddeus deciphered the spotted writing, he quickly found out why.

"Twenty Etas escaped the last battle." Thaddeus' hands trembled as read further. "They fled up north to the wild open lands between Duvarharia and Wyerland. Ten of the best dragons and riders went after them. They never came back. I'm going to find them and hopefully some answers."

Dropping onto the bench, Thaddeus let the words sink in. He couldn't fully comprehend the true weight of what he'd just learned.

Either they killed each other, or the Etas did.

Thaddeus opened his mouth, closed it. Words eluded him as he realized the horrifying conclusion. "So the Etas could still be alive and might have been alive for nearly five thousand years now." Thaddeus turned the note over. Jumbled numbers and letters decorated the back.

Coordinates, I assume, though nothing like the ones used now.

Thaddeus' mind raced. Though the logs stopped before mention of missing Duvarharians, one of them had listed twenty names. He'd found and memorized them in seconds. "We must find anything we can about these riders: why they were chosen, who they were, and why they might've failed in killing the last Etas. We need to find any city records from this time that speak of them, even just a birth statement or arrest."

Before he'd finished speaking, Kyrell took to the air and flew from bookcase to bookcase, racing along the platforms in search of city records. Thaddeus moved the logs and Eta books to the center of the library and arranged them; the logs he opened to their last entry next to the list of names and the note; the Eta books he opened to the sections on reproduction. His head spun as he did the calculations. Hidden from the world, the Etas would've been able to reproduce at an alarming rate. After five thousand years, they'd have amassed an army capable of wiping Duvarharia off the face of Rasa.

Thaddeus sank into a chair.

Yes, he needed Duvarharia destroyed, but not the way Etas would destroy it. If they were still alive and they unleashed their full might on Duvarharia, he'd have nothing left to build from.

The prophesized threat from the north must be the Etas. Everything I've done, everything I've lived through has led me to this moment. Were the Shadows of Light right? Am I . . . the savior? Though the idea of being the savior of Joad's prophecy made his skin crawl, he couldn't help but long for the power it'd bring him.

Kyrell's wings kicked up a cloud of dust as he landed and urged Thaddeus to join him. They flew to a small dark alcove in the far back of the library. *It's not much, but these are all the personal records of that time. You can use your magic from here to find what we're looking for.*

Thaddeus moved among the shelves, hands brushing against book spines, eyes closed, mind searching. Visions of the papers flashed before him: all twenty birth records, nearly three mating records, one divorce, two arrests, and four egg clutch records. The information droned on and on as his magic scoured the shelves.

Then his magic latched onto something more than just a record.

His eyes snapped open. Thaddeus climbed onto Kyrell's shoulders, holding onto the bookcase for balance as Kyrell lifted him to the second highest shelf. Balancing on wobbling tiptoes, Thaddeus wrapped the book with magic and pulled it toward him. It dropped safely into his hands. With bated breath, he hopped off Kyrell, hesitating to open the journal.

Malice spewed from the pages as he touched them. The heart of the author who'd spent many hours capturing his thoughts with a *juufu* had not done so with good intent.

A single name remained etched on the inside of the book's front cover, presumably of the author. *Auryn.*

Drawings of dark magic rituals eerily similar to ones the Shadows of

Light performed danced across the pages. But though these rituals and incantations resembled ones performed in Joad's name, the intentions behind them couldn't be more different. Many were reversed. The hair on his arms prickled as he flipped through the pages. His eyes darted over his shoulders with paranoia and guilt.

They took the book to set it with the others. Thaddeus felt he had all the pieces of the puzzle, if only they could make sense of it.

As Thaddeus read the journal's dark knowledge, connections became apparent. The author, Auryn, had long been fascinated with Etas. The main topic was how the Etas were intelligent enough to form systems of government and society but remained chained to instincts that demanded the death and consumption of Duvarharians. In their blood thirst, all previous intelligence disappeared.

But after studying how the neural pathways in the Etas' minds changed when filled with the hunger for Duvarharian flesh, the author theorized the Etas could be controlled and manipulated; he believed that was how Eta kings formed entire armies with the bloodthirsty monsters. By extension, he proposed if one were to control the Eta King . . .

Thaddeus snapped the journal shut, his heart slamming against his ribs. "It can't be," he whispered.

Thaddeus couldn't believe they were even considering the half-formed, hasty, even crazy ideas jumping between his and Kyrell's minds.

But it seemed too good of an opportunity to pass.

Steeling himself, he opened the journal again and read the final entry:

I've done the research. I know it is sound. The Eta Kings are the strongest and smartest of the Etas. By way of their psychic neural connections–as present in the split Elcores who share a mind–the Kings maintain absolute control over their armies. However, they themselves are not above manipulation. Another Eta with a stronger neural connection could take their place. I've discovered an object that possesses that connection.

The relic is a necklace with the emblem of the first dragon country, Adriva, except an Eta skull is molded into its center where a dragon's head usually resides. I found it while scouring the ancient ruins beneath the Dragon City, Yazkuza. Yazkuza was not the desert's first major city; something even older once called it home.

As soon as I laid eyes on the necklace, sitting among the dust of thousands and thousands of years yet as shiny, silvery, and bloodred as the day it was forged, I knew it had power beyond anything I'd found before. It pulsed with magic. It called to me. And I answered.

We let the Etas escape. I and nine other Duvarharian pairs believe the Etas were never meant for our destruction; they were meant for our use. With their power and their blind rage, we can unleash them on the rest of Ventronovia and rule without opposition.

We are leaving right away to track the last of the Etas. I have the amulet. We're prepared to put my theory to the test.

Thaddeus lowered the journal. For a moment, his mind was too overwhelmed, too horrified, too excited to think. Then thousands of thoughts battled for supremacy.

If the Etas were still alive, and if he found the necklace, he'd not only be able to protect Duvarharia from the Eta's annihilation, but he'd also have an ancient relic that would give him an army and potentially channel enough magic to destroy and rebuild Duvarharia exactly as it needed to be.

He and Kyrell in perfect agreement, Thaddeus took only the note and the journal, leaving the other books. Then he closed his eyes, whispered a simple tracking spell the Shadows taught him, and directed his intentions to the journal and its unique magic trace.

When he opened his eyes, a trail of red and black hovered opaquely in the air, leading through the library doors, out into the cavern, up where they had entered, then on to the exact location of the relic.

A sinister smile upon his lips, Thaddeus mounted Kyrell's back and followed the trail out into the cavern. He took one last look at the Shadows of Light door. It seemed so small and insignificant now.

Without a second glance, he exited the cavern and resealed it for a future day. Then he put behind him the weakness of faith and hope. He'd tried and failed to trust a god. Now if he wanted something done, he'd go and do it himself.

Chapter 40

Eastern Duvarharian Wilderness
Two Weeks Later

By the time Thaddeus and Kyrell crossed back into Duvarharia, their supplies were nearly gone. They were met with wary glances at their first stop in a small farming community; rumors had spread that the Peace Haven killer rode an Acid Dragon. Duvarharia crept ever closer to the truth, and Thaddeus didn't want to be near a city with guards when they found it.

Day in and day out, they mucked through the wilderness, following wherever the magic led them until nearly two weeks had passed.

Thaddeus? Kyrell's thoughts snaked their way into Thaddeus' wandering mind, stirring him back to the present. He'd been lost in a memory, a sweet one back before the pain, back before the fear, back when Syrinthia used to come and tutor with him and Thanatos before the evil reared its head. In the memory, he'd been able to forget everything else, to simply bask in the warmth of a simpler time. But the remembering made the pain of the present sting a thousand times worse.

He moved to rub the drowsiness out of his eyes but was met with an explosion of pain and the smell of something foul. Cursing, he turned his frustration to his dragon. *What is it?*

Do those trees look familiar?

Thaddeus wanted to throttle Kyrell for disturbing him for something so trivial, until he looked down and watched the same arrowhead-shaped lake pass below.

They were going in circles.

Dread dropped in his stomach. Blinking hard—his vision still blurry from the attack—he struggled to focus on the faint magic trail snaking through the forest and sky around them. It wavered, bent, and changed as if taunting them.

You didn't stay focused. Thaddeus snarled and drew on his magic to force the magic trace to straighten itself.

Now Kyrell shared his frustration. *I didn't stay focused? You were the one lost in a ridiculous memory!*

It's not ridiculous! Tears stung his eyes. *It's the only thing I have left of joy.*

As if I give a loizi! *Do I not bring you joy?*

Thaddeus regretted his words but couldn't take them back.

If you'd rather lose yourself in daydreams of a time that will never exist again, then fine. You can rot away in the forest. But that's not what we set out to do. That's not what I *set out to do. Are you not strong enough to continue what you started? I wouldn't have bonded with you if I thought you'd give up. Did I make a mistake?*

Gut-wrenching guilt stabbed Thaddeus' heart. *No. You didn't.*

Kyrell growled low. *You know why we've been going in circles, Thaddeus. And it's not just because* you *lost focus.*

Anger replaced the guilt. *And what else would it be? Look, it's straight again. It was a mistake, and it won't happen again. Drop it.*

Kyrell did drop it.

But Thaddeus was wrong.

It happened again.

And again.

And again.

Thaddeus' patience cracked. An explosion of acidic magic rippled through the forest below, burning everything in its path. A swath of once green and living forest now lay in a smoking, stinking swamp of purple death.

We should stop to rest. Kyrell's voice echoed unusually gently, but Thaddeus didn't let it soften the frustration in his heart.

No. It's hardly night yet and we've made even less progress today than the last. We go until nightfall. Gritting his teeth, he tightened his grip on Kyrell's scales as if he could physically hold his dragon in the sky. Kyrell began to descend regardless.

Thaddeus screamed and kicked Kyrell's neck. *Did you not hear what I said? Each day we make less progress. We're going to die before we find it at this rate!*

Kyrell abruptly banked to the side, lashing Thaddeus violently. He scrambled to gain hold again and keep from plummeting to his death. Blood filled his mouth as his teeth clattered together, catching his tongue between them.

We will *die if we do not rest! You are tired and you are in pain. You can hardly see the magic trace anymore, and* that's *why we're going in circles. If you keep ignoring your wounds, you'll die of a foolish infection. Is that how you want your story to end?*

Tears stung his eyes as he held a hand to his bloodied mouth. Though he didn't respond to Kyrell, he didn't protest as the dragon landed in a clearing and folded his wings.

Cold panic flooded Thaddeus' veins as he slipped from his dragon's neck and took some of his supplies with him. The bed roll and waterskins dropped in an unceremonious pile at his feet, and he didn't bother to pick them up when the skins started leaking.

The trembling of his hands came first, then of his knees as he collapsed to the ground. Kyrell's tail snaked around to offer him support.

You do not have to suffer this alone.

Kyrell was right. But Thaddeus had never felt so alone.

With tender hands, he reached up to his face where the blinding, throbbing pain had been growing steadily for the last month. A foul smell engulfed him as he drew away his hand. A thick, yellow ooze coated his fingers and he gagged, wiping it off on the grass. He'd kept up with the infection at first by washing it with water and spreading acid into it. But the forest had taken its toll on his soul and for a week he'd let it fester. For a week, he'd let the blood and infection gather into pustules and scabs. For a week, he'd let his near defeat at Artigal's hand break his resolve.

I can't. He drew his knees to his chest and rocked back and forth, shaking his head.

You must.

With a whimper, Thaddeus reached back to his wound and dug his fingers into the oozing, scabbed mess. Pain tore through his entire head, burning its way down his spine. Flashes of blinding white light streaked toward him, burning him, scaring him—memories of Artigal and the Pure Magic.

Hands trembling uncontrollably, he wiped the handful of infection on the grass and reached back for more.

Okay. Thaddeus gripped the grass in his hands, head bent low in case he threw up again. *I think that's all of it.*

Thaddeus.

I just need to rinse it, and it'll be fine.

Thaddeus.

With tear-streaked cheeks and blood trickling down his chin and neck, Thaddeus lifted his face to his dragon and stared deep into his unwavering gaze. "Please let me be done. Please don't make me do this."

A great tear of acid slipped from Kyrell's eye as he pressed his snout to Thaddeus' chest. *If you leave it in, it'll continue to fester, and the infection will fill your veins. You have to let it go.*

A guttural cry of pain and grief left Thaddeus' lips as he threw his arms around his dragon's neck and hugged him like he'd never let go. Kyrell pushed Thaddeus closer to him, and they stood like that, holding each other up against the weight of the world until the time came to let go.

Taking several deep breaths to steady his hand, Thaddeus raised his small skinning knife to his eye, just above his cheek bone. "Hold me," he whispered. Kyrell's tail wrapped around him as he pushed in the blade.

The screams that echoed through the forest scared away any other life, leaving them alone in the forest with their pain and grief until darkness claimed him.

Northeastern Duvarharia Wilderness
Two Weeks Later

THADDEUS.

Darkness swirled around him.

Thaddeus, you have to wake up.

Memories of the Pure Magic taunted him, frightening him out of the depths of his mind.

With a startled gasp, he sat up. Murky shadows greeted him. Every muscle in his body ached. A wretched smell welcomed him, and he gagged. Dizzy, he tried to lay back down but Kyrell's tail propped him up.

You did it. You did it. Mournful pride filled his dragon's voice.

At first, he could hardly remember what he'd done until the darkness on the left side of his vision brought the horrific act flooding back.

The knife burned at first, then grew cold. It scraped against bone, tore through flesh, severed nerves. The pain started as a spark, held back by adrenaline. Then the relief of shock failed as reality settled in.

He cast the knife away in horror, fingers groping the half empty socket in his face. Something hung from it, something thick, warm, and bloody.

"My eye," he rasped. "My eye!"

Then the screaming started.

A dull thud snapped him from the memory as Kyrell gently smacked him.

"My eye," he whispered, repeating the memory. He didn't want to check, didn't want it to be real, but his fingers betrayed him as they moved to his eye . . . or rather where it *should* have been.

Uncontrollable screams clawed up his throat as he scrambled backwards, trying to escape the horror, the reality of what he'd done. His nails dug into his arms, struggling to rid himself of the mangled vessel his flesh had become.

But he couldn't escape.

He could never escape.

This was who he'd become.

And he could never go back.

When his arms grew bloody, and his nails broken, when he'd crawled far enough away from the flesh he'd left behind so he could no longer smell its filth, he finally curled up next to Kyrell's warm body, contorted against the radiating pain, and fell into a fitful sleep.

THE DAYS ONLY GREW longer and more difficult. Each minute they spent searching the thick forests fractured the little sliver of Thaddeus' resolve, and slowly, the amulet's deep corruption and obsession began to leak in.

The growing tension moved past a few heated arguments between him and Kyrell, then progressed until Thaddeus rushed him with his raised axe, stopping only when Kyrell knocked him down with his tail.

Thaddeus' head cracked against a rock, and the heat of blood trickled down his temple. Stars scattered across his vision as darkness enveloped him, the first time it did so in months without nightmares. He wanted to remain there, in that pocket of blissful, death-like silence until the end of time.

Kyrell's roar dragged him back to the waking world, to the new pain in his head that only barely compared to the pain in his heart. Immediately, the horror of what he'd tried to do crashed down upon him, leaving him in a cold sweat and crying under his dragon's wing.

What's happening to me?

Kyrell growled low, a mournful sound that traveled deep into the forest, echoing into an unrecognizable rumble. A twisted, animalistic call responded, sending a shiver down Thaddeus' spine. He regretted not building a fire as the darkness of the waking night swallowed them whole. But even with the sounds of strange animals ringing in the night, he couldn't bring himself to move from where he'd dropped to the ground, exhausted.

He blinked his bloodshot eye feeling the way it grated against his lid. Rubbing it, he bit his lip against the emotion stuck in his throat. Tired, hungry, frustrated, he felt the call of the amulet crushing him under its power. Though he hadn't even found it yet, he could almost feel where it would hang around his neck. In his dreams it wrapped around him like a shackle, its chain thick and unyielding, dragging him deeper and deeper into the darkness of his own mind, into the corners filled with hate, revenge, and grief.

Finally, Kyrell pressed his nose to his rider's chest, sharing his warmth and strength.

Already the amulet is tainting your mind, your heart. We've yet to find it, but already your resolve is failing. I fear it will control you instead. You're hurting. You're desperate. And you're nearly at your end. We're nearly at our end.

Slowly, the tears escaped down Thaddeus' cheeks. *I don't want it to be the end. I'm not ready for it to end.* Though the memory of the bliss of death-like darkness tempted him, he willed himself to hang onto hope.

A little longer. Just a little longer.

Thaddeus sniffed and nodded. He curled up against his dragon's warm body and felt the steady beating of his heart. "Just a little longer," he murmured as sleep dragged down his eye and the amulet dragged him into relentless nightmares.

The next day, nearly a month after leaving the Cavos desert, the magic trail finally came to an end.

Chapter 41

Ruins of Eltrinth
Northeastern Duvarharian Wilderness

Triumph flushed Thaddeus' veins as the ruins of an old farming town stretched before them, nestled in rolling hills. The memories of the hardship they'd endured to find this place faded as he beheld the fruits of his labor, the place where he'd change his fate.

Pastures lay unnaturally dry and empty. The trees' bark was black, and the lack of leaves on the ground around them indicated they hadn't seen growth for an untold number of years. The only building still intact was an old temple. The architecture signaled its original intention was worship of the Creator, but the statues of various deities standing guard implied the later influence of the Wyriders' polytheistic religion.

Kyrell landed on the overgrown road, and Thaddeus dropped to the ground; it reverberated with an unnaturally hollow *thud*. Unease crept into his veins. Though outwardly the abandoned township seemed little more than a failed farming town, he sensed a thousand secrets hid in its soil.

Responding to the pull of magic from the temple, he picked his way to it through the rubble. Distorted creature-like shadows decorated some of the adjacent building ruins. Dark splotches, with uncanny resemblances to old blood, stained others. Shivering, Thaddeus directed his focus to the temple. The doors stood ajar. He didn't have to struggle to shove them open.

While the construction seemed distinctly Duvarharian, nothing inside represented the land of the dragons even remotely. Instead, the foreign, wispy, allegorical art and design of the Wyriders served as decoration. All that remained of old rows of semi-circle seating around the temple center were scars of splintered wood and burn marks after they'd been ripped apart.

Eight large columns rose in a ring around the center of the room. Between them lay the remains of countless ritual circles. Some of the designs contained paintings of symbols he recognized from the Shadows of Light. The most recent paintings he recognized from the journal.

Outside the wind blew, and a couple leaves danced along the temple floor. Then everything fell deathly silent and still again. Thaddeus reached for Kyrell's warm comfort.

Nerves rattled, he pulled out the journal and confirmed his suspicions. This had been the defective Duvarharians' main gathering place. From the magic burns on the walls, pillars, and décor, he also gathered that this was where they practiced spells.

Goose bumps prickled his arms. Everything before him reflected the magic the Shadows of Light warned him about, forbidden magic that feasted on hate, anger, revenge, nightmares, and fear. Magic that destroyed rather than cultivated. *Everything I'm looking for*, he reminded himself.

Following the magic trail, he moved past the temple center to the large altar spanning the back wall. He tried not to wonder where the blood stains came from or whether Wyriders, Duvarharians, or spell-weavers spilled it. The magic snaked under the altar to a place in the floor that appeared different than the rest.

Below their feet rested what they sought. As he raised his hands to command his magic, a flood of questions washed over him.

What if this is a bad idea? What if the magic is too much? We don't even know what happened to the other Duvarharians. Clearly, they left the relic behind, but why? If it didn't work, why didn't they warn anyone about the Etas?

I don't know the history of this temple or the horrible things it could've been used for. What if I unleash something even worse upon Duvarharia?

Kyrell moved to his rider's side and pressed his head to his arm. *We're here for a reason, Thaddeus. Regardless of if we know where we fit into the prophecy, we're a part of it. I feel something–or someone–orchestrated all this, and I think they're watching over us now. Maybe it's not Joad after all, but we must trust the higher powers of this world. If whatever we find kills us, then so be it. But it could also be the redemption of Duvarharia. We must take that chance; it's our destiny.*

Some of the knots in Thaddeus' stomach loosened. *The Shadows said they struggled to make a difference because of old infrastructure. They even said Joad easily ushered in the Golden Age because the elites destroyed Duvarharia themselves.*

Kyrell grumbled low. *So, you see? Maybe we're not the savior, but we might be the destruction which paves the savior's path. And when they reveal themselves, we'll stand next to them, ready to reshape Duvarharia into its true form.*

Creatures will die.

They already have.

Thaddeus thought of the Zoics he'd watched perish. He thought of Syrinthia, of the new riders and freed dragons who'd been slaughtered at the massacre. He thought of the thousands who'd died before them and the thousands who would follow. He thought of Zara, Anrid, his mother, and everyone else he loved who would suffer if he did nothing.

Then he remembered how good it felt to cast his brother aside and how free he'd felt while watching the headmistress choke on her own boiling blood at his feet. And now before him lay the chance to match the corrupt government, magic to magic, an army to an army.

Kyrell was right. Everything in his life had led to this moment. It'd been foretold in the stars, he was sure.

He'd already made his choice.

Hesitations gone, he wrapped his magic around the altar. With a grunt of exertion, he ripped it from the ground and cast it aside. It shattered into shards and dust. The crash echoed eerily; a fraction of the darkness lifted with its destruction.

After a few tiring minutes of wrestling against powerful magic sealing the floor, Thaddeus crumbled the old magic. A gaping hole opened before them, revealing a stone staircase that stretched into the darkness.

Steeling against what he might find, he began his descent.

If you need me, I'll tear apart the world to reach you.

I know.

Using a glowing ball of energy, Thaddeus banished the darkness, marveling at the tunnel's construction. It wasn't carved into the rock, as he had expected, but was pieced together with huge stones like a puzzle. Every stone, rock, and piece of gravel radiated with powerful magic. The passageway widened as the incline steepened and opened into a large cavern.

Dark murals of dragons and riders decorated the walls. Gone was the flowery, mystic, allegorical art of the Wyriders. Everything in this room resonated with the darker, hidden personality of Duvarharia—one that thirsted for war, power, control, and domination. But the more paintings he saw, the sicker he felt.

Dragons ate other dragons, draining their life force and amassing their magic through ingestion. Riders did the same with other magical creatures.

Thaddeus swallowed back the vomit in his throat. He'd heard legends and warnings of spell-weavers—usually non-magical creatures who obtained magic through the blood of magical Kinds—but he'd never heard of magical Kinds committing such atrocities to each other.

Turning from the horrific paintings and murals, he focused on the circular dais in the room's center. Like the temple above, magic scars cut across the floor and walls, and what parts weren't damaged were stained dark. At the center of the raised platform spiraled more ritual circles, which an object resembling a coffin sat upon.

Swallowing hard and wishing Kyrell was near him, Thaddeus

touched the tomb. As soon as his fingers came in contact with the solid stone, it disappeared.

Squawking like a frightened bird, Thaddeus jumped several feet back, heart leaping into his throat.

A rider lay on his back, perfectly preserved as if only napping. Dressed in remotely familiar Duvarharian clothes, the rider boasted of long black hair and light brown skin. His crossed hands gripped something close to his heart.

Fascinating. Kyrell chuckled as he peered through Thaddeus' gaze.

Horrifying, Thaddeus corrected.

He struggled to gain his composure and still his heart as he waited for the rider to sit up and fix a glassy dead stare on him. Slowly, he crept back to the tomb and peered at the objects in the corpse's hands: a journal and a necklace amulet.

Before he could reach to touch it, a hand of dark magic lunged out of its red gemstone and wrapped itself around Thaddeus' throat. He clawed at it, choking, until it pulled his soul into the body and memories of the dead rider.

Auryn's family—a woman, a little girl and a clutch of dragon eggs—laughed as they waved from a small house. The woman scooped up the little girl and called for the man to join them. Then a burning light consumed the home, and the screaming started. When the light lifted, the girl and woman lay dead among crushed eggs shells and lifeless hatchlings.

The sigil of the Shadows of Light rested over the heart of the perpetrator—a young pupil exercising newfound power and authority under the guise of an accident.

On a quest for vengeance, Auryn traveled to the Cavos Desert, searching for the Corrupt Magic. He joined the military and found others who cursed the Shadows. When he discovered the amulet, he devised a plan to control the Etas.

Though the cold air bit deep as they pursued the escaped Etas, the beginnings of spring lay heavy on the land. The smell of fruit blossoms filled the air as they neared the farming town. But the Etas reached it first. Blood mingled with the flowers.

Excitement flooded Auryn's veins, revenge fueling his magic as he drew the amulet from his chest to his hand. Magic pulsed, stinging his hand, warning of its danger, but he ignored it. Rallying his followers, he drew upon their strength, each holding a powerful energy stone in case their own power wasn't enough.

Tears in his conscious ripped open as he reached his mind and magic to the amulet. A scream parted his lips as agony surged through him. But still, he pressed on.

Then an unpredicted horror unraveled before his eyes. The souls of the other riders and dragons were fracturing, splitting from their bodies. Despite their precautions, they weren't strong enough. Not yet.

With all the strength he could muster, he severed the connection, forming a promise that he would do whatever he must to gain the strength to tame it.

The Etas fled, and the townspeople took shelter in last standing building: the temple. The riders trapped any survivors the Etas left, subjugating many to later experiments involving the amulet.

Traveling to the darkest regions of Ventronovia, the defective Dragon Riders collected the oldest and darkest forbidden magic—powers that grew their minds, bodies, and souls well beyond natural development. Within only months, they gained hundreds of years' worth of knowledge and skill. Then, by drinking the blood of other magical Kinds, they increased their power even further.

But no matter what they tried, none could tame the amulet.

They passed it back to Auryn. In desperation, he opened his whole mind and soul to it, holding nothing of himself back from it.

The amulet burned his hand, his mind, his soul. It gathered all the hate in his heart and the thousands of sorrows he'd caused in pursuit of strength and turned it against him. The price he'd paid for the power of the amulet consumed him. It drained him of his soul, memories, and consciousness until he remained only a hollow shell of the rider he'd once been.

Drawing his sword, he drew it across his own neck, and relief finally found him when darkness closed in and the amulet fell from his hand, breaking the connection, ending the nightmare.

Thaddeus sat up with a gurgling scream, sweat pouring down his body and saturating his clothes. Panic clawed at his chest and neck as he tore off his clothes; the fabric felt like greedy hands hungering for his own soul.

With a thundering roar, the ceiling caved as Kyrell broke through it. Acid burned into the floor as he and the rubble crashed to the ground.

Are you alright? What happened? Your mind went completely blank. Who attacked you?

Thaddeus hugged his knees to his chest, rocking back and forth as he breathed deeply. *Those weren't my memories,* he reassured himself. *I am Thaddeus, rider of Kyrell. I'm not bleeding out on the chamber floor. I'm not lying dead on a cold stone slab. I am alive. I am strong. And I will not fail as those riders did.*

Staggering to his feet, Thaddeus used Kyrell for balance as the world spun. The memory of the vision transferred to Kyrell's mind.

The amulet drove Auryn mad. It influenced his decisions until they weren't his own. It'll do the same for you.

No. Thaddeus blinked hard, shaking his head free of the dead rider's memories. *He took the lives of other magic creatures. He drank their blood and ate their flesh to gain the power he needed. That was what drove him mad; the amulet only showed him his sins. I will do no such thing. I seek to better the lives of my magical brethren, not build myself from their loss.* Thaddeus spat at the corpse. *I'll not make the same mistakes.*

No fear of the dead remained; instead, disgust served in its place. Thaddeus wrenched the journal and amulet from the body's hands. Moments after the amulet left his hands, the corpse rapidly decayed, filling the chamber with the stench of rot.

"Let's get out of here."

Together they flew out of the opening in the chamber ceiling that Kyrell had burned with his magic.

Back in the open air of the abandoned town, Thaddeus no longer felt unnerved by it. Instead, he sensed the land's deep sorrow. It was a place of death, regret, and loss. Places like this, forgotten to the rest of the world, were where renewal was desperately needed the most.

In his hands the amulet appeared small enough to be dismissed as regular jewelry, but when he put it around his neck, he felt as though he'd draped the weight of the sky upon his shoulders. Opening the two journals, he immediately recognized countless similarities. Between the two, nearly every spell or ritual they'd learned to gain unnatural strength and magical power was detailed step by step. Anything to do with draining the life and magic of other creatures he ripped from the journal and dropped into a pile of Kyrell's acid.

"Most of these spells can take up to three days to complete. Each stage of transformation is similar to a moth's or butterfly's, only spiritually instead of physically. I'll need protection and supplies. If anything goes wrong, you'll need to break the spells."

Kyrell nodded before rising to the skies to find the nearest town or farm for supplies.

Wanting nothing more to do with the sorrowful town and the evil left by the previous riders, Thaddeus left the temple and its bloodstained walls far behind. In search of peace and shelter, he walked all day until he could no longer see the town ruins and death's grip on the land wasn't so strong.

Finally, he found himself at an abandoned homestead. With a breath of relief, he picked a small cabin that still had most of its roof and a half dead tree out front.

He settled onto the faded wood floor and crossed his legs. Slowing his breath, he rested his mind and body, preparing himself for the exertion of the transformation he was to undergo.

More than once on his day's long walk, he'd been tempted to control the amulet before the transformations, but he held back, not wanting to risk a gruesome death. At least, that's what he told himself.

Deep down, he just wanted to be more powerful than Thanatos had been, than his father was, than all the Duvarharian elites. This was his chance to finally grow past the weak child he'd once been and develop his own strength and power. Though the Shadows of Light had warned him against the danger of such quick gains, they'd been wrong before.

When Kyrell returned with a large collection of preserved foods he'd stolen from a farm town a few miles away, Thaddeus stirred from his meditation and ate a quick meal. As he thought of the feat he was going to attempt, dread and anticipation crept into his limbs. His hands shook as he lifted a spoonful of canned peaches to his lips before washing it down with a swig of frothy alcohol.

You're worried you'll change too much. Kyrell lay on the porch, his head snaked into the main room where Thaddeus sat.

Thaddeus lowered his bowl and shook his head. But Kyrell knew him inside and out. *You're worried you won't recognize yourself when you emerge and that those you love won't recognize you either. You're afraid of losing yourself.*

"Yes. I am." Admitting it lifted a weight from his heart. He'd always wanted to be different, to be someone else, but he feared losing himself even more. Tears collected in his eye as he nodded. "What if I lose the parts of me that make me . . . me?"

Kyrell growled low. *I'm going to meld my mind with yours so whatever changes in you will also change in me. We'll go through this together, and I'll be there every step of the way to decide what changes and what doesn't. You can just choose the physical-altering spells. You don't have to use those that affect your mind and magic.*

"But what if it's not enough?" Thaddeus looked down at the amulet. The riders who'd first attempted controlling the amulet had changed everything about themselves, some even past recognition. Their souls had changed fundamentally. Even then, they hadn't been strong enough.

Then I'll stop you before it turns you mad, and we'll find something else. We'll adapt, learn, and move forward. But we will not compromise. You will not give up your soul, nor mine, and we will not take from the lives of others.

Though Thaddeus wasn't sure they'd be able to defy the amulet's demands once they gave in to it, his dragon's confidence gave him resolve.

"Do you think we're rushing this? Perhaps I should rest a few days first..." The words escaped unsolicited, voicing a deep concern that had been weighing on his heart. So little time had passed since he'd returned home from the Dragon Palace. So little time for so much change. Each day blended into the last, a mere blur in his mind. Each decision he made sped past him faster than the last, leaving little room for reflection or regret.

If not now, when? We've been wandering the wilderness for a month looking for this amulet and even longer looking for answers. This is what we've been waiting for. Do not hesitate when it matters most.

Thaddeus balled his fists. Part of him wanted to stay like this for the rest of his life—just another victim amongst many, another star burning out in the sky. This transformation would be rapid and irreversible. Days would pass like minutes, and he didn't know what or who he'd become on the other side.

But without the transformation, he'd spend his life always on the run, always searching for someone to accept him, help him, teach him. Never being enough. He'd always be the victim—another irreversible choice. And the bigger part of him would rather die than make that choice.

Kyrell was right. The only time was now.

Quickly, he finished the last of his meal and lay on his back, hands outstretched. He relaxed and slowed his breath until he entered the trance-like state of meditation he'd learned at the Dragon Palace. The comfort of Kyrell's mind merging with his stilled his soul.

With a deep breath, he whispered his intentions and the ancient words written in the journals. Then he called upon his magic.

The world faded into darkness as the magic took control of itself and him. He felt it the moment he crossed into a current and he'd never return the same.

North of the Ruins of Eltrinth
Northeastern Duvarharian Wilderness
Unknown Number of Days Later

DAYS PASSED WITH NO BEGINNING AND NO END.

The sun rose and set so quickly that it hardly seemed as if it were moving at all. Burning pain faded into deep cold aches, then flared again. Fevered dreams of blood and gore haunted him.

Sometimes, when his eye flickered open, he saw hundreds of bleeding, acid-ridden Duvarharians standing in the fields outside the cabin. They waited for him, hated him, desired their revenge on him. The visions drove him back into his mind, desperate to find a corner where it didn't hurt, didn't whisper dark, malicious desires, didn't encourage him to destroy Duvarharia in the way his hate begged him to.

Blood pooled under him. Swollen and distorted, his limbs lay unresponsive. His head throbbed. His damaged eye puckered, so distorted that he worried it would pop and ooze from its socket. Claws grew from the tips of his fingers, then retracted back into his bones. Longer and sharper, his ears heard more sound than he'd believed existed. Plants breathed in light and air; the sound clashed with screaming crickets, a roaring creek, and singing birds. His ears bled from the noise as his soul pleaded for silence.

The silence only came when the pain grew unbearable, and his body succumbed to the darkness.

It seemed the horror would never end.

He no longer cared how he would look, think, or *be* on the other side. He only wished he were there.

BIRDS CHIRPING THEIR morning songs filled Thaddeus' senses.

The sound mingled with the rustling and barking of a nearby fox and then Kyrell's scales on the patio wood as he stretched and groaned.

The overwhelming sounds had quieted. The suns and moons moved slowly in their passage across Hanluurasa. His head no longer throbbed; the damaged eye no longer strained against its fibers.

But everything had changed.

Though his body was still his own, he was now a stranger to it. His skin, no longer thin and weak, sat heavy on corded muscles and stronger bones.

Lengths of hair sprawled out beside him, caked with his old blood. His veins surged with new blood—the blood of dragons. Blood capable of carrying vastly more magic and energy.

With the ghosts of excruciating pain still radiating in his mind, he sat up with a groan.

Subconsciously, he rubbed the sleep from his eyes.

He froze, unable to believe what he'd felt. Slowly, he touched his face again, shaking fingers roving to his empty left eye socket.

Only it wasn't empty. Not anymore.

His eye lid had regrown, and something that felt the same as an eye rested under it. Confusion filled him as he opened it but still saw only darkness. Frowning, he let his fingers roam over the rest of his face. A thick scar remained, but it no longer lay open to fester.

Taking a deep breath, he closed his right eye and opened only his left in one last hopeful effort. Magic trickled through his veins, moving to the strange eye. Nothing else happened.

Gritting his teeth against his frustration, he took a deep breath. *So, it's connected to the new magic somehow,* he thought to himself as he opened his good eye. In time he'd learn how to use the gift the amulet had presented him, but until then, he'd adapted to his limited sight.

When he looked at his hands, his stomach turned. Gone were the small, soft hands of youth. Slender, capable fingers moved in their place. Veins pulsing with life wrapped around them and flexed with his muscles. When he curled his fingers, his nails moved from his fingertips like claws. He tried to make a fist without stabbing himself but couldn't. Groaning, he curled his fingers over and over until he mastered the muscles responsible for the claws. But even with his hands in the familiar shapes of fists, he didn't recognize them. Instead of delicate white nails, his magic seeped into his fingertips and nails, staining them dark purple. Little veins pulsed purple, drawing little shapes across his once flawless skin.

Still flawless, he reminded himself, desperate to gain autonomy over this new form. *Just different. Just different.*

Tripping over his own legs and feet, he struggled to stand. A wave of dizziness washed over him. With his new claws, he detangled the bloody knots in his hair. It'd grown down to his waist. He'd either have to cut it or find a stream for washing.

"Kyrell?" He jumped at his own voice. The soft high voice and cracks of adolescence were nowhere to be heard. Tears filled his eyes as he croaked his dragon's name again, hardly recognizing it on his own lips. "Kyrell?"

A loud crash and a roar spurred him forward, staggering as awkwardly as a dragon hatchling.

When he pulled the door open, it flung from its hinges and shattered into a thousand pieces upon hitting the floor. The new strength surprised him. Blinking against the morning light, he watched a sight unfold that looked exactly how he felt.

Kyrell flailed in a mess of wood, his tail snagged under the cabin's crawl space and his wings caught in the patio railings. With a roar, he reared back, stretched his wings, and tore the patio apart. A huge hole in the cabin's floor smashed open behind Thaddeus as Kyrell yanked his tail out from under it.

A laugh bubbled up in Thaddeus' throat. When it escaped his lips, it sounded as if someone else was laughing instead.

Kyrell froze and turned an eye to his rider. *Well, you certainly look and sound different.*

Thaddeus scoffed as he stepped to the splinter-ridden ground. "You're quite different yourself."

Kyrell twisted his neck and hopped awkwardly to survey his body. Stretching his wings, he marveled at their size and strength. *I'll never struggle to take off again.* With a deep, playful growl, Kyrell leapt into the air, testing his new capabilities and strengths.

His positivity helped Thaddeus feel less estranged from his own body. Taking his axe in hand, he marveled at how it had grown with him; it was now twice its original size. What had once been a struggle for him to wield, even with the Shadows' training, now felt as weightless as his own arm—the extension of himself it was always meant to be.

Reentering the cabin, he gathered his torn and ruined clothes and searched for other leftover fabric. Then he laid out his finds. Gathering magic in his hands, he drew upon the ancient words of a material-altering spell Syrinthia had taught him. The magic came effortlessly. Instead of changing some of the fabric, he transformed all of it.

When the spell was complete and he opened his eyes, he held a dark rider's cloak with a long, flowing back, loose sleeves, and a large red collar, along with matching pants, riding boots, and armored gloves. He quickly dressed, appreciating the soft suppleness of the fabric on his skin.

Soon I will do the same to Duvarharia.

Do what? Kyrell landed with a heavy *thud*, claws digging scars into the land as he adjusted to the weight of his new body.

Alter the ruins of Duvarharia into something beautiful. Look what I did with rags. He turned for Kyrell to see the craftsmanship in them; no trace of old torn clothes or the moth-eaten brown curtains remained. *Once I've brought Duvarharia to ash, my message spread far and wide for others to follow, I'll rebuild it just as I have these clothes, only a thousand times more beautiful.*

Kyrell's tail twitched with excitement. *We'll form extensive hatching grounds from the mountains, just like the dragons in Yazkuza, and make all the cities big enough for the dragons again while also accommodating beings with disabilities like Anrid.*

Thaddeus' heart fluttered and head spun as he searched for the limits of his new power; he found none. *With the strength we now possess, no one will stand in our way.*

Kyrell growled low as Thaddeus mounted his back.

"Now I just have to see if we're strong enough for the amulet." But without even trying, he already knew they were. He'd far surpassed the previous riders. *I'm different.* He was more certain of it now than he'd ever been since Rakland told him so years ago. *Because this is my destiny.*

Amulet in hand, he tapped into its magic.

It fought back, seeking to take control of his mind. Every rageful desire, hateful thought, thirst for vengeance—every moment he'd been made to feel weak, inferior, and humiliated—poured forth. But instead of fleeing from it, Thaddeus reached out and grasped it. Holding each emotion and desire tenderly, he embraced them, validated them, and promised they would see fulfillment. The amulet's power broke under his will and succumbed to him.

The amulet's life stirred inside him, opening a whole new world. He sensed the might of the Eta army and the strength of their thousand-year-old King; he felt their presence and life. When he opened his eyes, the path stretched out before him, leading him straight to them.

Where once he'd been uncertain in his decision to find the Etas and force them to follow him, now he felt only conviction and determination.

Kyrell pushed from the ground, taking to the air with rapid ease.

Thaddeus turned back to gaze with fondness at the cabin of his transformation. Then, with nothing more than a whisper, he sent down a raging ball of acid to destroy it. Minutes later, it was nothing more than a mud-like puddle.

He smirked as he flexed his hand, his Shalnoa glowing powerfully. Destiny had been calling, and finally, he was ready to answer.

CHAPTER 42

Uncharted Lands of Chinoi
Three Days Later

With the amulet's magic, they locked onto a new magic trail leading to the Etas. They followed it far north, past the border of Duvarharia and into the wild, uncharted lands of Chinoi. Though winter had begun its return to Ventronovia, it seemed to have never left Chinoi. After spending his first night in Chinoi shivering under Kyrell's wings, despite heating himself with magic, Thaddeus dedicated the next day to hunting mountain goats for meat and fur.

On the third day of frozen exploration, they reached their destination.

Spiky, colossal obelisks, buildings, portcullises, and impenetrable stone walls towered from the snowy landscape. One side of the fortress merged with the mountain; the other dropped off a cliff. A single long, winding road weaved to its main gates. For a moment, Thaddeus wondered if they'd stumbled across a hidden kingdom of Duvarharians or Wyriders. But the amulet hummed with anticipation; this was an Eta castle.

I didn't expect them to be so culturally advanced.
This contradicts everything the academy taught us.

Kyrell perched on a rocky ledge as Thaddeus recalled what he'd read about them in the cavern library. The notes made more sense now that he fully understood the Etas' true intelligence. *Some of them have the in-*

telligence of animals, but many are as intelligent as an average human. A small percentage are nearly as smart as the Duvarharians themselves. And of course, the King is the smartest of them all.

Closing his eyes, he extended his consciousness to the amulet. Its power ran deep and connected to the magic forces of Rasa itself. If Thaddeus could tap into it, his power over the Etas would be limitless. But the amulet whispered secrets about the current Eta King that caused him to worry. Different than the Kings before him, the current King had reigned for the last thousand years. It was under his command and leadership they were able to build such a castle—a feat previously impossible for their battle-hungry Kind.

Resolving himself, Thaddeus banished all hesitation. His plan would work. *It must work.*

Kyrell took to the skies again, and they glided toward the castle.

A long, bellowing screech resounded in warning. The fortress, which appeared abandoned only seconds before, swarmed to life with thousands of Etas.

Impressed, Thaddeus watched hundreds of red sparks light up the walls as the Etas changed shapes. He'd read about their shape-shifting abilities and seen it on the Cavos Desert murals, but to witness it firsthand was an experience truly mortifying and stomach turning.

A few rose into the sky, nearly as large as Kyrell. Bat-like wings carried them with ease. Their whip-like tails snapped menacingly. Though they shared similarities, each Eta was unique; some had feline heads, others the heads of horse-like creatures. The few with lizard heads looked uncomfortably like dragons.

Thaddeus . . .

They flew closer, howls piercing the air. More took flight.

Wait.

Thaddeus . . .

When the first Eta was close enough for Thaddeus to see its individual scales, he wrapped his hand around the amulet. The magic surged through him, feeding on his hate and anger. It collected in his palm.

Thaddeus!

With a bloodcurdling screech, the first Eta dove toward them, jaw open, revealing multiple rows of jagged black teeth.

Thaddeus cast the magic.

The Eta's scream cut off as its body exploded. Black blood splattered Kyrell's scales as the pieces of flesh plummeted. Three more met the same fate. Confusion swelled in their ranks as they struggled to turn back.

A pulse of the amulet's power struck them, consuming their minds and bodies with pain. Those too weak to face the torment plummeted to their deaths. The others gave in to the amulet's control and grew docile. Eyes dull and submissive, they glided next to Kyrell as if he were one of them.

Two more dove for Kyrell. But when their black blood joined with the stench of burning flesh filled the air, the others drew back, most falling under Thaddeus' control.

Thaddeus sucked in a strained breath. The dozens of new minds under his control weighed on his soul like an anvil. His head throbbed as his mind sought to find space for the new consciousnesses. Wrestling with their minds, he crushed and shoved them until they fell into the corners of his own, nothing more than strings of consciousnesses. Then he pushed through their minds, spreading his magic like a disease. Some exploded when his magic entered them, but he didn't bat an eye; he had no use for the weak.

Kyrell banked as they flew around one of the tall, dark spires. Thaddeus sneered as frightened Etas scattered, calling in warning or racing into the buildings for protection. Not many escaped the amulet's oppression.

Bypassing the walls, gates, and guard towers, they let the amulet pull them toward the large patio of the tallest spire. A powerful presence exuded from the room inside. Kyrell snapped his jaws as his tail demolished the patio railings. They'd found the King.

Expecting to be met by a grotesque monster, Thaddeus drew his axe as he slid from Kyrell's back. Footsteps thundered behind the patio doors before they swung open. Thaddeus grinned at the dozens of Etas, weapons brandished against him, and Kyrell licked his lips.

Oh, how we've waited for this.

Blood flew from his blade as it sang through the air. Flecks of acid burned anything they touched. With deadly precision and instinct, Thaddeus aimed for the heart or brains, either decapitating the Etas or slashing into ribs. Morbid fascination filled him; when his aim wavered and his axe struck an arm, the injured Eta grew a new limb while the limb grew a new body.

Elcores.

The books warned about the twin Etas. Because of their heightened unique psychic neural connection, Elcores possessed increased cognitive function and could plan complex, coordinated attacks.

He swung his axe at one of the Elcores, taking off its head, but the momentum unbalanced him, and he slipped on blood. Kyrell's tail caught him and dragged him out of a spear's path before it found his heart.

Shoving his way into the room, he spotted a dark mass sitting on a jagged throne. His patience gone and lust for blood satiated, Thaddeus tapped into the amulet's power and unleashed it upon the guards. A sliver of intestine struck his cheek when three of the Etas imploded. The rest turned against each other.

Axe raised, he stepped calmly through the fighting and bodies, knowing the Etas under his control would sacrifice their lives to keep him safe from the others. A mass of red sparks encompassed the dark creature upon the throne.

Thaddeus paused, feeling Kyrell's comforting presence behind him. No Eta would make it past his quick jaws. Thaddeus focused his attention on the throne.

When the sparks dissipated, four red eyes stared from a face hauntingly similar to his own. Rotting skin peeled from the Eta King's face, and while Thaddeus' hair and skin were light and clean, the Eta's hair was black and matted and his skin pale green. Stretching his arms as he tested his new form, he waved his fingers, and a ripple of red sparks encompassed his naked skin, covering it in a torn, dark robe.

"Why have you come here, dragon scum?" His voice grated like claws on polished stone.

Snarling, Thaddeus rolled his shoulders against his anger. With great effort, he plastered a smile on his face. "I request an audience with the King of Etas. I gather we have something in common."

Cloak trailing behind, the King descended the dais, eyes roving over the slaughter as the Etas under Thaddeus' control overpowered the ones under the King's. The throne room doors slammed open as a fresh wave of defense poured in. The King raised his hand, and the fighting ceased.

Look how effortlessly he controls them.

Soon that power will be ours.

"You've barged into my throne room, taken over my people, slaughtered them mercilessly, and displayed a magic I know I cannot fight, and you say you merely request an *audience*?" The last word rolled off his tongue with disdain.

The air was rank with the smell of rotting flesh—a stench it seemed all Etas possessed even if their flesh wasn't decomposing prematurely. Thaddeus crinkled his nose. Disliking how close the King stood, he gripped his axe tighter. The King's odor nearly drove him to make rash decisions—like taking his head from his shoulders.

"If I'd knocked on your castle gates, do you think your people would've welcomed me inside?"

His dark smile revealed a row of sharp gray teeth. A forked tongue slipped between thin, pale lips. "Well," he said, chuckling quietly, "no, I don't think they would've. Still, I don't find pleasure in you coming into my territory, my castle, my *home*."

"Yet you haven't let me plead my case."

The King flexed his arms. Red sparks crackled along his spine as his bones popped and distorted. Black wings sprouted out of his back.

Kyrell snarled and spread his own wings, tail swishing with anticipation. Thaddeus held out his hand, keeping Kyrell from tearing the Eta to shreds.

"You have nothing I want, dragon scum. Why don't you scurry back to whatever corner of Susahu spat you out and find someone else to kill for you."

Thaddeus ground his teeth, fists tightening around his axe. "I want to lay low the country of Duvarharia."

His words raised the King's brow. "So you want to annihilate your own people from the face of Rasa." He stepped back and gestured to Thaddeus' axe and dragon. "Yet you've partaken in their traditions and culture. What's driven you to such a decision?"

"Not annihilate. I said lay low. I wish to rebuild it the way it should've stayed after the Golden Years."

The King's resounding laughter boomed off the room's sharp edges. The other Etas stirred uncomfortably. "So, you take my army, and you destroy Duvarharia's. Somehow, you try not to kill the innocents, though really none of them are innocent since they've all in some way contributed to the degradation of society. You think you can take from your enemies what they took from you without sacrificing yourself. And then after you 'lay low' Duvarharia, you believe you'll somehow have the power to rebuild *everything*." He sneered. "Stop me when I'm wrong."

His rancid face paused only inches from Thaddeus'. Though he wanted to retch at the stench, he didn't move, didn't answer.

"And you expect me to just *help* you. To put aside a thousand years of my efforts to move past our near extinction and the bloodlust that led us to that battle, the very same battle that ushered in the Golden Years." His voice rose, booming through the room, piercing Thaddeus' ears. "You expect us to fight for you and repeat our darkest hour? Answer me!"

Thaddeus growled and wiped the King's spit from his face. "Yes, I do. Because without Duvarharian blood slipping down your throats, you'll never truly thrive. You're nothing but a bunch of worthless bloodthirsty animals who're good for fighting and dying, nothing more, and you know it."

The King threw back his head and roared. "I will not disrupt our peace for a fool like you! Get out of my castle!" His clawed hands slammed into Thaddeus' chest. His back hit the ground first, then his head with a sickening crack. Darkness spotted his vision; his lungs scrambled for air.

Kyrell roared and threw the King against the dais with his tail. A ball of red sparks encompassed the Eta as he changed shape, revealing a giant hound with black wings, three spiked tails, and the back legs of a lion. Six red eyes opened as he howled and charged.

The throne room exploded into chaos as the Eta guards charged each other, tearing through flesh with violent ferocity.

Thaddeus scrambled to his feet, drawing his fingers over the bloody gashes in his chest and resting them on the amulet. In a moment's whisper, the King could be under his control. But he didn't just want control; he wanted submission. Snarling, Thaddeus healed his wounds and took up his axe.

One of the King's tails whipped toward him, coated in poison. Dodging the attack, Thaddeus wrapped chains of purple magic around a pillar before pulling it down onto the King. Refusing to offer any chance of recovery, Thaddeus brought his axe up and through the side of the hound's face, tearing out two of his eyes.

The King screamed and threw off the pillar. Black blood poured from his face. Half blinded, he attacked haphazardly. Kyrell bit off one of his tails as Thaddeus ducked and weaved around the rest, testing out the reflexes of his newly obtained body. His unhinged laughter, so foreign to his own ears, reverberated with Kyrell's mocking trills.

"All my life I've taken no for an answer," Thaddeus hissed as the hound leapt. Ducking, he caught the Eta's underbelly. Black blood and stinking flesh drenched him. Screams shook the walls. Standing, he wiped the blood from his face and spat out the flesh. "But never again."

The Eta King lay on the ground. Steaming flesh and entrails spilled from his abdomen as he thrashed against the pain and his inevitable demise. Desperate red sparks crackled around the wounds, regrowing his eyes and stitching up the gash in his stomach. Thaddeus waited a moment, letting the King taste hope, before he raised his hand. The amulet's magic twined with his own and slid to the King in a heavy purple fog. It choked out the red sparks.

Running his hands through messy hair, Thaddeus let the magic wash over him. Blood and flesh slid from his skin and puddled on the ground. The gore moved from under his feet, leaving a clean path to walk. Even the dead Etas had no choice but to bend to his will.

"Please." The King's body contorted until he resumed the sickly form resembling Thaddeus himself.

Kyrell caged the King with his long claws. One of his claws pressed deep into the Eta's leg, drawing a pained groan, but the dragon didn't move.

The fighting in the throne room ceased as the Etas under Thaddeus' control slaughtered the last of the King's. No more came in through the doors.

"Please don't do this."

Thaddeus knelt beside the King, repulsed by how easily the leader had been reduced to a quivering mess of blood and tears "Do what?" Thaddeus caressed the side of the King's face. "You call yourself a King, yet you failed to protect your people from even one Dragon Rider. I'm almost reconsidering using you. I was told Etas were the bane of Duvarharians, but you're little more than a bedtime fable to scare hatchlings."

The King shook his head and coughed. Blood trickled down his neck. "No. I've been the best King in thousands of years. I reminded them of their intelligence and culture. Reminded them they don't need

Duvarharian blood to survive. We're more than bloodlust. Please. Leave us alone. Find someone else to fight your war."

Thaddeus stood and fingered the amulet. "Maybe I'd believe you." His eyes strayed to the crazed Etas waiting for the order to kill, eyes void of intelligence. "But I know better. You're a Kind of war, and nothing more than the blood of murderers flows in your veins."

The King sobbed as Thaddeus smiled coldly. "Don't be so upset. None of us can help what we were made to be. The Duvarharians were made to rule and to be free. They cannot attain that purpose unless they're torn from their own wretched reality. The same goes for your own people." He twisted the Eta King's head so he could see the other Etas. The ones Thaddeus controlled were nearly twice their original size, bulging with muscle.

"They're dying slowly without war. Is that what you want? To perish off Rasa with little more than a whisper of what you'd once been and could be again? That's not what I want for my people, and I *am* strong enough to choose differently for them, even if you are not. I will walk away today with an army, with or without your help. But I'd much rather you see the vision I have for Duvarharia. For you. For us."

The King thrashed against Kyrell's claws and howled when Kyrell sunk his teeth into his legs. Acid seeped into his veins, slowly dissolving him from the inside out.

"What do you say?" Thaddeus bit his lip against the magic bubbling inside him. The amulet was wrestling for control; it wanted to reduce the King and his army to nothing more than a black stain on castle ruins. Blinking hard, heart racing so fast he thought it would burst, he dragged his claws through his own chest. The stinging pain brought his mind into focus.

The King's eyes met Thaddeus' as he spat into his face. "Never. You'll have to force me. I'll never do it willingly."

"Too bad."

Thaddeus unleashed the magic.

The King's body contorted before his back arched. Thaddeus' skin crawled from the Eta's screams as he writhed on the floor, purple magic ripping through his body and mind. Any Etas not previously under Thaddeus' control distorted in pain. Sparks of purple magic fought the red.

Then the King fell still. The castle was silent.

Whatever pity Thaddeus might've felt for the King, he buried deep inside. Too many times he'd been taken advantage of, reduced to a sobbing mess of tears, humiliated, stripped of everything he loved, and forced to comply. It was time for someone else to feel the same.

With a kick, Thaddeus turned the King's body over. Red glassy eyes stared back.

"I'm surprised you didn't explode like the other weaklings." Wrinkling his nose, Thaddeus stepped aside as the King sucked in a rasping breath and coughed up a clot of blood. Slowly, he pushed himself to his feet.

He towered over Thaddeus now. Arms, no longer anorexic, bulged with muscle. Eyes flashed vibrantly with the thirst for blood and a deep hatred of Duvarharians. Dozens more Etas clambered to their feet as the castle stirred back to life, each of them connected to Thaddeus' mind with an unbreakable string. A flush of victory washed over him.

Kyrell flapped his wings and roared. *Finally, we have the power for our vengeance!*

"I hate you, Thaddeus, rider of this Acid Dragon." The King snarled and jerked his head as he resisted Thaddeus' control.

Thaddeus pressed his axe to the King's neck. No matter how much the Eta strained, he couldn't defend himself. He smirked in satisfaction.

"I will never willingly fight for you. But . . ." With shaking limbs and hatred in his eyes, the King knelt and lowered his head. "I have no choice."

Adrenaline surged through Thaddeus' veins. *This is it. This is what we've always needed—unyielding power and control. Everything we've dreamed of is finally within reach.* He'd spent his life being trampled by those bigger and stronger than him, silenced because of what flowed through his veins, and powerless to protect those he loved. But no longer. He was tired of running.

"Swear yourself to me, Eta King. Swear you'll fight for me and my vision." He drank in the Eta's every word.

"As we live, so long as you hold the amulet, we will fight for you. I, Veltrix, King of the Etas, and all my people are yours to command, Thaddeus, traitor of the Duvarharians."

CHAPTER 43

Just Outside of Peace Haven, Duvarharia
A Couple Weeks Later

BY THE NEXT DAY, Thaddeus had rallied his new troops and assigned new commanders. Many of the Etas hadn't wanted to fight, but after a bit of pain-based motivation, Thaddeus stirred the violence in their veins.

Getting the entire army through Duvarharia's border had been easier than he'd anticipated. Not only could he trick the border into accepting the Etas as Duvarharians with the power of the amulet, but it seemed no one had bothered maintaining the border between Chinoi and Duvarharia. Though the broken wall served its purpose now, Thaddeus vowed to fix it in the years to come.

Once they were safely on the other side of the border, Thaddeus laid out his war plan. After wandering the wilderness in search of the amulet and Etas for weeks, he'd had plenty of time to brainstorm.

Starting with the outermost cities, they'd attack with guerrilla warfare, targeting the *Xene'mraba* and the elites who condoned them. By converting the smaller border cities first, he hoped to slide under the Dragon Palace's notice until the Etas grew stronger and he perfected his tactics.

Upon arrival at each city, he would enter alone to announce Duvarharia's crimes and the justice he brought, offering anyone the chance to join his cause. Anyone who chose the abusive government instead would be marked for death.

I hope they all join us. Kyrell's thoughts filled Thaddeus' as they streaked through the night sky, an hour's flight from Peace Haven. The darkness wavered with morning light. A strange emotion twisted his gut as Thaddeus surveyed his army.

Some Etas rode upon the backs of the dragon-like Etas. King Veltrix rode the largest—an Eta bigger than Kyrell. A large scowl dipped the King's brows over his four red eyes as his teeth worried into bloody lips; though he didn't want to fight, he had no choice. The power of the amulet was total and inescapable. Thaddeus touched the relic to remind himself of that.

I'm sure they will. Remember how many we converted at the at the Xene'mraba?

Kyrell did, but he also remembered how easily the newly bonded pairs had been slaughtered by the elites.

That's why we have them. Thaddeus nodded to the Etas, the strange emotion washing over him again.

Have we really become traitors?

Thaddeus blanched at Kyrell's thoughts. King Veltrix's words echoed in his mind, "Thaddeus, traitor of the Duvarharians." His hands tightened around the straps of his dragon's new saddle.

I don't know. The confession wove doubt in his heart. It made him feel small and helpless again; he hated that feeling more than anything. *No, I do know. We brought the evil from the north—the Etas. We are the traitors. I see that now. But the Dragon Prophecy came from Joad, and Joad abandoned me long before I chose this path.* Thaddeus shook his head, brushing a strand of his long wind-tousled hair from his lips. *We may be the traitor in Joad's prophecy, but I am no traitor to my people. His words do not define me, and whether or not Duvarharia believes it, I am its savior; nothing can change that.*

Kyrell rumbled in agreement as he banked to the left. The Etas descended to the mountains while Thaddeus and Kyrell continued to Peace Haven. Today was the first day of the second winter month. The elites would be having their first springtime meeting for government changes. They'd be entering the Council Hall, the glass dome above them painted with murals of dragons and riders living in perfect harmony—everything the leaders below would vote against.

I almost don't want to give them another chance. Look what happened last time.

Kyrell blew a mist of acid into the air. *But we were relying on Joad then. Now we hold the power. This is not giving them another chance; this is giving them a final chance. There will be no failure or mistakes after this. It will not go wrong.*

If they refuse, I want to get my mother away before the Etas descend. I may have commanded them only to fight any elites or soldiers who fight back, but I won't take any chances. Will the dragons take her to the island?

Kyrell nodded. *They've no vendetta against the Zoics, and the dragons living on the island are already on our side. They'll help spread our message.*

Good. I'd pray to the gods for help, but I know they wouldn't answer.

For old Duvarharia.

For old Duvarharia.

THE CITY BLURRED beneath them as they descended straight toward the Council Hall. A few dragons looked up from where they slept on the adjacent roofs. Though several leaped to their feet and sounded the alarm, none were quick enough.

With one great breath, Kyrell blew out an enormous gust of acid. It slammed into the glass dome with a shattering roar.

For a moment, the world stood still. The suns crept across the horizon as if frightened to face the day. Birds halted their songs. Thaddeus sucked in a deep breath as Kyrell thrust out his wings, rapidly slowing their descent. Then everything sprang back to life.

The glass dome shattered from the acid and collapsed. Riders shrieked in terror as the dragons, cut by the shards, roared in pain.

Kyrell curled in his wings and dropped through the opening, shaking the walls as he landed. Remaining panes of glass shattered and fell from the vibrations.

Thaddeus watched as one of the painted dragons from the mural dissolved into a puddle of simmering acid and molten glass. He allowed a single moment to grieve the end of something so beautiful. *At least it will no longer be mocked by those beneath it.*

Turning, he stood on Kyrell's back and extended his hands. The doors of the room were locked and sealed shut, trapping everyone inside. "Elites of Peace Haven!" Amplified by magic, Thaddeus' voice carried over the chaos, silencing the audience. "I am Thaddeus, rider of Kyrell, and I come before you with a truce."

Ripples of awe and fear waved through the onlookers. Some watched with anticipation, most with hate. A woman in a back corner cried, but Thaddeus blocked his mind to her.

"Outside Peace Haven stands an army of nearly four thousand Etas. They will descend upon this city and tear down your rich places, your black markets, your games, your elitist structures, and society. Any who submits will be spared and protected for the recreation of Duvarharia. Any who resist will be considered a threat to the new age and killed upon sight. Do you surrender to me?"

Silence stretched, grew, consumed. Then a snicker broke the tension.

Thaddeus' blood boiled as it grew louder, bolder. Others joined in.

They were laughing. *Laughing.*

Heart rushed to his face as anger and embarrassment crashed over him and Kyrell. In seconds, the entire elite Council roared with laughter. Several of their dragons rolled on the ground, grunts and growls rumbling in their throats.

"Do you not believe me?" Spots dotted his vision as he held up the amulet. "This is a relic of our people. It contains a magic long forgotten because of your restrictive laws. It has the power to control the Etas—

Etas that survived thousands of years because elites like you were too indolent to finish the job!"

"Go home to your mother's *lubesh*, Thaddeus!" A woman clutched her stomach, face red with mirth. "You're nothing but a delusional child trying to crawl out of your brother's shadow. Your father would be—" Two pillars tore from their bases and crushed her between them. A red mist decorated their sides and the floor. The room fell silent as the Duvarharians stared at the gore with disbelieving horror. Then the woman's dragon screamed and dug his claws into his own eyes, trying to quell the pain of losing his rider.

Mass hysteria broke out.

Purple magic swirled around Thaddeus' hands. His heart raced. Bile rose in his throat. The smell of vomit and blood wafted to his nose. Panic wormed its way into his own mind and body. Digging his nails into his palms, he drew upon the amulet's strength.

"I do not want to kill anyone!" he screamed.

No one listened. They threw themselves at the doors, mercilessly trampling each other to save themselves.

I don't want to kill anyone, he repeated over and over. But his heart told him otherwise as their mocking laughter echoed in his mind. He wanted them to suffer like he had. The bloody spray upon the pillars was a testimony to how easy it would be.

Several dragons and riders drew their weapons and stalked toward Kyrell and Thaddeus, realizing the only way out was past them and through the roof. By extending his magic into the room, Thaddeus realized only five dragons and four riders held no violence toward him. All seventy-three others wished him dead.

They've no right to treat you like this, Thaddeus. Kyrell snapped warningly at an approaching dragon. *They've rejected your mercy. Now show them your fury.*

Kyrell was right. To create meant to destroy. He was ready to become the destroyer.

"You leave me no choice." With a flick of his wrist, the first rider's head twisted backwards; he was dead before he met the ground. The other two hesitated long enough for Kyrell's jaws to clamp around one and for Thaddeus' axe to tear through the other's arm, then her head.

A battle cry rose as one of the loyal riders and her dragon took up the fight beside Thaddeus and Kyrell. A triumphant grin spread Thaddeus' face as another joined.

Kyrell jumped onto the back of a much larger dragon and sank his teeth deep into the base of its skull. He pulled the dragon's head back, exposing its throat to Thaddeus. With a burst of magic, he drove a large piece of the broken mural deep into its flesh before dodging the sword of another rider.

The fighting continued until the hall was slick with blood and a horrible silence settled.

One of the riders who joined Thaddeus had met their end in another dragon's jaws. Their own dragon staggered around the room, insane with loss.

Then, as darkness swirled through the room, a single scream pierced the air. Thaddeus swallowed, shielding himself from the soul vortexes.

"What's happening?" The rider cried and cradled her friend. The dead rider's eyes were missing, and blood oozed from their orifices.

"It's a soul vortex," Thaddeus whispered as his magic cleaned gore from his axe, body, and Kyrell. "If you don't want to end up like them, don't look at the dead dragons and don't open your soul to them. If you're weak enough to get pulled in, you're too weak to fight this war with me."

Shaking herself free of the bloody horror, she held on to her dragon's leg for support and left her friend behind. The last remaining rider and two dragons joined her as they bowed before Thaddeus. "We are strong enough," she whispered with balled fists. "We believe in what you are trying to accomplish. We've waited a long time for someone like you. I won't let anything stand between me and making sure nothing is left of the stain they've left on my country."

The others nodded or growled in agreement. Relief washed over Thaddeus. *So, all is not lost. Some will follow.*

Kyrell nodded, eyes sparkling.

"What's next, Lord Thaddeus?"

The title sent a shiver down Thaddeus' spine. For a moment, his eyes lingered on the bloodshed around him. A portion of his soul grieved for those already killed; many were simply products of a failing system. But regardless, they'd stood between him and tearing down that system. No matter if they would've followed his cause in a different time or life. Right here and now, he could spare no obstacle.

"You"—he pointed to the woman, her dragon, and the riderless dragon—"will fly through the city and evacuate any dragons and riders who believe in the coming reformation." He pointed to the other rider and dragon pair. "You will rally any soldiers who stand with us. Warn them of the Etas and point them to the northern mountains where a fraction of my army waits. Then, when the rest of my army storms the city, you'll stand by the innocents and lead them to the safety of *Ulufakush*. Any dragons or riders standing in your way *must* be killed. Spare no one who defies me and the truth."

"Yes, Lord Thaddeus."

The riders mounted their dragons and took to the skies. The dragons' roars resounded through the city. Bells and alarms quickly followed. Chaos filled the streets as the innocents rushed to evacuate. He wished he could assure each one of them they had no reason to fear him, but they needed to evacuate as quickly as possible. Fear was the quickest motivator.

Thaddeus nodded as he mounted Kyrell. *Now, let's go home.*

THE FRONT DOOR HUNG OPEN. Darkness loomed inside.

Something felt horribly wrong.

"Mother?" His voice broke as he tried to keep from screaming. "Mother!"

The gate to the garden hung crooked on bent, broken hinges. A foul wind blew through the plants; they'd never been so dull and wilted.

Kyrell roared as they landed. Thaddeus' knees buckled when he slid to the ground. Tripping over his feet, he rushed into the garden, axe in hand.

A figure stirred in the center of the garden, then stood. It wasn't his mother.

The *Jen-Jibuź's* leader turned, his cloak snapping around his ankles, a long knife in his hands. Blood slipped from the blade, dripping slowly to the ground. A crow cawed in the distance.

"No."

Dark fabric sucked around a beak-shaped mouth and distorted as the cloaked leader drew in a shaking laugh. "I was worried you wouldn't make it in time, son of the prophet."

Thaddeus staggered, his knees growing weak.

"This is what happens to those who threaten Duvarharia's safety and the power of the *Jen-Jibuź*." With a slow swipe, he wiped his blade clean on his cloak. The blade shone sickeningly, flashing red and silver.

A scream started somewhere in Thaddeus' chest, rising, rising, rising.

For a moment, the world stopped.

Then reality set in.

"No!" Thaddeus threw his axe. The blade whistled as it streaked through the air. A loud crack echoed, and before the weapon split the cloaked man's skull, he was gone. The axe embedded into the wall of his mother's private garden instead.

"Mother!" Thaddeus rushed to the still form on the garden dirt. He fell to his knees beside her, words of healing pouring from his lips as he summoned all the magic he could command. Purple sparks crackled over her pale body; the single wound in her chest closed. The blood stopped flowing.

A scream pierced the forest, followed by a sickening crack.

"Mother, look at me. Look at me, please." Tears blurred Thaddeus' vision. Frustrated, he brushed them away and pulled her into his lap. Her soft black hair spilled over his arm and onto the ground. "Please, Mother. I healed you; you're okay. Please wake up!"

Thaddeus . . . Kyrell landed beside him, an unconscious *Jen-Jibuź* rider under his claws. Thaddeus ignored them.

"Come on, Mother." Gently, he slapped her cheeks before pressing his lips to hers, forcing breath into her lungs. Though her wound was healed, his knees were soaked in blood, and her body was so, so heavy.

"*Sulujnu*, wake up!" Thaddeus shook her still form as he screamed and buried his face against the crook of her next. "Just open your eyes. Please. Just once more, just once more."

Instead, she lay still.

Turning, he dry-heaved, spitting out foul acid. Then he rocked back and forth, trying to ease the gaping grief in his chest. Lying down, he wrapped his arms around her and laid his head on her chest as he had so many times as a child. "I love you, Mother," he whispered to her.

I failed, his heart whispered to himself.

But the ground didn't swallow him whole like he wished.

"I didn't deserve you," he sobbed. "None of us ever did. But I'm not ready for you to go. Not yet. Just not yet."

Thaddeus, we have to leave.

Thaddeus' heart broke. He turned to snap at his dragon, to yell at him that the battle wasn't worth fighting now that both Syrinthia and Naraina were dead. But when he saw his dragon's tears, the anger fell away to expose his grief. *I can't. I can't go on.*

You must. Kyrell pressed his snout to Naraina's chest, and his tears washed the blood from her hair. *We have to finish what we started. The Jen-Jibuź must be hunting down anyone with known affiliations to you. If we don't stop them, they'll find the Ovesens and then the Shadows of Light like Zara.*

Thaddeus' raspy scream, full of the desperation choking his heart, made the forest fall silent. Turning to his mother, he wrapped his arms around her one last time.

Magic flowed from him and Kyrell and encompassed her as it had Syrinthia. His embrace collapsed as the magic condensed her body, leaving a pendant in the shape of a swirling green plant, a sunset-colored flower in its center.

Attaching the pendant on the chain next to Syrinthia's around his neck, he took to shaking legs. He stalked to the *Jen-Jibuź* rider, who was just gaining consciousness. "Tell me what you know." Thaddeus grabbed a handful of the rider's hair and jerked back his head.

"Please . . ." the rider mumbled. His eyes widened. He smelled of urine and fear.

Tell him what you said. Kyrell's voice tore through the rider's mind.

He wailed, succumbing quickly to the dragon's power. "Your brother. He's . . . he's still alive. He's at the academy with your father. Please don't—" The plea ended abruptly as Thaddeus sliced through his jugular.

Blind rage consumed all other thoughts. His brother had defied death, had defied Thaddeus' vengeance. "No matter what it takes, I'll finish them both." Cold determination settled in him as he mounted Kyrell. "Even if I must burn this whole *tizuge* city to do so."

Chapter 44

"**Where is my father?** Where is Thanatos?" Thaddeus screamed at the guard whose neck was in his hands. When the guard did nothing but blabber, Thaddeus threw her to the ground. The crack of her head against the floor echoed darkly. "Where are they?"

A cowering guard pointed down the halls. "The old med bay," he whimpered. Sweat poured down his brow as he wrung his clothes with shaking hands. Snarling, Thaddeus shoved past him.

When another guard stood in his way, he left a corpse. With every life he took, he felt the balance of right and wrong even out. The walls of the academy had always been stained in blood; he'd only made them visible.

Instead of going straight to the med bay, he paused at the dining hall. He knew he was already too late, but he stepped inside anyway. Several bodies lay still on the ground, but one small body lying by the food stands held his attention.

Sorrow grew inside him as he made his way to Anrid and pulled the *Suźuheb* from his satchel. A long crack ran down the edge of it from being carried across Duvaharia. For a moment, he gazed upon it. The awe and wonder he'd felt while making it were tainted with lies and betrayal now. The Dragon Palace hadn't been what Anrid had hoped; it would've cast her aside just as quickly as the *Jen-Jibuź* had today.

But it had been her dream, just like it used to be his, and she still deserved to hold on to the beauty of it and remember it that way, even if she would never get to see it.

Crouching, he planted a kiss to her forehead and laid the *Suźuheb* on her chest, crossing her hands over it. His magic removed clotted blood from the gash in her neck and knit it back together. She almost looked as if she were sleeping.

"I hope your soul finds the love this world never gave you."

Without a second glance, he made his way out of the dining hall to Kyrell, stepping over the few lifeless bodies of students who'd stood up to the *Jen-Jibuź* and their lies.

Every life stolen from him built another wall around his heart. What use was it anyway if he had no one left to love? Numbness opened like a vortex inside him, swallowing up the pain he didn't know how to confront.

Three guards charged them. Kyrell snapped the head off one while Thaddeus met the others with his axe and acid. Blood splattered on his face, but he hardly felt it. One of the guards groaned as he staggered away, organs escaping from the gaping wound in his stomach. Their pleas for mercy fell on deaf ears.

Thaddeus shrugged his blood-caked hair off his shoulder and continued down the hall, leaving the guard to a slow and painful death.

When he rounded the corner, he spotted the cloaked man and three other *Jen-Jibuź* members standing before his father, yelling.

They don't deserve a fair fight. Out of the numbness rose rage.

Thaddeus manipulated the metal of the first one's blade, driving it into his heart. The second fell as her head swiveled around, breaking her neck. The last member scrambled to conjure a shield.

Locking eyes with the dedicated *Jen-Jibuź* member who stood protectively in front of her leader and Quinlan, Thaddeus smiled and reached out his consciousness. The shield was strong, but he found the woman's weakness easily. She and her mother were very close. Smiling, Thaddeus opened his eyes and nodded to the woman, filling her mind with images of his mother bleeding out in the garden; only instead of Naraina's face, she saw the face of her own mother. Confusion washed over her before her eyes rolled into the back of her head. The shield faltered just enough. Thaddeus' axe lodged deep into her skull. She dropped and twitched before lying still.

"Thaddeus, what have you done?" Quinlan's voice grated on Thaddeus like claws on granite as the coward stepped back behind the cloaked man.

Kyrell crouched low, snaping his jaws as acid dripped from his teeth and burned into the floor. Thaddeus' axe caught on bone only for a second before he wrenched it from the still body.

"I've only done what needed to be done. What no one else had the strength to do, Father." Thaddeus pointed to the windows. Fires from rebelling Combustion Dragons burned wild in the city as they struggled against the Etas. The dark silhouettes of the Etas darted through the sky, far more agile than the lazy, incompetent riders and dragons who rose to fight them.

"Thaddeus, you've no idea what you're doing." The cloaked man lifted his hands, magic crackling between his fingertips.

"You know what?" Thaddeus chuckled as years of bitterness bubbled forth. He'd spent his life wondering what his purpose was, wondering why the cloaked man plagued his family, why his brother had turned on him, why his father had played favorites, why his mother had been encouraged to terminate her pregnancies. "I think you're right. I *don't* know what I'm doing." He laughed maniacally, too broken to shed tears. He rested his hand on Kyrell's leg for support. "And you know why?" His voice boomed through the halls "Because all you fed me were lies!"

He lunged at the *Jen-Jibuź* leader, his axe crashing into the man's magic shield with a shower of sparks. "So tell me! What about this prophecy? What about this traitor and savior? What about being Quinlan's son!"

Over and over his axe slammed into the magic, but despite Kyrell's acid, it held. When he realized Quinlan and the cloaked man wouldn't fight back, he stopped his attacks. Tears fell down his father's cheeks.

"I've lived under this curse my entire life, simply because I had the misfortune to be born to *you*, but even now you refuse to tell me why I've been hated, shunned, hunted, and feared when all I wanted was to be loved and accepted? And you"—Thaddeus pointed his axe at the cloaked man—"don't you think you've done enough grief to my family? Are you here to kill my father as well? What did I do to deserve a dead mother?"

Quinlan's face drained of color as he turned to the *Jen-Jibuź* leader. "You said you wouldn't hurt her." A feral glint flashed in Quinlan's eyes as the cult leader laughed nervously.

"She would've helped Thaddeus. We couldn't just—"

Quinlan's sword ended the explanation as it pierced through his neck. Bubbles of blood foamed at his lips as Quinlan withdrew the blade. When the man collapsed, the hood fell from his face.

Thaddeus hissed in disgust. "What is he, an Eta?"

The man's face was distorted between something Duvarharian and something animal. Fur grew from half of it, and though his eyes were Duvarharian, the snout-like nose that jutted from his face was not. But unlike the Zoics, he wasn't beautiful—he was an abomination. Thaddeus spat on him.

Not so different than the creatures he spent his life hating.

Death is too good for him.

The clatter of a sword brought Thaddeus' attention back to his father. Quinlan stood shaking, hands held out. "I know I made mistakes. I've always known that. But if I didn't go along with what the *Jen-Jibuź* said, I believed they'd kill you. All of you." His shoulders sagged. "In the end, they did it anyway. I'm sorry. I'm sorry I was the prophet, and I'm sorry I didn't tell you about it. I'm sorry that in trying to avoid the prophecy, we brought it down upon you."

"Sorry doesn't fix this. Sorry doesn't bring Syrinthia or Mother back." He lifted his blade to his father's neck. "It's too late for apologies." He expected his father to beg for his life, to strike some deal with him as he had with the *Jen-Jibuź*.

He did neither.

"I failed," he whispered. "Everything I tried to do, I failed." Collapsing to his knees, he buried his face in his hands and wept.

Thaddeus' heart twisted as he listened to his father's soul break. His axe lowered. *What would I have done in his place? I know he loved Naraina, even when their love wasn't safe or convenient.* It was clear now; they didn't think they could have children since they were of different Kinds. The system hadn't taught them the truth; it'd failed them just as much as it failed him. And whatever deal Quinlan struck with the cult, it had kept Thaddeus and Thanatos alive longer than they'd hoped.

At the end of it all, could I have done any better? If he hadn't searched for the truth, he could've loved Syrinthia and protected her the same quiet way his father had with Naraina. If it weren't for him, maybe they'd both still be alive—in hiding, but still alive.

Growling, he brushed the tears from his cheeks. He didn't want his father to apologize. He didn't want to mend the gap between them. He wanted him to pay.

Grinding his teeth, Thaddeus pressed his blade to his father's neck again. "Tell it to me."

Quinlan winced. "Tell you what?"

"The prophecy. I want to hear it from you, the illusive, oh-holy prophet who believed he was responsible for the fate of Duvarharia. Tell it to me, word for word."

With trembling lips, the man nodded and spoke.

"Dragon folk now heed the call, from the wars of man's great fall.
In your days of sloth and peace, the hands of death shall find release.
But up from you, there shall rise, a keeper from this fear and demise.
Features pale with dark blood hair, eyes of red beyond compare.
Guide this girl, whether to or fro, she must come to the Stone Plateau.
Raise her up, to love not hate, never straying from her fate.
And to this girl, marked with my hand, a helper too, both fierce and grand.

Beware her helper, though young and wise, will need be steered from lust of prize.
Soon hard years, from death you cannot run, for a traitor from your ranks will come.
A young boy, Quinlan's own dear son, will bend to evil and then be won.
Listen, riders, that all may know, all this could be avoided so.
Turn back, my children, back to me. I'll set you from the Dark Lord free.
But if my voice, you do not heed, my urgent warning, I now plead.
Then know that I will then set forth, destruction, terrible, from the North.
And if you turn away from me, know this quite for certainty: no rider will retell your lives, no help for you shall then arise.
So, Quinlan, stand, the Stone Plateau, for in five years the moon will throw, the fate for all, written in stone, knowledge to learn and skills to hone.
Follow its riddles, follow to know, what the future then may show.
Go to your leaders, speak of this hope, to fight the evil and to cope.
Remind the people to seek me out, with a whisper or a shout.
For I, your Lord, am never far, and know each one for who they are."

Thaddeus bit his lip until he tasted blood. "I never could've been the savior. I couldn't have been anything but the traitor."

"We thought it was Thanatos." Quinlan's voice was so quiet, Thaddeus almost didn't hear him. "That's why we enrolled him in the academy. The later prophecies said the traitor would be a traditional Duvarharian. We thought if he was indoctrinated with the new culture, he wouldn't become the traitor."

"And you just, what, forgot about me? Didn't consider me your son enough to protect as well?"

He shook his head, sucking a deep breath between quiet sobs. "That's not it. Syrinthia—she . . . she thought you might become the traitor at first."

She'd confessed the *Jen-Jibuż* forced her to be friends with him and

Thanatos, but only now did doubt creep into his heart. Had anything they shared been genuine? Or had she been nothing more than a spy?

"Once she voiced her concerns, the *Jen-Jibuż* told her to shadow you and keep watch over you. She was supposed to keep you focused on the academy and hoped you'd follow Thanatos' lead. But then she lied to us . . ." His voice trailed off.

"If you stop speaking now, I'll cut your jaw from your head and make sure you never speak again."

Quinlan flinched. He looked so much older and more tired than Thaddeus remembered him being. "She told us you weren't becoming the traitor. Every concern the *Jen-Jibuż* rose about you, she shot down, recanting all her previous statements. It seemed every time they tried to clamp down on you, she found a way to shield you from them." The ghost of a smile spread across Quinlan's lips as his eyes met his son's. "She had an incredible magic that brought out the best in anyone, even in you, until it was all the cult could see." His eyes darkened. "That was before you left for the Dragon Palace, and they found out about her magic. But you were already gone, away from their reach. She protected you just long enough."

"Why . . . why would she do that?" The words stuck in his throat as he leaned against Kyrell for strength.

You know why, Thaddeus, Kyrell whispered.

He did, but he wanted to hear someone else say it, as if that would make it real.

"She cared about you. Deeply. You were *everything* to her."

All doubt about her loyalties rushed from his heart, replaced with incomprehensible grief over losing her. "Why didn't you protect her?"

Quinlan shook his head. "Because it was either her or Naraina, and I—"

"Get out of my sight."

His words echoed through the halls. The surprise in his father's gaze mirrored the surprise Thaddeus felt.

"I said get out of my sight. Leave this place and go crawl into whatever godsforsaken hole will take you. I'll be surprised if your dragon even wants you now. I certainly don't."

Quinlan's gaze lingered a little too long on the scar marring his son's face, enraging Thaddeus even more. He staggered to his feet, awkwardly pausing beside Thaddeus as if not trusting him to refrain from burying the axe in his skull the second he turned around. Thaddeus didn't trust himself not to.

"Son—"

Thaddeus didn't look at him. "I am not your son. Leave, or they'll have to scrape you off the walls."

"Don't kill your brother," Quinlan begged. "Please. He's nearly dead as it is, and I can't . . . I don't want to lose my entire family."

"You should've thought about that before you chose him over me." Thaddeus shouldered past his father just as Krystallos broke through the window. The two dragons stared at each other and nodded. Then Quinlan mounted Krystallos, and they fled.

The door to the med bay loomed before him. It was already cracked open, a pool of blood seeping under it into the hall. Taking a deep breath, Thaddeus shoved against the large door.

A body lay just inside, limbs askew. Thaddeus ground his teeth when he recognized the creature as the mouse Zoic who'd treated him years ago. Only now, they were much skinnier than he remembered, and more scars decorated their body. Three sword wounds lined their chest. Thaddeus hoped their death had been quick. Gingerly stepping over their body, moved farther into the room.

A groan echoed in the dimly lit hall. "Thaddeus? Is that you?"

Whatever pity and mercy he'd felt toward his father dissipated as he recognized the damaged, raspy voice. "You son of a *žebu quhuesu dasuunab*," he hissed.

A gargling scream left Thanatos' lips as Thaddeus' axe embedded into the headboard, inches above his head.

Thousands of hateful, bitter words bubbled into Thaddeus' throat as he grabbed Thanatos' shirt and wrenched him from the bed. Disregarding numerous casts and bandages, he throttled his brother, drawing screams from his cracked lips. "I hate you, Thanatos," he growled in his brother's ear. His hands wrapped around his neck.

Wide, scared blue eyes stared back at him. Thanatos gasped for air as he weakly clawed at his brother's hands.

"I hope you rot in Susahu for all the things you've done to me, to Mother, to Syrinthia, to Duvarharia. One death is not enough for you." Thaddeus spit on his brother's face, eager to watch the acid burn his coveted features. But the acid dissipated. It dripped harmlessly down his cheeks.

"What—" Throbbing pain shot through his body as something slammed him into the baseboard of the next bed over. Kyrell lunged forward but was knocked back just as effortlessly.

Blinding light consumed Thanatos' body, forming a shield around him. Thaddeus scrambled to his feet and muttered a healing spell over his cracked ribs. Then a man stepped out of the light.

He didn't have to wonder who he was.

"Joad." He spat in disdain. At one time, he would've thrown himself at Joad's feet, lips full of praise and worship. Now all he wanted to do was tear his traitorous head from his shoulders.

"Thaddeus." Quiet and soft, Joad's voice was in direct contradiction with the chaotic rage and panic filling Thaddeus' mind. "Why are you doing this?"

Every hateful word he'd kept buried in his heart rushed forth. "Is it not obvious? Maybe because you forced a prophecy upon me because my father was unfortunate enough to be in the wrong place at the wrong time. Sound familiar?" He stepped forward, pain radiating from him in waves. "Let me ask you this: did you ever love me? Or was everything I did for you, for your people, just a way to force me into this wretched destiny? Did I watch my loved ones bleed out just so you could display your magnificence?"

Tears rolled down the shining man's face. "This was never supposed to be your destiny, Thaddeus. This isn't what you were born for. You were born for beautiful, gentle things, but you let yourself be corrupted just as much as your brother."

Thaddeus followed Joad's gaze to Thanatos. His brother was healed; he stared at Joad with wide, adoring eyes. Thaddeus wanted to break every bone in his brother's body and wipe that ridiculous look off his face. He hated that it once had been on his own.

"No. I am not corrupt. I see the true corruption in this world, and I'm the only one willing to do what's necessary to pave the way for its rebirth—something you don't have the power to do."

The lack of anger in Joad's gaze only enraged Thaddeus more. "The path you're on does not lead to the renewal of Duvarharia. Two more lives besides yours are entangled in the prophecy, and all will be needed for Duvarharia's rebirth. Even Thanatos has a place in it all. You alone do not have the strength to rebuild all that has been lost and all that will be lost."

"Maybe I don't." Thaddeus spat at him as hot tears of betrayal rolled down his cheeks. Joad had once been his hope and hero, but he'd allowed his mother and Syrinthia to be killed; he'd allowed a prophecy to shape and harm so many lives; he'd abandoned him. Thaddeus' heart turned stone cold. "But that doesn't mean I need you."

Time slowed.

Thaddeus lunged forward and ripped his axe from the headboard. He swung it toward Thanatos' neck just as Kyrell reached his jaws around Joad.

A deafening crack split the air with an explosion of blinding, burning light. It flooded Kyrell and Thaddeus' bodies, rendering them helpless.

The last scene Thaddeus beheld before the light faded was Joad wrapping his arms around Thanatos as Thanatos' bright blue eyes burning into Thaddeus. Then they disappeared.

The room fell still.

"He took him. He . . ." Thaddeus choked back a sob as he staggered to his feet. "He saved him."

Kyrell lunged at the bed and tore it to pieces. Feathers and splinters littered the floor as acid burned through it to the rooms below. *We sacrificed everything for him. Everything! We were the faithful Duvarharians, true to the old ways, true to his message. And this is our thanks.*

"He chose Thanatos over me." Hate and rage clouded his vision, feeding the darkness inside him and the amulet. It fought for control. "Joad chose a dragon-killing, raping, lying, murdering, dragon-less *ñekol* over me!" Thaddeus screamed and gave in to the darkness.

The academy shuddered as his magic tore through it. Waves of acid burned through every book, chair, guard, pillar, and dome. As it began to collapse, Thaddeus leaped onto Kyrell's back. The ceiling caved around them as they rose into the sky.

Acidic flame consumed the school behind them, reducing it to stinking pools of waste.

"I will find the savior of the prophecy and her helper, and I will tear them from Joad's corrupt bosom of protection. Then their power will be mine, and I will finish what I have started. Then one day, I will stand in front of Joad and reveal him to be the true traitor of Duvarharia."

The purple flames below them spread to the rest of the city, and Peace Haven burned. Screams of terror and pain rang through the air, mingling with the screeching of Etas and dragons.

He loosened his control over the Etas. They surged upon the Duvarharians, dragons and riders alike, magic and magicless, young and old, male and female.

Emotionless, Thaddeus watched as a wave of Etas descended on the fleeing refugees. They fell eerily silent as their weak numbers were reduced to a river of blood and mountain of torn flesh in a matter of seconds.

"Let them perish, and let their deaths pay tribute to my power. I want

Duvarharia quivering in fear and begging for mercy when I descend upon it."

Thanatos' mocking blue eyes flashed before him, a smirk upon his dark face—a smirk of victory as he was chosen by Joad, not Thaddeus.

Thaddeus clenched his fists and cursed his brother in the Ancient Language. "If I must, I will wait a thousand years to feel your blood on my hands and taste your death on my lips. So I swear."

Digging his nails into his palm, he let the wind catch his blood, sealing his promise.

"The reign of the traitor begins now."

Hidden Identity

The Abandoned Mountain Fortress
Dragon Palace, Duvarharia
Year: Rumi 6114 Q.RJ.M
Present Day

Stephania gasped for air as her eyes snapped open. The world burned around her. Echoing screams mixed with the smell of acidic fire dissolving flesh. Nausea rose into her throat as the slaughter of thousands of innocent Duvarharians played over and over in her mind.

Staggering to her feet, she felt her legs give way.

Strong arms wrapped around her, catching her before she collided with the hard ground, and lowered her back onto the soft bed. Someone was speaking as they pushed tangled, sweaty curls from her face. But she could only see a pair of piercing blue eyes, staring into her soul, mocking her, hating her, claiming victory over her.

Not her—Thaddeus.

Her own emotions, entangled with Thaddeus', were impossible to distinguish. They clashed, confused each other, and finally escaped from her lips as harsh sobs racked her chest. Bile crept into her mouth. She fumbled for the glass next to the bed and threw up in it.

Vaguely, she sensed Farren outside pacing anxiously and pouring strength and comfort into her rider.

"Breathe, Stephania. Just breathe." A familiar voice pierced the memories clinging to her mind. A cold rag wiped her lips. Another pressed against her forehead.

Eventually, the room stopped spinning, and the visions of a burning city and dying Duvarharians began to fade. But the haunting blue eyes never vanished.

"What did you see? You have to tell me, Stephania. Please." She heard the man's voice more clearly now.

She nodded, focusing on breathing like he'd encouraged her too. "It was—it was—" The only sounds that followed were sobs.

The man pulled her into his arms and held her close, whispering comforting words she could barely hear over the whirlwind inside her mind. "Shhh, it's alright. Just breathe and take some time. Just breathe." A hint of impatience laced his voice.

"I saw him."

His body tensed. "Who?" he asked, but they both already knew.

"His brother. I . . . I finally saw his brother."

The man nodded quickly. "Alright, alright. What did he look like? What happened? Did he kill him? Did he escape?"

Stephania tried to form words but kept tripping over them. "His father killed the cloaked man, but he didn't kill his father."

The man frowned as he pulled away far enough to look down at her face. She clenched her eyes shut, trying to halt the sudden vertigo. The man reapplied the cold wash and rubbed her back. "He didn't? Are you sure?"

"Positive. He let him live." Desperately, she wanted to press her forehead to the man's and share everything she'd seen with him from her own memories, but the thought of connecting to another rider's mind right now seemed impossible.

Take your time, little one. We've waited this long; we can wait a few more minutes. Farren's warm voice sent a wave of strength through Stephania, and she nodded.

A few breaths later, she continued. "He went into the room, into the med bay, to kill his brother. He hardly said anything. He just . . ." A vivid recollection of her hands—Thaddeus' hands—wrapping around the Dragon Rider's neck as he gave in to overwhelming hate reminded her too much of her own hate as a child. She wanted to forget it all—his memories and hers.

Think of pure, good things. Think of Dalton's love for you. Think of him and Trojan and Frawnden and Aeron. Release the hate and anger. This is Thaddeus' memory of the Corrupt Magic, not yours. You do not have to succumb to his hate and pain.

Stephania bit her lip, meditating on Farren's every word. *I am not a slave to my anger. I am not a slave to my vengeance. I am not slave to my hate*, she repeated over and over to herself.

"Did he kill him?" the man pressed again. "Stephania, I know this is hard, but you have to tell me what you saw. We need to know everything we can about Thaddeus, and we know his brother was a weakness. If somehow, he survived—"

"He did." She barely heard her own whisper.

"What?"

She shivered and leaned into him, tears welling up in her eyes. "A man came out of a light—Thaddeus believed it was Joad—and saved Thanatos. He saved him from Thaddeus. He took him away . . . somewhere through *Dasejuba*."

The man shook his head as he ran a hand through his long hair. "Why? Why would he save Thanatos?"

"I don't know." She'd seen what Thanatos had done. She couldn't believe the Joad she knew would choose someone as wretched and evil as him. But that's what she'd seen, and that's what Thaddeus believed.

"But if Joad actually saved him and took him somewhere, then that means . . ."

"He could still be alive." The realization spoken sounded even more ludicrous.

He grabbed her shoulders and shook her gently. "What did he look like?" His words were panicked, eager, excited. This was the breakthrough they'd spent so many hours, days, weeks, months searching for. Everything she had suffered, following Thaddeus through his memories, had led them to this.

Closing her eyes, she recalled Thanatos' face, clear in Thaddeus' memories no other time than the last time he saw him. Thaddeus hadn't wanted to remember his brother's face, but he couldn't forget that last smirk no matter how hard he tried.

"He looked like . . ." She shook her head, trying to find the right description. Her eyes met his, and her heart lurched in her chest. "You."

The room quieted.

"What?" His mouth hung open as he shook his head. "What are you saying?"

"It's you." Tears of confusion filled her eyes as she leaped from the bed. How had she been so blind? How had she not seen the resemblance? Even now she didn't believe her eyes, but she was unable to deny the truth. "You're Thaddeus' brother."

Pronunciation Guide & Glossary

Pronunciation Guide

Artigal— AR-ti-gall
Deimos— DAY-muss
Duvarharia— DU-var-HAR-ee-uh
Elcore— EL-core
Eta— EE-tuh
Gauyuyáwa—GAH-yoo-YAY-wuh
Hanluurasa— han-loo-RA-sah
Igentis— aye-GEN-tis
Kijaqumok— KEE-jah-QUH-mock
Krystallos— kri-STA-lose
Kyrell— KY-rul
Quinlan— QUIN-lan
Raythuz— RAY-thooz
Sankyz— San-keez
Shalnoa— shal-NO-ah
Sházuk— SHAY-zook
Shushequmok— SHU-sheh-QUH-mock
Stephania— Steh-FAW-nia
Susahu— Soo-SA-hu
Syrinthia— sir-IN-thee-ah
Thaddeus— THAY-dee-us
Thanatos— THAN-uh-tose
Trans-Falls— trans-falls

Veltrix— VEL-trix
Ventronovia— VEN-troh-NOH-via
Wyerland— WHY-er-land
Wyrider— WHY-rider
Zoic— ZOE-ick

GLOSSARY

DUVARHARIAN *(Rażugub)*

Benierku—The legalized arena games in Duvarharia (arena victory)
Chue—Shitty
Dasejuba—World between worlds, the path between all realms, time, space, and matter
Dasun(ab)—Idiot(s)
Dasuun qevab—Egg sucker (vulgar insult)
Elus-ugu—Duvarharian with dwarfism
Femi—Duvarharian currency
Fuse—A very large breed of buffalo-like pack animals
Hanluurasa—The sky realm
Huladau(b)—Asshole(s)
Jen-Jibuż—Black poison (name of the cult in Duvarharia that came from the Shadows of Light)
Juufu—An information recording device made of magic that transposes observed actions and personal reactions into words
Kijaqumok—Corrupt Magic
Klushuuv sub—Flirting whore
Klushuub—Flirt
Lubesh—Breast
Lurujmu fuju—Malt whiskey
Nesa—Bitch

VI

Nuben ehash vul. vul ehash nuben. Lisu nuflu żufaź—Matter into energy. Energy into matter. Forever safe with me

Nufa seż—Fuck you

Nufaqulu—Fuck this

Qeżujeluch—Frog dragons (water lizard)

Qumokuhe(b)—Magic image(s) (basic photographic image made from magic)

Rabur-Fechamu—Shadow Nest (Mountain fortress in the Dragon Palace Valley)

Rubuż Xeneluch—Blooded dragon (common execution of draining the magic {via blood} from a creature)

Rusadabe—Generic mountain goat native to Duvarharia

Shekkamub—Lesser rider (a slur Duvarharians call Wyriders)

Shushequmok—Pure Magic

Sufax—Bastard

Suf'furruj—Marsh nut (high-end snack imported from the Human Domain)

Suiseż—Thank you

Suluj—Damn

Sulujnu—Damnit

Susengube—Tourist

Sużuheb—Physical memory (a painting/photograph made from magic that preserves the artist's emotions)

Ue—Shit

Ug, fursuu—Fire, please

Ulufakush—Hidden paradise (name of the dragon island near Peace Haven)

Umu qucha esh num—Scale within my wing

Unurarujax—A celestial event that only occurs once every five thousand years

Urku-qurkoźo—Story artist (storyteller)

Uvu—Grow
Vukko—Conviction
Vuk Quse(b)—Game master(s)
Xeneluch-frasuub—Dragon Slayer (murderer)
Xene'mraba—The illegal arena games involving the slaying of dragons (Dragon massacre)
Xeneluch-Rani—Dragon Sea (just outside of Peace Haven)
Xeneluch-shuvub—Dragon Trainer
Xeneluch ue—Dragon shit
Żebu quhuesu dasuunab—Mother of rotten (bad) eggs

WYRIDER *(Džoxsenä)*

Arella—The sun goddess in Wyrider legend and myth
Daufa—Mythical Wyrider gods of chaos
Džoxsenä—People of New Birth (Wyriders)
Elush—Coffee
Eshisifoz džou—Demon spawn
Kinätyä gudi—Sprout brother (term of endearment common among terrestrial Zoics)
Kinätyä segi—Little sprout (term of endearment common among terrestrial Zoics)
Läshiglunov—Plebean style sweet beer
Loizi—Fuck
Ozi—Shit
(Se)ñekol—Bastard(s)
Shäsevel—Toast
Shäshisä—Thank you
(Ti)zuge—Curse(d)
Tyän (se)tyäg—Term of endearment

Zinligil-shätshgugi—Sunset flower (the flower Zoic type Naraina is bonded to)

CENTAUR/FAUN *(Sházuk)*

Elu lásheñ—Ass cloth/wipe

Gauyuyáwa—Tree of our Fathers (or ancestors)

Ñáfagaræy—Blue four eyed nocturnal rodent living in Trans-Falls (four hop)

Ñáshaid—Fool

Shaze-dow—Heart of the Moon, Esmeray's staff

Sházuk—Kin (Native word for Forest Children Kind, Centaur language)

Zheborgiy—Witch dream (psychedelic mushroom type)

Zuru—Damn

ACKNOWLEDGEMENTS

To kick off the acknowledgements, I have to start by thanking my two brothers, Zachary and Blake. They've been with me my entire life and know me better than most. They've been through all the ups and downs, and they've loved me and cared for me through it all. It's because of them I learned how important siblings are and how much they can affect the baby of the family (that's me!). I'm very lucky to have such amazing older brothers who've taught me how to have fun and be both tough and sensitive. I've always admired them both and looked up to them, just the same as Thaddeus did to Thanatos. Unfortunately, Thaddeus didn't luck out quite like I did, and his sibling story didn't have the happy ending mine does. But it's because I have such loving brothers that I was able to write a book showcasing what can happen to the baby of the family when their older siblings aren't so loving and supportive. So, thank you, Zach and Blake, for always sticking with me so I got to have a happier childhood and adult life than poor Thaddeus did. You're the real ones.

Next, I of course have to thank H.A. Pruitt for once again going above and beyond with editing Son of the Prophet. She's been with me this entire series including working on *The Legends of Rasa Vol. I* on the side, and I can never thank her enough for taking on this massive series with me. She always does a fantastic job with her edits, and I'm so grateful to have her in my corner.

Samantha Mendell did the final proofread and I am so grateful for her eye for detail and dedication to her craft. She really gave this book the last and final whipping it needed to shape into the masterpiece it is today. She's an absolute gem of a human being and I can't wait to work with her again.

Huge shoutout to those who support me as a person and by listening to me talk nonstop about my books and even complain about them sometimes! This list is not exhaustive, but my mother, father, and Nathaniel Luscombe all definitely get the brunt of it. Thank you for putting up with my fantasy and emotional shenanigans!

Now for a very exciting part of this acknowledgements section! I did something a little different with this release and ran a Kickstarter in order to afford some of the editing and marketing I'd need to get this book off the ground the way it deserves. I had an EXTRODINARY number of people pledge to this Kickstarter and help make this book possible, and it's time to shout out each and every one of them:

Aaron Nieson, Abby Johansen, Alexander Grant, Alexandra Corrsin, Alexandria Frederick, Anne J. Hill, Antonio Oliver, Andrew Euston, Avra Blake, Bethany Meyer, Brandon & Victoria, Brandt McDonald, Caleb Kleveter, Cheryl, Dawn E. Dagger, Franchesca Caram, GC Annison, Jacob H Joseph, Judy Liu, Julie Payne, Kate Korsak, Kate Lawhon, Katrina Nappi, Kyle, LeAnn B., Linda Carmack, Lu Salmieri, Margaret Claire, Melissa Vink, Myka Silber, Nathaniel Luscombe, Rosetta Eclipse, Sam, Samantha Mendell, Samantha Newberry, Shivam Khanna, Tracy Bradley, Z Halo, Z.S. Diamanti, & The Creative Fund by BackerKit.

Last but not least, thank YOU, reader, for picking up this little book child of mine and giving it a chance. Whether it's your first time stepping into Rasa or if you're an old fan, I hope it delivered everything you needed and wanted when you picked it up. And I hope you'll visit Rasa again soon!

See you in the next book!

May the suns smile upon your presence,

—Effie Joe Stock

COMING SOON:
BOOK FOUR OF THE SHADOWS OF LIGHT

RIDER OF THE SUN-FLASH DRAGON

TWO ESCAPED CAPTIVES.

TWO UNPLANNED LEADERS.

ONLY ONE DESTINY TO FULFILL

Follow Effie Joe Stock and Dragon Bone Publishing online for updates on the fourth installment of The Shadows of Light Series.

More From
The Rasaverse

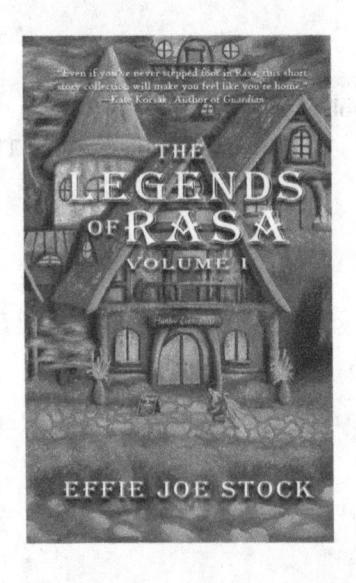

- Child of the Dragon Prophecy — Effie Joe Stock
- Heir of Two Kingdoms — Effie Joe Stock
- Son of the Prophet — Effie Joe Stock
- The Legends of Rasa, Volume I — Effie Joe Stock

More By
Dragon Bone Publishing

MOONSOUL
Nathaniel Luscombe

BLEACHED REMINDERS
Effie Joe Stock

UNLEASH THE COSMOS
A Space Poetry Anthology
Compiled By
NATHANIEL LUSCOMBE
& JENNI SAUER

THE PLANETS WE BECOME
NATHANIEL LUSCOMBE